Anybody's Sports Medicine Book

Anybody's Sports Medicine Book

THE COMPLETE GUIDE TO QUICK RECOVERY FROM INJURIES

JAMES G. GARRICK, M.D.

PETER RADETSKY, PH.D.

Ten Speed Press
Berkeley Toronto

Ten Speed Press
Box 7123
Berkeley, California 94707
www.tenspeed.com

Distributed in Australia by Simon & Schuster Australia, in Canada by Ten Speed Press Canada, in New Zealand by Southern Publishers Group, in South Africa by Real Books, in Southeast Asia by Berkeley Books, and in the United Kingdom and Europe by Airlift Books.

COVER DESIGN: Jennifer Crook Design
COVER PHOTOGRAPHY: Yvonne Israel-O'Hare
BOOK DESIGN AND COMPOSITION: BookMatters, Berkeley
ILLUSTRATIONS: Joyce Jonté, Valerie Kells (VK), and Karen Jacobsen (KJ)

LIBRARY OF CONGRESS CATALOGING-IN-PUBLICATION DATA

Garrick, James G.
   Anybody's sports medicine book: the complete guide to quick recovery from
      injuries / by James G. Garrick, Peter Radetsky.
      p.   cm.
   Includes index.
   ISBN 1-58008-144-4 (pbk.)
   1. Sports medicine — Popular works. 2. Sports injuries — Popular works.
      I. Radetsky, Peter. II. Title.
   RC1210 .G37 2000
   617.1'027—dc21
   00-022974

Printed in Canada
First printing, 2000
1 2 3 4 5 6 7 8 9 10 — 05 04 03 02 01 00

CONTENTS

Introduction

THIRD AND 12. Richard Green, a twenty-year-old wide receiver for the University of Iowa, waits for the snap. He's about to run a cross pattern, one that requires him to speed downfield, then cut sharply to the inside to receive the ball. If the timing is right the play should gain at least fifteen yards, and there's always the possibility that Richard, with his great speed, will break it to the outside for much more.

The snap. Richard charges downfield then pivots, his entire weight on his right leg, and cuts toward the middle of the field. Meanwhile the quarterback drops back and throws the ball to the spot where he knows Richard will be. He can taste it—first down for sure, maybe a long gainer.

It is not to be. When Richard planted his foot to cut, his cleats caught in a seam in the artificial turf, turning his ankle beneath him. Now, rather than cutting to the inside, Richard continues downfield in the air before crunching onto the carpet. There he lies on the artificial turf, clutching his ankle, wishing he could take back that instant when he slammed his foot into the invisible seam.

All that Marilyn Bernardi is wishing right now is that she could've avoided the weak forehand she just dribbled into the net. How embarrassing! The pro is standing not ten feet away, the rest of the students are looking on, and the doubles party in the next court is probably chuckling among themselves at her ineptness.

Marilyn is thirty-eight years old and took up tennis just a few months ago. She knew she had to do *something*, and it was either that or running or aerobics. Well, running just didn't appeal to her—too lonely and just plain boring. And besides that, she didn't much care for the idea of traipsing all over the city by herself. She didn't much care for the idea of stuffing herself into a leotard and bouncing around in front of all those people in aerobics class, either. Tennis was the best alternative, especially so when she signed up for a series of clinics sponsored by the local rec district. She met some nice people, found she enjoyed getting out in the sunshine three times a week, and she *was* learning how to play tennis. Before this, the last time she had stepped on a court had been during a required PE class in college, and what little she learned then had long since flown out the window. But now she can hit the ball back and forth with reasonable accuracy and reasonable frequency. Having never been much of an athlete, Marilyn's delighted with the progress she's made and the fun she's having. She's even lost a couple of pounds—or maybe that's just wishful thinking.

All the more reason to get to this next ball in plenty of time, swing the racquet back, and stroke a good one over the net. Bong! The ball slams off the racquet of the player in the opposite court, skims the net (that's even better; it gives her an extra second to pull the racquet back), and heads about seven feet to Marilyn's right. Marilyn rushes to the ball, all the time going over the things she should remember: swing racquet head back on a line—good. Keep wrist stiff—good. Keep knees bent—good. Now *hit* all the way through the ball, and. . . .

She never gets that far. While concentrating on the ball flying toward her, she fails to notice a stray ball rolling at her feet. She steps directly on top of it, turning her ankle beneath her, and with a shriek falls to the court clutching her ankle.

Neither Richard Green nor Marilyn Bernardi are real people. But they might as well be. They've just experienced the most frequent injury in all sports, a sprained ankle, in a couple of typical ways. That much they have in common. What they don't have in common is what happens to them *after* the injury. And what happens after the injury is the motivation behind this book. Please read on. It's likely that the same thing, or something very nearly like it, has happened to you.

Within seconds Richard Green is no longer clutching his ankle. Now someone else has hold of it, an orthopedic surgeon, with the team trainer looking on. The referee has called time, and most of the team clusters around Richard to find out what happened.

The beauty of it all is that already the doctor is almost completely sure what has happened. He has cut off Richard's shoe and sock and, as there's no swelling yet because the injury has been attended to so promptly, he's able to examine the ankle almost as readily as though it weren't injured at all. He's virtually certain that nothing's broken and there's no muscle or tendon damage—it's a sprain. Once the attendants pull Richard to his feet, the fact that he's willing to put weight on the ankle reinforces the doctor's diagnosis; if Richard had refused to walk on it the likelihood would increase that it may be fractured. And as Richard limps off the field to the applause of the crowd, the doctor is already mapping out his treatment strategy.

If there's still any doubt, it's about to be dispelled once and for all—the x-ray machine is just down the tunnel to the locker room. Most colleges can have x-ray equipment available within ten minutes. The pros are similarly attentive—it's an NFL rule that there must be an x-ray facility at every stadium. So, to be absolutely certain, the doctor escorts Richard into the x-ray room. Five minutes later the verdict is in: no broken bones. A sprain it is, and a severe one.

And that's that. Even before the x-ray results were in, Richard's ankle was put into a compression binding consisting of crushed ice with a firm wrap around the outside. Now he rests comfortably, his leg elevated, in a cart that allows him to be wheeled to the mouth of the tunnel to watch the rest of the game or into the locker room to catch up with the outcome on TV. Everything has been done that can be done for the first day; tomorrow Richard will start rehabilitation.

When Marilyn turned her ankle and fell to the court, she too was surrounded by people wondering what had happened. The difference is, none of these people know what to do about it. The tennis pro may have an inkling of what happened—he's certainly suffered sprained ankles in his time—but there are thirty people taking the clinic, spread out over five courts, each at six bucks a session, and he simply doesn't have time to take care of Marilyn. He makes sure she gets off the court, tells her to stay off her feet, assures her he'll check on her soon, and hurries back to the other backhands and forehands and tentative serves.

So there Marilyn sits in a chair on the side of the court, her ankle beginning to throb like crazy, terrified to put weight on it, not knowing what to do next. Maybe she should go to the emergency room. But it's her right foot, so she can't drive, and the tennis clinic still has an hour to go. She doesn't know anybody well enough to ask them to give up their practice time and take her, and, even if she did, she doesn't want to be a burden. So she sits, her injured ankle hanging below her, waiting for the clinic to end. She does, however, manage to pull off her tennis shoe. Ahh, that gives some relief.

By the time the clinic ends, her ankle, deprived of even the modest compression her shoe would have provided, is ballooning to softball proportions. And even though it's throbbing like mad, Marilyn has decided that she doesn't want to go to the emergency room after all. She hates the thought of an emergency room—who doesn't? Besides the kids will be home soon, and then her husband, and there's dinner to arrange. There's probably nothing seriously wrong with the ankle. It'll get better.

After a friend drops her at home, Marilyn finds that she hurts too much to do anything around the house. She's simply got to do something about this ankle. Let's see, what is it that you do to a swollen ankle? It's either ice it or put heat on it—she can't remember which. When the kids hurt themselves in soccer the coach said to ice the injury, didn't he? So she hobbles to the refrigerator and takes out some ice cubes. Ouch! It couldn't be ice—that hurts too much. A hot bath would feel much better.

And so it does. But by the time the kids burst through the door and her husband comes home a bit later, her ankle is beginning to resemble a purple cantaloupe. Soaking in all that hot water felt lovely, but by promoting blood supply to the ankle, she caused even more swelling. Marilyn's husband, who played high school football and so remembers a little something about how to treat injuries, says, "Why didn't you ice it? We've got to get you to a doctor." So they put a bag of ice on the ankle, leave the kids to scrounge for dinner, and go off to the emergency room.

It's 6:30 in the evening. The emergency room is packed. The first question the registration clerk asks Marilyn is, "When did this happen?"

"At 1:30 this afternoon," she replies.

Well, thinks the clerk, if it happened at 1:30 and it's almost 7:00 now, it certainly isn't an emergency. And she puts Marilyn at the bottom of the list. So again Marilyn sits down in a chair to wait, again with her foot hanging below her, although this time it has a bag of ice on it.

Forty-five minutes later, the nurse leads her into the emergency room. Twenty minutes later the doctor walks in, throws away the bag of ice because by now it's dripping all over the floor, takes one look at her Hebrew National salami of an ankle, and says, "We better take x-rays." It's about the only thing he can do because by this time you can't even tell what the anatomy of the ankle is—it's nothing more than a giant, taut balloon.

Now Marilyn sits in a wheelchair, with her ankle—if no longer hanging, not yet elevated either—stretched out in front of her, waiting to go into the x-ray room. There's a line for the x-ray room, and only one technician on duty at night. An hour later, the x-ray taken, she's wheeled back into the emergency room, and there she sits for another half hour until someone has a second to peek at the x-rays.

Finally the doctor comes back. He has a big smile on his face. "Good news! Nothing's broken. You've just sprained your ankle."

Marilyn, who is by now very nearly numb with worry, fatigue, and hunger, heaves a sigh of relief.

Realizing that the ankle will probably swell more during the night, the doctor decides that a cast is not a good idea, wraps the ankle with an Ace bandage, fits Marilyn with crutches, writes out a prescription for codeine to help with the pain, and tells her to see her doctor in the morning.

"But what should I do in the meanwhile?" Marilyn asks.

"Keep it iced," the doctor says. "Good luck." And he's off to the next patient.

It's now 10:00 at night, almost nine hours since the injury occurred, and Marilyn has finally found out what Richard knew within a few minutes: the ankle is sprained. But whereas Richard's ankle was compressed, iced, and elevated immediately, thereby keeping swelling and pain to a minimum, Marilyn's ankle was hardly treated at all. In fact, she did all the wrong things—simply because she didn't know any better—and so made the problem worse. She's in for a rough night, and when she wakes up in the morning—if, indeed, she gets any sleep at all—her ankle will most likely be swollen into a fat cylinder, stretching the confines of the wrap, and will hurt more, not less. And this is just the first day. The worst is yet to come.

To make a long—and painful—story short, Richard Green starts the game two weeks later. The day after the injury, as soon as the swelling stopped, he began rehabilitating the ankle. With a small army of doctors, trainers, physical therapists, and nurses to assist him, and a clinic full of rehab equipment to utilize, and with all the time in the world to work himself back into shape, Richard was jogging gingerly in a matter of days, sprinting soon thereafter, running noncontact drills with the team soon after that, and was back in full pads ten days after he hurt himself. Although he plays somewhat sparingly in his first game back, he catches a touchdown pass and doesn't reinjure his ankle. He goes on to finish the season, playing every game, and starts getting some nibbles from pro scouts even before his senior year begins.

Marilyn, on the other hand—and this is the painful part—still complains of a weak ankle three months after the injury. She walks with shortened steps, her foot twisted to the outside, won't go near rough ground, turns her ankle at least once a week, and, needless to say, has not stepped on a tennis court since that fateful afternoon. She eventually had to wear a cast—put on by the doctor she visited after four days of agony—for days, had problems with her knee and hip and lower back because of the abnormal way she moved while struggling to walk on the ankle, spent almost $800 on the whole business from the emergency room and subsequent doctor's visit and, although she doesn't really *blame* anybody for what happened, she wonders why it has taken her so long when the athletes she sees on TV seem to bounce back right away.

It was hard enough for Marilyn to make her initial foray into the world of sporting activities—it'll be a good while before she makes another one.

Two people, identical injuries. Why are the results so different? Two reasons: Number one, Richard simply has access to terrific medical care. Not everyone does. As a college football player at a good school, Richard has available some of the best sports medicine in the world. And he's not alone. Other college and professional athletes are similarly taken care of, and, fully as important, they have the time to devote themselves to getting well—a luxury Marilyn and millions of others just can't afford. If you make your living with your body, and suddenly your body is unable to perform, all that time you used to spend at your trade you can now devote to rehabilitation—a great boon.

But it's just not realistic to think that Marilyn and others like her will ever have access to such superlative care. Although things are getting better—largely because recreational athletes have noticed that people like Richard quickly come back from injuries that could sideline most people for months and have wondered why the same care wasn't available for them—there's still a huge gap between the medical care offered to top athletes and that available for everyone else, and probably there always will be. But there's one area in which there's no reason for a gap of any kind. It's at the heart of the second reason why Marilyn's experience was so much more difficult than Richard's—that is, *knowledge of how to treat yourself.*

It doesn't have to be much. Had Marilyn known enough to wrap her ankle right away, and ice and elevate it, many of the problems she experienced could have been avoided—even if she didn't go to a doctor until later on. But Marilyn didn't know, and there's really no reason why she should have. For many people—perhaps most of us—the workings of the body are a mystery best left to the experts, and many get away with that kind of ignorance all their lives.

But these days people are more active than ever before. The fitness boom keeps booming, and people who never before dreamed of pulling on a pair of tennis or running shoes, or a swimsuit or leotard, are doing just that. Along the way they find that things come up—things like sprained ankles and the rest of the wide world of sports-related injuries—that they never had to deal with before.

But we should know how to deal with common athletic injuries. Why spend months limping around as a result of ignorance when you might be back on the courts or the track, or in the pool, the studio, or the gym, doing the things you love to do? Why waste time and money dealing with problems long after the fact? The consequences of so many injuries are determined by what you do *immediately* after they occur—why suffer needlessly?

So, where do you go for such good advice? To a doctor? It's hard enough just to get in to *see* a doctor, much less *talk* to him. To a book? You turn to the section on ankle sprains, and the book tells you to ice it and wrap it—that's better than nothing, but it doesn't tell you *how* to wrap it, it doesn't tell you that ice cubes won't do much and that it's crushed ice you want, it doesn't tell you lots of other good things. Besides, it's either so dull or so technical that you have trouble staying with it.

But there's no reason why everyone shouldn't know about these things. Read on. This book explains how the body works, what injuries commonly occur during sports and exercise, how to recognize those injuries, how to treat them ourselves, and how to get good help if we can't—all in an accessible and lively manner that presents our bodies as just what they are: wondrous machines that work in very interesting ways.

This is a revised, revamped, and redesigned version of a book that first appeared in 1986. The world of fitness and sports medicine has changed since then. For example, we're now seeing the vanguard of the running boom of a few decades ago inching toward retirement age. These people are more active than their predecessors and carry with them the scars of a lifetime of athletic activity. Thus they're experiencing more problems than earlier generations, either due to recurrences of previous injuries or because of the fact that being more active gives them more opportunities to get hurt.

There are substantially more women participating in sports and fitness activities than a decade ago when the original book came out. Females face a higher risk of certain injuries than males (anterior cruciate ligament sprains, for example), and often they're not particularly well prepared to handle them. The unfortunate fact is that middle-aged and older women were allowed little organized sports experience in their younger days. They've not been exposed to appropriate first aid measures or rules of thumb by which to judge the severity of injuries, as they would have had they been part of a team attended by sports medicine doctors or athletic trainers. At the Center for Sports Medicine in San

Francisco, we're seeing more of these people—aging athletes and women of all ages—all the time. They're particularly well served by this book.

There's another, extremely practical reason that this book is timely. Today's health care system makes it very difficult to consult with a sports medicine physician. HMO's and insurance companies consider sports medicine doctors specialists. In their eyes a visit to a sports medicine clinic requires a referral from a patient's primary care physician. That referral may or may not be forthcoming. It's also equally difficult for an injured fitness athlete to receive adequate rehabilitative care—this too requires a referral. And even if a referral is arranged, in today's busy world the injured athlete may simply not have time to devote to lengthy physical therapy sessions. In such cases this book can be a life—or at least a fitness activity—saver.

Finally, the ability to recognize and deal with your own injuries saves money for you, the consumer (as well as for your insurance company). Going to an emergency room when the problem is not really an emergency often results in a battle with your insurance carrier, which is loath to pay for nonemergency visits. But how are most people to know if the injury is really an emergency without making that visit? And even if the insurance company does pay, you the patient are often responsible for a co-payment or 20 percent of the tab, either of which is almost certainly more than the cost of this book.

Knowledge is power—that adage is certainly true in this case. For athletes, fitness enthusiasts, and all active people, knowledge of how to recognize and deal with sports injuries provides economic power, the power of health and well-being, and the power to fully enjoy your favorite activities. That's a lot to gain from a book.

HOW TO USE THIS BOOK

This book is arranged mostly by body part. If your ankle hurts, you'll find the possible culprits in chapter 2, "The Ankle," followed by some suggestions of what to do about it, including specific rehabilitation exercises. More general exercises appear at the end of many chapters. If you can't lift your arm above your head, look in chapter 8, "The Shoulder." Each of these chapters includes a map of the area involved, with arrows pointing to various likely trouble spots. So if the back of your ankle is sore and swollen, there's a pretty good chance that an arrow labeled "Achilles tendinitis" points right to the spot. Simply turn to that section of the chapter, and you're in business. It's easy, simple, and straightforward. Most people will be able to find most of their ailments this way.

If you can't, turn to the sports injury index at the back of the book. There, injuries, and where they can be found in the text, are listed by sport. Under "Tennis," for example, you'll find "tennis elbow," "tennis leg," and "Little League elbow," among others, along with page numbers so you can turn right to them and start doing things that will make you feel better.

HOW TO USE THE REHAB EXERCISES

We've included some general exercises at the conclusion of many of the following chapters. Because treatment of virtually all of the injuries described in the book requires a rehabilitation program to reestablish strength, endurance, and flexibility, these exercises can help. Many of them can be started immediately after you discover the injury. While many conditions will require specific exercises aimed at strengthening specific muscles (best gotten from your physician or physical therapist), these exercises can often serve as a starting point.

Some caveats

+ The exercises should be done through a painless range of motion. This is not a "no pain, no gain" situation. Instead, pain usually means no gain and may even worsen the condition.

+ The exercises should *never produce any numbness or tingling.* If they do, better see a physician.

+ You should *warm up* before doing the exercises. Walk around before doing the leg/thigh exercises. Move your shoulders and arms around (gently, not violently) before doing the shoulder/arm exercises.

+ The exercises should be done *slowly and with control.* Lift or push the weight, hold it briefly in the lifted position, and slowly let it down. The letting down part of a lift is probably the biggest contributor to increasing strength.

+ Exercises should *never hurt joints.* A little muscle burning is to be expected, but a joint should never hurt.

+ Unless otherwise noted we suggest three sets of ten repetitions of each of the exercises. Repeat this series of sets up to three times a day.

CHAPTER ONE

Some Do's, Don'ts, Truths, and Misconceptions

THERE ARE THREE LEVELS of athletic injuries. The first involves *getting in shape*. Almost all the problems at this level come under the category of muscle soreness. Usually these problems are magnified beyond their real significance because at this level you've probably never hurt anything before and don't know how to interpret the pain you may be feeling. Part of becoming an athlete is learning to put up with being injured. But if you've never been hurt, probably because you've never stressed anything hard enough to injure it, you won't know what to be worried about and what to ignore. It's easy to make the wrong decisions. You may go to the doctor for a problem that means nothing and ignore something that a doctor really should see. You may wake up in the morning, not be able to get out of bed, and think you're in real trouble; but it may be nothing more than the result of doing too much stretching the day before. Or you may walk around for days with a ligament tear that needs attention. People at level one simply have no good frame of reference.

Stick with your athletic activity long enough, and you'll find yourself at level two: *learning the activity*. Once you get in shape, once you learn to handle muscle soreness, and shinsplints, tendinitis, and the rest of the common initial injuries in sports, you'll find yourself facing a second constellation of injuries that occur while you're learning your activity. Each activity makes its own particular demands on the body, and, once you've gained a general sense of what your body can and cannot do, you must learn how to handle these specific demands. That process takes time. For example, 60 percent of all football injuries occur *before* the first game, while the players are trying to adapt to the particular needs of the sport. In time you'll learn how to do the things that work and not do the ones that hurt. Figure skaters, for example, learn how to fall. Instead of stretching out their arms to break a fall and ending up with a broken wrist, skaters learn to crumple onto the ice and take the shock on their rear ends, where they're well padded.

The third level involves the risks of actually *performing the activity*. Some injuries are simply more likely to occur from performing particular movements. Baseball pitchers, for example, often develop arthritis and lose motion in their elbow joint from throwing so much.

So the question is, as you pass through the various levels of injury, what can you do about them? Most people go to the doctor. If you do, you'll want to find a doctor who knows your activity almost as well as you do. If not, many of these injuries can be puzzling to someone trying to treat you. If you're a right-handed person who throws things—a quarterback or a pitcher, for example—and you have a sore right knee, you'll probably begin to deliver the ball differently because you won't want to hurt the knee even more. You may release more quickly, start depending more on your arm, so you don't have to come down on the knee with any force. That can lead to other problems—a sore elbow, say, or an injured shoulder. And the new injury most likely won't go away until you return to your old delivery. Unless your doctor understands the dynamics of your sport, and so can see that treating the elbow injury involves clearing up the knee problem first, little will change. Sports medicine is a world unto itself.

INJURY TIP-OFFS

There are some general tip-offs that are common to all these chapters, things to be aware of while you're doing whatever it is you like to do. The helpful thing about sports injuries is that, with the exception of back problems, you always have the uninjured side for comparison. So for all the symptoms we're about to discuss, use your uninjured side as a barometer. If your ankle just doesn't feel right, but there's nothing obviously wrong that you can point to, compare it with the other side. Is it swollen? Does it feel weaker? Are you less able to bend it? If the answer to these questions is "yes," then you may have a problem.

Some injuries are immediately evident. You know when you've hurt yourself; you know what the consequences are. Other injuries—most of them, really—sneak up on you. They may be even more serious in the long run, but they can be harder to identify in the beginning. The subsequent chapters deal with both kinds of injuries in detail. In general, though, there are six general signs of injury that you shouldn't ignore, no matter where they appear:

1. **Joint pain.** Don't ignore joint pain, especially in those joints not covered by muscles—the knee, ankle, elbow, and wrist. Muscle pain may not be a significant problem. If muscle pain doesn't come on rapidly, it may be no more than a bit of soreness from overdoing your activity. But joint pain can be another story. If it lasts more than a couple of days, you'd better see a doctor.

2. **Tenderness at a specific point.** Does it hurt when you push your finger against a particular spot? If you push against a bone, a joint, or a muscle, and it really hurts, but the corresponding area on the other side doesn't, you may have a problem that requires medical attention.

3. **Swelling.** Sometimes swelling is obvious—your ankle looks like a softball, or your wrist is twice as fat as the other one—but sometimes swelling is not obvious at all. Sometimes you *feel* swollen long before anything seems to show up. The knee can be that way. Often people have a tough time noticing swelling in the knee, even though the joint may feel funny. Here's where comparing it with the other side can be invaluable.

   If the swelling is obvious, often other things will start to go wrong as well. Body parts don't slide over one another as well as they should. Your knee, for example, may develop a clicking sound, as the tendons start snapping over each other because they've been pushed into different places by the swelling.

4. **Reduced range of motion.** If you can't see or hear any signs of swelling even after comparing the injured area with your other side, check for reduced range of motion. If there's any significant swelling, in all likelihood you'll lose the extremes of motion. Can you straighten out your knee as far as on the other side? Can you bend it as far? Or if you can, does it feel odd at the extreme of motion? And is there *pain* that keeps you from straightening or bending it all the way, or is there a definite *block*? If the latter, something (a piece of cartilage, for example) may be in the way.

5. **Comparative weakness.** Look for weakness compared to the other side. Sometimes weakness is hard to notice, a little more subtle than swelling or reduced range of motion. One way to identify weakness in the legs is by going up and down stairs. Is this harder on one leg than the

other? And, of course, if you have access to a weight facility, you can test your strength by comparing your lifting on one side to that of the other.

6. **Numbness and tingling.** Never ignore these sensations. They're the kind you get when you hit your crazy bone, or when you sleep on your arm and wake up with it feeling dead. If you can't readily explain such a sensation, it's usually an indication that you have a problem that requires your doctor's attention.

With all these signs of possible injury, first look for an obvious external cause. A crease in a figure skater's boot can cause pain in the front of the ankle. Tying toe-shoe ribbons too tightly can give a ballerina all the symptoms of Achilles tendinitis. Clothing that's too tight, a wrinkle in your sock, something in your ski boot, an ill-fitting handball glove—sometimes what seems like the knottiest problem can have a simple cause and solution.

But if there's no obvious cause for any of your symptoms, you need to find out why they're there. It may be that a day or two of swelling or pain or weakness or reduced motion is no cause for alarm—sometimes things, unexplainable things, go on in our bodies and soon disappear just as mysteriously. But if you're no better in the next couple of days, or if things get worse, then you should see your doctor.

What to do about injuries

At first it's simple: don't injure yourself any more seriously than you have already and minimize the secondary symptoms. In other words, *don't let whatever it is get worse, and don't let it get any more swollen.* The goal of first aid, of any initial treatment of any problem no matter what it is, is precisely that.

So, to begin with, *if it hurts, don't use it.* That's really a matter of listening to your body and acting accordingly. More often than not you know if you've been hurt badly; there's an innate sense that warns us when real damage has been done. (For example, a quick indication of whether you've broken or sprained an ankle is whether you're willing to put weight on it. If you are, you've probably sprained it; if you're not, you may be faced with a fracture.) But sometimes people go against their best judgment and continue to use the injured part—the supposed virtue of gutting it out, playing even though hurt, and all that business. So, listen to your body and do what it tells you. It doesn't lie.

The rest of your self-care involves *keeping any swelling down.* Swelling is the enemy because it causes pain and loss of motion, which in turn makes you lose the ability to use your muscles. When you don't use your muscles, they waste away, and, once gone, muscles resist returning. Anyone who works out knows how much longer it takes to build strength than it does to lose it. Miss working out a few days and it's almost as though you never worked out before—a process that accelerates with age. It's important to keep muscles strong, especially after an injury.

Applying *compression* to the injured part, *icing* it, and *elevating* it are anti-swelling tools available to just about everyone. All of these fight swelling—elevation by keeping blood from pooling at a low point, ice by causing blood vessels to contract and thereby decreasing circulation, and compression by physically maintaining the normal contour of the injured area.

For acute injuries, the ones that happen suddenly and tend to swell quickly, compression is the most important of these tools. Applied correctly (and we'll suggest how in the chapters to come), it can do more than anything to keep swelling to a minimum. Ice certainly won't hurt, but people can more readily carry around a couple of Ace compression bandages in their tote bags than they can a bag of crushed ice. (And you should always use *crushed* ice, rather than cubes or chemical ice, because crushed ice, or even a bag of frozen vegetables or fruit, will mold itself to the contour of your body, is less likely to cause frost-bite, and is cheap.)

Above all, *don't apply heat to injuries*. Stretching in a hot shower, Jacuzzi, or sauna before you exercise can promote circulation and help you warm up, as stretching applies internal heat. Likewise, a hot shower can feel mighty good after exercise, but, in either situation, don't stick your injured part in the hot water. Increasing circulation is the last thing you want to do for an injury—not at first anyway. Stay away from heat because it promotes swelling and prohibits healing.

Again, if you hurt, don't make things worse by continuing to use the injured part. Wrap the injured area with a compression dressing, keep it cold with a bag of crushed ice, and elevate it. That's about all you or anyone else can do at first.

SOME GENERAL TRUTHS ABOUT SPORTS INJURIES

Occasional exercise is not as beneficial as regular exercise. A person who exercises just once a week does not reap the conditioning benefits of regular exercise. You have to stick with exercise for it to do you some good. And the occasional exerciser has a greater likelihood of being injured than someone who exercises at least three days a week. You tax your muscles but do not strengthen and condition them if you exercise only infrequently.

Deconditioning occurs faster than conditioning. You lose conditioning faster than you gain it—at least twice as fast. Twice as fast, that is, if you simply stop working out. If you're sick with the flu, say, or otherwise indisposed, the rate can increase to perhaps five times as fast. The moral of the story is: to stay in shape you have to keep up with your activity. And if you hurt yourself, find a healthy way of continuing to exercise and strengthen the injured part. The longer you're out of the habit of regular exercise, the harder it is to get back in shape.

If you don't use it, you lose it. And that's not just true for strength and endurance, it's true for range of motion, cardiovascular health, your muscles' ability to contract, and just about anything else you can think of. For example, if you have tennis elbow and somebody puts you in a sling for ten days, when you get back to using the arm you'll find that you've lost range of motion in your shoulder even though there's nothing wrong with the joint. The same goes with the knee, ankle, toes, and so on. It's important to stay active.

Misuse is worse than disuse. When you misuse something, you have to use other parts of your body inappropriately. If you can't walk normally after an ankle sprain, for example, it's better to go on crutches until you can than it is to hobble around with your ankle stiff and foot turned out. That awkward motion puts unaccustomed strain on the knee, the hip, even the back, and sometimes the resulting problems are more difficult to deal with than the initial ankle sprain. Our bodies are designed to function in specific ways. They rebel against inappropriate demands.

Strength and motion coexist. You can't have one without the other. The body is so smart that it won't allow a range of motion that it can't control. Take shoulder injuries, for example. If, after an injury, you don't use your shoulder for a long time, it will lose much of its range of motion. Sometimes the loss is so severe it leads to a condition called "frozen shoulder." On the operating table, however, under anesthesia the same shoulder can be completely flexible. With the muscles deactivated, a surgeon can turn the shoulder through a full 360 degrees of motion. After the patient wakes up and the muscles return to action, the shoulder goes right back to where it was—frozen. It's not that there's anything wrong with the shoulder, it's just that the muscles need to be stronger to control its motion.

If you're not strong enough to handle a full range of motion, your body just won't let you have it. So regaining strength is as important to rehabilitating an injury as regaining range of motion—they go together.

Don't live on anti-inflammatory medications. Taking "pain pills" day after day in order to carry on in athletics is not a good idea—unless you're being paid to sacrifice your body. Most nonsteroidal anti-inflammatory drugs (NSAIDs; see sidebar, p. 19) both combat inflammation *and* are potent pain relievers (analgesics). (Indeed, in some cases, readily available medications such as ibuprofen can be as effective as narcotic-type drugs in combating postoperative pain.) After seven to ten days the anti-inflammatory component of a NSAID will have done its job; after that the drug's effects are due to its pain-relieving function. That pain relief can create a dangerous situation. You can actually make some conditions worse by not receiving pain signals warning you that you're doing something wrong.

SOME COMMON MISCONCEPTIONS

Tight- or loose-jointed people suffer more injuries. Not so. Just because you happen to have loose joints doesn't mean that you'll be more prone to ligament injuries. Just having tight joints doesn't mean you should look out for more muscle injuries. You run no greater or lesser chance of these types of injuries than anybody else.

If you have tightness or looseness *because* of injury, however, that's a different story. That kind of situation usually means that you've never completely rehabilitated the injury, and unrehabilitated injuries often lead to more injuries. Make sure you completely recover from any injury.

And there's one other time when tightness can cause problems: when we age. Aging usually means tightening, and anyone who continues to be involved in activities that require a great deal of flexibility may be in for problems. It's hard to be a competing gymnast at 45 years of age, say, or a professional dancer. Aging is the great equalizer; just to remain as flexible as you are now requires more and more effort.

Muscle pulls are forever. It can seem that way if you're a runner and you've pulled your hamstring every year for the last ten years. But recurrent muscle pulls are usually the result of never having quite completely rehabilitated the original injury. It's the

+ Pulled Muscles +

A muscle pull, also called a strain, is really a partial tear of the muscle. In a full-fledged tear, muscle fibers completely separate, leaving a gap. In a pull, some fibers hold together, others separate, but mostly the muscle remains intact.

The biggest problem with muscle pulls is that they tend to come back, usually as the result of inadequate rehabilitation. Stretching the pulled muscle is the remedy most people think of for this type of injury—because pulled muscles feel tight—but the need to build up strength is not so apparent. Yet it's probably more important. Unless the injured muscle is strong, the beneficial results of stretching will not become permanent, which means the tightness will simply recur. You have to stretch *and* strengthen pulled muscles. (See more on how to rehab muscle pulls in chapter 6, "The Thigh and Hip.")

+ Older Athletes +

For the most part, sports injuries are equal opportunity afflicters: they plague anyone, regardless of age (or gender, for that matter). But older athletes do have the following special problems:

Number one—*you pay for old sins.* Previous injuries can come back to haunt you as you age. For example, joint injuries suffered in youth are among the most common causes of arthritis later on.

Number two—*it takes more effort to sustain the status quo.* As you age, you lose conditioning more rapidly, and it takes longer to build it back up. (It also takes longer to recover from injuries.) Yet older athletes often try to continue their high level of activity ("I did it when I was thirty, and, by gum, I can still do it") without additional training. Cross-training or weight training becomes increasingly important to compensate for the strength loss that accompanies aging. And engaging in a variety of athletic endeavors—helping to spread the conditioning, and the stress, around—may even be more important to older athletes.

old story—flexibility won't come back without strength, and tight muscles, muscles that aren't flexible, are likely to be reinjured. No, muscle pulls aren't forever, but you must thoroughly rehabilitate them.

Rehabilitation programs come to an end. If you've had a major injury, then, no, your rehab program probably will never end—especially if you demand a lot from the injured part. It may be that you can eventually discard some specific rehab exercises, but the likelihood is that while you were injured you developed habits that compensated for the injury and so misused other parts of your body. It can be a good idea to continue to do general rehab exercise a few days a week. That's not a huge commitment, and it may compensate for those subtle misuses that you do all the time.

We can always become stronger, faster, more flexible. What we're about to say may not be popular, but there *are* limits. Work though we may, sweat and suffer as we can, there's a point beyond which we won't be able to go.

So much for the bad news. The good news is, that as a practical matter, most of us *will* be able to better our own lowly performances, at least at first. But the better we get, the harder we work, the more nearly we approach our limits, the more difficult it is to reach them—and the more we get hurt. Injuries increase as we approach our limits. Top-level athletes live constantly on the edge. Push too hard, and you fall off into injury. The trick is to walk the line without falling off—find a level that strikes the balance between performance and injury and stay there.

The element that constantly destroys the balance is, of course, aging. It's the melancholy serenade of athletics, the unknown variable that throws every equation out of whack and makes life interesting. The good news here is that getting older does not necessarily mean getting worse. Our bodies grow smarter as we grow older, and even if we can't maintain strength and speed through the years, we can rely on increasingly rich experience and so, in some activities, actually better our performance. Even though the clock may say that our abilities are decreasing, our minds and hearts can experience increased pleasure in the doing. Such can be the enduring joy of athletics.

+ NSAIDs +

Over-the-Counter Nonsteroidal Anti-Inflammatory Drugs

NSAIDs have been around for most of our lifetimes. Aspirin, the granddaddy of them all, is still an excellent medication for bone, joint, and muscle problems. The newer preparations, ibuprofen, naproxen, and the rest, are better only in that they may have fewer side effects (mainly gastrointestinal effects such as stomach upsets, ulcers, etc.) and require less frequent doses—once or twice a day rather than every four hours. In addition to their anti-inflammatory properties (important because with sports injuries, inflammation is often the root of pain), all NSAIDs are powerful pain relievers (analgesics). They can make you feel better just because of their pain-relieving properties.

For most conditions inflammation will be decreased by taking NSAIDs for a week or ten days; after that these drugs function primarily as pain relievers. Taking these medications regularly in order to participate in a sport or activity may not be in your best interests—especially if you haven't first tried other means of dealing with the underlying problem, such as working to regain strength, endurance, and flexibility. While the medication may mask any pain you're feeling, whatever is causing the pain might actually be getting worse.

There are some conditions, however, for which people take these medications regularly, even after they've exhausted the benefits of exercises and other measures. Rheumatoid arthritis and degenerative arthritis are two. With these conditions, the only alternative to pain relief from NSAIDs may be total joint replacements.

When used appropriately, NSAIDs can be effective anti-inflammatories and pain relievers. But in most cases regular use is *not* appropriate. As with most drugs, you should take NSAIDs sparingly and only when absolutely needed.

CHAPTER TWO

The Ankle

BREATHES THERE A PERSON who has not turned an ankle? It might have been caused by stepping into a hole while running, coming down with a rebound in basketball, landing after a grand jeté in ballet. The quick starts and stops of tennis will do it—more tennis players sprain their ankles than develop tennis elbow—as will running in place in aerobic exercise, especially when you're tired. Gymnasts dismounting after a routine, soccer players dribbling, running backs making quick cuts, even swimmers who slip on the deck—all are prey to ankle sprains. And you don't have to sweat to produce a sprain; simply pushing awkwardly out of your chair can do it. Eighty-five percent of all ankle injuries in sports are sprains.

To look at the ankle, however, it seems to portend better. It is a simple, straightforward structure, with none of the inherent instability, say, of the knee or the complexity of the shoulder. The ankle is a kind of mortise and tenon joint in which the lower leg bones, the tibia and fibula, combine to form a concave, vaulted receptacle (a mortise) into which the anklebone, the talus, fits like a tenon. Dense tissue called cartilage cushions the meeting of those bony surfaces, and ligaments along the outsides of the bones hold the joint together. There is virtually no muscle at all around this joint.

The joint would seem to be a solid, stable structure, and so it is, with one important discrepancy: the lip of the bowl

<table>
<tr><th colspan="2">✚ WARNING ✚</th></tr>
<tr><td colspan="2">If You Experience Any of These Conditions, Seek Medical Help</td></tr>
<tr><td>✚</td><td>Inability to bear weight on the ankle;</td></tr>
<tr><td>✚</td><td>Any obvious deformity;</td></tr>
<tr><td>✚</td><td>Inability to rise onto the toes (stand on tiptoe);</td></tr>
<tr><td>✚</td><td>Numbness or tingling in the foot or ankle;</td></tr>
<tr><td>✚</td><td>Tenderness over the ankle bones (malleoli);</td></tr>
<tr><td>✚</td><td>Abrupt loss of the arch of the foot (fallen arch).</td></tr>
</table>

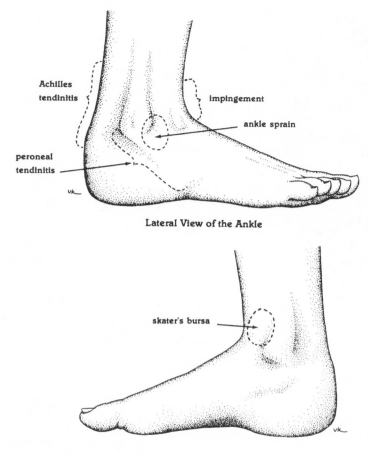

Achilles
tendinitis

impingement

ankle sprain

peroneal
tendinitis

Lateral View of the Ankle

skater's bursa

Medial View of the Ankle

formed by the tibia and fibula, the mortise half of the arrangement, is not uniform. On the outside of the ankle, it protrudes farther down toward the foot than it does on the inside, and the outside lip is thicker than the inside as well.

The result of this uneven construction is that the anklebone is more easily able to roll toward the inside of the joint, where the bowl is shallower, than to the outside. When that natural inclination is fueled by some outside agent—a pothole in the track, say, or an off-balance dismount—the upshot too often is that the ligaments on the outside of the ankle, those tough bands of fibers that connect bone to bone, cannot take the stress of the violent roll inward, and they stretch, strain, or tear.

The ankle is full of ligaments. They're flexible but not elastic. Like Saran Wrap, ligaments will bounce back if stretched, but if stretched too far or too vio-

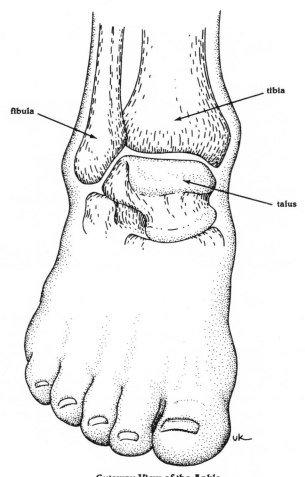

fibula

tibia

talus

Cutaway View of the Ankle

lently, they remain stretched, or they tear altogether. And the result of that over-stretching or tearing is the sharp pain, the swelling, and the drawn-out discomfort of an ankle sprain.

HOW TO RECOGNIZE AN ANKLE SPRAIN

People often are surprised that a professional athlete they've watched hobble off the field from an ankle sprain is back at it within days, while the amateur suffers for what seems like an eternity before being able to run, or play, or dance again. The difference is largely the result of what's done in the first few minutes following the injury. The professional's injury is diagnosed and treated instantly; the amateur may fumble around for hours before hitting upon an effective treatment, if then. With sprains, the first few minutes are critical. If you can diagnose and treat your sprain immediately, you'll save yourself untold time and discomfort later.

How do you know if you've suffered a sprain, rather than a more serious injury? Some rules of thumb:

✦ Did you test your ankle? The first thing that most people do when they sprain their ankle is to see if it works. Put a little weight on it, twist and turn it a little. That may hurt, but if you're able to do that, most likely it's "just" a sprain. Most people have an inherent sense that prevents them from even trying to move or bear weight on an ankle that is significantly fractured. If you're afraid to even try moving or standing on your ankle, better go to the emergency room. Your instincts are probably right.

✦ How to Wrap and Ice a Sprained Ankle ✦

A simple and effective way to counteract swelling right at the beginning is to take any soft, pliable material—a pair of socks, an old T-shirt, disposable diapers (some Bay Area Little League teams buy boxes of disposable diapers at the beginning of every season as part of their first aid supplies)—and cut and fold it into the shape of a horseshoe. Place this impromptu horseshoe around the ankle knob, with the closed, curved part of the horseshoe cupping the bottom edge of the ankle knob, then wrap the entire ankle, horseshoe included, with an Ace compression bandage. The result is a snug bandage with roughly equal compression applied to all areas of the ankle, not just on the anklebones. Other, more elaborate devices are available—a sponge-rubber donut to be placed over the ankle knob, for example—but none will provide more effective treatment. It might be worthwhile for athletes to keep an Ace bandage and a couple of disposable diapers in their gym bags for instant medical care.

Compression does not have to be tight. If your foot gets warm and tingly or starts to discolor, loosen the Ace bandage. But compression must be applied in the right place. Compression against just the ankle knob will do nothing for the sprain. Be sure, by use of the horseshoe, to make the pressure firm and equal throughout the injured area. And keep your bandaged foot elevated for the first twenty-four hours after injury.

If *ice* is available, use that too; also the sooner the better. But not just any ice. Crushed ice. Just as the value of compression is reduced if it isn't constant over the entire area involved, so icing does little if the cold doesn't contact all the injured parts. The ice must be contoured to the shape of the ankle, and it's pretty hard to contour a block of ice

HOW TO WRAP THE ANKLE

✚ If, against your better judgment, you try out your ankle and you feel something grind in there or feel a strange gravelly sensation, you'd better get your weight off it and go to the emergency room. Something other than a sprain has happened.

✚ If your friends help you off the field by supporting you on either side while you hop on your good foot and your injured ankle can't tolerate the jarring, better go to the emergency room.

✚ If your ankle feels numb or tingles, or if your foot feels initially cold, then you should go to the emergency room.

HOW TO WRAP AND ICE A SPRAINED ANKLE (CONTINUED)

or a bag of ice cubes. Physical therapists who work with professional sports teams carry crushed ice, no other. (If crushed ice is a unavailable, use a bag of frozen corn or peas. It contours nicely, provides appropriate compression as well as cold, and can be refrozen and reused for further icing.) And re-member, icing and compression must be alter-nated —you need to unwrap your ankle before icing and recompress your injury afterward.

Ice has much the same effect as compression. The cold is a natural condenser, constricting blood vessels and other soft tissue to keep swelling to a minimum. Don't ice directly against the skin but rather with a loose layer of Ace bandage under-neath. Icing hurts. After a while your ankle will ache as though it's sprained again; later it may go numb. Stay with the icing as long as you can stand it, then compress the ankle again. When alternated with compression, icing is especially effective—the two are a dynamic duo when used this way.

As effective as icing can be, perhaps the pri-mary reason for recommending it is so people *will not* consider heat. *There is no acute athletic injury for which you should use heat*—at least not at first. No matter how good you think it might feel to take that sprained ankle and soak it in a warm tub,

don't. It may go into the tub looking like an ankle, but it'll come out looking like a salami. Heat has precisely the opposite effect as cold: it opens blood vessels and expands tissues. It is a great way to increase circulation, but increased circulation is the last thing a newly sprained ankle needs. Maybe later, after the bleeding and swelling have stopped, but certainly not now. If you expose a just-injured ankle to heat, you will only delay its recovery. *Don't use heat.*

Later, after you've compressed and iced and the swelling has stabilized (which should happen in about twenty-four hours), there are other things you can do. It's important to remember that none of the things you have done so far will make any injury other than a sprain worse in the first twenty-four hours. Even if you've misdiag-nosed your injury and treated it as a sprain when it's really something else—a fracture, perhaps—you've done no harm. The worst thing that might happen is that the injury will continue to hurt like crazy, keep you up all night, and fail to respond to any treatment. In that case, better see a doctor. But in 70 to 80 percent of such cases, the injury is not serious, and in two or three days it will be in pretty good shape.

These tests will indicate 95 percent of all possible fractures. Otherwise, you almost certainly have a sprain.

✚ **What to do about it** ✚ The most important thing you can do is apply compression to the sprained area. That's more important than getting off the ankle, more important than icing, more important than elevation—all these things can come later. Compressing the ankle immediately will prevent more discomfort than anything else you can do.

But not just any compression will do the trick. To be effective compression must constrict the site of the injury itself, rather than the surrounding area. It's easy to make the mistake of simply wrapping the ankle with an Ace bandage and letting it go at that. The problem with such a wrap is that it provides little pressure in the soft places—the hollows immediately surrounding the protruding anklebones—where the injury has occurred. It only provides pressure over the anklebones, which stick out further than the rest of the ankle. Because the soft hollows are not affected by the wrap at all, they tend to swell out to the level of the wrap. Rather than keeping the swelling to a minimum, you actually encourage it. Upon removing the wrap you find an ankle swollen to precisely the contours determined by the bandage, as though the swelling were formed in a mold.

Swelling hinders recovery. Almost all initial swelling is from internal bleeding. When ligaments tear, so does the soft tissue capsule that surrounds the joint; and that tissue is laced with tiny blood vessels, which bleed. Because swelling makes the ankle stiff, it must dissipate before the ankle can regain its mobility. The pressure of the swelling itself is the cause of much of the lingering pain of an ankle sprain. Swelling affects not only the injured parts but the surrounding ligaments, tendons, and other soft tissue, causing areas that previously had no contact to rub against each other and increasing the possibility of irritation and, consequently, more swelling—a vicious cycle. And because swelling hinders movement, any muscles involved in the area tend to atrophy during the period in which they're immobilized. The recovery process then becomes needlessly complicated: you must work to reduce swelling to decrease pain and regain motion, then work to restrengthen the parts weakened by the swelling. Why not minimize the swelling in the first place? What you do during the first 30 minutes following your injury can either shorten or lengthen your recovery period by about six weeks. The trick is to compress and ice the sprain immediately.

Later treatments

Now, at least 24 hours after the initial injury and with swelling stabilized and pain no longer increasing, it may be time to increase the circulation around the joint. At this point, the increased blood flow will leach out some of the accumulated fluid and debris from the bleeding and promote healing. Timing is crucial here. As long as your ankle continues to swell, you don't want to increase circulation. The time to reap the benefits of increasing circulation is when the swelling has stabilized. One way to proceed is by using *contrast baths*.

Another way to reduce swelling is by *movement*. Movement of the ankle is a form of internal massage, twisting and turning the tissue much as a masseur kneads it from the outside. This movement promotes circulation at the same time as it milks away the swelling. In addition to these therapeutic effects of movement, the quicker you begin to move your ankle, the less muscle wasting you suffer, and the sooner you recover. Let pain be your guide. If you can bear weight without hurting an hour after suffering a sprain, then it's fine to walk on the ankle. You might have to take six-inch steps because it hurts to do more, but even with an extensive ankle injury you can walk—you just take small steps. Rehabilitation involves gradually taking longer and longer steps, increasing the ankle's range of motion. In this process you are your own physical therapist. Push, but not so much that it hurts. If you find you've done too much (swelling or pain in your ankle the next morning will tell you), then back off a little. As long as you're not in pain, you're not harming your ankle.

The longer you baby the ankle, the longer it will take to regain range of motion and strength. Yet you won't be able to get back to your favorite activity until you regain them, and you won't get them back singly—strength accompanies range of motion and vice versa. As a general rule, your body won't allow you to have a range of motion that it can't control with strength. You may be able to stretch out the ankle, but that flexibility won't last if the muscles aren't up to controlling the motion. You have to bring strength and flexibility back simultaneously.

Flexing and walking are ways to regain both strength and flexibility. Bicycling, especially on a stationary bike (hard to fall off, no potholes to run into), is another. Soon after your injury, place the bike pedal directly beneath your ankle rather than the ball of your foot. That way the ankle remains relatively stationary, but you keep your leg strong. As more and more ankle motion returns, move the pedal further forward beneath your foot. Bicycling provides an effective, relatively risk-free way of regaining strength. The motion is up and down, so there's little danger of turning the ankle again, and you're giving your calf muscles a good workout.

Conditioning the muscles near the ankle is more important than it may seem. Once you've stretched or torn ligaments through injury, they will never again be as tight as they were. But everyone's ligaments are loose, sprained ankle or no. That's because ligaments are the joint's second line of defense. Ligaments hold joints in alignment, but they don't provide strength. That is provided by the first line of defense, the muscles in the area. If the muscles are strong, then you've got your own built-in splint. You don't need a splint of wood or plaster because the muscles will hold things together. So the best defense against reinjuring your ankle (or injuring it in the first place) is to build up the muscles in the lower leg.

Bicycling is a good way to do that. Another is to strap on a water ski flotation vest and "run" in the deep end of a swimming pool. The vest provides buoyancy—keeps you from sinking—and since the pull of gravity is greatly

---

+ How to Give Yourself Contrast Baths +

Contrast baths, of alternating warm and cold water, can help to increase blood supply by first constricting the blood vessels with cold then opening them with warmth, draining the afflicted area. The nice thing about contrast baths is that you can easily do them at home. The secret to taking care of yourself at home is to use the things you already have on hand. Filling a plastic bucket with warm water and another with cold will work just fine for a contrast bath. Or you could fill the bathtub with warm water and fill a bucket or wastebasket with cold. You can even use the toilet for the cold bath—the water in the toilet bowl stays cool if you flush it now and again.

But the heat won't do much good unless it's active heat, meaning that you have to keep your ankle moving in the warm water (and "heat" does not mean "hot"—100 degrees Fahrenheit, just above body temperature, will do just fine).One way to keep your ankle active in the water is by writing the alphabet with your big toe, in letters as large as you can tolerate. The movement forces you to use all the motions of your ankle, up and down, side to side, in complex ways, which approximate what the ankle and its muscles do when running over rough ground. Any movement of the ankle in the warm water will do, but writing the alphabet may be less boring than simply moving up and down and side to side.

Try four minutes in warm water alternated with one minute in the cold (and the cold water should be as cold as you can tolerate—spike it with ice cubes). Repeat these alternating cycles of hot and cold for 20 minutes every day. The regimen should help reduce swelling, although if you've taken care of yourself properly from the beginning (with compression, elevation, and icing) you shouldn't have much swelling to get rid of.

reduced in the pool and the water itself provides resistance, it takes just about as much muscle to push a leg down in the pool as it does to pull it up. This provides, among other things, a terrific cardiovascular workout as well. Fifteen minutes of vigorous "running" in the water will cause even the hardiest person to gasp for breath. Just don't forget that flotation vest.

> ### + How to Care +
> ### for a Sprained Ankle
>
> 1. Apply immediate *compression.*
> 2. Apply crushed *ice,* if available.
> 3. *Move* the ankle as much as comfort will allow.
> 4. Once the swelling has stabilized, use *contrast baths* to help reduce further swelling.
> 5. *Exercise* to regain motion and strength. Walk, bicycle, balance on your toes, and do other exercises as comfort allows.

The peroneal muscles in the lower, outer calf are your first line of defense against ankle injuries. To strengthen these muscles, you can use a piece of bicycle inner tube, surgical tubing, or a Thera-Band®. Nail the ends of the tubing or Thera-Band® to a piece of board and stick your foot under the loop. Since the peroneal muscles allow you to pull your foot to the outside, exercise them by repeating that motion—lower the inside of your foot and pull up and out. As you develop strength, tighten the tubing to provide more tension. If you can't find tubing or a board, you can use your uninjured foot to provide resistance. Simply rest one foot on top of the other and pull against it. You'll notice a difference sooner than you think.

Another way to strengthen the muscles around the ankle—and a test to see how the ankle is progressing—is to balance on your toes on the injured side. Push up onto to your toes and, wobbly or no, hold on as long as you can (*without* clutching a chair, door jamb, or friend to help you stay there). You'll feel this in your calf muscles as well as in the ankle. It's a good workout for all the muscles in the ankle area and, if you're successful, an indication that your ankle may be strong enough to allow you to resume your favorite activity. Many of our patients have found that a good way to remember to do the exercises—and do them frequently enough—is to take all phone calls balancing on the injured foot. First on the whole foot and later, as your strength improves, on the toes.

MEDIAL ANKLE SPRAINS

We've been talking about the kind of ankle sprain in which you roll your foot in, toward the midline of the body. This type, called a lateral sprain, is by far the most common and is accompanied by pain and swelling on the outside of the ankle (when the foot rolls in, outside ligaments tear). The other kind of sprain, the medial sprain, is caused by rolling the foot out, away from the body, and involves pain on the inside of the ankle. It is relatively rare because the ankle's construction (discussed earlier) makes it difficult to roll the foot to the outside. It takes some doing to accomplish a medial sprain—but when you do, it's likely that the injury is much more severe.

In soccer, for example, a medial sprain may be the result of a runner cutting in one direction while her cleats catch in the ground and force the foot the other way. It may involve someone inadvertently stepping on the foot, or it may be caused by running into a hole. Because so much force is required to roll the foot outward, medial sprains are often accompanied by other kinds of rotational injuries—like a fracture. And because of the extra distance the foot has to travel to roll to the outside, the ligaments on the inside of the ankle often completely tear off, rolling up like a window shade and sometimes lodging in the joint itself. Sprains like these may require surgery.

So if you experience pain on the inside of your ankle, you may want to pay particular attention to the warning signs discussed earlier. If any of them apply, see a doctor.

ACHILLES TENDINITIS

The Achilles tendon is the largest tendon in the body. Named for the Greek hero who was invulnerable everywhere except in his heel, the Achilles tendon is the taut cable that runs down the back of the leg from the lower calf to the heel. No other tendon is quite so obvious or exposed, and, next to sprains, tendinitis, or inflammation of the Achilles tendon, is the most common ankle problem. Tendons connect muscle to bone; this tendon connects the calf muscles to the heel bone. Without the Achilles tendon, ballet dancers wouldn't be able to rise up on their toes, much less point them. Nor could the rest of us run or even walk up and down stairs.

Like ligaments, tendons are strong but not particularly elastic. They will stretch only so far—then something has to give. Usually what gives is not muscle (which is able to contract and expand), or bone (which is unyielding), but tendon, the weak link in the chain. In contrast to ankle sprains, however, the onset of tendinitis is usually not a dramatic event. Achilles tendinitis is an overuse injury. You notice that your tendon hurts a little bit in the morning after you've run too far the day before. Later in the day it loosens up, and you ignore it. A few days later you find that it hurts a bit at the end of your run, or after your tennis match, but you continue to ignore it. Three days later it's hurting in the middle of the run, and then it begins to hurt at the beginning as well. Pretty soon it hurts so much you can't work out at all. By then you *are* aware that something is wrong with your Achilles tendon. This is the usual way people deal with Achilles tendinitis—ignore it until it starts compromising your activity so much that you can't ignore it anymore.

It may seem as though Achilles tendinitis is caused by overstretching, but that's not usually the case (although it may be in women who are used to wearing high-heeled shoes and start doing a lot of hill climbing, for example. The Achilles tendon is shortened from the high heels and suddenly is asked to stretch as the ankle flexes in the opposite direction). Much of Achilles tendinitis is the result of weak calf muscles. The process by which this works is described below.

Muscles don't have many ways to tell you what's going on. If they're hurt or fatigued, they tighten up; and if they tighten up, they hurt more. That's why it's a good idea to stretch after doing an activity. Muscles that are fatigued tighten up and stay that way all night, and the next morning they don't work very well. But if you stretch them out at the end of your activity, the stretching (and flexibility) lasts.

Muscles become tired from overuse. If you keep working a fatigued muscle, it continues to tighten until finally it's significantly shorter than it was when you started exercising. And then something gives. So Achilles tendinitis is not the result of *over*stretching, but of *normal* stretching that the tendon is unable to bear because the calf muscles are shorter and tighter than usual. It's a vicious cycle: The more you use the muscles, the more tired they become. The more tired the muscles, the shorter they become, and tighter. The tighter the muscles, the greater the strain on the Achilles tendon.

Tendinitis probably starts as minute single-fiber tears. The tendon is made up of thousands of fibers; you're not going to miss a few. But where the fibers tear they also swell. As you continue to use the tendon, the swelling increases and begins to hurt. The Achilles tendon is enclosed in a kind of loose sheath, and as it swells it can begin to rub against this sheath. That irritates the sheath, which can then swell, compounding the whole problem. In extreme cases the swollen tendon and sheath stick to one another—there simply isn't room for the tendon to slide in the sheath. This can lead to a condition called snowball crepitation, in which the tendon squeaks in the sheath, sounding much like the noise made by squeezing a handful of snow. Ballet dancers are prone to snowball crepitation. You can sometimes hear a dancer's Achilles tendon squeak from across the room, as though someone were pulling fingernails across a blackboard. That degree of severity is rare, however. If your Achilles tendon is squeaking, see a doctor.

+ Strengthening Figure + Skaters' Ankles

One good way for skaters to strengthen their ankles is to stroke with successively fewer hooks laced together. For example, try stroking daily for ten to fifteen minutes, twice the amount of time forward as backward (forward is more work). During the first week, don't run the laces through the top hook of your boots. During the second week, don't use the top two hooks. During the third week, don't use the top three hooks, the fourth week the top four hooks, and so on until you get down to the eyelets. Then lace only through the eyelets for all your stroking.

The stronger your ankles, the better your boots will fit. The less external support you need, the less reinforcement the boot will have to provide, and so the more flexible it can be. Thus, a better and closer fit.

Your ankles will strengthen noticeably because you'll no longer be able to depend on the boot for support. When you jump and turn and do other things that could be dangerous to attempt with only a partially laced boot, lace all the way up. When you go back to stroking, lace down again.

+ **What to do about it** + Since Achilles tendinitis usually starts insidiously and then feeds on itself, the thing to do is to break the cycle of injury before it has a chance to settle in. If you notice your tendon hurting after a workout, stretch well and ice the area to decrease the blood flow. To stretch, stand with your foot pointed straight ahead, keep your heel on the ground, and slowly bend your body forward over your ankle. You'll feel the tug in your Achilles tendon. (Keeping your knee straight stretches the gastrocnemius, the large muscle in the calf, as well. Bending the knee stretches the smaller muscle, the soleus. More on that in chapter 4, "The Lower Leg.")

Don't do your usual workout the next day. Do half as much and then stretch and ice as before. Most likely the problem will then go away. As with ankle sprains, it's crucial to catch the problem immediately. As a general rule with overuse problems like Achilles tendinitis, it takes as long to get over the injury as it does to realize that it's there. If you choose to ignore the pain for three weeks, it will take at least three weeks to get over the injury.

After the pain disappears, you can gradually go back to your usual workout schedule. Be sure to stretch well before and after each workout. And if the pain returns, break the injury cycle again by curtailing your activity, stretching, and icing.

Strengthening the calf muscles is another way of reducing the impact of Achilles tendinitis and reducing the risk that you might get it in the first place. Strong calf muscles can take more use and are less likely to tighten up at the end of a workout. To strengthen your calf muscles, do toe raises. With your feet pointing straight ahead, rise up onto your toes—with your knees straight to strengthen the gastrocnemius or with your knees bent to strengthen the soleus. Rise up, hold the position for a few seconds, then let down. Keep repeating the exercise until you get tired, then do it one more time. Gradually increase the number of toe raises until you're doing three sets of twenty each—that's a reasonable goal. As with ankle sprains, doing toe raises while taking phone calls is a good way to remember to do the exercise.

And, as with ankle sprains, balancing on your toes is a good way to strengthen the calf muscles as well as provide a good workout for the muscles around the ankle. For this exercise, it doesn't matter if your knee is straight or bent; it's your choice which calf muscle you prefer to work on.

Recently a new treatment has become popular. People with Achilles tendinitis often find that their first few steps in the morning are the most painful of the day. They've slept all night with their feet pointed, and it's hard to get the injured heel down to the ground when they take a step. But now commercially available night splints can hold the ankle at a right angle, maintaining a calf muscle stretch throughout the night. Upon arising, you take off the splint and, voilà, your heel is on the ground. This device has done more to help us treat Achilles tendinitis than anything else in the past decade.

If, after all this, Achilles tendon pain persists, better see a doctor.

ACHILLES TENDON RUPTURE

As the Achilles tendon is the largest and most exposed tendon in the body, it's also the one most commonly ruptured. But ruptures don't happen often—even less commonly in women. An Achilles tendon rupture usually afflicts a man over 30 years old, usually someone who has been athletically active and who has had a previous bout with Achilles tendinitis. Often this person has had some kind of warning—pain or weakness in the tendon—which has been ignored. The injury usually results from a sharp, quick movement: pushing off the ankle to return serve in tennis, going for a rebound in basketball, even jumping from a boat onto a deck. The movement puts a sudden strain on the tendon that it simply cannot tolerate; as a result, the tendon rips.

Achilles tendon ruptures are strange injuries in that the pain, or, more precisely, the lack of it, is entirely out of proportion to the severity of the injury. The entire tendon may be severed, but often it doesn't hurt at all—at least not at first. The first response of people who rupture the Achilles tendon is to look over their shoulder to see who has hit their ankle. This immediate looking over the shoulder is the primary diagnostic tip-off for this injury. Tennis players swear that their partner hit them with the ball. Basketball players are ready to punch the person who kicked them in the ankle. Dancers think someone's thrown something at them from the wings. There's no warning at all. You may hear a big pop (your friends may hear it, too) and feel as though someone's whacked you in the ankle. And that's it. No pain. No sense of being injured.

Except you can't push up onto your toes any longer. You may be able to point your foot, as other tendons are involved in that movement, but you can't go up onto your toes. For that reason, this is a devastating injury for ballet dancers.

Another way of checking for Achilles tendon ruptures is to run your finger down the back of your tendon. If your finger drops into a hole, you've ruptured the tendon. (Try that test immediately—soon the hole will fill up with blood.) And your ankle feels strange. It's hard to control your foot, which has a tendency to flop around.

✛ What to do about it ✛ See a doctor. There's no home remedy for a ruptured Achilles tendon. You can make the diagnosis yourself (and probably as accurately as the doctor can—the injury is frequently misdiagnosed), but you'll need professional treatment. Until a doctor can see you, though, there are two things you can do: Let your foot hang down, toes pointed toward the ground, so you won't pull the ends of the torn tendon any farther apart than they already are. Because any treatment you receive will be designed to facilitate those ends healing back together, you can begin to help the process along by keeping your foot in this position. And a firmly wrapped compression bandage, much as with a sprained ankle, will help keep bleeding to a minimum.

A doctor will do one of two things: recommend surgery or put the ankle, in the toes-down position, into a cast for six weeks to two months. Both approaches aim to help the tendon grow back together. In surgery, the doctor can actually place the ends together, and, theoretically at least, you may end up with a tendon that more closely approximates its length and strength before the injury.

Controversy continues to exist regarding whether or not to operate for this condition. Studies have uncovered little if any difference in strength or range of motion between ruptured Achilles tendons treated surgically and those put in a cast to heal on their own. For years—perhaps centuries—doctors have treated children born with tight Achilles tendons (clubfeet) by actually severing the Achilles tendon during the first few months of the child's life, putting the ankle in a cast, and allowing the tendon to grow back together normally. There's no attempt to stitch or otherwise line up the severed ends—the tendon simply heals on its own. On the plus side for surgery patients is the fact that newer techniques usually result in less total time in a cast or brace than if the injury were treated by immobilization alone. But, of course, you have to deal with potential surgical complications. Infection is a risk because the blood supply isn't particularly abundant to the area.

There is no right or wrong way to treat this injury. Just make sure you see a doctor and get the injury treated professionally. And know that *there are options*. Regardless of the approach you and your doctor decide on, there's a nervous one-month period when the ankle comes out of the cast and begins to regain its strength and range of motion. That process requires effective rehabilitation. Stretching exercises such as those discussed with respect to Achilles tendinitis can help, but even more important is regaining strength. In the long haul, regardless of how it's treated, the Achilles tendon ultimately stretches out to normal length. But your calf muscles won't regain normal strength without a lot of work and exercising. Failure to regain normal strength results in continued pain and disability and increases the chance of reinjury.

Don't let your doctor simply remove the cast and tell you that you're on your own. Make sure you're pointed in the direction of a good rehabilitation program. If treated effectively, Achilles tendon ruptures recover remarkably well.

OTHER ANKLE INJURIES

Fractures

You'll know it when you fracture an ankle. The pain is terrific. It doesn't *feel* like a sprain or Achilles tendon problem. But before you see a doctor, treat it as though it were an ankle sprain by compressing, elevating, and icing it. You won't hurt the fracture that way and may help keep swelling and pain to a minimum. Keep movement to a minimum (you won't feel like moving it, anyway) and see a doctor.

Impingement

A strange thing sometimes happens in the ankles of ballet dancers, gymnasts, and football linemen. The bone and soft tissue in the front of the ankle build up, making it hard to plié—bend the knee over the front of the foot. It might seem odd that these three groups of athletes have anything in common, much less an unusual ankle problem. The common denominator is the fact that all rely on the plié as a basic technique. In ballet all jumps begin and end in plié, as do many turns. Dancers use it at the barre to stretch and make the muscles and tendons flexible. Gymnasts land in plié position after dismounting an apparatus. And football linemen constantly plié when going into down position before a play.

The plié position puts great pressure on the ankle. The skin and soft tissue over the bone compress and wrinkle like an accordion. Sometimes in reaction to this pressure, the bones grow ridges that lock against themselves and the tissue swells, further reducing flexibility. When gymnasts miss a dismount and land short, the problem is intensified. The result of this impingement can be a great deal of pain and an inability to plié effectively—aesthetic death for the dancer, annoyance and discomfort for the others.

✛ What to do about it ✛ There is no cure for impingement, short of surgery. The operation involves removing excess soft tissue and chipping away at the bone until it regains normal clearance and thickness. This procedure can solve the problem for a time, but there is no assurance that the joint will not thicken again. Some people simply seem disposed to recurrence of this problem. (See the appendix, "Ballet," for more on impingement surgery.)

Before choosing the extreme of surgery, though, there are some things you can do to mitigate impingement. Gymnasts can strengthen their calf muscles to be able to use them as shock absorbers when they land from their dismounts. If their calf muscles are exceptionally strong, gymnasts can lean into the Achilles tendon before crunching the front of the ankle on dismount—the Achilles tendon is better equipped for that kind of shock. Dancers and football players can similarly strengthen their calf muscles. Dancers can learn to cheat a little—they can get away with lifting their heels in plié, and in football it doesn't matter how you look as long as you get the job done.

Ballet dancers also suffer impingement in the back of the ankle, making it hard for them to go up onto their toes, much less on pointe. Again, surgery is the only real solution, but dancers can cheat to reduce the discomfort. They can sickle, or roll in their feet, just enough to reduce the pressure on the back of the ankle. As little as 2 degrees will cause some relief, and few people will notice the difference—but the dancer has to be very strong to be able to sustain the position. All such techniques are little more than stopgaps, however. Eventually the body is going to lose the battle.

Bursitis

Bursas (from the Latin for "pouch") are small, moist envelopes that occur around joints, wherever things slide over one another. They're the body's friction reducers, its ball bearings. The walls of a bursa slip back and forth, allowing things on top of the bursa—soft tissue—to slide easily over things beneath—bone. Sometimes, though, the bursas can become irritated and inflamed. When that happens, they can swell and fill with fluid. This problem is called bursitis.

Bursitis is an occupational hazard for figure skaters. Champion figure skaters have inflamed bursas; so do ten-year-olds who are just cutting their teeth on the ice. These fluid-filled sacs along the front and sides of the ankle are no problem for dancers—ballerinas can simply tie their toe-shoe ribbons around the bursas. Runners won't notice them, for their shoes don't reach high enough to make contact. But for skaters, who require a superb boot fit from side to side, inflamed bursas can be dangerous as well as simply annoying. The stability for taking off and landing comes from a snug, strong boot, as most skaters' ankles are not strong enough to absorb the pressure of jumps by themselves. If a boot cannot fit snugly because a swollen bursa is in the way, then the skater cannot take off and land correctly. The risk is an injury much more serious than an inflamed pouch of fluid.

No one knows exactly what causes bursitis, but most likely the bursas become inflamed as a protective response by the body to stress. Football players get them on the elbow, for example, perhaps to provide a cushion against the constant pounding on the ground (bursas are especially common among players on artificial turf). Figure skaters always get bursas in the same spot, the inside of the ankle, most likely to counter the pressure and rubbing of their boots and the stress of frequent push-offs and landings. But the body works against itself. The fluid begets more fluid, which stretches and irritates the skin, producing more fluid.

✚ What to do about it ✚ It may be that bursitis can be prevented, but once established it's tough to get rid of. Bursas can be drained, but often they simply fill up again. The only remedy may be surgery to remove the entire sac. Once the sac is gone, bursa problems are unlikely to return.

Osteochondritis Dissecans

The name alone is forbidding enough; the fact that no one knows just what causes this problem provides even less comfort. Osteochondritis dissecans (OD, for short) is a condition in which a piece of the anklebone loses its blood supply and simply flakes away. The bone fragment might remain where it is, loose in its bed, or float away, leaving a crater behind. The diagnosis is very difficult; treatment should be professional.

OD sufferers are people with bizarre ankle complaints. You wake up one morning, and your ankle just won't work. It's stiff and hurts like crazy. By mid-morning it's fine, and it stays that way for the next few weeks. Then one day you get up from your desk, and it feels as though somebody's stuck an icepick in your ankle. It stays like that all day, even swells up a bit. But by the next morning it feels great again.

You can't explain it. It isn't because you were running uphill, or breaking in new shoes, or lacing your boots too tightly. It's not your first week on pointe, and you haven't suddenly taken up racquetball. But the problem keeps coming back. Then it goes away, and by the time you forget that you ever had it, it shows up again. Better go to a doctor.

Once in the examining room, you may find that physicians are as puzzled as you are. They'll probably take x-rays, but OD doesn't necessarily show up on x-rays. And even if they do suspect that the culprit is OD, they'll be hard-pressed to tell you why it happens. No one is quite sure.

✚ What to do about it ✚ If the fragment of bone has come completely loose, surgery is usually necessary. Occasionally the fragment can be pinned back in place; otherwise it has to be removed.

Peroneal Tendon Dislocation

It's almost impossible to sprain your ankle skiing—you could hardly twist your ankle in ski boots if your life depended on it. But if you go over the tops of your skis, you can dislocate or tear your peroneal tendons.

The peroneal tendons connect the peroneal muscles, which run along the outside of the lower calves, to the bones of the foot. These muscles enable you to pull your foot to the outside. The tendons run behind the outside ankle knob in a little groove with a gristly roof on it. You can easily find them with your fingers. They usually don't pop loose, but going straight forward over your skis (or slipping backwards off a flight of stairs) can do it. The muscles are particularly tight, and when the foot flexes forward—dorsiflexion, it's called—they give very little. But something has to give, so the tendons simply pop out of their groove.

The tip-off to peroneal tendon dislocation is that it is *not* a result of twisting the ankle, as is a sprain. This is straight-ahead, over-the-top dorsiflexion. You usually feel something pop out of place. And you get a great deal of swelling that comes up very quickly just behind the ankle knob. In no time at all, it looks as though a sausage has lodged beneath your skin.

✚ What to do about it ✚ At first you can treat this condition as you would Achilles tendinitis—compression, ice, rest. That will minimize discomfort, but any lasting treatment needs to be offered by a doctor. It may be that a doctor will simply push the tendons back into their groove and place your ankle in a cast for four to six weeks, letting time and inactivity heal the injured area. Or surgery to reconstruct the torn area may be necessary. In either case, rehabilitation to regain motion and strength is a must.

Posterior Tibial Tendinitis

The tendon for the posterior tibial muscle—one of the groups of muscles in the calf—lies behind the inside anklebone (or medial malleolus). It attaches to the foot at the navicular, that bony bump beneath and ahead of your inside ankle knob. Its major job is to support the arch of the foot. In older women, the tendon can become tight and irritated—presumably because of years of wearing high heels, but no one knows for sure.

This problem is heralded by pain, tenderness, and swelling below and behind the inside anklebone. Ultimately a woman might notice that her arch has fallen, compared to her other foot, and that other regions of her injured ankle and foot are now painful. This is a serious problem. These signs indicate that the tendon is irritated and inflamed and, if ignored, might rupture, leaving a permanently, painfully, fallen arch.

✚ What to do about it ✚ See a doctor. Sometimes the foot must be immobilized to allow the irritation and inflammation to subside. This is then followed by a careful rehabilitation program to reestablish both strength and flexibility. Often the use of a custom-made orthotic (arch support) will take some stress off the tendon and not only speed healing but prevent recurrence. If the tendon ruptures, orthotics might still help, but often surgery is necessary. Best to catch this problem early.

Constriction Tendinitis

If you lace your running shoes too tightly and then run for your usual few miles, you may wake up the next morning with a swollen and painful ankle and a roaring case of tendinitis. A number of small tendons run down the front of the ankle into the foot. They are very sensitive to pressure. These tendons move under the ridge of your shoelaces with every stride you take. An overly tight middle buckle of a ski boot can cause the same problem.

✚ What to do about it ✚ Loosen your footwear. And as with tendinitis elsewhere in the ankle, ice and rest will most likely do the trick.

COMMONLY ASKED QUESTIONS ABOUT ANKLE INJURIES

When can I run again?

That's what everyone wants to know. After you've injured your ankle, when can you get back to training? There are three quick tests you can try on yourself at home:

1. You can run again when you can walk fast, without limping and without hurting, with a long stride—almost as though you were race walking.

2. You can run again when you can balance on your toes on the injured side for as long as you can on the good side.

3. You can run again when you can hop up and down on your toes on the injured side ten times without dropping your heel and without hurting.

Then go ahead and try running. On level ground, after walking a bit to loosen up, jog for about a block. If it hurts after the third stride or so, then stop. You're not ready yet. Try again a couple of days later. A bit of discomfort is okay, but it shouldn't hurt.

A good test is to have a friend run behind you to take a look at your gait. If you're limping, better not run. Limping forces you to use the wrong muscles, and that can lead to other problems—tendinitis of the hip or knee, for example. And besides, you're not training effectively. . You don't do yourself any favors by limping when you run.

You're better off doing other things: bicycling to strengthen your leg, rapid walking (walking rapidly over hilly terrain gives a strong aerobic workout), or "running" in the deep end of a swimming pool while wearing a flotation vest.

Can I walk or run while my ankle is still swollen?

Yes, if it doesn't hurt, you probably can. And if the swelling doesn't increase, you probably can. Most ankle injuries remain a bit swollen even when you're back to full activity, at least for a little while. So if the injured ankle doesn't yet look identical to the uninjured side, you're okay, as long as your ankle's comfortable and isn't getting worse. Remember to ice and stretch after you're done.

Why is my ankle stiff in the morning?

Generally, morning stiffness is nothing to worry about. With the night's inactivity, the ankle swells, causing stiffness. The swelling will go down with the day's movement. Motion milks the fluid out of the ankle.

There aren't large tolerances in any joint, not much space for extra baggage. If the soft tissue—the tendons and ligaments—and the surrounding capsules are swollen, then things don't slide the way they're supposed to, and motion around the joint depends on things sliding over one another. That's why the first few steps in the morning are short ones. Slowly they'll get longer and longer. Motion has the same effect as applying intermittent pressure—the circulation carries away the swelling.

Will ligaments heal so they're as tight as before the injury?

Probably not. But it really doesn't matter, *if* they don't bother you. The tightness of a joint is mainly determined by muscle strength, not ligament tightness. Everyone has loose ligaments, but usually we're not aware of this because the muscles take up the slack. That's why a good muscle-building rehab program is essential to recovering from any ligament injury.

Is a sprained ankle worse than a broken ankle?

No, not by a long shot. The reason people sometimes think so is that when you break your ankle, most likely you'll go to a doctor to get it treated, take good care of it while it's healing, and then rehabilitate it carefully. When you sprain an ankle, you may not see anybody—indeed, you may not do anything except wait it out. So often sprained ankles can take forever to heal, if they ever do.

Sprained ankles should be treated and rehabilitated as thoroughly as broken ankles. This is an injury that responds well to good treatment but can linger for what may seem like a lifetime if neglected.

I sprained my ankle six months ago. Why does it still hurt?

Because you're not strong enough. Almost without exception, that's the answer. Strengthening the muscles acting on the ankle will almost certainly solve your ankle problem. If you're diligent, even two to three weeks of work is enough to make a difference. That's spending ten minutes a day—not a big investment in time, but all you need to show impressive results. Remember, peroneal muscles are the first line of defense against ankle sprains. Build them up as suggested in the section on sprains.

Do I need a cast for a sprain?

Probably not, as long as you're able to stay off the ankle when necessary. Some people have to get casts because they just can't function without bearing weight on the injured ankle. Climbing on and off the school bus, negotiating flights of stairs, getting to and from the subway—doing all this while wearing a cast for a few days might be easier than dealing with crutches. (Climbing stairs with crutches is one of life's more memorable experiences.)

The problem with walking with a cast is that because of the cast-induced limp you won't build up the strength to walk normally. We try to treat very few problems with casts. The odds are that you're not going to do anything without a cast that will cause you permanent damage, and you might do some good by beginning strengthening exercises. You can't do these exercises in a cast.

Are taping, ankle supports, or braces any good?

Sometimes taping or using an ankle wrap will do some good. By providing a little external support, a hedge against disaster, a support may nudge you into a higher level of activity than you would be ready for otherwise. There are a number of varieties available. None of them is bad.

Generally, the little elastic anklets don't help much. They may give you a sense of security by reminding you that your ankle is not yet well, but they won't keep you from rolling over on it. If something is going to prevent you from

---

+ Thera-Bands®, Surgical + Tubing, and Inner Tubes

Thera-Bands®, surgical tubing, inner tubes, and other homemade devices are elastic appliances used instead of weight to provide resistance for exercising muscles. Their primary advantage is their portability (easier to carry in your luggage than ten-pound weights) and low cost. By altering your body position, you can use them to exercise almost any muscle.

Their disadvantage is that as they are stretched their resistance goes up progressively, so the extremes of range of motion often aren't exercised adequately. Your muscles may encounter too little resistance at the beginning and too much at the end.

respraining your ankle, and it's not your own strength, then it's going to have to be substantial and often not terribly comfortable.

Braces fall into this category. A brace may help, and it won't harm you unless you wear it in lieu of exercise—that'll make you weak. But a brace is not a short-cut. It may help you back to doing the things you like to do a little quicker (and there is some evidence that wearing the brace for the rest of the season or for six months or so after the injury provides some protection against a recurrence of the sprain), but ultimately it won't solve the problem. What will is rehabilita-tion—good, diligent restrengthening work, with or without a brace.

REHAB EXERCISES

For sprains

The following exercises strengthen all of the important muscles that provide stabil-ity to the ankle, using such aids as Thera-Bands®, surgical tubing, and inner tubes.

Pull your foot to the outside and up against resistance. This exercise, which strengthens the peroneal muscles, is the most important, as the peroneal muscles are the anti–ankle sprain muscles. Take care to just move the ankle, not twist the entire leg from the knee down. If you're doing the exercise correctly, you should feel the muscle on the outside of the lower leg tighten.

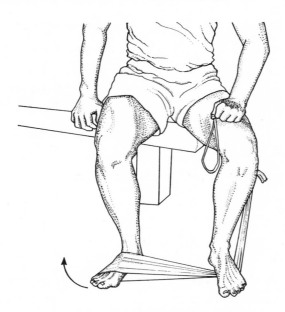

PERONEAL MUSCLE STRENGTHENING

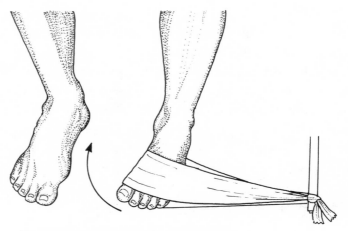

POSTERIOR TIBIAL MUSCLE STRENGTHENING

Pull your foot to the inside and up against resistance, keeping your toes pointed. Take care to move just the ankle, not twist the entire leg from the knee down.

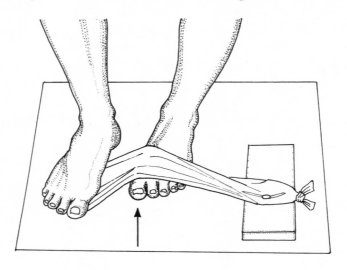

DORSIFLEXER MUSCLE STRENGTHENING

Pull your foot up and toward you against resistance.

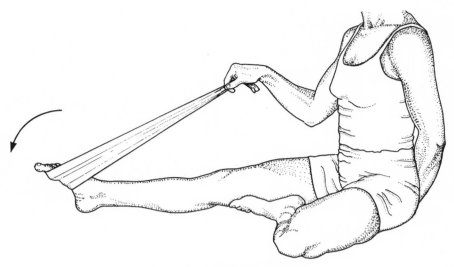

CALF MUSCLE STRENGTHENING

Push your foot down against resistance.

For Achilles tendinitis

After an ankle sprain, the calf muscles (and Achilles tendon) have a tendency to tighten up. These are calf-stretching exercises. The first (holding your knee straight) stretches the gastrocnemius (upper-calf) muscle, the second the soleus (lower-calf) muscle. Hold the stretches for thirty seconds.

GASTROCNEMIUS MUSCLE STRENGTHENING

SOLEUS MUSCLE STRENGTHENING

CHAPTER THREE

The Foot

FEET ARE MISTREATED and maligned, decried for being too large or too ugly or for having toes too long or too short, stuffed into all manner of uncomfortable shoes—in short, taken for granted. We ask our feet to support hundreds of pounds, day after day. Flexing, bending, turning, pitching and yawing, navigating changing and uneven terrain, gripping with the toes (and in the case of ballerinas actually balancing on them)—no wonder there are times when life offers no greater joy than being able to get off your feet.

But the foot is no passive bearer of weight. Rather it's a flexible, ingeniously designed organism in its own right. It contains 26 separate bones with a complex web of ligaments to hold them together, muscles and tendons to animate them, and nerves to control them and give them feeling. Some of the muscles and tendons found in the foot originate in the lower leg, some in the foot itself. Some are large and easily visible beneath the foot's thin skin; others are so tiny you'd never become aware of their existence—if things didn't go wrong. And all work together as part of a complicated scheme of guy wires, pulleys, and levers that afford the foot its remarkable resilience and range of motion.

No wonder your feet get tired, and no wonder things go wrong. In aerobic dancing, foot problems account for almost a third of all complaints. Overall, feet rank behind only the knee for gradual-onset overuse problems and behind the knee and ankle for acute injuries. A huge industry has arisen as a result of foot problems: shoe inserts, cushioned soles, heel pads, shock absorbers (with air cushions, even) for

+ WARNING +

If You Experience Any of These Conditions, Seek Medical Help

+ **You're unwilling or unable to bear weight after an injury; or**
+ **Your arch suddenly collapses.**

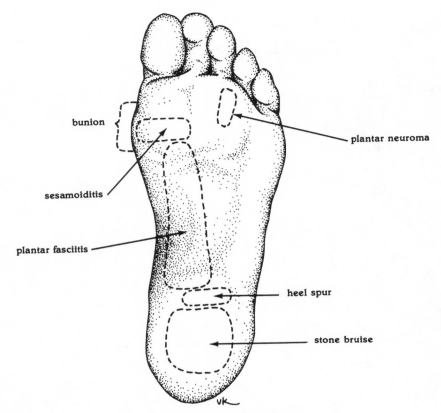

bunion

plantar neuroma

sesamoiditis

plantar fasciitis

heel spur

stone bruise

vk

BOTTOM VIEW OF THE FOOT

sports shoes, and so on. But even though foot injuries rank among the top ten problems requiring a visit to a physician, there are plenty of injuries doctors never see. People simply put up with them, complaining about their feet but rarely doing anything—as though aching, painful feet were our lot in life, especially when engaged in any kind of sports activity.

The following sections suggest ways to pinpoint and handle these aches and pains. We'll start with the back part of the foot—the heel and vicinity—and work forward to the toes. And we'll end with suggestions on how to pick footwear. Believe it or not, it *is* possible to find shoes that are good for your feet.

THE HEEL

Stone Bruise

One of the most painful foot injuries is a stone bruise, which can occur when you step with your heel onto something irregular, like a rock, pebble, or scrap of

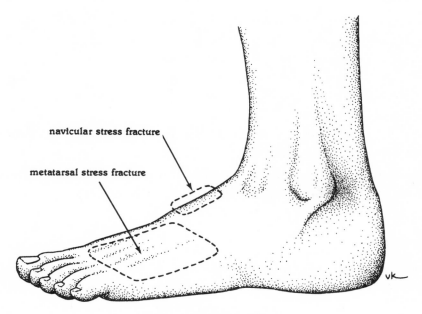

navicular stress fracture

metatarsal stress fracture

LATERAL VIEW OF THE FOOT

wood. It can even result from excessive pounding on the feet in aerobics class. A stone bruise can cause your heel to be so tender that you can't bear to put weight on it, forcing you to prance around on your toes for days.

The heel is cushioned to handle just such emergencies. It is filled with fat, but in a manner unlike other places in the body. The fat in the heel is held securely in place by a honeycomb of tiny, vertically running fibrous ligaments. You can't shift around this fat the way you can the fat on the back of your arm or leg, for example. The fat in your heel stays in one place, so it makes a great cushion.

But as we get older these little ligaments stretch and break down, and the heel pad of fat begins to lose some of its firmness. It then becomes more like the fat in the rest of your body, subject to being squeezed out of place. With age, your heel becomes less capable of cushioning you when you land on things like a sharp rock.

✚ What to do about it ✚ The treatment for a stone bruise is simple and ingenious. If the bruise is painful because your heel pad has lost its original firmness, simply restore that firmness and let your body continue to use its own cushioning. The device that can do the job is a rigid plastic heel cup, widely available in shoe stores and running shops. You might think that if it hurts to bear weight on your heel, the last thing you'd want to do is put a rigid piece of plastic in your shoe. But the plastic cups the heel, and because it's rigid it constrains the fat, re-forming the heel pad to its original shape. When you step down, your heel fat no longer shifts out to the sides—it cushions your foot as it's supposed to.

The heel cup works very well for this type of injury, and you don't need to go to a doctor for it. You can buy one over the counter. It can offer one of the most dramatic recoveries you'll ever see. Just be sure to use a *rigid* cup. It's always tempting to buy the ones with padding, but it's the rigidity that does the job, reconfiguring the fat the way it was in the first place.

Bursitis

A *bursa* is a slim, self-contained envelope (or sac) with walls as thin as tissue paper. The walls are moist, lubricated so that they can slide. Bursas show up in the body where things move over one another—in and around joints, in places where ligaments and tendons pass over bones. The bursas help to reduce friction, making it possible for us to move.

There is a bursa in the heel, between the skin and the spot where the heel bone connects to the Achilles tendon. In some people the back of the shoe, called the counter, can rub against this spot, irritating the bursa. If the irritation goes on long enough, the bursa's walls can thicken and, like any inflamed part of the body, produce fluid. This fluid enlarges the bursa sac, further irritating the walls, which become thicker and produce more fluid—and so it goes, a vicious cycle. A bump on the back of the heel can be the result, spongy at first, but gradually hardening to the consistency of a hard-boiled egg. The larger and more rigid this bump becomes, the more it presses against the shoe counter, producing pressure that brings about pain and more irritation. This condition is called *bursitis.*

Because bursas occur in a variety of locations in the foot besides the heel, bursitis can show up throughout the foot. Usually it's the result of a footwear problem—a shoe that's too narrow, too pointed, too tight—that's irritated the bursa. Some people have a tendency to roll inward excessively when they walk or run, irritating bursas on the inside of the foot. Bursitis also can be caused by a direct blow to a bursa. If the tiny blood vessels in a bursa rupture, they can bleed into the sac, enlarging the bursa and beginning the vicious cycle of irritation and enlargement. Unchecked, an inflamed bursa can become a significant problem.

✚ What to do about it ✚ You need to stop the cycle as soon as possible. Treat a bursa as you would anything that's inflamed: apply ice after activity, try NSAIDs and use contrast baths if the bursa is really swollen. But the best medicine is always preventive: find out what caused the bursitis in the first place.

Properly fitting shoes will go a long way toward preventing inflamed bursas (see "Footwear—How to Choose Shoes" later in this chapter). A hint: if the counter of a new athletic shoe begins to rub against the back of your heel, there's an effective—and dramatic—way to remedy the situation. Take off the offending shoe. Place it on the floor, heel toward you. Then crush the counter of the shoe with the sole of your shod foot. The shoe won't mind. It will spring back to something resembling its original form—now, however, more flexible in the back. Good news for your hard-working bursa, your Achilles tendon, and the rest of the area around your heel.

✚ WARNING ✚

If you try the things suggested in this chapter and you continue to hurt, see a doctor.

In extreme cases, the only remedy for bursitis is surgery—cutting out the inflamed bursa. You and your doctor should view this as a last resort.

"Lumpy Heel"

There's another condition that results in "lumpy heels" or "pump bumps," so named after the pumps women wear. The condition is an enlargement of the heel bone. Because of its prominence, the bump is irritated by the shoe and enlarges—a common problem for figure skaters because of the pressure from unyielding boots. The bump projects from the back corners of the heel bone, on either side of the Achilles tendon. Comfortably fitting into a shoe can become a real difficulty.

✚ What to do about it ✚ Treatment for "pump bumps" is initially like that for bursitis. You can also pad the area around the bump. Although these bumps can be surgically removed, padding and making shoe accommodations such as stretching the leather are preferable early on, as removing the bumps results in a longer period of recovery than most people are willing to tolerate. It's often two to three months before you can return to athletic activities and even longer to get back to dancing.

+ Orthotics +

There are orthotics and there are "orthotics." The former is an insert worn in the shoe, precisely fabricated (usually by prescription) by a podiatrist, that can assist in treating plantar fasciitis, Achilles and other forms of tendinitis, shinsplints, and even knee pain. "Orthotics" are customized insoles often available at booths at fairs and sometimes even in running stores. "Orthotics" are really molded insoles designed for comfort rather than to alter weight bearing or gait, the function of true orthotics. While "orthotics" may indeed enhance comfort, they are unlikely to assist in managing injury problems.

If all that weren't confusing enough, there are many kinds of real orthotics. There are soft orthotics, semi-rigid orthotics, and rigid orthotics, each with fervent supporters. There is little scientific evidence suggesting which is best—no surprise because what is good for one condition can be totally inappropriate for another. The podiatrist who prescribes the orthotic is the best judge.

However, with all the changes in health care management, obtaining orthotics has become a bit of a problem. Because they're expensive (up to $500 in some

Plantar Fasciitis

If you sit barefoot and relaxed, with one leg crossed over another, you might notice that the arch of your foot more or less resembles a bow. Pull back on your toes and you can see and feel the bowstring: the *plantar fascia*. This is a ligament-like rope of fibrous tissue that starts at the heel of your foot and runs along the inside of the sole, where it fans out into little fingers and connects to the metatarsal bones at the base of the toes. It's really dense, each strand of the rope about one-eighth of an inch thick. Its primary function is to maintain the arch by not allowing the ends to pull too far apart—the same thing a bowstring does for a bow.

As you use your foot, the plantar fascia stretches and contracts. A great deal of pressure—for runners, a sudden stop, start, turn, or simply too much mileage; for dancers, prolonged periods on half-pointe or repetitive relevés—can overstretch the fascia. Normally, if the muscles in your foot are strong, your feet can absorb this pressure because the muscles bear the brunt of such punishment. But if you're tired, or your muscles are wearing out, your feet tend to sag into the plantar fascia. If it stretches so much that it loses its flexibility, it can actually tear. This condition is called plantar fasciitis

Plantar fasciitis is not hard to recognize: the bottom of your foot hurts, anywhere from the heel forward. If you gently pull your toes back and make the fascia stand out, you can pinpoint the spot—it's usually at the inside front edge of the heel bone. Sometimes it will turn black and blue, sometimes become swollen. It's a common overuse problem, especially for runners and dancers. And it can be a particular problem for people with high arches. In such feet the fascias tend to be tight, just as bowstrings are tightest when the bow is flexed. A tight fascia has less give and so can be more easily overstretched—it doesn't allow much shock absorption. People with flat feet, while susceptible to all sorts of other foot problems, do not often suffer from plantar fasciitis. Their fascia are not tight enough to hold an arch in place, much less tear.

✚ What to do about it ✚ Treat plantar fasciitis as you would tendinitis or bursitis: stop doing what hurts, apply ice, take an anti-inflammatory drug for a week, give yourself contrast baths. And try to take some of the load off the bowstring. The idea is to artificially create an arch by bringing your heel and toes closer together, thereby easing the pressure on the fascia. One way to do it is to put an arch support in your shoe. But sometimes the arch support supports your arch in the very spot where it hurts. It may be that you have to see a podiatrist who can make you a customized arch support, an orthotic. Orthotics are not the answer for everything, but in this case they can make a huge difference, as the pain can be so severe that you can't even walk. So if rest, anti-inflammatories, contrast baths, and over-the-counter arch supports don't work, a visit to a podiatrist might be the ticket.

Plantar fasciitis can also feel just like a stone bruise in the heel. Sometimes the fascia can stretch and tear so violently that it actually pulls a piece of bone loose at the heel where the fascia connects, causing what's called a heel spur. Heel spurs can produce spectacular x-rays—a nasty-looking spike of bone up to three-quarters of an inch long floating in the heel—but in many instances removing the spike isn't going to solve the problem. What will is removing the pressure on the fascia and getting rid of the inflammation. Removing the pressure can often be accomplished with a donut-shaped heel pad. These are made of silicone rubber with a soft spot (for the tender area) in the center.

One of the biggest problems with plantar fasciitis is taking those first few steps after getting out of bed in the morning. That initial flattening of the arch—and re-irritating the fascia—is often the most painful activity of the day. But there's a solution for the problem: the right-angle night splint. This splint

OTHOTICS (CONTINUED)

cases), their purchase is often questioned by insurers. In addition, insurance companies may have contracts with particular orthotics fabricators, perhaps not the company your podiatrist is accustomed to using. What to do? Sometimes a letter from your physician will break up this bureaucratic logjam, but frequently the patient—you—is stuck with the cost. If appropriately prescribed and properly made, however, orthotics are worth the hassle and expense.

Orthotics can do a world of good for certain problems, but there is no evidence that they will *prevent* them. For example, just because your feet are flat doesn't mean you need orthotics—certainly not if you're not having any problems. Indeed, if you're not suffering pain, meddling with the way you naturally walk or run might cause problems. Elsewhere in this book (where Achilles tendinitis, knee pain, posterior tibial tendinitis, etc., are discussed), we have indicated the conditions for which orthotics might be helpful. Be careful. Indiscriminate use of orthotics comes under the category of attempting to fix things that aren't broken. If you're not having problems, don't fool around with them.

partially encircles the back of the calf and lower leg and holds the foot/ankle at a right angle to the leg, keeping the fascia stretched out overnight so it need not be reinjured every morning. The use of this splint has increased our success in treating plantar fasciitis more than any other single thing.

Plantar fasciitis is not something to ignore. Like Achilles tendinitis, once it become entrenched getting rid of it can be a long process.

THE MIDFOOT

Tendinitis

Just as anywhere else in the body, the bulk of foot problems are overuse injuries. You try something new, or do more of your usual activity, and overuse the muscles, which subsequently tighten up and pull against the tendons, which, being the most vulnerable link in the chain of bone-muscle-tendon, cannot bear the strain and tear. It's an old story, repeated often in this book. The foot, however, offers a couple of unique wrinkles.

One is that you can get a kind of tendinitis that you don't see anywhere else: tendinitis that is the result of *external* pressure. Think about it. We really don't put constraining clothing around our arms, our legs, the rest of our body. But we wedge our feet into all sorts of confining footwear, sometimes for reasons that have little to do with comfort or protection. This footwear can cause tendinitis in and of itself. When dealing with feet, therefore, we're in a world in which *clothing* can cause problems. (More on that later.)

The other thing about the foot is that it enables you quickly and accurately to identify problems, more so than other areas of the body. There's not a lot of fat in the foot, not a lot of muscle. You can see almost all the tendons. Anything that's kind of rigid, that feels like a little rope, is a tendon. When you move your feet, these little ropes move—you can't mistake them. So if one of them hurts when you move your foot, then you probably have tendinitis. Sometimes you'll get the same thing that's possible with Achilles tendinitis: snowball crepitation—where the tendon actually may squeak. And because there's little padding in the foot between the skin and tendons, the injured area may become red and swollen. So self-diagnosis of the foot is pretty easy.

Now, back to footwear. Because there's no padding in the foot, just lacing your shoes too tightly for one three- or four-mile run can cause so much irritation that you may be on the sidelines for three or four weeks. The tendons that run along the top of the foot are virtually on the surface. They're extremely sensitive to pressure. As you run, the tendons slide beneath the skin. Running puts the foot through a wide range of motion, and the tendons must move a long way. If there's outside pressure curtailing their ability to slide, the tendons can easily become inflamed. So, particularly when you're breaking in new shoes and haven't yet figured out how tightly or loosely to lace them, opt for loosely.

The same problem may arise in skiing. A too-tight center buckle on a ski boot is a common cause of tendinitis. Sometimes people have ill-designed or ill-fitting boots and find that they can't keep their heel down inside the boot. The first thing they do is tighten the center buckle over the instep of their foot. That probably won't keep the heel down, but it will keep the tendons down—mash them, in fact. And sometimes it can pinch one of the little nerves that run along the tendons. Like the tendons, the nerves in the foot are virtually unprotected. It's not uncommon in November and December to hear people complain that two or three of their toes are numb. These toes will probably stay numb through the entire ski season and into the summer, all from one day of skiing in boots that are too tight. It's not a major problem, but it can be very annoying to have a constant tingling feeling in your foot.

✚ What to do about it ✚ Treat tendinitis of the foot as you'd treat tendinitis anywhere: back off from doing what hurts. Also you might try a shoe with a more rigid sole to block some of the motion of your foot. If there's swelling, give your foot contrast baths. Take anti-inflammatories. But the most important thing is to stop doing whatever it was that caused the problem in the first place. Then ease back slowly. Let pain be your guide. If it doesn't hurt, you're okay. If it hurts, you're doing too much. Back off for a while, and then push forward again.

Stress Fractures

One of the most common foot problems, stress fractures occur more often than not in those small bones between the toes and the top of the foot called the metatarsals. (See chapter 4, "The Lower Leg," for a thorough explanation of just what a stress fracture is.) You can easily feel the metatarsals. Some people think that if you have what's called "Morton's foot"—your second toe is longer than your big toe—that you may have a tendency to suffer stress fractures, but this point of view is controversial. You don't incur stress fractures because there is something wrong with the mechanics of your foot, but rather because there is something wrong with the mechanics of your head—you went off and ran nine miles when you're used to running two, that sort of thing. Stress fractures are almost always the result of training mistakes like that.

You can get a stress fracture at the base of the fifth metatarsal, that area marked by a bump on the outside edge of your foot. Dancers, and basketball players even more so, are susceptible to stress fractures in this location. Jumping sports like basketball can also cause a stress fracture of the navicular, the bony ridge on the top of the foot. These are horrible to deal with—difficult to see on x-rays, slow to heal, sometimes even requiring surgery. Navicular stress fractures in gymnasts also are quite common. They are nasty injuries. Don't ignore anything you suspect might be a stress fracture in the middle part or outside of your foot.

Fortunately these bones are right there under the skin, visible and easy to keep track of. You'll see and feel swelling. And like stress fractures of the shinbone, there will be a discrete area of tenderness. You can cover it with a dime or a nickel. In contrast to tendinitis, in which the painful area is more diffused, if you put your finger on a stress fracture, it will *really* hurt. A caution: the most common cause of pain on the outside of the foot is shoes that aren't wide enough. So the first thing to do if you suffer any of these symptoms is look at your shoes. If you hurt only when you wear one particular pair of shoes and are fine the rest of the time, you're in luck. It's easy to replace a pair of shoes.

✛ What to do about it ✛ If the symptoms persist no matter what shoes you wear, stop doing whatever it is that makes you hurt. Rest is the primary treatment for stress fractures. That and dealing with the swelling by icing and taking contrast baths. Wearing a stiff-soled shoe that reduces the movement of your foot can also help. Boots are very good in this regard. Hiking boots, cowboy boots—both can help. (However, the big problem with cowboy boots is getting them on and off. Once you're in them, they can temporarily solve a great many problems.)

If a few days of rest and reduced activity doesn't seem to make any headway, or if you stop your activity, the pain goes away, and then comes back as soon as you begin again, it's a good idea to see a doctor. Because of. . .

Fractures

If ignored, stress fractures can turn into overt fractures, where the bone is actually severed and displaced. The navicular bone, which occupies a position in the foot somewhat like the keystone of an arch and is therefore particularly vulnerable, can be fractured in this way. So can the base of the fifth metatarsal.

There are a couple kinds of fractures that you can get at the base of this metatarsal (the bump on the outside edge of your foot, in front of and below the ankle knob). One kind results from a severe ankle sprain, which can pull off the peroneal tendon where it attaches to this metatarsal. The peroneal tendon connects the peroneal muscles, which run along the outside of the lower calf, to the foot. You can easily see and feel the tendon coming down from the ankle knob. These muscles are part of your protection against ankle sprain because they keep you from inverting your foot. If you step in a hole, say, and your foot begins to roll underneath you, the peroneal muscles tighten up strongly in an effort to hold back the foot and keep you upright. But if your foot continues to roll in, something has to give. Sometimes that something is the tendon (see "Tendinitis," above), but sometimes it's a piece of the metatarsal bone itself.

✚ **What to do about it** ✚ Usually the bone doesn't travel very far, just a couple of millimeters. In that case, the injury might heal by itself if you simply do the things that you'd normally do for an ankle sprain (see chapter 2, "The Ankle"). In some activities, like basketball and dance, where there is a lot of side-to-side movement, it's especially crucial that these injuries heal perfectly, so you may have to endure a cast. The important thing, though, is to realize that it's difficult to make this judgment on your own. So if you sprain your ankle and the outside of your foot becomes sore and black and blue, better see a doctor.

You can also suffer a fracture at the base of the fifth metatarsal. Dancers are plagued with these. Sometimes they start as stress fractures, are ignored, and turn into overt fractures. They can be nasty, difficult to deal with, and have a horrible reputation for not healing together. This is an area of the foot where the likelihood of having to resort to surgery is very high. Another injury to see your doctor about.

Medial Sprains

The worst thing that can happen to the inside of the foot results from another kind of ankle sprain, the less common medial sprain, which involves rolling the foot *out,* away from the body. This motion can put strain on the posterior tibial muscles—one of the groups of muscles in the calf—and on the tendon that connects them to the foot. The tendon attaches to the foot at the navicular, that bony bump beneath and in front of your inside ankle knob, and its major job is to support the arch of the foot. With some people, especially those with flat feet, the navicular is very prominent. Frequently it protrudes just at the top level of shoes. (Sometimes ballet dancers roll the foot out so much in an attempt to increase turnout that their navicular area actually hits the floor. A callus then forms over it.)

If your foot rolls out too severely, the tendon can tear, or it can pull so sharply that it pops a piece of bone loose, much as on the other side of the foot at the base of the fifth metatarsal. And like the metatarsal area, there's little padding around the navicular. This is usually an extremely tender injury. Fortunately, it's rare. It's another injury that should be seen by a doctor.

✚ What to do about it ✚ Other small bones in the midfoot can fracture as well, some as a consequence of ankle sprains. So, a word to the wise: if you injure your foot anywhere from the midpart back to the ankle and it *really* hurts, with a lot of swelling (in the foot, not around the ankle itself) and black and blue discoloration, *then caution is very important. See a doctor and get an x-ray.*

Contusions

Contusions are very common. Dropping something on your foot or having somebody step on your foot can cause them. The foot is not well suited to being scrunched. We wear shoes to protect not only the bottoms of our feet but the tops as well. Badly bruising the top of your foot can be terribly painful and debilitating. Remember that the black and blue color of a bruise represents blood under the skin, and when there's blood under the skin in the foot, there's nowhere for it to go. It simply pools on top of the bone. Because all the bones in the foot are just under the skin, the tendons on the top of your foot must slide directly over the bone. If there's a big sea of blood there, the tendons won't slide very well. Tendinitis can easily result from such an obstruction.

✚ What to do about it ✚ Foot contusions should be treated the same way you treat contusions anywhere: apply a compression bandage as soon as possible. The more blood that pools under the skin, the longer it will take to get rid of it. Ice can help to prevent swelling, and contrast baths can reduce swelling once it has formed.

Dislocations

The ultimate sprain is a dislocation, which actually displaces the bones from their normal position, and there are some horrible dislocations that occur in the foot. These are devastating injuries. There are so many bones in your foot, and so many things can go wrong with them. Again, if you *really* hurt your foot, and it swells and turns black and blue *especially under your arch*, don't even dream of not seeing a doctor.

THE TOES

Fractures

We can no longer put off mentioning the bane of foot injuries: stubbing the toe. It hurts even to think about it. And more than just hurting, stubbing your toe can cause a fracture. If you're ambling along at four miles per hour or so, your foot is actually moving at a speed more than twice that. If you're walking fast, your foot may be traveling ten to fifteen miles per hour. And if you're running, forget it. Every once in a while we see an x-ray of a toe that looks as though somebody put a firecracker beneath it. You think, how could anyone fracture a toe this badly? Then you remember that these are tiny bones, and if your foot is going ten miles per hour and it hits a coffee table in the middle of the night, or a door jamb while setting off for your workout, or a wayward tree root in the middle of your cross-country run, you can do an incredible amount of damage.

✚ **What to do about it** ✚ The toe swells up, turns black and blue, looks horrible. But as a general rule, if it looks straight as well, you probably won't have to do anything more than tape it to the adjacent toe. Toes, like fingers, are different lengths, and the space between the joints in the toe are different lengths too. Generally your toes fit against one another like building blocks. If you want to stabilize a toe, just tape it to the next toe—presto, a built-in splint. Remember to put something absorbent between the toes—a little piece of lamb's wool, say, which is available at running stores—to absorb the perspiration.

Tape the toes lightly enough that you're still comfortable. You may want to get into a stiffer-soled shoe to further protect the toe and reduce movement. Keep the toe in its homemade splint for a couple of weeks, until the pain goes away. That should be all that's necessary.

You can give the same kind of homemade treatment to the big toe as well. You don't as often stub the big toe, but when you do the injury can be a beaut. It's particularly critical that there not be any deformity or displacement of the big toe; if you're reluctant to bear weight on it, it probably isn't a bad idea to have it x-rayed. It's a sizable joint, and you must have good big toe motion for pushing off in most any sport, not to mention simply running and walking. It can't hurt to err on the side of caution when the big toe is involved.

Dislocations

If sprains are injuries to ligaments, dislocations are injuries to bones and ligaments—specifically the displacement, or dislocating, of bones from their normal position in joints. Sports dislocations are most common in activities like gymnastics and dance, in which the footwear is soft. A gymnast's foot may have a tendency to stick to the mat. Especially if barefoot, in the midst of floor exercises, say, a gymnast can get stuck on the big toe and go right over it. A ballet dancer on pointe can force the big toe to knuckle under with full weight on top of it. That kind of injury is not terribly common, but it can be devastating. There's so much weight on the big toe that sometimes the bone will actually pierce the skin. Needless to say, these injuries should be seen by a doctor. In most sports the shoes you wear have soles rigid enough to prevent the toe from going under.

Most of the time you could probably get away with putting a dislocated big toe into a stiff-soled shoe or a splint. If you can walk comfortably in a wooden-soled shoe or a clog, that's fine. But often people find it more convenient to have the foot put in a cast. And, again, as you need a completely healthy big toe to function well in so many activities, it can never hurt to get professional help.

You can stub your other toes and dislocate them, too. But we usually don't see these injuries because often people simply grab the toe, gently pull it straight out, and pop it back into place. And if it's not deformed, taping to the adjacent toe and going with a stiff-soled shoe can do the trick.

There's one more sport that is turning up dislocations these days: football. Football players have gone to lighter and lighter shoes. Football shoes are really quite flimsy now, and they contribute to football players getting something called turf toe. The shoes are so flimsy that when a lineman pushes off, he's allowed a great deal of motion in the big toe, sometimes too much. He can overstretch the joint, like a ballet dancer going up on relevé and falling forward all the time. It turns into a chronic sprain, which is resprained every time the lineman pushes off. (This respraining occurs on artificial turf, thus the name, "turf toe." On a grass surface the cleat can dig into the ground and make a little hole, allowing the toe to sink in and not overstretch every time.) The toe can become hugely swollen and constantly tender. Even a little motion can hurt. The condition can lead to a dislocation, as a dislocation is the ultimate sprain.

The problem also plagues other sports, as all athletes want light-weight shoes, especially when playing on unyielding synthetic turf or, as in indoor soccer, on hard floors covered by rugs.

Bunions

Bunions are *de rigueur* for dancers, a normal adaptation to the confining things dancers are always stuffing their feet into. In fact, most of the problems that follow are simply a fact of life for dancers, whose feet resemble nothing less than a combat zone most of the time. But in the general population, bunions can be a cause for comment, even embarrassment. Those big knobs at the outside of the big toe joint can be unsightly and can make fitting into shoes something of a trial. And as we age, our bunions tend to grow larger.

An overly tight shoe is a common cause (one reason that bunions are much more common in women than in men); the other is that some people are simply born with bunions. The big toe drifts out at the joint, forming a mound that rubs against footwear. In response, the skin around the bunion thickens, increasing the pressure against the shoe, which then rubs more firmly, causing the skin to grow thicker—and so it goes. Compounding the problem is the fact that usually a large segment of the bunion is made up of a bursa between the skin and the bone. If the friction between foot and shoe occurs at the level of the skin, you get a thickening of the skin—a callus. But if the skin presses against the shoe so firmly that the skin actually slides over bone, the result can be bursitis. And although filled with fluid, the bursa can feel as hard as bone (see the discussion of bursitis earlier in this chapter).

✚ **What to do about it** ✚ Most people simply learn to live with bunions. The important thing is not to let them get the best of you. Wear shoes that are not too tight and go barefoot as much as you can—bunions rarely hurt when there's nothing for them to chafe against. A crescent-shaped pad that goes *around* the bunion (in general, never pad *over* the thing that hurts; pad around it, behind it, next to it, so that you can take the pressure in some other area) can help. There's also something called a "bunion splint" available; you can find it at the Dr. Scholl's counter in the drugstore. It pulls your toe out a little straighter, which helps take pressure off the bunion. Arch supports will often help as well—elevating the arch often straightens the big toe. Sometimes it's most effective if the arch support is custom-made by a podiatrist—in other words, an orthotic.

If your bunion becomes particularly sore and inflamed, ice the area after activity, try contrast baths, and take two anti-inflammatory pills with meals to reduce swelling. If the pain persists, you might see a doctor, but think more than twice if that physician recommends surgery. Athletes should be *very* cautious about having any kind of surgery on their feet, especially bunion surgery (that's especially true for ballet dancers, for whom a bunion might be viewed as a functional adaptation). The hazards far outweigh the possible benefits, for three reasons primarily. Infection rates are higher in the foot than in other areas, and circulation is often not good (especially in older people), so surgical wounds heal more slowly. And foot surgery is particularly inconvenient, as you may spend anywhere from a week to two months or more recuperating on crutches or in a cast.

And certainly people who are athletic should *never* have any kind of cosmetic surgery on their feet. Women tend to have bunions more often than men, and women sometimes want their bunions cut off just because they look so awful. It's simply not worth it.

Calluses

Calluses, those thick, hard mounds of dead skin on the bottom, or sometimes the side, of your foot are caused by friction and pressure, and like bunions and bursas they can become self-aggravating injuries. As they grow bigger, they cause more friction and pressure; as there's more friction and pressure, they grow bigger. There are some activities, like dance, in which calluses are desirable because they can protect the feet against the constant pounding dancers put them through. When dancers have been off for a while and their calluses have reduced or disappeared, they're at a real disadvantage. (Gymnasts want calluses on their hands, which they soak in all manner of potions—brine, for example—to make the calluses bigger.) But when the calluses become hard and dense, they can become painful. They feel as though they're being pushed into the foot much as if you were standing on a pebble. Softening them makes them easier to tolerate. Often dancers help soften calluses and corns—but not remove them—by soaking their feet in tea. The acid in the tea helps control the calluses.

If calluses become too thick, they may crack—sometimes all the way through the callus. Once you get a crack through a callus, which may have taken three years to build up to an eighth of an inch thickness, it will take you another three years to fill in the crack. The thicker the callus, the less resilient it becomes; the less resilient it becomes, the more likely it is to crack. And a cracked callus can bleed. Then infection can be a problem because the crevices are so deep that they have a tendency to close over, trapping any infection within.

The other problem with large calluses is that occasionally you can get blisters under them. That is one of life's less appealing experiences. We've seen people with silver dollar–sized blisters under a callus. They're horribly uncomfortable. The pressure caused by the blister's accumulation of fluid can't dissipate underneath a callus—there's no place for it to go. The upshot is pain. And if the blister breaks, the whole callus may come off. You can end up with a piece of raw skin the size of a silver dollar. It may take months to heal. So there are some long-term reasons not to let calluses get out of control, even if you're just a recreational athlete.

+ What to do about it + There are surgical procedures that can make calluses less prominent, but it's much easier simply to spend ten minutes once a week sanding them down with a pumice stone or sandpaper. You may not solve the problem that way, but you can keep it from getting worse. Take a bath to soften the calluses, then sand them down. Let comfort be your guide—get them down to where they feel good. Since they will most likely form again no matter what you do, keep them under control.

Corns

Calluses and corns are the same thing in different places. Calluses occur on the bottom, or sometimes the side, of your foot. Corns occur in places where you're not bearing weight, most often on or between the toes. If you have a high arch and your toes tend to buckle up like claws, you may be particularly susceptible to corns.

+ What to do about it + Look at your footwear. If your shoes rub along the top of your toes, it's time to change styles. Corns can be a particular problem for women because women's shoes rarely have a deep toebox. If your toes are clawing inside your shoes, you most likely will have problems. A hint when trying on shoes: when you step down you shouldn't be able to feel the tops of your toes against the shoe. If you can already feel them rubbing in the store, then they're certain to rub more once you've bought them.

Corns between your toes are often soft because they're moist all the time from perspiration. They can be best dealt with by inserting a wad of lamb's wool between your toes to spread them and keep the corn dry. Spreading the toes takes the pressure off the corn, and sometimes they'll just go away. Keeping corns dry also reduces the possibility of infection. Because soft corns are moist, they're much more likely to become infected than dry corns. The temptation is to put something handy like foam rubber between the toes. Foam will keep the toes apart, all right, but it won't absorb perspiration as lamb's wool can. Simply keeping the toes apart won't help things. You must get rid of the moisture.

If all else fails, corns can be removed surgically. But unless the underlying cause is dealt with, they will simply recur.

Black Toenails

Black toenails are the result of bleeding under the nail. The easiest way to get a black toenail is to drop something on your toe—and you don't need to be an athlete to do that. In sports they're most common in long-distance runners, although they show up in dancers and other athletes as well. They're usually the result of an overly long toenail banging into the front of your shoe over and over and over. Eventually the nail shears off, and the skin underneath begins to bleed.

✚ What to do about it ✚ If the bleeding comes on gradually, the toe usually doesn't hurt very much. But if the blood gets in there quickly, it can hurt like crazy. The thing to do is to drill a hole in your toenail to let the blood out and reduce the pressure. Don't worry, it may sound awful, but actually it's a simple procedure. You can sterilize a little one-eighth or one-sixteenth-inch drill bit in alcohol and then work it through the nail by spinning it between your fingers. A particularly good trick is to take a paper clip, bend one of the ends out, and heat it over the kitchen gas burner until it's red hot. Then simply push it through the nail. It sounds as though this would hurt, but remember that there's a pool of blood under the nail, and as soon as the paper clip melts through the toenail and hits the blood, it cools down. It can be a wonderfully gratifying moment when the blood seeps out—instant pain release.

When the toenail turns black, you're eventually going to lose it. But you want to keep it as long as you can. It gives your toe a nice, sterile protection. As long as there's no sign of infection—it's not red, there's no pus—it makes sense to leave the nail in place. You might even tape it to keep it in place. After the nail falls off, another will grow in its place; depending on your age, this can take six to eight months. But one way to avoid having to go through the whole thing in the first place is to keep your toenails trimmed.

Ingrown Toenails

Trimming toenails is not the most exciting thing in the world to talk about or to do, but it's important for two reasons: it helps avoid black toenails, and, if you keep your toenails trimmed properly, you won't get ingrown toenails. An ingrown toenail is literally that—a toenail that curls at the edges and grows into the fleshy part of your toe. It may not sound like much, but it can be more devastating than an ankle sprain. A severely ingrown toenail can be extremely painful and easily becomes infected. Sometimes it never heals, and sometimes the nail has to be removed—that means *real* pain. Fortunately, though, ingrown toenails are almost all preventable. Trimming the nail properly is the key.

✚ **What to do about it** ✚ Toenails should be trimmed straight across, so that the corners clear the fold of skin at the edges. For women in particular it's important to trim the nails properly because female footwear tends to be constrictive. If you're on your feet a lot in tight shoes, the flesh of the toe can roll up over the nail, especially if you taper the edges rather than trim the nail straight across.

If the nail does become infected, you can soak your foot in warm soapy water. That can help draw out the infection by softening the hard skin. A doctor might put a wisp of cotton under the corners of the nail to push the skin away while the nail's growing—you can do the same thing. Once the corners of the nail grow beyond the skin, you're all right. Don't let ingrown toenails get away from you. The longer you ignore them, the worse they are to deal with.

Plantar Neuroma

The nerves to the toes run between the metatarsal bones of the foot. Sometimes the nerve between the third and fourth toes can become pinched between the bones that straddle it, a condition called plantar (or Morton's, after the man who first described it) neuroma.

The pain that results feels like an electric shock that starts at the ball of the foot and travels to the tips of the toes. If you squeeze your foot, driving the metatarsal bones together, or pinch the webbed area between the bones, it can be a shock as dramatic as hitting your crazy bone. And if you ignore the problem, the nerve can not only become swollen but permanently scarred. The bigger the neuroma gets, the more easily it gets in the way, and the more it hurts. Sometimes the only resort is surgery.

Almost always plantar neuroma is caused by overly tight shoes. That's why it doesn't hurt when you go barefoot—your foot can spread out and take pressure off the nerve. In fact that's the best way of diagnosing the problem: if the pain goes away when you take off your shoe, you can be pretty certain that it's plantar neuroma.

✚ What to do about it ✚ The best way to treat plantar neuroma is to take off your shoe whenever you can. That's not always practical, however, so there's a neat trick that can help you when your feet are inside a pair of shoes (which, by this time, should be a new pair, roomier than the ones that caused the problem). Make your foot narrower by putting more stuff in the shoe—to wit, a little pad on the bottom of the foot, right behind the area that hurts. The pad creates a bit of an arch, which raises your foot and makes it narrower, further reducing pressure on the aching nerve. You can buy these metatarsal pads at drugstores and shoe stores.

If you eliminate the pressure on the nerve, it will eventually go back to normal. But if you try these things and the pain persists, better see your doctor.

Blisters

A blister is a callus that hasn't had enough time to fully form. That is, instead of resulting from a long process involving a small amount of friction that slowly builds up dead skin, a blister is caused by heavy friction that over a period of an hour or two causes the skin to separate into layers, slide over itself, and form a pocket that fills with fluid.

✚ What to do about it ✚ By far the best way to deal with a blister is to catch it before it forms, when it's still only red and hasn't any fluid in it. Then (and this is one instance when it's a good idea to put something *directly over* the problem) cover it with Spenco Second Skin, a slippery pad widely available in drugstores—or even with just a piece of adhesive tape if nothing else is available. The Second Skin will absorb the friction, allowing the blister to heal. Usually it will, that is. The only problem is that more often than not you'll notice the emerging blister three miles into your seven-mile run, or in the middle of ballet class, and your Second Skin is back home in the bathroom.

So, the blister fills with fluid. Now what? If it's less than half an inch, say, you should probably leave it alone. If it's larger than that, and it's really hurting, then puncturing it will speed the healing process. First sterilize your foot, and then a needle, with alcohol. At the edge of the blister, right where it meets the skin, make a tiny hole and let the fluid leak out. Then apply an over-the-counter antibiotic ointment to help prevent infection. Cover the blister with moleskin (if you spread the ointment completely over the blister, it won't stick to the moleskin), and leave it there. The blister is sterile, and if you do all this without contaminating it, you've got a clean, built-in sterile bandage, exactly the right shape and size.

In three or four days the dead skin will work itself loose, but by that time the new skin underneath will have had a chance to toughen up. You may want to cover the area with Second Skin until it's no longer tender. Unfortunately, blisters are simply a fact of life—athletic life, anyway. You can get to be an expert at this kind of treatment.

Sesamoiditis

If your big toe hurts right at the base where the ball of the foot begins, especially when you push off the toe in running or jumping, you may have sesamoiditis. The term is a catchall description for any irritation of the sesamoid bones, which are tiny bones within the tendons that run to the big toe. Like the kneecap, the sesamoids function as a pulley, increasing the leverage of the tendons controlling the toe. Every time you push off against the toe the sesamoids are involved, and eventually they can become irritated, even fractured. Because the bones are within the tendons, sesamoiditis is a kind of tendinitis—the tendons around the bones become inflamed as well.

Runners tend to get sesamoiditis. So do dancers (female show dancers are at particular risk because doing anything in high heels throws more weight on these bones). And in the worst cases the bones refuse to heal. It can require surgery to remove fragments of the sesamoids, an especially difficult and nasty procedure. Avoid it if at all possible.

✛ **What to do about it** ✛ You treat sesamoiditis as you do any tendinitis or stress fracture: rest, ice, anti-inflammatories, with pain as your guide. If it continues to hurt, keep resting. If it feels better, gingerly go back to your activity, but not enough that you cause it to hurt again. If you remain pain-free, gradually increase the activity until you're back at your accustomed level. Putting a small pad below the area can help reduce the pounding the sesamoids take. But if everything fails, see a doctor.

FOOTWEAR—HOW TO CHOOSE SHOES

First of all, when you buy any kind of athletic shoes, be sure to take along the kind of socks you'll be wearing when you use them. Don't try on running or aerobic shoes in your dress socks or nylons. And whatever your activity, be sure to wear absorbent socks. Cotton socks absorb moisture and wick it away from the foot. They're usually considered better than synthetics. Everyone's feet sweat—the more you can do to absorb the moisture, the less chance of infections, and the more comfortable you'll be.

Next, don't be in a hurry. There's only one way to select a pair of shoes that are right for you—do to the shoe inside the shop what you're going to be doing to it outside the shop—and that takes time. The more thoroughly you get to know the shoe before you buy it, the less grief you'll experience later. If it's a running shoe you're after, try to run in it as much as you can without mowing people down. (Some shoe stores provide treadmills.) If it's an aerobic shoe, get up on your toes and bounce around. If it's a ski boot, at least walk around it in for a while.

Leave one of your old shoes on one foot, put one of the new ones on the other foot, and walk around—that gives you a valid means of comparison. Then reverse the process. Then put both new shoes on and see how they feel. If you measure the length of a shoe, it should always be while you're standing up. It's even a good idea to shop at the end of the day, when your feet are a bit swollen—if the shoes fit then, they'll always fit. Above all, test for comfort. Generally shoes will not stretch in length at all, although they may spread a bit in width. But for the most part, new shoes are never going to feel much better than they did in the shop.

A few other things to remember:

1. If there's a problem with fit, forefoot versus heel, it's easier to put something in the heel—a heel cup, for instance—than it is to change the front part of the shoe. Heel cups, which come in styles from soft leather to rigid plastic, can readily fill in the back part of the shoe, but there's not much to do about the front. If in doubt, *fit the shoe for your forefoot.*

2. When you step down on the heel of a shoe, particularly a court shoe, you shouldn't sink into it. Often shoe manufacturers will raise the heel of a shoe by softening part of the innersole in the heel area. When you try out the shoe, you should push up onto your toes, then sink back into the heel,

go up onto your toes, sink back into the heel. Try this sequence a few times, and if you find yourself sinking down into the shoe a quarter of an inch or more, then it's likely that when you're actually using the shoe it will rub into your Achilles tendon. Besides the irritation, the result can be bursitis and tendinitis.

The proper way to cushion a shoe is to put the resilient material *outside* the shoe, between the soft innersole and the hard outersole. That way, when you step down the whole shoe sinks rather than you sinking inside it. But the manufacturers know their customers. It's so appealing to stick your thumb in a nice, soft heel and say, "Gee, that feels great." But it won't feel so great when you wear it. Until you flatten out the foam in the heel for good, you're going to be sliding up and down whenever you take a step. So look for shoes that cushion *below* the heel area rather than inside it.

3. Another problem with heels is that they are contoured to what the manufacturers consider a "normal" foot. Shoes cup forward in the heel. In profile, they resemble a shallow C. But all feet aren't so regular and symmetrical. Some people's heels are indeed nicely cuplike, but many others are more nearly straight from the Achilles tendon to the bottom of the heel. These people, in tennis shoes in particular, will find that the counter of the shoe cuts into their heel. The solution: crush the back of the shoe with your foot. It won't hurt the shoe, and it could make life lovely for your Achilles tendon.

4. In young people's outdoor athletic shoes, look for the ones that have cleats molded to the sole. These are much safer than the longer, conical, screw-on cleats. There are fewer knee and ankle injuries with the shorter and more numerous molded cleats. The long ones tend to get stuck in the ground. They dig in too far, and your foot won't release readily—the result, a higher frequency of injuries. Some high schools have even forbidden these older-style cleats.

A problem is that most of these shoes are flat—no raised heel. There's nothing intrinsically wrong with a flat heel, of course, but these days most young people go to school in running shoes (which are well designed but don't last very long), or a variety of other styles, most of which have raised heels. In and of themselves, there's nothing wrong with raised heels, either. The problem arises when the students change to the flat heels during school sports, the most active part of their day, dropping their heel a good three eighths of an inch. It's as though they're doing Achilles tendon stretching exercises every time they run. (Except for sprinters. The only shoe that really doesn't need a heel is a sprint shoe. When you sprint, you're up on your toes the whole time.) Then they change back to the raised-heel shoes, shortening the tendon, until the next day, when they again don their athletic shoes and give the tendon an abrupt workout. That kind of abuse often leads to Achilles tendinitis.

Manufacturers pay lip service to the problem by making the cleats under the heel longer, so when the shoe is sitting on the store shelf it looks as though the heel is raised. Don't be fooled. When you lace it on and start running in it, the cleats will simply sink into the ground, leaving you with a flat shoe. We suggest that people buy a quarter- or three-eighths-inch heel pad to stick inside their athletic shoes. These can be made of cork, or you can use real felt—just as long as the pad doesn't flatten under pressure.

Athletic shoes don't have much of an arch, either. There's a soft, little foam rubber pad in the shoe, but it collapses easily. A fairly rigid over-the-counter arch support can make a real difference, especially in young people—Spenco and Dr. Scholl's make good ones. Kids can grow so quickly that they actually outgrow their muscles, which puts strain on the tendons attaching those muscles to bone. When the tendons are tight, they're particularly susceptible to injury. If the arch is not supported, or the heel is allowed to drop, there's even more of a tendency to injury, particularly tendinitis. Arch and heel supports can go a long way toward keeping young people healthy.

5. Be sure to look at quality control in shoes. Shoes should be mirror images of each other, but sometimes they're not. There's no reason for shoes to be asymmetrical unless they're designed that way. Some shoes are made so badly that they actually affect your gait. They can force you to pronate. You can usually trust name-brand companies that have had particular models on the market for a couple of years. Problems in those shoes have most likely been weeded out by now.

6. The days of breaking in ski boots are gone. Now, with boots made of rigid plastic foam, what you must do is break your foot in, hoping that you get used to the boot. But if the boot doesn't feel comfortable in the store, it certainly isn't going to feel more comfortable later. So, give ski boots par-

ticular attention. If you have other equipment to buy as well, look at boots first; then, when you find a pair that feels good, walk around in them while you look at skis, parkas, and goggles. If they begin to hurt in the shop, they're certainly not going to feel any better outside.

7. There are nearly as many kinds of aerobic shoes on the market as there are running shoes. At first glance the shoes may look different, but they're all pretty much the same—a bastardized running shoe, with less shock absorption at the heel, which is a good idea, and a nod in the direction of increased shock absorption in the forefoot. That, too, would be a good idea if manufacturers didn't equate shock absorption with softness. If you step into a pair of shoes and they feel soft, that probably means you're not going to get much shock absorption out of them. If they're soft enough to feel soft, then you'll bottom out in them quickly, and when you're jumping up and down with your full weight, it's unlikely that there is going to be any significant amount of energy dissipation. It's similar to walking on synthetic turf—it can be spongy, and you kind of float. You may think, "Boy, this is neat." But when you run on synthetic turf, it's a different story. It's like an old mattress—once you get to the bottom of it, it's as hard as asphalt. Players who run on synthetic turf regularly will tell you that it causes aches and pains and promotes the recurrence of old injuries.

But any shoe absorbs banging better than your bare foot. Some of the original aerobic studies were done when a lot of dancers went barefoot. The studies directed a lot of the blame for injuries toward those over-worked bare feet. In our culture we're not prepared to do anything bare-foot. When you're barefoot and you get onto your toes, you take the weight of your entire body at the base of the big toe, the bunion joint, first and then at the base of the little toe. If you put anything with a halfway rigid sole on your foot, you're going to spread the force into a triangle that's perhaps five times as large. That seems to solve most injury prob-lems. So if you're doing aerobics, you should wear shoes, and if you wear shoes, look for the firmest pair you can find that are comfortable.

Test the shoe by doing some exercises in the store. Get up onto your toes and bounce around some. Make certain the shoe is not too short or the toebox too low. There's a certain amount of lunging in aerobics, and your big toenail can go into the end or top of the shoe pretty easily if the fit is not right. That can become mighty uncomfortable after a while and can in time lead to a black toenail.

Point your toe to see if the counter in the back of the shoe cuts into your Achilles tendon. Sometimes manufacturers put padding in the counter to make the shoes look attractive, but that soft padding can rub against the tendon every time you point your foot. (Other dance shoes don't come above the anklebone—their manufacturers have learned how to deal with the problem.) Some shoes have a split counter, so nothing rubs against the tendon. They're hard to get on, however. Make sure such a shoe is comfortable for you.

In a survey we did of the popular brands of aerobic shoes, there was no difference in the injury rates at all. None! The most popular shoe was the best looking, but in every one of the other seven categories in which we compared them—including durability—it was below average or tied for last. And still people buy them. Unfortunately, it seems that the most important feature of aerobic dance shoes, as far as customers are concerned, is looks.

8. Bottom line: The main thing you should look for in a shoe, no matter what athletic demands you're going to place on it, is comfort. The shoe should simply feel good, with no pressure anywhere. All the business about traction, shock absorption, durability, and the rest won't make a bit of difference if your feet hurt. So, *buy a shoe for comfort*. Consider anything else frosting on the cake.

CHAPTER FOUR

The Lower Leg

YOU KNOW THE SCENARIO: You've broken through to the next plateau, and now you're running an extra two miles a day. Or you've advanced to the intermediate aerobics class and are in the studio five rather than three times a week. You know that soon you'll feel—and look—better than you ever have before. If it just weren't for that nagging pain in your leg.

You first noticed the pain after you ran—a dull ache along the shin. Or it hurt while you were walking home from aerobics class, and that evening it hurt while you were watching the late news. You're sure it's nothing. You're simply tired—it'll go away by itself.

But it doesn't go away. And soon it starts to hurt at the end of your run, or the end of class. Still, you figure, it's nothing. You'll simply work through it. What is it they say, "No pain, no gain"? It'll go away in a couple of days.

A couple of days go by. It doesn't go away; instead, it gets worse. Now the leg hurts at the beginning of your run. Soon it hurts when you're warming up. And still you decide to ignore it.

But when it begins to hurt when you wake up in the morning, gets worse *before* you even warm up, and continues to throb when you fall into bed at night, you might start thinking that it's time to stop ignoring it. And you'd be right. You're probably suffering from an overuse injury, the most

---

+ WARNING +

If You Experience Any of These Conditions, Seek Medical Help

+ You experience severe pain in the front of the leg that does not disappear when you stop exercising;

+ You hear a pop just above the heel and/or are unable to rise onto your toes;

+ You experience pain, swelling, and redness in the upper calf.

---

common problem that afflicts the leg between the knee and the ankle. Better not ignore it.

Overuse injuries almost always result from change. Change in distance run, change in stride length, change in speed, change in terrain. Change in floor surface, change to a new instructor, change in shoes. The change may come about because of illness. If you've had the flu, for example, and you go back to your old activity too quickly, you may suffer an overuse injury. Muscles deteriorate unbelievably fast. They fall apart twice as quickly as they build up, *at the least*. If you've had the flu for a week, it's as though you haven't run in two weeks (and most likely worse than that because the illness itself decreases muscle tone and strength). And the change may be the result of another injury. If you have an ankle sprain, say, that isn't completely healed, you may start favoring that ankle and putting inappropriate stresses elsewhere. The result: two injuries instead of one.

In such cases your body is crying out for attention. And the more attention you can give it sooner rather than later, the better off you'll be. The key word is "overuse." Once these injuries gain a foothold—or, rather, a "leghold"—they will only get worse. A word to the wise: nip overuse injuries in the bud.

STRESS FRACTURES

It seems an unlikely combination of words. "Fracture" suggests a break, conjuring up the image of a skier, say, breaking a shinbone as the result of a fall or collision. "Stress" suggests something much less violent—tension, pressure, or strain. How can tension cause something to break?

The answer is that in a stress fracture the bone doesn't really break in two, not quite. It *almost* does. Imagine an airplane wing. It looks rigid, indestructible. Indestructible? One hopes so. Rigid? Not so. It may be disconcerting at 30,000 feet to look out the window and see your airplane wing flapping, but if it didn't flap it would break. The flapping dissipates the stress that the wing undergoes. Bones work the same way. They bend under pressure. A stress fracture occurs when the bone bends almost to the point of breaking. The result may be a hairline crack, too fine to show up on x-rays but not too fine to cause you pain.

The situation is made more interesting by what is known as Wolf's Law: when you change an activity, your bones adjust appropriately. For example, a continuing problem for astronauts is that they lose bone strength at zero gravity. It's as if their bones say to themselves, "There's no force on us, why should we be strong? We'll let the body use energy for other things."

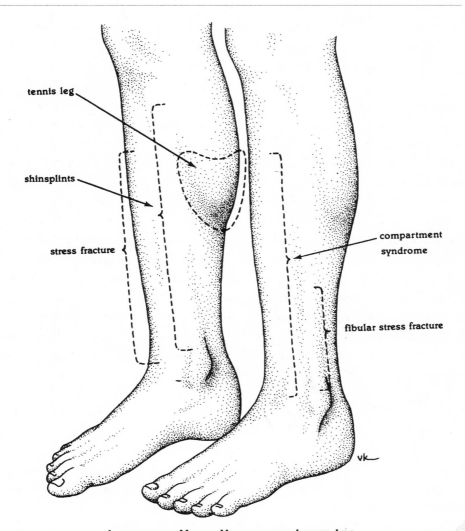

tennis leg

shinsplints

stress fracture

compartment
syndrome

fibular stress fracture

LATERAL AND MEDIAL VIEWS OF THE LOWER LEG

Bone also adjusts when you subject it to more force, but in a curious way. When you put heavier demands on bone by increasing your activity, it says to itself, "I'm too weak. Not only am I not dense enough, I'm not designed right." And rather than simply laying down new bone on old bone, it actually eats itself away, removing some of the old bone tissue so it can then lay down new bone more effectively. All well and good, but while the old bone is disappearing like mad and the new bone has not yet established itself, you run a particularly high risk of stress fractures.

The tip-off for stress fractures is that they're tender before they're painful, and the area of tenderness is well-defined. At the beginning your leg might hurt when you pull your socks on or get into leotards, but it might not hurt during the actual activity. So if you are changing your activity in any way, it might not be a bad idea to run your hand down your shinbone from time to time to check for a stress fracture. If you feel a discrete area of tenderness, a spot you could cover with a fifty-cent piece, you might start being concerned. All the more so if you move your finger up an inch or down an inch from the spot, and your leg doesn't hurt at all. That kind of pinpoint tenderness usually indicates a stress fracture. And if, over time, the pain grows worse, takes longer to disappear after activity, and gradually creeps into the activity itself, you can be sure you have a fracture.

✚ What to do about it ✚ The most important thing is not to let the stress fracture become serious in the first place. The sooner you recognize its onset, the better you will be able to treat it. That takes awareness—a little foresight— something all athletes develop (or should develop) anyway. The longer you let your injury go, the longer it will take to heal. The rule of thumb is that it will take you at least as long to get well as it took you to get injured. If you've ignored the stress fracture for two months, it'll take you at least two months to get back to your original level of activity. And what's worse, an ignored stress fracture can eventually snap in two, just as though you broke it in a skiing accident. Normally a stress fracture crack affects only part of the bone, but if subjected to pressure over too long, it can work its way all the way through. Then what you have to look forward to are all the joys of caring for a serious fracture—cast, immobilization, long rehabilitation—and none of the compensations of being able to describe the spectacular accident in which it happened. The moral of the story: it's not wise to ignore stress fractures; they'll get you in the end.

So, you've discovered your stress fracture. Now you want to back off and let the bone heal. But you don't want to rest too much because while you're resting you're wasting the conditioning you've already built and face the prospect of having to start all over again. If you simply stop exercising, the bone says, "Gee, nothing's happening. I might as well get weak again." The trick is to find a level of activity that is as strenuous as possible and at the same time pain-free. Then you're killing two birds with one stone: you're treating the stress fracture, because the way to promote healing is to maintain a pain-free level of activity, and you're continuing your conditioning, pushing the bone to become stronger so that when you're able to resume the level of activity that caused the problem in the first place, the bone will be able to handle it.

It's not as hard as it may sound. First, do *whatever's necessary to become pain-free*. Usually it takes only a day or two of complete rest, perhaps including a short bout with crutches, to rid yourself of the pain. Then very gradually begin experimenting with what you can and cannot do. This is a test you don't want to fail. If you push yourself so severely that the leg hurts again, you'll have to start all over. So you sneak up on your activity so carefully that you never push yourself over the brink. None of us is that smart, unfortunately, so occasionally you may push yourself to the point of discomfort just to gauge where you are.

For example, if you're a runner, you may start back into exercising by rapid walking. Three to four minutes the first day; then, if it doesn't hurt, six minutes the next day. When you can walk twenty minutes without pain, try running the first three minutes and walking the last seventeen. Then four and sixteen, six and fourteen, gradually changing the ratio of walking to running. Be sure to do the more stressful exercise—in this case, running—at the beginning, when you're not tired.

Gradually get back to your activity, letting discomfort be your guide. If your leg doesn't hurt, then you're not doing too much too fast—if it does, you are. In that case, drop back to the previous pain-free level, stay there for a few days, then pick up your level of activity again. Once you're back to where you were before the fracture, and especially if you change your level or type of activity again, be mindful of the danger signs for stress fractures—tenderness before pain and a tender area the size of a fifty-cent piece. That way, if these warning signs show up again, you'll be able to respond appropriately.

Remember that in response to increased levels of activity, bone destroys and then regenerates itself—and this takes time. The high-risk period is around the third week of any new training regimen—that's when the bone removal is at its maximum. So you can really hit it for the first couple of weeks, then flatten out at the end of the second and through the third week. Don't increase your activ-

---

+ Running on the Beach +

It may be that there's some value in the added work running in the sand demands from your feet and legs. But in general, for most people, running in the sand won't do any more for you than running anywhere else. In fact, it may do you some harm. The main reason is that your foot sinks into the sand as you run, and your heel, which bears the brunt of your weight, drops lower than the rest of your foot. There's nothing wrong with that in and of itself, but it's opposite to what we're used to. Most shoes raise the heel—running shoes certainly do—which in time tends to shorten the Achilles tendon and calf muscles. Suddenly lowering the heel stretches that entire linkage. The upshot can be injury (see chapter 2, "The Ankle").

The other reason that running in the sand can be hard on you is that usually you have to deal with a side slope. The sand slopes down to the water, sometimes fairly steeply, throwing off your center of balance as you run and shortening one side of your body as it stretches the other. Make sure you return the same way you came to balance the effect of the slope.

ity level at this time; even back off a little bit. Maintain that pace for a week to week and a half, then pick up again. That bit of caution might keep you from getting a stress fracture in the first place.

A little caution can go a long way, but if all these measures fail and your leg pain continues to get worse, better see a doctor.

CHRONIC COMPARTMENT SYNDROME

Sounds like a luggage problem—and the analogy is not as far-fetched as it might seem. The muscle groups in the body are enclosed in cases: tough, gristle-like envelopes called fascia. Muscles swell with exercise, and the fascia, being slightly elastic, allow this swelling to happen. But the muscles just behind the shinbone are bounded on three sides by inflexible things: the shinbone (or tibia) in the front; the fibula, the other, smaller bone in the lower leg, to the side; and a big, ligament-like membrane in the back. When these muscles swell after aerobics class, a long run, a tough game of tennis or soccer or basketball, they quickly press against the fascia, which, hindered by its inflexible neighbors, is unable to stretch in response. The result can be what's called chronic compartment syndrome—the muscles keep on swelling, up to a third more than their total volume, but the fascia compartment can't keep pace. The muscles strain against the fascia like clothes in an overstuffed suitcase, and the compartment grows tighter and tighter. At this point, the blood vessels bringing blood to and from the muscles begin to be pressed closed. As the veins shut down, the blood within the muscles becomes trapped, and when the arteries collapse, they shut off the blood supply to the muscles.

At this point, a number of things can happen. The least of these, and the most common, is that the area toward the outside of your shinbone starts to hurt. A compartment syndrome hurts over a larger area than a stress fracture, and, rather than hurting a little earlier on and more as activity aggravates it, a compartment syndrome hurts at precisely the same moment every time you exercise. That may be a third of the way through your barre, four miles into your run, twenty-two minutes after the beginning of aerobics class—your leg always hurts at the same time. It won't hurt if you only run three and a half miles, or only take a twenty-minute class. It happens at the same time every time, because that's the point at which the muscles swell enough to begin shutting off the blood supply. And when you stop the activity, giving your muscles a chance to relax, the pain usually goes away.

Often a tip-off that your pain is from compartment syndrome is the presence of what are called fascial hernias. These are little balloonlike bulges under the skin in the lower, outside shin area, just above the ankle. Normally tiny holes in the fascia allow blood vessels and nerves to get through. Sometimes the holes grow bigger, allowing muscle itself to poke through, and sometimes muscle and nerves become pinched against the edge of the fascia. These fascial hernias can cause tenderness and even numbness and tingling in the foot. And at least half the people with chronic compartment syndrome suffer fascial hernias as well. You can test yourself by running your fingers down your shin after exercise. Dab some hand lotion or baby oil on your fingers—this makes them much more sensitive to feeling all the little nooks and crannies. If you feel little balloons or defects under your skin, and if your leg aches at the same point during exercise every time, you can be almost certain that compartment syndrome is the culprit.

✚ What to do about it ✚ See a doctor. You *can't* work through compartment syndrome on your own. No one knows why chronic compartment syndrome may suddenly appear when an athlete has enjoyed years without injury. Sometimes it shows up in your mid-twenties. In women it may appear more frequently just before menstruation, when there is a tendency to retain fluid and the muscles become a little bigger. You might get off your feet, elevate your leg, apply ice, and hope that the swelling goes down, but once the pattern of swelling to the point of constricting blood flow is established it's awfully hard to change.

There are very sophisticated ways of confirming chronic compartment syndrome. With tiny needles doctors can actually measure the pressure inside the compartment and compare it to the other leg. Sometimes the only remedy is surgery. It's a relatively safe and effective procedure, although not too common today. The ability to measure pressure in the compartment has made a big difference in prescribing treatment.

A caution: sometimes compartment syndrome can result from a blow to the leg, a swift kick in the shin during a soccer game, for example. In such cases the muscle and surrounding soft tissue can actually *bleed* into the fascia compartment, with devastating results. This doesn't happen often, but sometimes the swelling can be so dramatic that it will *shut off*, rather than simply curtail, the incoming supply of blood. The pressure from the excess swelling becomes so great, and the arteries and veins so constricted, that blood cannot flow into or out of the compartment. Without nourishment, the muscle can die—in a matter of hours. Almost always this acute, dangerous form of compartment syndrome is diagnosed late, because people think they're going to get better despite the pain and take heavier and heavier doses of pain medications. A rule of thumb: *injuries between the ankle and knee that result in pain and any kind of numb-*

ness or tingling, or pain that doesn't go away with rest, might be medical emergencies. Get yourself to a doctor or emergency room as soon as possible.

CONTUSIONS

When we studied soccer players at the high school level (perhaps surprisingly, there weren't many injuries), one of our conclusions was that kicks to the shin were the major source of injury.

A contusion results from a direct blow. You don't have to play soccer to experience one. Anybody who has ever hit a shin against a coffee table knows how much it can hurt and how long it takes to heal. That kind of contusion can be tender for six months, and the knob created *never* seems to go down. A direct kick in the shin can hurt even worse. If the kick occurs right over the bone, it usually won't cause a fracture. But it can cause bleeding under the bone, and that's why it hurts so much. The resulting swelling lifts all the nerve endings away from the bone, baring them to the environment. They can be excruciatingly tender and stay tender for what seems like an eternity.

A kick in the soft tissue adjacent to the bone can cause even more bleeding (and can lead to acute compartment syndrome). Pain, swelling, and discoloration are the results here as well.

✛ What to do about it ✛ Compression and ice can help keep the swelling down; staying off the leg may keep pain to a minimum. But a contusion is one of those things you simply have to gut through. You know it will heal, eventually. There's little to do but wait it out.

Except, that is, taking care to make sure that it doesn't happen again. A good preventive measure is to wear shin guards during activities like soccer in which contusions are a strong possibility. People grouse about wearing shin guards. They can't imagine that the padding on the back of a little piece of plastic can make any difference. But shin guards disperse the impact of a blow. They can mean the difference between taking the force of a kick over an area of eight square inches instead of one. Shin guards do a good job of protecting the leg, and they don't impede ankle motion.

TENNIS LEG

It happens to tennis players who give a little bit extra to get to a ball that's just barely out of reach. It occurs in hikers who strain to jump a stream that's wider than it appeared when they took off. Baseball, football, basketball, and soccer players, racquetball and handball players, participants in running sports that demand quick thrusts and sudden changes of direction—all are susceptible to tennis leg. Especially so if they're between the ages of thirty and forty-five. Tennis leg never shows up in children and rarely in people past middle age.

It also goes by a much more mundane name: calf strain, the ripping away of part of the calf muscle from the Achilles tendon. (It's similar to an Achilles tendon rupture, only higher up in the leg, and usually not so severe. And the onset is similar as well.) It feels as though you've been hit in the calf. A tennis player thinks she's been hit with a ball; a hiker reports turning around thinking his wife has thrown a rock at him. There's little pain, usually, and sometimes you'll hear a noise—a popping sound. Frequently you can continue doing what you're doing for a while, because a good 75 percent of the calf muscle is still attached to the Achilles tendon. You know something's wrong, but everything still works.

Eventually the muscles will go into spasm, contracting violently, and you'll find that your foot begins to point downward. No matter what you do, you can't bring your foot back up to neutral—women often report that the only way they can walk is in high heels—and this awkward position is accompanied by a lot of internal bleeding. Sometimes the entire calf will turn black and blue. Sometimes, because the blood flows down with gravity, you'll see discoloration in your ankle, in your foot, or even in your toes. The blood travels downhill until it can find its way to the surface. It can be alarming to look down days after being treated and see that your toes are black and blue. And you can end up with a huge, puffy calf as well.

If you run your fingers along the inside part of your calf muscle, you'll usually feel an area that is just extremely tender, and sometimes you can actually feel a hole. The tender area marks the point where the muscle fibers flow into tendon fibers. It is there that the tennis leg rupture takes place.

The upper-calf muscle, which is called the gastrocnemius (or "gastroc" for short), attaches at the top in the lower thigh, runs behind the knee about two-thirds of the way down the lower leg, and connects to the Achilles tendon, which itself attaches to the heel bone. Thus the gastroc spans two joints, the knee and ankle. Muscles that rupture, like the gastroc, almost always span two joints. The hamstring muscle in the thigh, which spans the pelvic and knee joints, is another. You have double the capability of stretching a two-joint muscle.

Usually the body protects against too much stretching. For example: in walking, when the knee is straight, thereby stretching the upper end of the gastroc muscle, the ankle is relaxed. When the ankle is flexed, stretching the lower part of the gastroc muscle, the knee is bent. It is when you get into positions that stretch both ends of this muscle at the same time that you flirt with tennis leg.

✚ **What to do about it** ✚ Stretch right away. Keeping your knee straight, foot pointed forward, and heel on the ground, slowly bend forward over your ankle and then bring your foot back to neutral. The motion stretches out the gastroc and also provides some internal compression for the injured part, slowing down the rush of blood into the area, thus reducing swelling. (See the illustration on page 87. The exercise is the same as that for stretching the Achilles tendon.)

Another way of stretching this muscle is by sitting with your leg straightened out in front of you. Hook a towel around the front portion of your foot and pull it back toward you. It may be a bit harder to stretch that way—gravity doesn't help you out as before—but if you just don't feel like standing on your feet it might be the technique for you. As with the standing stretch, you'll be able to feel the pull against the gastroc from the ankle all the way to the knee. It may be uncomfortable, but slowly, firmly stretch as much as you can. The results will be worth it.

Next apply ice and compression. Start at the toes with an Ace bandage and wrap all the way up to the knee. If you wrap your leg only at the calf, you could wind up with swelling below the bandage. You want constant compression all the way so the blood won't pool. But immediate stretching lessens the likelihood of much swelling. It even makes ice and compression less crucial. All three together—stretching, ice, and compression—make an especially potent course of action. And combining them with the use of the right-angle night splint (see "Plantar Fasciitis" in chapter 3) can also help, as the splint keeps the muscle stretched while you're sleeping, obviating the need to re-stretch (and hurt) every morning.

Most likely you'll have to have the injury treated by a doctor sooner or later. People with untreated tennis leg can take months to get their injured foot back to neutral, much less return to action. Even if you're treated, it may be four to six weeks before you're back to playing reasonable tennis. It used to be that doctors put tennis leg in a cast, with the foot pointing downward, which meant that the leg healed in that position, and it took up to five months to get the foot back up to neutral. Nowadays, especially if you stretch right away, you may be able to bypass all that and begin rehabilitating much more quickly. We continue people on a gentle stretching program and begin a restrengthening program as well, because the rest of the muscle that is still attached will waste away if you don't use it.

Eventually the muscle reattaches to the tendon, but not in the same place. It heals a bit shorter than it was. So why not sew the muscle and tendon back together? It doesn't work. The tendon takes stitches very well—it's nice, gristly stuff—but sewing muscle is like sewing hamburger. It looks very nice, but as soon as the muscle contracts all the stitches come out. Tennis leg responds well to nonsurgical treatment. The trick is to do the rehab exercises diligently. And be patient.

FRACTURES

First the bad news: When you think of a broken leg, you think of skiing. With reason. There's an occasional broken leg in soccer, but lower leg fractures in sports other than skiing are relatively unusual. Now the good news: ski fractures look spectacular in x-rays, but they occur in a better spot than they used to. When plastic ski boots first came out, they were very stiff but not very high, and fractures involved the ankle joint. Those were devastating injuries because they disrupted the construction of the joint itself. Not much could be done about those. Boots are still stiff today, but they're higher; so ski fractures are higher as well. Now isolated bones break, rather than joints. It's usually the shinbone, the tibia. That's a big bone, and it takes a long time to heal, but it *does* heal.

Fractures that involve the knee joint (tibial plateau fractures) still do occur, however. They're potentially devastating injuries. Often they masquerade as a knee sprain, with swelling and pain when you step onto the leg.

✚ What to do about it ✚ See a doctor. A fracture is one injury you simply can't treat yourself. But there is one thing you can do: be sure that your doctor—or someone else who knows what to do—prescribes a good course of rehabilitation exercises. Too often people come out of a cast with a stiff ankle and a calf that looks like a chicken leg and no idea of what to do next. What you *won't* do next is get right back to skiing or anything else. That will become abundantly clear the minute you start to bear weight on your "new" leg. You'll wonder what that funny, useless thing is beneath your knee. (Sometimes fractures require that the joint above the injury be immobilized, which means that you might find yourself in a cast up to your groin. In that case, we might as well be talking about thigh muscles. See chapter 5, "The Knee," for advice on how to rehabilitate your thigh.) During this period, your cast will probably be changed at least once, but not because it will have stretched or your swelling gone down. It will need to be changed because your muscles will have shrunk. Muscle wastes away at least twice as quickly as it builds up. If you've been immobilized for a month, it will take you two months *at the least* to get back to where you were before the injury. The most graphic way to become aware of the problem after you're out of the cast is to look over your shoulder into a mirror while you go up onto your toes. Notice the nice bulge in your healthy calf, then look at the matchstick that's supposed to be your other calf. Until the two legs begin to look symmetrical, you've got work to do.

Sometimes people just don't get very good advice—either because they don't ask for it, they don't listen, or they simply aren't given it. Often people are so happy to be out of the cast and done with doctors, they never want to talk to them again. Don't penalize yourself by assuming that when your leg comes out of the cast, your recovery is complete. Your fracture might have been managed very well—set right, held in a cast for the right period of time—but if you don't build back your strength intelligently the residuals of the fracture can be almost as troublesome as the fracture itself. The results can include some of the things we talk about in this book: Achilles tendinitis because you've got a stiff ankle, calf problems because your muscle has virtually disappeared, ankle sprains because you don't have enough muscle to protect this area, knee problems from favoring the withered leg. A word to the wise: after you get out of the cast, rebuild the strength of your leg in a solid rehabilitation program.

SHINSPLINTS

Depending on your point of view, shinsplints are either a brilliant, all-encompassing category, or an embarrassment to the medical profession. It is a diagnosis of exclusion. We know all these other fine things about causes of pain in the lower leg; everything we don't know falls under the umbrella of shinsplints.

There seem to be two kinds of shinsplints (if you can say there are two kinds of something you can't define): those that disappear in two to three weeks, and those, perhaps as many as 20 percent, that simply don't go away. These are the ones that are tough to treat.

The onset is familiar to most people. You change your training regime in some way—you run greater distances or over different terrain (a day of walking around San Francisco can do it)—and your leg begins to ache. It's usually the front of the leg, not right on the shinbone but where the muscle and bone meet. A tip-off that it's shinsplints and not something else: run your fingers down your leg. If the soreness encompasses a large area, the length of two dollar bills laid end to end, say, rather than a spot the size of a fifty-cent piece as in stress fractures, it's shinsplints. At first your leg aches after activity, then during, but if you stop for a few days it goes away. And after a few weeks of this on again, off again behavior, it simply goes away for good.

The most readily acceptable explanation for shinsplints is that it involves muscle pulling away from bone. Muscle is attached to the tibia along its length, except for that front area that's directly under the skin. There really isn't any tendon along most of the bone's length—these muscles attach directly to bone. Probably the pain of shinsplints is the result of tiny muscle fibers pulling loose either because they tighten up from fatigue, or the activity is too violent for them, or some such thing—no one really knows for sure. In any case, the condition is the result of an activity for which you're not prepared.

+ **What to do about it** + In the great majority of instances shinsplints are not a problem because by the time you've sorted out the fact that something's wrong and you want to treat it, it's already gone. But sometimes it doesn't go away, and if our knowledge of the cause of shinsplints is vague, treatment can be even more so. The medical literature on shinsplints reads almost like witchcraft. People describe similar symptoms and then describe a myriad of treatments, some of which are bizarre, and all of which seem to work, at least some of the time.

> ### + Slimming Down +
> ### Calves and Ankles
>
> Spot reducing isn't easy. Perhaps your best bet is a combination of lifting weights (see chapter 11, "Exercising to Stay Fit") and diet. Aerobic exercise, while not particularly effective for reducing weight, reorients your metabolism to burn excess fat more efficiently. A general rule of thumb is that the more fit you are, the better you look. Muscle is more attractive than fat, and, in contrast to fat, muscle can be toned.

Some people apply a concoction called tobacco poultice, a mixture made with moist tobacco. It works—for some people. Others rub in red-hot or analgesic balm and cover the balm with tape. Some simply tape the leg to constrain the muscles, reasoning that the tearing was caused by too much muscle movement. This can work as well. If you put a band around certain people's legs just a couple of inches above the anklebone, they're able to run without pain. And some years ago a sports trainer felt that improper use of the toes led to shinsplints. He made a cigarette-sized roll of fabric and inserted it in runners' shoes just below the curl of the toes. Allowing the toes to curl over the roll changed the length of the muscle-tendon groups, he reasoned, and it worked—for some people. *All* these things work *when* they work, which makes it difficult to sort out just what's making who well. It probably means that the problems doctors call shinsplints are really eight or ten different things, none of which we understand very well, but which we group together out of desperation.

The most common initial treatment for shinsplints involves an effort to increase the flexibility and strength of your lower leg muscles, especially the dorsiflexors, those muscles that pull the foot back toward the leg. The simplest way to strengthen them is to nail the ends of a piece of inner tube or surgical tubing to a piece of board and stick your foot under the loop. Pull your foot up against the tubing. As you develop strength, decrease the slack in the tubing to provide more tension. Stretch your calf muscles before and after your activity, and apply ice as well.

Sometimes putting an arch support in your shoe can help. You can get a Dr. Scholl's or Spenco semi-rigid arch at any large drugstore or running shoe store. Sometimes raising your heel a little bit will help. Heel inserts or pads are also widely available. These are all experimental things, but none of them are expensive or a big hassle, and none will make your injury worse if they don't work. Stretching and strengthening are things you can do at home. Ice, arch and heel supports, even anti-inflammatories—you just start working through these things from the least expensive, least time-consuming, to the most, and hope you get well. If nothing seems to work, see a doctor, and the two of you can experiment together.

REHAB EXERCISES

For stretching and strengthening the calf and Achilles tendon

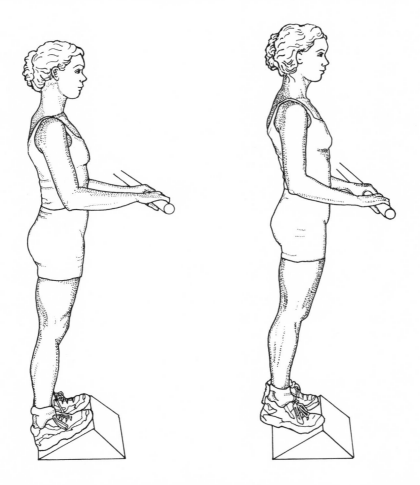

You can use a slant board or simply place the front of your foot on an inch- to inch-and-a-half-thick book. At first do the exercise with both legs, but once you're strong enough, exercise the injured side alone.

CHAPTER FIVE

The Knee

WHEN IT COMES TO THE KNEE, "instability" is the word. Over 25 percent of all sports injuries involve the knee (75 percent when it comes to surgery), and many of these involve instability of some kind. But it's not that the knee is necessarily ill designed. It's just that it has to put up with all manner of stresses and strains. In fact, when you think of it, the knee is very well designed—ingeniously so.

Imagine you're a mechanical engineer, and you've just been given a commission: Create a hinge. But not just any old hinge. This hinge must be flexible enough to bend a good 150 degrees front to back, another 3 or 4 degrees side to side, and it must be able to rotate 60 degrees as well—all at the same time if need be. It must be able to withstand anywhere from 100 to 2,000 pounds of pressure. It must be self-lubricating—no periodic grease jobs allowed. And it must be decidedly high tech: This hinge must be able to adapt to the changing demands made upon it. If it undergoes great stress on one side, it must be able to strengthen the other side, in order not to break.

And that's not all. The hinge must be durable, able to last sixty, seventy, eighty years. And it can't be too big. It may be the largest hinge in the machine of which it's a part, but if it extends more than three inches across in any direction, that's just too much. And, by the way, leave some extra room inside because the power train for the rest of the machine has to go right through this hinge.

So, you begin. The first problem is

+ WARNING +
If You Experience Any of These Conditions, Seek Medical Help

+ Your knee feels unstable or bends the wrong way;
+ Your knee is locked or won't straighten out;
+ Within a few hours your knee becomes obviously swollen;
+ Your knee won't bear your weight.

flexibility. Since this hinge (which we might as well start calling a joint) must bend and rotate at the same time, there's no possibility of a rigid linkage like a door hinge. And you can't get too exotic in design, because the more flexible you make this joint the less stable it becomes—and it has to hold together for a long time. So you decide simply to have the two parts of the joint abut, one against the other, so that they can bend and twist and do all sorts of maneuvers. You mold them so the top part ends in two convex mounds, much like two scoops of ice cream side by side in a single cone. The bottom part you hollow out, making two shallow cups. When you place one part against the other, the ends—the mounds and cups—fit. Next you protect the ends by coating them with some tough, white, rubbery stuff called cartilage; between them you place rings of thicker cartilage called a meniscus to further cushion the joint and provide shock absorption as well. So far so good.

Now, how to hold the two ends together? With stays and guy wires called ligaments and tendons. You hook them up in the middle of the joint and along the outside (the collateral and cruciate ligaments) so that they're able to loosen and tighten their grip as needed, as though there were a minicomputer controlling everything. Now your joint can bend, twist, push and shove, and withstand immense pressure. It may give, but it won't break. And you enclose the whole business in a tough, flexible sac that not only protects the joint from the outside world but produces its own lubricant as well.

One problem remains: the business of the power train (muscles). Finally it comes to you: why not let the joint function as a pulley? From the power source above, run a cable across the joint and tether it on the other side. As the power source contracts, it reels in the cable along the joint, lifting the weight (which happens to be your lower leg) on the other side—just like a prototype giant crane. And to increase leverage, thereby increasing lifting power and making the joint more efficient, simply make the pulley larger. But, of course, this joint has no turning wheels. Its pulley uses a sliding mechanism. To increase efficiency you must increase the angle over which the cable slides. So, a bold stroke: you place a small, lens-shaped piece of bone on top of the joint. The cable now must run *over* the piece of bone, which itself slides along the upper side of the joint. As the cable moves, the bone increases the angle between the power source and the weight to be lifted. The result: more strength.

Finally, make sure you leave some slack. If the tolerances are too tight, the fit too precise, this joint of yours will degenerate too quickly—just as your car's transmission will grind itself to death if its gears are too tightly aligned.

The result? Voilà: the knee. The lens-shaped piece of bone is, of course, the kneecap. The sides of the hinge, above and below, are the femur—the large bone in your thigh—and the tibia—the shinbone. That ingenious power train begins in your thigh with the quadriceps, the body's largest and most powerful muscle, and turns into tough tendon that extends all the way to the lower leg. This artful conglomeration of bone, muscle, soft tissue, and gristle makes up the largest and most complicated joint in the body and the one most frequently injured in sports (although ankle sprains are the most common single injury, the variety of knee problems outrank those of any other joint).

As you can see by now, the knee isn't ill designed. It has changed less in our long evolution than any other joint. It's just that we subject it to so much abuse. And because it's so large a joint, and so busy, there are a lot of things that can go wrong. There's lots of bone in the knee; seven distinct ligaments; more and thicker cartilage than anywhere else in the body; one huge tendon, as well as smaller ones; and a full complement of bursas that can develop bursitis at any time. But by far the greatest number of knee injuries have to do with what is called the extensor mechanism.

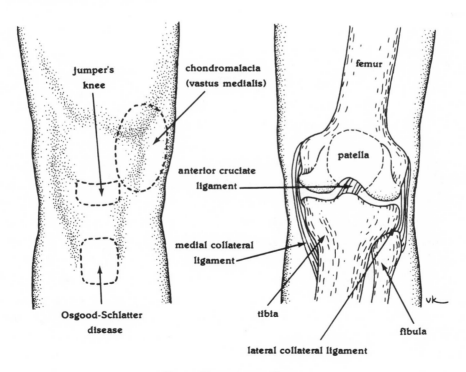

FRONT VIEW OF THE KNEE

THE EXTENSOR MECHANISM

Your knee functions in two ways: as a joint that you stand on, that bends and twists, and as a lever that allows you to move, jump, run, and kick. The power train that drives this lever begins as the quadriceps muscle in your thigh, consolidates into a tendon that runs through the knee joint, and finally attaches to the shinbone. It's called the extensor mechanism because it allows you to extend your lower leg. The key to it all is the kneecap, which actually resides within the large tendon that crosses the knee. It is the kneecap that forces the tendon away from the joint, increasing the angle and thereby the efficiency of the linkage. As the tendon moves, the kneecap slides over the bone beneath.

You can do without your kneecap if you have to. If for some reason your kneecap has to be removed, you can function pretty much as before, even continue to play professional sports. With one major difference: because the tendon would then drop back onto the joint—the pulley become smaller, in effect—you would have to be 30 percent stronger just to do the things you did before. The muscle would have to compensate with brute strength for the loss of mechanical advantage. Imagine what a demand for another third as much strength would mean for the quadriceps, already the largest and most powerful muscle in the body. The kneecap, the smallest part in this joint's linkage, is simply vital.

And vital to the kneecap itself is how efficiently it's able to slide over the end of the thighbone beneath it. As you bend your knee, your kneecap slides up and down the femur. It touches an entirely different part of the bone when you're sitting on the floor, say, than when you're standing up (it never touches the shinbone—the tibia—which is at least an inch away). But this sliding is no free and fancy flight. The kneecap must tolerate tremendous pressure. Just walking down a flight of stairs will put three times your body weight across an area that's little larger than a fifty-cent piece. A full squat can subject the kneecap to pressures up to seven and a half times body weight. For an average-sized person, that's around 1,000 pounds per square inch, an incredible amount of force. The cartilage that covers the end of the bone is thicker in the knee than anywhere else in the body—up to a quarter of an inch—just to cope with these forces.

The kneecap navigates the best possible course—in this case a groove in the femur—almost as if it were on a track. But rather than being smooth, the cartilage covering the back of the kneecap is faceted like a gem. When you bend your knee and the kneecap travels up or down the femur, this cartilage absorbs the pressure generated by the movement on one and then another of its facets. As the cartilage moves, the angle between it and the femur changes, and more of its facets come into play. This is a highly synchronized and sophisticated progression, and usually it works very well.

When it doesn't, a whole range of problems can ensue. Most common of these problems is the kneecap's tendency to jump off track.

It doesn't have to jump off by much. The engineering of the extensor mechanism is so precise that the tiniest deviation from its prescribed course can cause trouble. That's where the knee's ability to adapt to different circumstances becomes so important. Because the guy wires that hold the knee in place are not static and can change their tension constantly as your knee moves, the kneecap is able to stay on line. Your knee may bend and twist as you run, scrunch together as you dismount an apparatus, or extend as you stretch for a lob, but all the while the kneecap stays in its groove, sliding up and down as always, because some of the guy wires loosen up and others tighten as necessary.

Most of these support wires are tendons attached on one end to the kneecap, on the other to various areas of the quadriceps muscle. They are able to tighten and loosen because the quadriceps constantly contracts and expands. But—and this is a big "but"—there's something in the design of our bodies that can work against the efficient functioning of this extensor mechanism. It's apparent when you stand with your knees together in front of a full-length mirror, even more apparent when you look at an anatomical drawing of the lower torso and legs: we are wider in the hips than we are through the knees. The thighbones on either side of the body angle inward from the hips to the knees, and from there each leg's tibia and fibula (the other, smaller bone in the lower leg) drop pretty much vertically to the ankles and feet. The effect is a "Y" shape, certainly not the most direct route from beginning to end. As a result, the quadriceps muscle and tendons have to turn a corner at the knees before attaching to the lower leg. When the muscle contracts, however, the tendency is to try and establish a straight line—the shortest distance from point to point. The contraction tends to pull your kneecap to the outside, and that pull can, at the least, cause the kneecap to momentarily jump its track or, at the worst, to dislocate.

Your insurance against this happening is a tiny section of the quadriceps muscle called the vastus medialis. It's located just above and to the inside of the kneecap—you can feel it—and its job is to counteract this tendency of the kneecap to drift to the outside by tugging at it from the opposite direction and holding it in place. Unfortunately, the vastus medialis is the first muscle to get weak when you don't use your thigh properly and the last muscle to get strong when you're coming back from an injury. Which means that the first thing that happens when you limp, or favor your knee, is that this stabilizer goes.

It needn't be a knee problem that weakens the muscle—almost any injury can do it. An ankle sprain, for example, will cause you to lose strength in your thigh because you no longer walk normally. Achilles tendinitis, even ill-fitting shoes—anything that makes you limp—can make you lose muscle in the thigh. And heading the disappearing muscle act is invariably the vastus medialis. The result: a painful, swollen knee. So if we posted a sign that said

> IF YOU STRENGTHEN YOUR VASTUS MEDIALIS,
> YOU WILL NOT HAVE TO READ ANY FURTHER

probably three quarters of the people with knee problems could close this part of the book. Proper alignment of the extensor mechanism is that important. (If you're still here, stick around. In a few pages we'll suggest how to do the strengthening.)

So, onward to extensor mechanism problems and other knee injuries resulting from overuse, misuse, and abuse. (The sudden injuries, caused by such things as stepping in a hole or falling off a skateboard are more dramatic, but it's hard to take care of those by yourself. We'll take a look at such acute injuries in the latter part of the chapter.)

OVERUSE INJURIES

Extensor mechanism injuries—(chondromalacia)

They go by many names—runner's knee, quadriceps insufficiency, chondromalacia—and like most overuse injuries they are a result of change. For a runner, these injuries can be the result of a new pair of shoes that changes your gait or of changing from a pair that's badly worn in the heel to a new pair of the same brand. They can result from starting to run hills: when you run uphill you run with more of a bent knee and thus shorten your stride; downhill you lengthen your stride because the earth is falling away from you and your foot doesn't hit the ground as quickly. They can occur from training on a track. About 60 percent of a typical quarter-mile track is curved, and when you run on an unbanked curve, you bank yourself.

For a dancer, extensor mechanism injuries simply may be the result of working up to a new role, one that involves a lot more jumping, say. For a gymnast, the trigger for these injuries can be nothing more than changing floors. Hikers often develop knee problems more readily while trudging downhill than up. The reason may be that it's harder on the muscles to constantly lengthen than contract.

Ironically, fitness programs, one purpose of which is to make your knees stronger, can cause the extensor mechanism injuries they purport to prevent. As far as the quadriceps is concerned, lifting weights by extending your leg is just like going upstairs. Essentially what you're doing is hanging a weight on your foot and trying to straighten your knee out against it—not a terribly natural thing to do. People subject their knees to this kind of abuse because it's an effective way to isolate muscles, but if the vastus medialis isn't strong enough to hold your kneecap in place and you hang seventy or eighty pounds on your foot, your kneecap may try to find a new groove. It's important to build up slowly, with weights light enough for the vastus, then gradually increase.

Squats can be the most harmful exercise of all. At the least a squat subjects the back of your kneecap to about seven and a half times your body weight—around 1,000 pounds per square inch. Imagine the forces on the knees of people who do their squats with 200 pounds of barbells on their shoulders.

The pain of an extensor mechanism injury is like all overuse injury pain in that it creeps up on you. Frequently you first notice it *after* completing your activity. Then you start noticing it toward the end of the activity, then during the activity, and pretty soon it's there all the time. Usually it hurts in the front of the knee, but in a diffuse way. It's not like a torn cartilage (which we'll get to later on in the chapter), where you can put your finger against a spot on the knee and say, "*That's* where it hurts!" When you ask people where an extensor mechanism injury hurts, three quarters of them will rub a finger up and down along the inside of the kneecap. For another 15 percent it will be on the outside of the knee; and the last 10 percent can't quite figure out where it is—except they know it's somewhere around the front of the knee. It's worse with activity, better with rest. And as it gets worse, you develop problems elsewhere. From now on we'll call this kind of injury "chondromalacia." *Chondro* means "cartilage," *malacia* "wear"—together, "cartilage wear." Often the kind of problem we're talking about may not actually have anything to do with cartilage wear; nevertheless chondromalacia is the term is used to describe it. (More on that later.)

One of the next tip-offs to appear with these extensor mechanism injuries and the last to disappear is what is called the positive theater sign: you're unable to sit with your knees bent for a long period of time. People with this problem are the ones you're always tripping over in a crowded theater because they sit on the aisle and stretch their legs out. These are the people who have a hard time in the coach section of airplanes, or who can't take long rides in small cars. If you're one of these people and you've been sitting for a long time, you may get up and discover that your knee just won't work. It might take you four or five steps to straighten it out. The knee isn't locking, really, but doing something that's called gelling (as in "gelatin"—it's rubbery; hard to move).

Next the knee may start to swell. That causes it to ache, usually in the back, where the capsule surrounding the knee is softest and fluid accumulates most readily. When you bend your knee, the fluid squirts into the back, and it may feel as though there's an orange stuck there. At the least it will feel tight, like something's in the way. Something is indeed in the way: fluid. But people usually don't realize that that's the problem. They just know that they can no longer get into a squat. Not because the knee hurts so much, but because it feels tight, full, sort of boggy. As fluid continues to accumulate, your knee will begin to look, as well as feel, different.

It takes quite a bit of fluid in the knee to call attention to itself—a shot-glassful, about an ounce to ounce and a half, will just begin to be noticeable for most people. But if you really know how to look at your knees, you can tell. Stretch them in front of you on the floor, or on top of a coffee table, all the way out, without tightening up the muscles (if you tighten your muscles you push all the fluid to the back of the knee). Then check to see if both knees look the same. There should be hollows on either side of each kneecap—look for them. If one knee is less delineated than the other, then it's time to stop ignoring that knee and see your doctor.

One thing leads to another: now the pain in your knee may be sharper. If there's a lot of fluid in your knee, your kneecap can't possibly be where it belongs. It may have been displaced a bit to begin with; now it's more out of place, pushed to the side by the fluid. It may start rattling around a bit, making clicking sounds, or popping—repetitious noises. And now you're using your knee differently. You're reluctant to straighten it—that's an extreme motion and it hurts—and you're just as reluctant to bend it all the way. In fact, you *can't* bend it all the way; it's stiff, as though filled with Jell-O. So you start limping, keeping your leg somewhere between too straight and too bent. Which means that you must walk on your toes because your partially bent leg isn't long enough to do otherwise.

When you walk on your toes, your calf starts to hurt, as your calf muscles are the ones that keep you up on your toes. Because the gastrocnemius muscle in the calf begins above the knee, the strain on it may cause further knee pain. Or the hamstring muscles may begin to hurt where they connect in the back of the knee because they're helping to keep the knee partially bent all the time. And your quadriceps isn't being used normally, so it gets weaker, especially the vastus medialis, which was too weak in the first place. Then your knee may start giving way. It just won't hold you up. You'll be walking and suddenly feel as though you stepped into a hole, nothing there for support. But before you fall you catch yourself—until the next time.

All these things feed on themselves. The more problems you have, the less normally you're going to use your knee. The less normally you use your knee, the weaker it gets. The weaker it gets, the more likely you are to have problems. And once this cycle gets started, it's *not* going to get better by itself. Especially so because it sneaks up on you. Without thinking much about it, you start altering your activity to fit your diminishing capabilities. You used to run five miles a day—after a month it's down to two, then one. You used to take an aerobics class five times a week; now you take it three times; a month later you barely take any classes at all. A month after that, you have trouble walking to the studio from the parking lot. You always take the elevator now, and you drive around the block four times just to find a parking place that's three blocks closer because it's going to be hell walking down the hill to the office.

Gutting it out is *not* the answer. Neither is simply stepping up your activity rate. Some people figure, rightly, that if the knee is weak there's only one thing to do: make it stronger. So they lift weights even more than they used to, walk, run if they can, no matter the pain. And the knee simply doesn't come around. It's not that these activities aren't making you stronger, it's that they're making both sides stronger at the same time. So the injured side remains weaker by comparison. You've got to do something to get the weaker side up to the level of the strong one—otherwise the discrepancy will remain, along with the pain. You've got to do something *extra* with the side that's bothering you.

✚ **What to do about it** ✚ The solution (and, indeed, the solution for other problems as well) is to make the quadriceps on the injured side, specifically the vastus medialis, stronger. If you can cycle, one-legged cycling will make it stronger. But frequently by this point you're no longer able to do weight exercises (and cycling is really a weight exercise). Usually about the only things to do are tightening exercises.

It's simple: Straighten out your leg in front of you. You can sit on the floor, or sit in a chair and rest your leg on a coffee table, or you can even sit on the edge of your chair and extend your leg, with your heel on the floor, so that the knee is perfectly straight. Just make sure the knee's relaxed. Then place your fingers about an inch above the top of your kneecap and an inch to inch and a half toward the inside of your leg (toward the midline of your body), and tighten your thigh. If you're doing it right, you should feel the small muscle below your fingers get tight—*really* tight. If that's the case, you've found your vastus medialis. Tighten up and hold it for six to eight seconds, relax for a couple of seconds, tighten and hold for six to eight seconds, relax for a couple. Do three or four of these sets ten to fifteen times a day.

Sometimes it may be difficult to tighten this muscle. You may find that when you tighten your thigh much of the muscle is rock hard, but the portion beneath your fingers remains soft. In that case it's a matter of learning how to control the muscle in order to exercise it. One easy method is to roll up a towel and place it beneath your knee. Then push the back of the knee down into the towel. When you do that, you'll find that the vastus medialis beneath your fingers tightens automatically. You can accomplish the same thing by putting your fist underneath your knee and pushing down. It really doesn't matter what you have to do to persuade the muscle to work—a rock-hard contraction is the bottom line. Continue doing the exercise in this way until you find you can tighten the vastus without anything beneath your knee. Again, tighten for six to eight seconds, then relax, tighten again, and relax, three or four cycles in all. And do these sets ten to fifteen times a day. (If every method fails, you may want to try an electrical muscle stimulator to help you figure out how to do the exercise. Now you'll have medical bills—doctor, physical therapist, machine rental—but it's better than not getting the exercise at all.)

It may sound horrible, but what we're really talking about is no more than seven minutes of work—thirty seconds of exercise ten to fifteen times a day. You can easily fit that much effort into your schedule if you tie it to things you already do a lot. If you're in school, do the exercise set every time the bell rings. If you're in the office, do it every time the phone rings. If you're at home watching television, do it at each station break. *Don't* try to do fifty of these at a time, thinking that if four are good, fifty must be better. Not so. It's almost impossible to do more than a few really good quality tightenings at any one time. Don't worry, you'll be able to *see* the increase in muscle in two to three weeks. And the odds are better than eight in ten that you'll get better.

Sometimes the kneecap is so badly out of alignment that it hurts even to do the tightening exercises. If that's your case, pushing the kneecap toward the center of your knee with your fingers can make the exercise more comfortable. Some people prefer to wrap their knee with an Ace bandage or wear a neoprene knee sleeve. Such sleeves are available at hospital supply shops and some sporting goods stores. Pro, Ortho-Tech, and Bauerfeind are the brand names of a few good ones. Knee sleeves keep the knee warm and may help hold the kneecap in place. Icing after activity helps reduce inflammation, as will anti-inflammatory drugs. But all these things are no more than adjunctive treatments. They may make life a little easier for you, but you're not going to get rid of the problem—if you can get rid of it at all—until you make the injured leg stronger.

You may discover that you're among the 15 percent or so of people who just don't respond to this kind of treatment. It may be that the problem has gotten so bad that the back of your kneecap is chewed up (see the following section), or the capsule may have been scarred and has become too tight. If the exercise hurts (as a general rule you shouldn't try to strengthen things that hurt) and displacing the kneecap with your fingers or a bandage doesn't help, then perhaps you should see a doctor. The exercise simply may not work for everyone.

But if you've experienced the symptoms we've described and the swelling isn't too bad, your knee isn't locking or doing any other frightening things, and doing the exercise doesn't hurt, then it won't harm you to let up on the pain-producing activity and try the exercise program for at least two to three weeks before you even think about going to a doctor. Doctors who deal with these kinds of injuries regularly are going to give you the same advice, anyway. They may give the knee a thorough exam, take x-rays, test your strength, but at the end of the visit they're going to tell you to make the muscle stronger—and it'll cost you $200.

If you do the exercises and develop lots of good muscle, and this doesn't change things, then you're between a rock and a hard place. You may have to do something more spectacular, like seeing a surgeon. Surgery for chondromalacia is a last resort. It may provide relief but should never be considered without first trying a thorough rehabilitation program. Surgery is *not* a substitute for rehabilitation; indeed, after surgery there is even more rehabilitation to do.

First things first. Try the exercises. Odds are you'll have to do nothing more. And once back on the track, on the court, or in the studio, *keep* the muscle strong.

The vastus medialis—so much depends on so little.

Chondromalacia—Degeneration of the Cartilage

As promised, here's a word about the "real" chondromalacia, the kind that is more closely associated with the meaning of the word itself—wear and tear of the cartilage. In the precise use of the term, chondromalacia suggests that the back of your kneecap is wearing out, that the normally smooth, faceted surface of articular cartilage has begun to roughen like sandpaper. Sometimes the surface of the back of the kneecap softens and literally falls away in strands, a hanging garden of cartilage.

This degeneration of the back of the kneecap may be caused by the slow, subtle extensor mechanism problems most of us suffer to one degree or another, or it may be the result of a fall that drives your kneecap into the thighbone so hard that it cracks the cartilage. The initial injury may have happened ten years ago, and you've only begun to suffer the consequences now. It's a tough condition to deal with and may even require surgery, but in general strengthening the vastus medialis will help here as well. (It's not uncommon to find chondromalacia when operating on the knee for some other reason. Often it's been there for much longer than symptoms have been apparent. Many people do remarkably well with some wear and tear of the back of the kneecap. Just because chondromalacia is present doesn't mean something must be done about it—especially if your knees never hurt in the past.)

+ What to do about it + This kind of chondromalacia is rare compared to the problems that the more general use of the term describes. But if you try the treatments suggested in the previous section and your pain just won't go away, you may be in the select group that has the real thing. Better see a doctor.

Patellar Tendinitis (Jumper's Knee)

One of the big differences between the effects of patellar tendinitis (that is, tendinitis of the patella—the kneecap) and those of chondromalacia is that tendinitis sufferers are much better able to locate the pain. Whereas people with chondromalacia may rub their fingers up, down, and around the knee to indicate where it hurts, when you have tendinitis you can put a fingertip right on the spot. You can put the top of a ballpoint pen right on the spot and just about levitate yourself into the air with pain. And that spot is right at the bottom of the kneecap, where the tendon that connects to the shinbone begins—hence the name, patellar tendinitis.

It's also called jumper's knee, as it was first described in the takeoff leg of high jumpers. But it turns out that basketball players probably have more jumper's knee than anybody else. You also see it in dancers, runners, volleyball players—anyone who runs and jumps regularly may suffer from it. And like chondromalacia it sneaks up on you, first hurting after your activity, then toward the end of the activity, then during, at the beginning, and finally all the time. It's not nearly as common as chondromalacia—nothing is—but it's more difficult to treat. It's probably the second most-frequent overuse knee injury.

But no one understands patellar tendinitis very well at all. Judging by the discomfort it can produce, you might expect a great deal of inflammation, but when surgeons operate on these people, often they can't see anything wrong. Sometimes the tendon looks red and inflamed, but many times it doesn't. These changes in the tendon may be very, very subtle.

Not so subtle, however, is *acute* patellar tendinitis—that is, tendinitis caused by a specific incident rather than a problem that develops gradually. It can be the result of a misstep while running (a hurdler, for example, who confuses steps between hurdles and tries to correct, or a sprinter who slips out of the blocks), a blow on the knee, even snapping out your leg while dancing—anything that puts an undue amount of load on the knee *quickly*. And you'll know it when it happens. You'll have sharp pain at the bottom of the kneecap, swelling, difficulty in moving the knee. In this case part of the tendon actually tears away from the kneecap, but often much less than you'd think to cause so much discomfort. It may be that only a few of a couple thousand fibers in the tendon have broken away, but it is enough to cause pain.

It may be, however, that you've actually pulled your kneecap *apart*. Sometimes, though not often, the tendon is actually stronger than the bone, and instead of giving way, the tendon stays intact and the bone splits in two (a patellar fracture). Patellar fractures can also occur as the result of a direct blow to the kneecap, such as falling on a bent knee.

Again, the tip-off that it is patellar tendinitis that's troubling you: the pain is sharp, specific, and easy to locate—right at the bottom of the kneecap.

✚ What to do about it ✚ If it's acute patellar tendinitis, the result of a particular incident, then two anti-inflammatories with meals, icing three times a day, a rest from your activity, and maintaining muscle strength during that period is a way to begin. But if it really hurts and your knee is hard to move as well, you should probably see a doctor.

Some people think that the overuse variety of patellar tendinitis, the kind that sneaks up on you, can result from an inappropriate balance between the strength of your quadriceps and hamstring muscles. That's not at all well documented, but there does seem to be some association with tightness of the quads. That goes along with the general philosophy concerning tendinitis: tight tendons are tendons that are likely to be irritated. The thing to do, then, is to stretch out the patellar tendon, and the way to do that is to stretch out the quadriceps muscle itself. You can lie on your stomach and have someone gently bend your leg to the point that your quadriceps feels tight. (You should only feel the tightness in the quadriceps, *not* in the tendon. If it hurts in the tendon, you're doing the stretch improperly.) Hold the position for a few seconds, and then do it again. You can do the same exercise yourself by lying on your stomach, reaching behind you with the arm opposite to your injured leg, grasping the foot of the injured leg, and gently pulling your heel toward the small of your back. Or stand supporting yourself with a hand against the wall and pull your foot toward your back as you did on the ground. The important thing is to stretch *without* pain. If it hurts, don't stretch so far. Gradually it will come.

Interestingly, about half of the people with jumper's knee find it hurts to extend the injured knee and tighten their thigh muscles—the kind of vastus medialis strengthening exercise described in the proceeding section. But if you put your fingertip on the outside of the kneecap and push toward the inside of the leg just a tiny bit, sometimes an imperceptible amount, the pain disappears. That suggests that the vastus medialis is involved in this injury as well. It's probably an alignment problem. The tendon isn't pulling in quite the right direction because the muscle is weakened, allowing the kneecap to stray too far to the outside. Vastus medialis strengthening exercises are always a good bet.

So, vastus muscle strengthening exercises and quadriceps stretching exercises most likely will help, as will doing all the other things that you do for tendinitis in general—warming up well before activity, icing afterwards, perhaps wearing a neoprene sleeve over the knee (which can help push the kneecap to the inside—basketball players seem to like that), taking anti-inflammatory drugs, and, just in case there's anything to the quadriceps/hamstrings strength ratio theory, making sure that the hamstrings in both legs are equally flexible. Just lie on your back with your legs straight, and then lift one leg up, then the other. If there's a noticeable difference in flexibility, stretch the tight leg—but gently.

Both patellar tendinitis and chondromalacia, because they involve kneecap alignment problems, can sometimes be helped by orthotics. Anything that decreases the angle in the knee around which the quadriceps has to pull decreases the likelihood of the kneecap slipping out of alignment. If your arch collapses, forcing you to pronate to the inside when you walk or stand, then your knee rotates to the inside. That makes the angle on the outside of the knee greater. Arch supports or orthotics can help straighten things up and decrease the angle. Seeing a doctor for an evaluation may be a good idea. But it costs you nothing to try exercises first.

Sometimes patellar tendinitis can require surgery. The operation can be successful, but it's a last resort. You always want to treat things in the simplest, least invasive way you can. Try the easy things first. If they don't work, then you can try the more invasive, and expensive, things. But the vast majority of people are going to get well by doing the easy things. It's just a matter of recognizing the problem and knowing how best to go about handling it. That's what this book is for.

Osgood-Schlatter Disease

Osgood-Schlatter is not really a disease, but rather a form of tendinitis at the *lower* end of the patellar tendon, where it goes into the shinbone. You can easily locate the spot. Simply run your fingers up the shinbone toward your knee. When you come to a small lump a couple of inches below the kneecap, you've found the place. That would be enough said about the problem—how to deal with tendinitis should be pretty clear by now—were it not for one thing: Osgood-Schlatter disease only affects people who are growing. That is to say, young people, usually between ten and sixteen years old.

The reason for this being a young people's problem is interesting. When bones grow they don't just stretch like elastic; rather they expand at certain spots near the upper and lower ends of bones called growth centers. It is in these centers where new bone is made, pushing out to lengthen and thicken the existing bone and grow kids up to adult size. Once children finish growing, the growth centers close down (although the bone, like the rest of the body, constantly regenerates itself, it simply doesn't become appreciably larger). It just so happens that the patellar tendon connects to the shinbone at a growth center. Which means that in young people the tendon encounters *forming* bone, bone that is not yet as hard and resilient as it will become. It's between bone and cartilage at this stage, not quite one or the other. In x-rays it resembles a cloud in the midst of the more solid bone at either end. Normally, if a tendon pulls away from the bone the tendon tears, not the bone. But when a tendon strains against a bone's growth center, it can pull away pieces of the soft, forming bone instead.

That's exactly what happens in Osgood-Schlatter disease. The tendon pulls against the forming bone, tearing away tiny pieces of it. But wait—the story isn't over. The forming bone, now connected to the tendon rather than the shinbone, isn't about to stop doing what it's doing. Its job is to turn into new bone, and so it does, right there at the end of the patellar tendon. The result? A lumpy knee. You already had a lump at this point—now you've *really* got one.

✚ **What to do about it** ✚ Because the patellar tendon is so near the skin, often it will get red and swollen, and very, very tender. Treat it with ice, anti-

+ Kids and Sports Injuries +

When it comes to most sports injuries, kids are miniature adults. The same problems attack them that afflict bigger and older people, and for the same reasons. Overuse and abuse are the major causes, with an occasional acute injury striking children just as it does adults. For most of these problems, the suggestions we offer throughout the book will help kids as readily as adults. Look for your child's ailment in the text (we make special note if the treatment is different for children than it is for adults). And the general injury tip-offs discussed in chapter 1 are as true for kids as they are for grown-ups:

1. Joint pain;
2. Tenderness at a specific point;
3. Swelling;
4. Reduced range of motion;
5. Weakness;
6. Numbness and tingling.

If any of these symptoms show up in your child, better see a doctor.

But, as any parent knows, kids are much, much more—and less—than little adults. They have special talents and problems that adults just don't have. When it comes to sports injuries, those special problems are almost always a result of their size, or lack of it, and the fact that they're constantly making up for that lack—that is, growing.

Think about it. We adults become used to our bodies. The changes that active people experience are usually those resulting from concentrated effort to increase skill and conditioning, injury, or that inexorable process that we know only too well: aging. But most of these are gradual changes, subtle and in the long run relatively minor. We hold on to the general shape

inflammatories, and rest until you're not limping during everyday activities. And, as before, you must strengthen your quadriceps. Especially so because people who are growing very quickly often have tight muscles. The bones grow faster than the muscles can stretch—they just can't keep up. So the quadriceps muscles of people with Osgood-Schlatter disease are often tight. Or more likely it's vice versa: tight quadriceps muscles can lead to Osgood-Schlatter disease. It's important to start long, gentle, sustained quad stretching exercises, as described in the earlier sections of this chapter.

The only other treatment besides strengthening, stretching, and getting rid of the inflammation is to wear a horseshoe-shaped pad around the lump. These are called Osgood-Schlatter pads and are available at medical supply stores. You'll be amazed at how often you fall or kneel onto the lump, or bump your knees into all sorts of things. As with any injury, you become very conscious of the tender part of the body. But don't expect the lump to go away. Most likely it's yours forever. Unfortunately, decreasing the lumpiness surgically is a tough, involved operation. You have to take the tendon off the bone, shave down the bone, then reattach the tendon. Most people are better off with a lump.

Hamstring Tendinitis

Chondromalacia, jumper's knee, and Osgood-Schlatter disease are the most frequent knee problems, but there are a number of less common kinds of tendinitis that can attack the back of the knee. One of these is tendinitis of the hamstring tendons. These are the tough wires in the back of the knee, one toward the outside of the leg, two others toward the inside. If you place your hand at the back of your knee and bend your leg, you'll feel them. They're obvious to the touch as well as the eye. They connect the hamstring muscles, the large muscle group in the back of your thigh, to the lower leg. It's these muscles that pull your lower leg up toward the body, allowing you to bend your knee. If any one of the hamstring tendons become sore and inflamed, it's probably due to tendinitis.

Usually the tendinitis is from overuse. You can get it from running hills (running downhill, especially, stretches the hamstrings and can cause hamstring tendinitis if the muscles are tight), and limping with a bent knee to favor another injury can bring it on as well. It's the hamstring muscles that keep the knee bent—too much limping can overtax them, straining the tendons. Sometimes you can cause hamstring tendinitis by trying to solve other problems in your knee. If you bandage your knee too tightly, for example, the hamstring tendons will chafe against the wrap every time you take a step. Even wearing a knee sleeve can give you tendinitis.

Another possible cause is less obvious: changing to a lower-heeled shoe. It's easy to associate Achilles tendinitis with a low heel, because it makes sense that if you lower your heel you stretch the Achilles tendon. It takes a bit more thought to realize that the hamstrings are part of the same chain. When you run and your heel hits the ground, your knee is partially bent. If your heel doesn't come down as quickly, as when you're running downhill, or

KIDS AND SPORTS INJURIES (CONTINUED)

and size of our body from our late teens to the day we die. We become used to walking with the same size feet, reaching to the same height, squeezing through the same tight places. In sports that familiarity translates into a confidence in our bodies that allows us to perform on a roughly consistent level day after day, year after year. If you're an adult, chances are that living in your body is pretty darn comfortable.

Not so for kids. Especially during rapid growth spurts, kids have to contend with a new body virtually every six months. A body that's different in size, shape, center of gravity, and flexibility. You just get used to one body, more or less discover your angles and leverages, more or less figure out how much push comes to how much shove, and all of a sudden you're hit with an entirely new one. And the changes don't have to be all that dramatic to throw off the best laid plans. A sudden extra inch of height is plenty to foul up the best coordination. A few new pounds in an unaccustomed spot will cause the most steady balance to waiver. And then, just as you're finally figuring out this new body, wham!—here comes another one. You can't win.

So pity the poor child athlete. But not too much. That same energy that fuels their growth gives kids a resilience and flexibility that adults just don't have. Kids catch on quicker than adults. They usually bounce back from injuries far faster than adults. They need less time to prepare for athletic activities than do adults, less time to recover afterwards, and less care to keep going in the meanwhile. And for kids, the performance curve just keeps going up. None of the leveling off that adults constantly contend with. Kids continue to run faster, jump higher, balance better, and grow stronger until . . . well, until they're no longer kids.

if you lower the heel of your shoe, your knee must extend a bit farther for your foot to make contact with the ground. That can stretch the hamstrings. But if they don't stretch, something has to—that something is the hamstring tendon. The result can be tendinitis. So running in a tennis shoe, which has almost no heel at all, rather than in a running shoe, which has a raised heel, can often cause hamstring tendinitis. As can running on the beach barefoot. It's like running in a negative-heeled shoe because your heel sinks into the sand.

✛ What to do about it ✛ The first thing to do is take care of the inflammation. Try ice, aspirin, gentle stretching, and strengthening of the hamstring muscles, as suggested earlier. But none of those treatments will have a lasting effect until you find out *why* you have tendinitis in the first place. What change have you made in your training, in your footwear, in the kind of activity itself? When you figure that out, avoid the activity for a while and continue to deal with the problem by strengthening and stretching. When you feel better either ease back into your training or change back to the kind of activity—or footwear—that caused you no problems earlier. And one temporary thing you can do while recovering is to raise your heel a quarter of an inch or so with a cork heel pad. That'll help relax the tendon while you're sorting things out.

The important thing is to get on with a treatment program quickly. The longer you walk with a limp or an abnormal gait, the harder it will be to get rid of the underlying problem. But if your hamstring tendons don't get better, or if they're red and swollen and really tender to the touch, you might be better off seeing a doctor. A doctor can prescribe stronger anti-inflammatory drugs and suggest physical therapy that might get you on your way a bit sooner.

Tendinitis of the Iliotibial Band (IT Band)

There's a long, thick, rigid tendon that runs from the upper part of your hip (the ilium) all the way down the outside of the thigh, through the knee, and connects to your shinbone (or tibia). It's called the iliotibial band. You can feel it just above the hamstring tendon on the outside of the knee. It feels like a cable and, indeed, acts mostly as a stabilizer, almost as though it were a ligament. It's also involved in straightening the knee, for about the last fifteen degrees of motion, and in flexing it as well. It can be irritated by the difference in gait demanded by running downhill or by other gait problems in runners.

✚ **What to do about it** ✚ Stretching and strengthening can help if you catch iliotibial tendinitis early. Gently pull your injured leg to the outside and toward the back to strengthen. You can do this exercise standing or lying on your side, and it doesn't matter if you point or flex your foot. To stretch, stand up and cross your injured leg behind your other leg—it's called a cross-leg stretch. And, as with any other tendinitis, try ice, anti-inflammatories, and rest. But you may have to see a doctor, as the exercise programs involved with iliotibial band tendinitis are very specific and require demonstration.

Popliteal Tendinitis

There is a tiny muscle in the back of the knee called the popliteus. It helps to flex your knee. Its tendon winds its way up and around and crosses the outside of your knee, the only tendon that's really inside the knee capsule itself. Popliteal tendinitis will give pain in the outside of the knee, most often when you're running downhill.

✚ **What to do about it** ✚ See a doctor. This is a tough problem: it's difficult to stretch or strengthen the muscle, as it's so small and its role so specific.

In fact, with problems of the outside of the knee in general, if a little bit of stretching, a footwear change, and an activity change don't help, you'll probably have to see a doctor. These problems can demand a lot of precision in diagnosis and very specific rehabilitation programs. And there are a number of other things that can cause problems in this area. It's simply beyond the capabilities of most people to handle these injuries at home. Indeed, some of these problems are so difficult to treat that they're beyond the capabilities of physicians.

Bursitis

Bursas are envelopes of paper-thin, slippery tissue that act as the body's slipping and sliding mechanism, its friction reducer. Wherever two things in the body rub over each other—tendon over bone, tendon over ligament, tendon over tendon—you might find a bursa greasing the way. Because so many tendons run through the knee, there are more than a dozen different bursas around the area. They can become irritated and inflamed. Usually they don't swell enough so that you'd notice it, but they can hurt.

The exception is what's called prepatellar (in front of the kneecap) bursitis. Here the bursa directly over the kneecap swells, most likely as the result of a fall or a blow.

(It's also known as housemaid's knee, after those legions of women who through the years spent much of their time on their hands and knees.) This bursa can grow so large that it looks as though someone has stuffed a lemon underneath your skin.

✚ What to do about it ✚ Once the bursa's that size, you should definitely see a doctor. It may have to be aspirated and injected with cortisone to decrease the inflammation. Until that point you can try icing it three times a day for twenty minutes and taking two anti-inflammatories with meals. If a few days of this treatment produce no results, better visit your doctor.

Baker's Cyst

Unlike baker's yeast, this has nothing to do with bread; but it does rise. A Baker's cyst (named after the surgeon who first discovered it) is a large swelling in the back of your knee. In adults, it usually forms because you've got something else going on in the knee that is producing too much fluid. The knee capsule is much firmer in the front of the knee than in the back. When you tighten your quadriceps muscle, the capsule tightens around the kneecap, and the fluid gets smooshed to the area of least resistance, the back. If enough fluid is pushed to the back of the knee enough times, the capsule can become permanently deformed, ballooning outward like a bulge in an inner tube. Sometimes people have a bulge the size of an orange.

✚ What to do about it ✚ The idea is to get rid of whatever it is that's causing the fluid to form in the first place. If you let air out of a bulging inner tube, the bulge disappears. If you persuade the knee to quit forming fluid, the Baker's cyst disappears. Often the cause is a torn cartilage. That may require surgery. But the cause can be chondromalacia or arthritis as well. Whatever it is, if you deal with the underlying problem you almost never have to take out the Baker's cyst. It simply goes away. Better see a doctor.

Children sometimes develop something called primary Baker's cyst. The symptoms are the same, but in this case there's nothing wrong with the knee. The cyst forms for unknown reasons. Often it has to be removed surgically. See a doctor.

Meniscus Cysts

What we think happens in this injury is that you tear part of a meniscus (the cushioning cartilage in the knee), it tries to heal, and it heals abnormally. In the process, cells that are capable of forming fluid somehow get trapped in the meniscus and form a cyst filled with jellylike fluid. As the cyst grows, frequently to marble size, it pushes toward the outside of the knee. You'd think that something that small wouldn't cause as much pain as it does, but things are pretty tight in the knee, and as the cyst grows it pushes against the ligaments and the knee capsule itself. That hurts. Often you can feel and see these cysts. As you bend and straighten your knee, the cysts appear to change in size, but they're only reacting to the amount of tension exerted against them.

✚ What to do about it ✚ If these cysts hurt enough that you simply can't live with them, sometimes they can be aspirated and injected with cortisone to shut down their ability to make more fluid. But they can be difficult to drain because the fluid is gummy, the consistency of cold maple syrup, and it clogs up the needle. Usually, however, as the cause of the cyst is a torn meniscus, surgically removing the tear gets rid of the cyst as well. Here the arthroscope can be very useful. (See chapter 13, "So, You're Going to Have an Operation.")

DEGENERATIVE DISEASE IN THE KNEE

It's not something most of us like to think about, but little by little our bodies wear out. If we live long enough, we're going to wear out our joints, and often the knee is the first to go. Although our body makes day-to-day repairs, it simply can't keep up with the abuse we heap on our knees. As we get older, we wear down the knee's cushioning structures, the articular cartilage (joint surface), and the meniscus. They become less rubbery, more granular, and begin to get microscopic tears. These tears gradually become larger and can start getting in the way of the joint. And if you've had any major problem that disrupts the mechanics of the joint—a torn meniscus removed, a ligament tear, long-term chondromalacia so that the kneecap doesn't track properly—then this overall degeneration of the knee is accelerated.

Degenerative arthritis is one term used to describe these changes. People blanch when they hear it, but it *is* a form of arthritis. Not rheumatoid arthritis, which can deform the joint, but wear-and-tear arthritis. And that may sound worse than it actually is. For most people, the consequence is that their knees become less tolerant of the kinds of problems we've discussed in this chapter. If it would normally take a 50 percent change in your daily running mileage to bring on tendinitis, say, now you might get those same symptoms with just a 20 percent change. If running up and down hills never bothered you before, now your knee may ache after a workout. If five days a week of tennis, or racquetball, or aerobics class used to be your norm, now you may notice that your knees are talking to you at the end of the week (or the middle, or the beginning).

So the upshot is that you lose the luxury of being able to ignore things. Little problems are less likely to go away by themselves. You're less tolerant of change. And it can be very frustrating for an active person to realize that the little aches and pains that always simply disappeared by themselves are now things that have to be attended to. That now it's necessary to become *aware* of what's going on in your knees and plan your activities accordingly, instead of simply bludgeoning through as before.

These degenerative changes will show up in the guise of overuse problems. Your knee may ache after an activity, say, and stiffen up. Usually as the day goes on you get a little stiffer, notice a little more loss of motion. But you can't put your finger on any particular spot that hurts, nor can you point to any particular cause. The knee just hurts. And if the pain goes away after a night's sleep, there it is again the next day, this time before you're done with your workout. Soon the knee aches while you're lacing your shoes. And so it goes.

✛ What to do about it ✛ The realistic way to deal with degenerative changes is to do all the things that you would do for overuse problems: ice, anti-inflammatories, and rest. Also, the over-the-counter supplements chondroitin sulfate and glucosamine appear to give relief to over half of the people who use them—and side effects are rare. While techniques for joint surface cartilage replacement exist, none seem applicable to the large areas of destruction seen with degenerative arthritis.

It's also important to maintain as much strength and flexibility as you can. There's some information to suggest that if you remain strong, you can better handle degenerative changes because the joint is held together more firmly than if you were weak. And if you stay strong you retain a greater range of motion.

So degenerative changes usually mean that you'll have to alter your activity but not necessarily stop it. For example, if you're a runner and your knees are wearing out, you may have to start training without running. Alternate running with cycling. That cuts in half the amount of weight your knees have to bear while continuing to maintain strength and cardiovascular conditioning. A few years down the road you may have to do three quarters of your training on the bicycle and only one quarter running. After you run a ten-kilometer race you may have to cycle exclusively for the next two weeks to give your knees a breather.

Eventually the day may come when running simply isn't in the best interests of your knees, and you may have to figure out a way to maintain your conditioning and have some fun while running only occasionally—or not at all. It's a matter of adapting. No one can reverse these changes. Knee joint surgical replacement techniques do exist, but so far they're more suitable for salvage operations than anything else.

REPLACING THE KNEE

You see people with artificial hips on the tennis courts all the time. Why not artificial knees? The answer is that you *can* replace the knee joint, but the surgery doesn't permit the abundance of activity a hip replacement does. For a simple reason: The hip is a very simple joint, a ball and socket, the easiest kind of joint to work with. But the knee is a very complicated joint, a hinge that can rotate as well as bend, and which is held in place by a system of restraints rather than a positive linkage. You have to depend on the body's natural guy wires—the ligaments and tendons—to hold the artificial joint in place, and that's often a problem because they're not in such great shape after the joint has become so worn out that it needs replacing.

The second problem with knee replacement surgery is that the knee is a huge joint, the largest in the body. It has four or five times as much surface area as the hip. So you're faced with inserting big pieces of metal or plastic in an area that's just under the skin, not covered and protected by muscles as is the hip joint. The body likes to get rid of foreign things that are near the surface, and because of the immense forces acting on the knee, those things are more likely to loosen and break down.

Especially so because you have to replace both sides of the knee joint at the same time, whether they need it or not. No one has yet come up with a compound that will coexist with the cartilage and bone in your knee. If it's too hard, the compound wears away the cartilage on the other side of the joint; if it's too soft, the cartilage remains but the artificial bone compound wears out. So you have to insert two synthetics that are mated to each other—usually plastic on one side, metal on the other. And, if the kneecap needs replacing as well, it must be done in conjunction with the joint replacement. Putting in a new kneecap in your existing, worn-out joint doesn't work for the same reasons that prevent you from replacing only one side of the joint—the synthetic replacement material is simply not compatible with what it has to rub against.

The moral of the story: hold on to your knees. Treat them *right*.

Overuse Checklist

+ About 60 percent of all overuse knee problems involve chondromalacia—a kneecap out of alignment. You'll know because with chondromalacia it's hard to put a finger on the pain—it seems to spread around the knee. If this condition persists, it can become submerged by other problems. Best get to it right away. Ice, rest, anti-inflammatories can help, as can exercise: *strengthen the vastus medialis muscle.*

+ About 15 percent of overuse knee injuries are other tendinitis problems: jumper's knee, hamstring tendinitis, popliteal tendinitis, iliotibial band tendinitis. They, too, can involve the extensor mechanism. Try ice, rest, anti-inflammatories, and exercise.

+ Another 15 percent are degenerative changes. They show up in the guise of common overuse problems. Nothing to do but treat them as you would the overuse problems themselves. And stay strong. The healthier your muscles, the healthier your knee joint.

+ The remaining 10 percent are various little things: bursitis, cysts, etc. These are difficult to diagnose and difficult to treat. They require somebody pretty good at doctoring.

ACUTE KNEE INJURIES

Overuse injuries creep up on you. A minor discomfort turns into nagging irritation, which turns into chronic pain, and before you know it you're hurting all the time. And you can't figure out when and how it happened. Not so with acute injuries. These you can date from a single incident. In fact, you can probably recall the hour, the minute, the second it happened, and *precisely* what you were doing at the time.

All this to say that if you suffer an acute knee injury, you'll know it. You'll simply be able to *feel* that something serious has gone wrong, something that has never happened before and that you want *never* to happen again. Trust your own insight in such a situation and go with your better judgment, not against it. In other words, don't deny that something serious has happened and try to ignore it. No one likes to go to the doctor, no one wants to have surgery (and acute knee injuries are the most frequent cause of surgery in all sports), no one wants to have to do all those awful things to rehabilitate the knee. The temptation is to go home, hit the sack, and hope that when you wake up it will all have been a bad dream. Just as when your car acts up, you put it in the garage for the night and hope that miraculously it will start the next morning.

Well, in the morning your car still may not start, but it will be no worse—your knee will be. And not only will it be worse, it will be a lot harder for a doctor to figure out what's wrong with it. If you're examined quickly after an injury, you're half again as likely to get an accurate diagnosis as when you wait. The reason is simple: when you injure your knee severely, the muscles in your thigh go into spasm—that is, they contract violently and immobilize the knee, just as though you were wearing a splint. The longer the muscles are in spasm, the more tightly they hold the knee. The tighter the knee, the more it hurts. And the more it hurts, the more difficult it is for you to relax enough so that someone can move the knee as necessary to examine it. And soon the knee will start to swell. If you finally go in to a doctor after a couple of days and your knee looks like a softball, then there's little alternative than to resort to x-rays—at some cost—or, because in about 95 percent of acute injuries x-rays won't disclose the problem, to more expensive procedures like an MRI scan.

One of the reasons that professional athletes receive such good care is that someone is always available to examine an injury within a minute—literally—after it occurs. At that point an athlete is still in shock, with no pain, so it's possible to do a superb examination. You can manipulate the knee in ways that an hour later would probably get you a punch in the nose. You can make an accurate diagnosis and start the athlete on a rehabilitation program almost immediately. So if you suffer one of these dreadful injuries, it may not be necessary to call an ambulance, but do have somebody drive you to an emergency room right away. That kind of fast response will save you much unnecessary difficulty later.

Acute Injury Tip-Offs

If you're not sure what happened to you and any of the following kinds of behavior describe your knee, you'd be wise to get to a doctor and have your knee looked at.

1. **Noise.** It is not good to hear things in your knee. A lot of people may have a creaky knee, a knee that makes noise when they go up and down stairs, say, or bend into a squat. That's a different sort of thing. It's been around a long time; it's nothing new. The kind of noise that should snap you to attention is a noise that's the result of *doing something* to your knee—changing direction, slowing down, speeding up, landing after a jump, cutting hard. A pop or a snap—a sharp, short sound—can signify a torn car-

tilage or ligament. A dislocated kneecap is marked by a long, drawn-out sound, like a chicken leg being disjointed. And certainly if you hurt your knee and *someone else* says, "What was that?" you'd better have it looked at by a doctor. Knee sounds that other people hear bode no good.

The sound is important, for although your knee may hurt, you can't always otherwise tell that something serious has happened. For example, most people don't know when they've dislocated their kneecap because as soon as they straighten their knee, the kneecap slips right back into place. They look down, and the knee looks all right. The tip-off is the noise. So sounds that you either sense or hear, or that other people hear, should be viewed almost as absolutes. Get your knee to a doctor.

2. **A sense of instability.** If the knee doesn't feel the same as it did before the incident, before you heard the sound, then there's a good chance that you've torn a ligament. It may be an obvious difference—your knee now bends the wrong way—or it may be subtle, no more than a *feeling* that something has changed. And it may not hurt enough to otherwise raise your suspicions. Be smart—see a doctor.

3. **Rapid swelling.** Certainly if swelling occurs before your eyes—which will happen with a dislocated kneecap—you should see a doctor immediately. If your knee is obviously more swollen now than it was a half hour ago, better make a trip to the emergency room.

With some injuries, like a torn anterior cruciate ligament (among the most common acute knee injuries), the swelling occurs a bit more slowly. It may not be until morning that you realize that your knee is swollen. You'll notice it first in the back of the knee, where the capsule that surrounds the joint is softest. And even then you may not *see* the swelling as much as *feel* it. You'll notice that you can't bend your knee back as far as you used to. It feels tight, sluggish. Then the next thing you know you can't stretch it out completely, either. The extremes of movement tighten the capsule, packing the fluid that causes the swelling tightly around the joint, preventing motion. And then you'll begin actually to see the swelling. Waste no more time—let a doctor see your knee.

4. **Locking.** It's important to understand just what locking is. It is *not* your knee becoming stiff after you've been sitting for a while. That's not really locking; it's something called gelling, probably caused by swelling that

eventually is absorbed away when you move your knee. Locking is just what the term suggests: a sudden rigidity that occurs abruptly and then stops just as abruptly. True locking implies unlocking. So if you think your knee is locking, ask yourself what you have to do to get it moving again.

If the answer is that walking around and getting the kinks out unlocks it, then it probably isn't of much concern. Simply walk around and get the kinks out. But if you're forced to twist it with your hands, or jiggle your foot, or have a friend pull on it, and if then you feel a snap like the one when you originally hurt your knee and suddenly the knee works again, you've got honest-to-God locking. And that means something is getting in the way inside your knee.

That something may be a loose piece of cartilage, or cartilage and bone, that's caught in the joint. And that means that it won't go away by itself. It may be that you have an operating room in your future. Better see a doctor.

Once again—noise, a sense of instability, the rapid onset of swelling, and locking, these are the primary tip-offs for acute knee injuries. Two other things, as well, might cause you concern:

5. **Compromised use of the knee.** If you hurt your knee and afterwards you're unwilling to bear weight on it, better let a doctor take a look at it. As with ankle injuries, people often will try to get back on the knee, sometimes successfully. That's how you find out if it's loose or tight, or it doesn't work at all. But if something happens to your knee and you're simply unwilling to put your foot down afterwards—you just *know* that it's not a good idea—it could mean that something significant has happened.

Likewise, if you're unwilling to move the knee at all, you should have it looked at. With most knee injuries, people will try to move the knee, and often it will move, at least in one direction. But if something tells you that you shouldn't move your knee at all, don't. See a doctor.

6. **Bruising around the knee a couple of days later.** You can have a lot of bruising with an ankle sprain, and it may not mean much. But if your knee develops a bruise larger than, say, a silver dollar—and often these bruises will involve an area four to five inches in diameter—it means that there's bleeding underneath the surface, a tip-off that something is going on in the knee that shouldn't. Better have a doctor take a look.

Now, on to specific injuries.

Torn Cartilage

It is the most famous knee injury. In fact, you sometimes hear people with undiagnosed knee problems stating, unequivocally, "I've torn a cartilage." And they might be right, for if cartilage tears are not the most common acute knee injury they are plenty common enough. And they can result in all sorts of problems—pain and a locked knee most notably. Often cartilage tears lead to surgery. But you don't have cartilages removed just because they're torn—they must cause problems (locking, catching, sharp pain). MRIs tell us that many knees are afflicted with torn cartilages that never cause any symptoms. In such cases, removing them offers no improvement.

Your knee contains two types of cartilage. The ends of the two large bones in the knee, the tibia and femur, are coated with one kind, the articular cartilage. If you crack open the joint between a chicken leg and thigh, you'll notice that the ends of the bone are covered by a glistening, white cap. That's articular cartilage. The ends of our bones are white and glistening, too—at least when they're in good shape—as though they've been dipped in liquid latex. This articular cartilage cushions and protects the bone. But it's hardly indestructible. You can dent it with your fingernail and it stays that way. Try it with a chicken bone sometime. If your articular cartilage becomes dented, or cracked, or a piece is knocked out, it stays that way. It's not like bone; it doesn't repair itself. You start out with all the articular cartilage you're ever going to have, so you might as well be nice to it.

(Recently a method has been developed to culture and grow cartilage in the laboratory, allowing us to replace cartilage defects. There have probably been fewer than a thousand of these replacements, but the technique has received a lot of exposure through the media and Internet. It will most likely endure but never become terribly popular because for the replacement to be successful, the defect must be surrounded by a wealth of normal cartilage. In knees that have seen wear and tear, normal cartilage can be hard to find.)

The other kind of cartilage is the meniscus (menisci, plural—pronounced men-*isk*-eye). They are rings of dense, rubbery shims that perch on the end of the shinbone, the tibia, and act as shock absorbers between the two parts of the knee joint. But they don't just rest there. They're attached to the capsule that envelopes the joint; when your knee moves, they move. When you flex and extend your knee, the menisci move with the tibia. When you rotate the knee, they move with the upper leg bone, the femur. In that way they're always in the most advantageous position to absorb the forces in the knee. And the movement of the bones themselves is not simple. They sort of twist, glide, and slide at the same time.

So it's very important that these menisci stay whole and function as they're supposed to. That doesn't always happen. If you twist your knee while bearing weight, you can tear them. If you tear them badly enough, the torn piece can float away within the joint, in the worst cases lodging between the moving bone like a wedge stuck between gears. Your knee is so sensitive that something the thickness of a credit card loose in the joint would hurt so badly that you can't bear to stand. A quarter-inch-thick piece of meniscus can be excruciating. It's these floating pieces that can cause the locking and pain cartilage tears are known for.

The medial meniscus—the part on the inside of the leg, toward the midline of the body—tears with cutting-type maneuvers. The classic example is a football wide receiver who goes down the field, plants his foot, cuts, feels a snap in his knee, and can no longer straighten out his leg. Medial tears are more likely to cause the knee to lock and are more easily diagnosed.

The lateral meniscus, on the outside of the knee, tears when you're bearing weight on a bent knee. A wrestler on the mat with his knee bent underneath him, an aerobic dancer folding her legs behind her and leaning back over them to stretch, a person simply squatting and inadvertently twisting a knee—all of these are likely causes of torn lateral menisci.

People in their teens and early twenties are more likely to have abrupt, spectacular meniscus tears than older people. As we age, our menisci lose some of their fluid content and become brittle and granular. So often meniscus tears in older people begin as degenerative conditions and gradually extend, like a crack in a windshield, until finally the torn piece may break away within the joint. It's much harder to diagnose a meniscus tear in older people. The signs are often more subtle.

With ligament injuries and dislocations—as well as certain overuse problems, as we've seen—you may hurt, certainly, but the pain is spread over a large area. But with a torn meniscus, you can usually tell *exactly* where it hurts. You can put a fingertip right on the spot. If any of the tip-offs discussed above sound familiar, and you can pinpoint the pain, it's likely that a torn meniscus is the culprit.

And you need not have a swollen knee with a meniscus tear. Seventy percent of the meniscus has no blood supply. You can tear it and it won't bleed inside the knee. You may get some swelling later, because the inside of the joint becomes irritated and produces fluid to protect itself, but not necessarily. Your knee may even lock and not swell appreciably.

✚ What to do about it ✚ Sometimes the meniscus will simply heal by itself, especially if it's within that 30 percent that receives blood. There are times when we look into a knee with the arthroscope and it's hard to tell just where the tear was—it's all kind of pushed back together. But usually something needs to be done. If the tear is in the part of the meniscus that receives blood, then it's possible to sew it back up. But nine out of ten times a doctor has to remove the torn portion. You might ask, "Isn't it harmful to have the meniscus taken out? Don't I need that shock absorption?" The answer is yes, you do. And yes, it isn't particularly good to have it removed. But it's better than having a torn piece lodge in your knee. It's simply not good to ignore these things. Best to bite the bullet and get medical attention.

Torn Ligaments

Now we're in a different world. The hazards of a torn cartilage involve reduced shock absorption, increased wear and tear, and the possibility of locking—and pain, of course. With ligaments we're dealing with the guy wires of the knee, the stays that hold it together. If one of these goes, the knee suddenly finds itself able to move in brand-new directions, none of which it was designed for. You experience that dubious freedom as looseness, instability, the "trick knee" that painfully bends in directions you never dreamed of, and always at the wrong time.

Anterior Cruciate Ligament (ACL) Tear

Here's the classical description of an anterior cruciate ligament tear: You hear a pop or a snap and fall down, but you're not quite sure why you're on the ground. It's not terribly painful, but you have a sense of instability, although you'd be hard-pressed to say just where. The knee doesn't feel right, but you're not quite sure just why. Some people say that their knee shifts in position—which it actually does. Others more nearly *feel* the pop rather than hear it and just know that something's wrong, although they can't tell you what. It's one of those serious injuries whose onset can be disarmingly . . . well . . . *friendly.*

An ACL tear may be the single most common acute knee injury. No one knows for sure, as it's just in the last fifteen to twenty years that tests have been developed to make possible a dependable, accurate diagnosis. It's likely that there are a lot of people walking—or running—around with anterior cruciate tears who were never treated for them, who never even knew they had them. And some of them don't have any problems, never have, even though it's a big ligament, the size of your little finger. Some people can tolerate not having an ACL without batting an eye. Eventually they'll come to the clinic for something else, and you'll examine the knee, discover it's loose as can be, and ask them, "Do you have a lot of trouble with your knee?" They'll look at you as though you were from another planet, and then they remember: yes, twenty-three years ago, while playing high school basketball, they missed half a season because they did something to their knee. But they can't quite remember what, and it makes no difference, anyhow, because it hasn't bothered them since.

While we don't understand as much as we should about why these ligaments become injured, most often the reasons for the injury are similar to those for cartilage tears: cutting from one direction to another, decelerating quickly (especially if you jam your foot in front to stop yourself), coming down from a jump awkwardly. Basketball players frequently suffer anterior cruciate tears—they're knocked off balance in the air and come down wrong—as do volleyball players and dancers. Usually your knee is relatively straight when this happens, so it doesn't often show up in racquetball or tennis players, whose knees usually are—or should be—bent. Skiers sometimes tear this ligament, especially as the result of a twisting fall. But you rarely see it in runners, unless they step into a hole.

One of the most puzzling things about ACL tears is that they occur more often in women than in men, especially in sports such as basketball, soccer, and volleyball. Girls are four to six times more likely to sustain this injury than are boys. Girls are also more likely than boys to sustain a second ACL injury—to either the previously injured or other side. And we simply don't know why.

✛ What to do about it ✛ An ACL tear is a difficult injury to deal with because people have such a wide range of reactions to it—from nothing—just a lot of looseness during an examination, to real disability—in which your knee goes out on you all the time. The treatments are correspondingly various—and none are right or wrong. In fact, other than ice and compression on the spot, and getting off the leg—which are only stopgap measures—we really don't know the best way to treat it. Part of the reason is that there's no way of determining whether someone is going to be in that one-third who don't even know there's something wrong or in the larger number who will have at least some noticeable disability. If you operate on everybody, you know that a third of the people are going to get great results because they never needed the operation in the first place. But who is in that third? This uncertainty makes it hard to evaluate how effective surgery is. How to deal with anterior cruciate tears is one of the most controversial issues in sports medicine.

One thing that most people will agree on is that sewing this particular ligament back together generally doesn't work. Because it's in the middle of the knee, inside the joint capsule, the ligament is constantly bathed in fluid, and fluid prevents a clot from forming around the stitches. For a ligament or anything else to heal it needs a clot around it. A clot forms a kind of seal, and new blood vessels grow into it. Without a clot, healing is inhibited.

So if people do go ahead and operate on these tears, they actually build a new ligament rather than repair the old one. They borrow a tendon from somewhere else around the knee, then attach it directly to the bone. (People have tried using synthetic ligaments for over two decades. Probably because they don't have the ability to maintain themselves by repairing the minor damage that occurs with day-to-day living, these have all failed. Even worse, most have to be removed later because they act as irritants to the knee.) There are over half a dozen ways of doing this ACL surgery, all of which claim essentially the same results. And there are those who don't do surgery at all, just rehabilitate the knee, and they also claim the same results.

It comes down to the approach—and wisdom—of your orthopedic surgeon. You have to find someone you can trust. But realize that whomever you see will be used to following a certain approach. A second opinion may be worth the effort, especially if the first doctor is too quick to prescribe surgery as the *only* treatment. At the Center for Sports Medicine we assume everybody is going to be in the group that has no long-term disabling problems. Or at least we try to give everybody the opportunity to find their way into that group. No one knows the answer to who ends up with which outcome for sure. If anyone says they do, be suspicious that they simply haven't treated enough anterior cruciate tears to know better.

A rule of thumb: younger, more active people are more likely to need—and receive—surgical ligament reconstruction. They have more opportunity to reinjure the knee. And recurrent problems with instability can damage the menisci. That can lead to arthritis.

Posterior Cruciate Ligament Tears

This is not very often a sports injury. It's more likely to happen in automobile accidents, say, in which you're thrown into the dashboard, which hits the front of your shin and drives it back under the femur. Most of the time people can manage to recover from this injury without having the ligament replaced.

Sometimes instead of tearing, the ligament pulls loose a piece of bone. These injuries are usually operated on, because you get great results—bone-to-bone healing—when healed bone regains its original strength.

Medial Collateral Ligament Tear

Another biggie. Next to the anterior cruciate ligament, it's probably the most frequently injured ligament in sports. The medial collateral (middle supporting) ligament runs along the inside of the knee, connecting the thighbone, the femur, to the shinbone, the tibia. To injure it, you generally need an outside force. The common cause is a hit from the outside—a clip in football, say— that collapses the leg sideways, in toward the other leg, forcing open the inside of the knee and tearing away the medial ligament. It's almost impossible to injure your medial collateral ligament by yourself unless you step in a hole—or unless you're wearing skis. Medial collateral ligament tears are the most common ski injury. You catch one ski in the snow and continue skiing on the other, driving your legs apart and causing yourself to fall into the center. That wrenches open the inside of your knee. (See chapter 11 for tips on how to ski more safely.)

As painful as they sound, these injuries are deceiving: you can completely tear the ligament and hardly know it. Often the more severe the injury, the less pain involved. It hurts when you feel the ligament rip, but the pain rarely lasts more than a minute. Then you can get back up on your feet as though nothing happened. Over half the people who injure themselves on the slopes ski down *after* the injury. And their subsequent complaints rarely involve pain: my knee bends the wrong way; it feels loose; I can't turn because my knee won't hold me. It's likely that the majority of football players who injure their medial collateral ligament go on to play another down or two. Only then will they figure out that something is wrong.

So, with this injury the question to ask yourself is, how does the knee feel? Not, does it hurt? If it feels loose—even if there's no pain—you might have a significant problem requiring medical attention.

✚ What to do about it ✚ We used to operate on all these tears. We don't operate on many any longer. They heal well on their own. We use a hinged splint and, because the quadriceps muscles are capable of taking up almost any slack resulting from the torn ligament, we prescribe extensive rehabilitation exercises. If you rehabilitate faithfully, you'll be okay.

So, if you've fallen while skiing, or been tackled from the outside, and your knee feels loose and unstable, ice the area as soon as possible, apply compression, and see a doctor. And count yourself lucky in your misfortune. This is one injury that heals well and may bother you very little.

Lateral Collateral Ligament Tear

Not much to say about this injury. The lateral collateral ligament is the smaller sibling of the medial collateral ligament. Its jurisdiction is the outside of the knee. It's not very often that this ligament is injured in sports. The reason: the kind of thing that would stretch the ligament enough to tear it would be a blow on the *inside* of the knee. That takes some doing, as your other leg is usually in the way. It's more likely that the other leg would absorb the force itself, putting the pressure on its own medial ligament.

Dislocation of the Kneecap

Finally we return full circle to the extensor mechanism. Remember how important it is that your kneecap be seated properly? That it travel smoothly along its groove and not drift to the side? Now we're back in the same territory, but during an acute phase of injury. A patellar dislocation is the culmination of all the subtle and not-so-subtle tendencies we discussed earlier, accomplished in one climactic stroke. That is, the kneecap simply jumps its track once and for all.

First-time dislocations are the most dramatic. They can sound like chicken bones being separated—crruuunch! They usually occur with the knee partially bent and the foot turned out—and out, and out. It's a twisting injury that wrenches the kneecap out of its groove and to the side, stretching and tearing the securing ligaments and muscles along the way. When you straighten your knee the kneecap will usually pop back into place, but it may not stay there. With its medial support gone, the kneecap will tend to drift back to the outside as soon as you bend your knee.

The physical quirk that predisposes us to such injuries has to do with the fact that we're wider in the hips than we are at the knees. The quadriceps, the body's largest muscle, begins at the pelvis and runs all the way along the thigh, across the knee, and finally ends at the upper part of the shinbone. The kneecap resides in the lower quadriceps tendon and acts as a pulley for this extensor mechanism linkage. When the muscle contracts, your knee straightens. You might think that this linkage transcribes a straight line. Not so. Because the body is wider at the pelvis than at the knee, this extensor mechanism actually pulls around a corner. (See illustration on p. 134 in chapter 6.) The more you turn your knee in and foot out, the more of a corner it has to pull around. But it would rather find the shortest distance between two points—enough of this turn-a-corner-at-the-knee business. So when it pulls, it exerts pressure to the outside, and nowhere greater than against the weakest part of the linkage, the pulley.

Your pulley, the kneecap, is held in place from side to side by small ligaments that are part of the capsule that surrounds the knee joint, and by the vastus medialis muscle, a tiny part of the quadriceps. These connectors are reasonably efficient in their job but not particularly strong. It doesn't take too much of a twist to tear them loose. And when they go, the kneecap jumps off track and sets up shop where the rest of the extensor mechanism has been pulling it all the while, on the outside of the knee.

Kneecap dislocations are more common in women than in men. In general women have wider hips than men, and so the angle from the pelvis through the knee to the lower leg is greater. Women's kneecaps are under proportionally greater pressure to jump the track. And frequently women are not as strong as men and so don't have as much vastus medialis to hold the kneecap in place. Young women—teenagers, specifically—suffer more dislocations than their elders, for the simple reason that people are most active during the high school years. Basketball, volleyball, tennis, cheerleading, dancing—all are good breeding grounds for kneecap dislocations. Because of its exaggerated turnout, ballet would seem another prime cause of kneecap dislocations, but not so. If ballet dancers have been trained properly, they dance very precisely and under great control—lessening the chance of kneecap injury. And their turnout should come from the hips rather than the knees, so there really is no great increase in the extensor mechanism angle.

These injuries can swell amazingly quickly, especially the first time. Because so much soft tissue tears away, there's a huge amount of bleeding into the knee. It's one injury that allows you to look down and watch your knee grow before your eyes. People with first-time dislocations can swell so much in just an hour that you have to cut their clothes away to take a look at the joint.

✚ What to do about it ✚ As always, ice and compression can only help matters. Then see a doctor as soon as you can. It's likely that you'll be able to avoid surgery. With most dislocations, immobilizing the knee in a splint and then going through a rehabilitation program will do the trick. It's a long and rigorous road back, because if you're going to keep your kneecap in place you've got to strengthen the little muscles that hold it in the center. These will have been torn during the injury. They'll heal back, but most likely they were never very strong to begin with. Otherwise you might not have dislocated your kneecap in the first place.

The danger is that there's so much force involved in the injury you can shear away a piece of the back of the kneecap or the inside of the joint, giving you a fracture to deal with as well as the dislocation. And a loose piece of bone can prevent the kneecap from getting back on track. In this case, surgery is the answer. Not only to remove the loose piece of bone, but to reattach the vastus medialis.

A word to the wise: it may be that there's no practical way to prevent kneecap dislocations, but it certainly can't hurt to keep your thigh muscles in general, and vastus medialis in particular, strong and healthy. Since strength is one of the main ingredients in the smooth functioning of your extensor mechanism, and since a kneecap dislocation is no more than an extensor mechanism malfunction in the extreme, it stands to reason that a strong vastus medialis muscle might keep you out of all sorts of trouble.

Knee Fractures

The preceding example to the contrary, fractures in the knee are uncommon. Occasionally injuries that will cause ligament problems in adults will produce growth-center fractures in children, but not very often. This is something you don't have to worry about.

Loose Bodies in the Knee

Sometimes injuries such as kneecap dislocations may knock off a piece of the joint surface—cartilage and bone, or just cartilage—inside the knee. It may be a flaked-off piece no larger than the end of a pin, but, because most of your cartilage receives its nutrition from the fluid in the joint rather than from your blood supply, the loose body can grow while it's floating free in the joint. Through the years it can grow large enough to make trouble by lodging inside the joint and causing locking.

Sometimes we don't know where these loose bodies come from. Some of them may be the result of a portion of the joint surface somehow losing its blood supply, so that that part of the surface simply flakes away. The condition is called osteochondritis dissecans (see chapter 2, "The Ankle"). It's not that unusual, but we just don't know why it happens. And these loose bodies won't show up until they're big enough to cause trouble.

If you have a loose body in your knee, you'll know it, even if it isn't bothering you. More often than not you'll be able to make the diagnosis every bit as accurately as any physician. Sometimes you'll even be able to find the culprit, push it around with your fingers. It's when the body is middle-sized that it causes problems. If it's tiny it can travel the back roads of your knee with impunity, slipping away from all sorts of sticky situations. If it's large, the size of the end of your thumb, say, it's just too bulky to do much of anything except find a corner somewhere and stay out of trouble. But if it's the size of a bean, it can wreak all sorts of havoc. It's small enough to travel the knee easily, small enough to hide, yet large enough to lodge somewhere and cause locking and pain.

✚ What to do about it ✚ For most people, the locking caused by loose bodies is an annoyance rather than anything else. These folks develop a system to unlock their knees quickly and go about their business. But for those involved in certain activities, loose bodies can be more than an annoyance. With hikers and rock climbers, for example, it may be very important to find these particles and remove them. You don't want to be deep in wilderness country, twenty-five miles from any ambulance, and suddenly catch a loose body in the knee and be unable to free it. When a body lodges in the knee, all the muscles momentarily give way so that there's no danger of injuring the joint. That's why you invariably fall to the ground when it happens—everything immediately stops working. If you're lost on a remote trail, or inching your way up the face of a cliff, a lodged loose body can quickly become more than a mere annoyance. It can be life-threatening.

So, it can be important to remove these loose bodies, but often that's easier said than done. The knee is so big that a foreign particle the size of the end of your finger can get lost when you go to remove it. You simply can't find it. And these bodies are very slippery, with sides worn smooth from tumbling through the knee. The best way to deal with a loose body is for the physician and patient to attack it together: trap it between your fingers, then put local anesthetic in the knee and skewer it, impale it with a needle. Then you can either take it out using the arthroscope or simply make a cut directly over it and lift it free.

Dislocation of the Entire Knee

This is a really devastating injury, but it doesn't occur very often in athletics. Maybe a couple times a year in football, once in a while in wrestling—but most of these injuries are the result of automobile accidents, parachute jumps, and the like. Because you can tear the blood vessels in the back of the knee that supply the whole leg, a knee dislocation can result in amputation below the knee. The blood vessels tear in an area where one vessel branches into three, so surgically repairing that junction is very difficult. You can lose the blood supply to your leg. All the ligaments in the knee tear as well, and there's extensive tendon and muscle damage.

✚ What to do about it ✚ Hope it doesn't happen. The knee is pretty stable—to sustain that kind of injury requires monumental force. If it does happen, see a doctor.

COMMONLY ASKED QUESTIONS ABOUT KNEE INJURIES

If I have an acute injury, will my knee ever again be as healthy as it was?

If you've had any of the acute injuries we've discussed, then no, your knee will never be the way it was—but you may never know it. If you tear a ligament, say, it may be that after you rehabilitate your knee you can go back to doing pretty much everything you did before, but if you worked at it hard enough you'd find things that you could no longer do. Most of us aren't going to work at it that hard, and if we do it may be that those things aren't so important after all. So, most people will find themselves functioning pretty much as before.

That's not always true, of course, and it's hard to predict exactly who will be able to get back to what activity. If you tear an anterior cruciate ligament, for example, getting back to basketball or volleyball will be tough, maybe impossible. But you'll be able to run, play tennis, ski, even play football (there are pro football players doing just fine without their anterior cruciate ligament). What happens is that other mechanisms in the knee rise to the occasion and take over the function of the missing part. It's as though your knee has a number of built-in redundancies. Training helps, however. With an anterior cruciate tear, you train the hamstring muscle to act as a surrogate and keep the shinbone in line. More often than not, it will.

Torn cartilages present a different picture, because rather than causing instability they reduce shock absorption. And there's nothing in the knee to act as shock absorber surrogates. The entire joint has to absorb the extra pounding.

The result is that there's a significant increase in wear and tear in the knees of people who have had a meniscus removed. Still, the difference may not be of any real consequence. By the time your knee gets bad enough so that you notice it, your activity level may have dropped to the point that it no longer matters.

But you must become vigilant and aware of what's going on in your knee. If it starts acting up, do something about it. You just don't ignore things in your knee if you've had any significant injuries. If you do, you not only run the risk of more knee problems but problems elsewhere as well. If your knee begins to hurt when you run, say, especially going up and down hills, and you ignore it and persist in running up and down hills, your body simply won't stand for it. Without you realizing it, your running gait will change to accommodate the pain, and the next thing you know your ankle will hurt, or your hip ache, or your back stiffen up, and then your knee will begin to act even weirder.

If you've had any serious knee problems in the past, stay on top of the situation so you won't have any more problems, in the knee or elsewhere, in the future.

If I have a cartilage removed, what will replace it?

Nothing will replace it. There's no such thing as an artificial meniscus. You've just got to learn to live without it. It takes a while to get used to it, longer if you've lost your lateral (outside) meniscus than the medial meniscus, but sooner or later you'll be able to go about your business as before without pain. The knee compensates.

There are techniques being examined wherein a cadaver meniscus is transplanted into a knee that has had its original removed. This is a substantial operation requiring weeks to months of healing and rehabilitation. The best candidate for this procedure is probably a young person who has had nearly the entire meniscus removed. Replacing it *before* wear and tear arthritis sets in would seem to make some sense. Replacing it *after* the arthritis is already present doesn't seem to make as much.

If I *don't* have surgery for a torn ligament, will my knee heal?

Depends on the ligament. The cruciate ligaments won't heal by themselves, but the collateral ligaments (the ones on the outside of the knee) will. When you repair them surgically, all you do is put the torn ends together (stitches provide little strength)—but the torn ends are never that far apart in the first place. They'll heal by themselves, and they may heal as tightly as they would have had you sewn them back together. Even if they don't, though, going through surgery may be harder on you than dealing with a little bit of looseness. Any surgery involves trauma and risk. It should be well thought-out, done as a last resort, when it's clear that leaving things as they are is more hazardous than the operation itself. Your knee may not be as tight as before, but it may not be necessary for it to be as tight as before. You may function very nicely with a looser knee.

In fact, most of us do, all the time. Everyone has some instability of the knee; a lot of people have almost breathtaking instability. The system is not so precise that it doesn't have any slack in it. Like the clutch in your car, things work best when there's some play. If there's too much, we have muscles to tighten things up.

If rehabilitation is a lot of work, can I just have surgery instead?

That's not the choice. The choice is, are you going to have surgery and go through rehabilitation? Or are you just going to rehabilitate your knee? Surgery may or may not be necessary. Rehabilitation always is.

Is fluid in the knee serious? Should I have it removed?

That the knee can become inflamed and swollen is common knowledge—not so the fact that there's *always* fluid in the knee, at least a little bit. The knee constantly lubricates itself. More than that, it feeds itself. The cartilage in the knee doesn't have a blood supply of its own, and it has to get its nutrition from somewhere. It gets it from the knee capsule, that sac that surrounds the entire joint. Normally the wall of the capsule is no thicker than wet tissue paper, and its underside is very slippery, covered with a fluid-producing lining called the synovial membrane. The membrane secretes all the time, bathing the cartilage and the rest of the joint in a fluid that's full of nutrients, much like blood with the red cells removed.

If the capsule is irritated in any way, it reacts by producing more fluid. And any injury to the rest of the knee tends to irritate the capsule, which surrounds the joint in a kind of protective embrace. Producing fluid is the only way it can react—how else can it tell you it's being picked on? So it makes fluid, and more fluid, and if you've been overusing the knee, running too many hills, taking too many dance classes, pretty soon you're going to have to cut back and be nice to it because it simply isn't going to bend anymore. The excess fluid functions as a splint. It's as though your knee is trying to tell you to lay off for a while, and if you ignore it it'll *make* you lay off by forming enough fluid so that it simply doesn't work.

The fluid in the knee is dynamic, in an equilibrium of coming and going. The synovial membrane has the capability of absorbing the fluid as well as producing it—the fluid that's in your knee tonight most likely will not be the same fluid that's in there tomorrow night—so usually there's no reason to take out the fluid *until the knee is ready* to have it taken out. The important thing is to find out why it's there and do something about the underlying cause of the fluid production. Otherwise, it'll simply continue to form.

If the fluid is drained prematurely, or, worse yet, you have cortisone injected into the joint (cortisone is great for reducing swelling—it will shut off the fluid, but it will also stop the healing process in the joint), you may never discover why the fluid was there in the first place. Once the effect of the cortisone wears off, the fluid will come back as before, and you'll be right where you started. And perhaps worse off, because now you may have caused some damage in the joint itself. Be very cautious with cortisone, especially with children. But in older patients facing the prospect of a total knee replacement, an occasional cortisone injection might buy some time. Other kinds of anti-inflammatory medications may be better, because they don't have the side effect of shutting down the healing process. Such remedies may get you through a game or a performance, but sooner or later you'll have to find out why the fluid formed and do something about it.

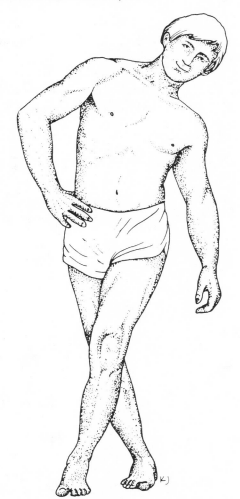

REHAB EXERCISES

For iliotibial band tendinitis

To stretch, stand up and cross your injured leg behind your other leg.

Gently pull your injured leg to the outside and toward the back to strengthen. You can do this exercise standing or lying on your side, and it doesn't matter if you point or flex your foot.

For strengthening the thigh

The following three exercises are called knee extensions. They strengthen the quadriceps muscle, the most important muscle in rehabilitating the knee. You

ILIOTIBIAL BAND STRETCHING EXERCISE

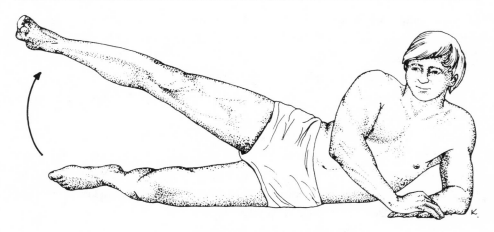

ILIOTIBIAL BAND STRENGTHENING EXERCISE

can use Thera-Bands® or surgical tubing, wall pulleys, or a knee extension bench. Be cautious—doing these exercises if you have kneecap problems (chondromalacia of the patella) may be painful or irritate the knee.

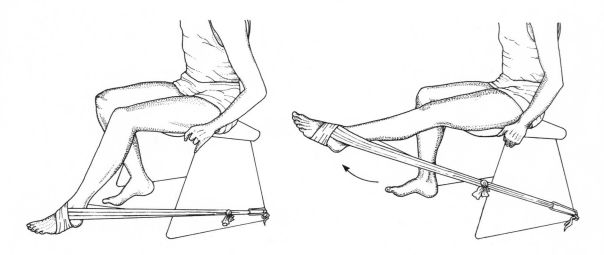

ELASTIC MATERIAL OR WALL PULLEYS

As you extend your knee the angle of pull changes, often lessening the resistance.

It may be difficult to attach the material to your leg or foot. See the illustration above for how to do it.

WALL SITS

This exercise employs the same action as climbing a step or getting out of a chair. With your back against a wall, support yourself in a semicrouch, as though sitting in a chair. Hold for as long as possible. You can also add up and down motions. When strong enough, try the exercise on just the injured knee.

These are squats, or presses, done on two different kinds of leg press machines. Be careful *never* to allow your knee to bend more than at a right angle, ninety degrees. If the exercise is uncomfortable, try changing the position of your foot by rotating it slightly clockwise or counterclockwise. Ultimately you should do the exercise with just the injured side.

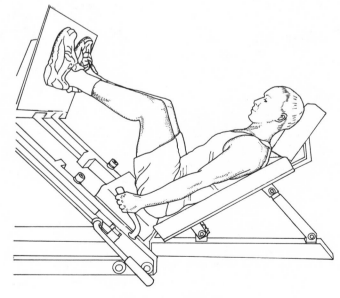

SITTING LEG PRESS

This exercise primarily strengthens the quadriceps. You can adjust the seat back and forth for more or less knee bend.

SINGLE-LEG PRESS

Better for assuring equal strength in both legs. Other varieties of leg presses may allow cheating without the exerciser being aware of it.

CHAPTER SIX

The Thigh and Hip

THE HIP IS THE MOST STABLE JOINT in the body. It's well protected, as it lies deep inside the body, surrounded by muscle on all sides. It holds together very well, and it allows a lot of motion—front to back, side to side, and rotation. The joint is formed by the end of the thighbone, the femur, which inserts into the lower part of the pelvis, that thick ring of bone that anchors all manner of muscles and bones and provides a transition from your body's torso to your legs. Imagine a butterfly resting flat in a collector's display box—the pelvis looks something like that. The body of the butterfly corresponds to the lower part of the spinal column, which descends between the two "wings" of the pelvis to taper into the tailbone, or coccyx. Like the butterfly's wings, the pelvis is wider on top and narrower toward the bottom. You can feel the top portion of your pelvis—it's where you hang your skirt or pants—but not the bottom, which is deeply embedded in muscle and flesh. And that's good. It helps to keep the hip joint safe from most injuries..

The stability of the hip comes from the design of the joint itself. It's truly a ball and socket, with a deep socket in the pelvis and a lovely, round ball at the end of the femur. In contrast to the knee and shoulder, other large joints with a wide range of motion, the hip doesn't depend on muscles and ligaments to hold it together. It's designed to

> **+ WARNING +**
> **If You Experience Any of These Conditions, Seek Medical Help**
>
> + **Pain in the upper thigh, hip, or groin that recurs every time you run, dance, jump;**
> + **Pain in the hip that radiates down the thigh and lower leg;**
> + **Pain in the hip accompanied by numbness or tingling of the lower leg or foot;**
> + **Pain that awakens you at night or keeps you from going to sleep;**
> + **Having your hip collapse under you while you're walking or running.**

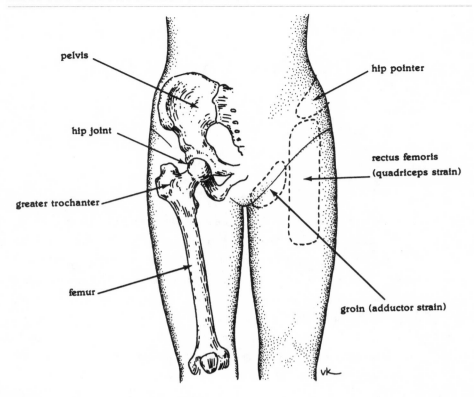

FRONT VIEW OF THE THIGH AND HIP

hold together on its own. There are few substantial ligaments in the hip, and the muscles that surround it serve to move it rather than keep it from falling apart. So there are few joint problems in the hip. Injuries tend to show up in the muscles and tendons themselves.

The ringlike structure of the pelvis, all that bone, makes it ideal as a muscle attachment. Appropriately enough, the muscles of the spine and abdomen, above, begin at the pelvis, as do the hip muscles, the hamstrings, and part of the quadriceps, below. Except for the gluteal muscles in the buttocks, which are large and allow you to rotate, extend, and abduct your legs or pull them apart, these muscles in the hip tend to be smaller than those in the thigh, shorter and fatter, more suited for precision work like rotation and stabilization. But they're no less important than the bigger muscles. Many problems around the hip arise from these short muscles being forced to do things other than what they're supposed to be doing.

The thigh is not much more than a big bone surrounded by big muscles. The bone, the femur, is the largest in the body, and at least half of the thigh, the entire

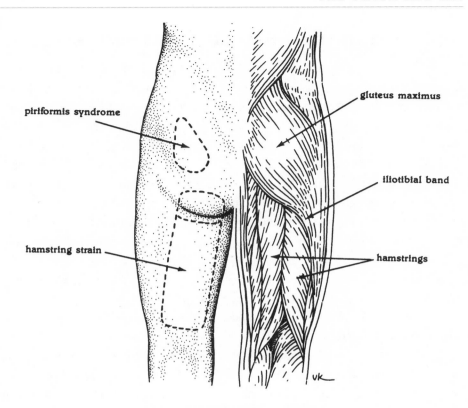

BACK VIEW OF THE THIGH AND HIP

front portion, is dominated by the quadriceps, the body's largest muscle. Almost the whole back of the thigh is taken up by the hamstrings, and the upper inside is defined by the groin muscles, or adductors. These big muscles are responsible for big, propulsion-type movements, like walking, running, and going up and down stairs and hills. All knee bending, as well as all knee straightening, comes from the thigh muscles. You depend on the thigh muscles to adduct, or pull your legs together, and to stabilize your hip as well. They're very strong and absolutely necessary for the most basic needs of most sports, not to mention simply getting around from day to day. There aren't many subtle things about the thigh.

Interestingly, however, the largest and most powerful muscle in the thigh, the quadriceps, is so sensitive that no other muscle in the body atrophies more quickly when it's not used, as after an injury, or misused. As we discussed in chapter 5, "The Knee," lack of quadriceps strength can be at the heart of a myriad of problems, and it's as easy to have weak quadriceps as strong ones. Something to watch out for.

ACUTE INJURIES—MUSCLE TEARS AND STRAINS

These affect the thigh, primarily, and are some of the best-known injuries in sports. Who has not heard of, or experienced, a hamstring strain or pull (the most common), or a torn quadriceps muscle? These injuries are endemic to running sports. And except for contusions—the result of direct blows—they are pretty much the *only* serious problems to affect the thigh and hip area. (People don't break their femurs very often, and it takes a lot to dislocate a hip. These are such awesome injuries that you're not going to run home and look them up in a book. Rather you'll be writhing on the ground awaiting an ambulance. Suffice it to say that there's no question about fractures and dislocations in the hip and thigh area—they don't happen often, but you'll know it when they do. Go quickly to an emergency room.)

A muscle tear might occur in a sprinter who's trying to accelerate harder than usual, or a football player who needs a couple of extra long strides to get under a pass that's overthrown. Whether it's because the muscle itself tightens and can't tolerate the increased demands made upon it, or because the opposite muscle tightens and forces the first muscle to work harder to accomplish the same task, you suddenly feel something pop. Other times it may feel as though someone has thrown a rock at your thigh. Either way, the next thing you know, you're on the ground. There's no doubt that something serious has happened.

*Over*stretching can cause tears. This can occur if you miss your footing, say, presenting your body with a situation it doesn't anticipate. (The body does anticipate movement.) Everyone has had the experience of going down a flight of stairs and encountering one more (or less) stair than expected. In these instances, it takes a real effort to overcome the body's inertia and not land flat on your face. Why? Not because one more stair is inherently so dangerous, but because you just didn't expect it. The same thing happens in sports. A runner coming out of the blocks anticipates a certain kind of surface, a certain degree of traction. But if she slips, all bets are off. A slip of no more than an inch can fool the muscles. They're going to go ahead and contract powerfully because they expect the resistance of the surface to slow them down, but if that resistance isn't there, the muscles can't readjust in time. The contraction continues, becomes monumental, and something's got to give. The result, a muscle tear.

Not being warmed up can also cause tears. Track meets early in the spring are a problem because it can still be cold outside and thus difficult to stay warmed up. When a muscle gets cold, it gets tight. And just stretching it out isn't going to help—you have to keep it warm, working, and flowing well.

Another source of thigh tears is, of all things, stretching for exercise. Stretching has become something of a cult activity, as though being well stretched in and of itself is good for you. It may be, but probably stretching is more useful in combination with something else—before and after another activity, to prepare the muscles for action and relax them afterwards. As with any cult activity, some people don't do it properly. They throw themselves into stretching, start by doing bouncing toe touches and quick torso twists rather than long, slow stretches. Sometimes the result is a torn muscle.

Sports medicine doctors usually separate these injuries into three categories: Grade Three indicates the worst ones—in which the muscle actually pulls apart. It feels like there's a hole in there (reminiscent of ruptures of the calf muscles—see chapter 4, "The Lower Leg").

Grade Two strains are not as bad. You may feel a pulling sensation, you know something's wrong, but it really isn't dreadful, and, rather than causing you to collapse, these strains allow you to slow down and then get off your feet.

Grade One strains involve the least pain, the least discomfort. It's as though your thigh just tightens up over a few strides. You know something's happened, but it doesn't seem like much. Rather than stopping their activity, people often go ahead and try to keep doing what they're doing.

✛ What to do about it ✛ For the worst of these, if you feel something pop and you're immediately unable to move, you should see a doctor. And that doctor should know how to treat athletes. If you go to a doctor who isn't used to treating athletic injuries, the likelihood is that you're not going to get proper care. You might be told to rest for too long, be put on crutches, or be put in a splint. These injuries must be treated aggressively—rest is *not* the answer here— or it'll take you forever to recover. The milder ones you may want to try and take care of yourself. Here's a way to go about it:

All muscle tears and strains, no matter how severe, probably involve at least some tearing of the muscle fibers. (A tear is no more than an extreme strain, or pull. In a tear the fibers completely separate, leaving behind a gap. In a strain, the tearing is more subtle—some fibers hold together, others separate, but the fabric of the muscle remains whole.) And since muscles are generously supplied with blood, the tearing means that many blood vessels tear as well. As a result, the severed vessels bleed into the muscles. With big tears, there can be a lot of bleeding. A pint of blood can flood into the muscles just like that. Bruising may not show up until a few days later, and usually not at the site of the injury. The blood migrates where gravity takes it, and you won't see it until it gets close

+ Recurrent Hamstring + (or Quadriceps) Strains

Almost without exception, hamstring strains recur because the muscle has never gotten strong enough. It may be flexible, but it's not strong. So it keeps getting injured.

The reason is that people think they can exercise themselves back into shape after these injuries by doing the same things they always did. If they run, they run again. If they play tennis, it's back to the courts. Or back to the studio, or the gym, or the health club. That's all well and good, but once one of these muscles gets weak, it no longer starts at the same level as your other muscles. As you exercise, all the muscles get stronger, but you never erase the discrepancy between the injured muscle and the others. So even though your injured hamstring may be stronger than it was when you began, compared to the rest of your body, it's still weak.

You must do *specific exercises* for the *specific muscle* that was injured. That doesn't mean more exercise, necessarily; it means different exercises. And that's why it's vitally important to discover just what it was that went wrong in the first place. If you don't know what muscle was injured—precisely what muscle—you won't know what muscle to exercise.

enough to the surface to show up. A hamstring tear today may mean a discolored calf next week.

So, *you* may not see it, but the *muscles* know all that blood is there. The problem is that they don't know what to do with it. They're used to blood that's contained in vessels. Now it's as though something foreign has been injected into the body, and the muscle is capable of only one reaction to any foreign invasion: go into spasm. It's a protective reaction, just as a turtle retreats into its shell or a snake winds tightly into a coil. Scrunch! The muscle tightens violently, as though you have a cramp.

Once the muscle goes into spasm, it tends to stay in spasm. And the longer it stays in spasm—days, weeks, months—the longer it'll take to straighten out. Meanwhile, as the muscle is starting to heal, the likelihood is that it will heal in spasm as well. That means you end up with a shortened muscle.

So one thing you can do immediately is try to limit the amount of bleeding into the muscle. Ice and compression are good for that, but compared to the ankle where compression is very effective after sprains, it's hard to apply ice or compression to the thigh. There's too much fat and muscle, making it difficult to apply enough pressure to do any good. If you've suffered a hamstring tear, sitting on a bag of ice is a pretty good way to achieve icing and compression at the same time, but for injuries in other muscles it's tough to do. (How do you sit on a torn quadriceps?) If the tear is in a place you can reach, pressing your hand against the spot that hurts for ten or fifteen minutes can help. But there's another thing you can do to treat a tear that may be even more effective but is certainly less obvious: stretch it.

All the time the muscle spends shortened in spasm is lost recovery time. Even though the muscle remains tight, it really doesn't do anything. It gets weak. It gets smaller. It gets flabbier. And when you finally get around to stretching it out, it won't stay that way—it just isn't strong enough to stay stretched out. You stretch it, you get back to your activity, the weakened muscle gets tired much too easily, and it goes right back into spasm. That old adage about recurring hamstring injuries—"once a hamstring tear, always a hamstring tear"—is often true, simply because people don't realize that the muscle has withered during the time it wasn't used. So a tight muscle is not only an uncomfortable muscle, one that will tolerate only limited motion, it's a muscle that's weakening right before your eyes.

The best way to deal with these injuries is, never let the affected muscle get weak in the first place. As soon as you can, begin gentle stretching (immediately, if possible; within 24 hours or so if not) even though it may be uncomfortable to do so. Pain is your guide. Keep the stretching just on the edge of being really painful. The more stretched-out you can make the muscle sooner, the better off you'll be later.

And the better off you'll be sooner, too. Muscles are contained in tough, gristly tubes called fascia. Even though a muscle may tear, it's likely that its fascia will not. When you stretch, you stretch the fascia as well as the muscle, making the tube longer and narrower, tightening it around the injured muscle and reducing bleeding. You *internally* compress the muscle, curtailing bleeding, which is good, while stretching the muscle, which is also good. A neat trick.

So, it's important to do something soon. If you suffer only a mild strain and get up the next morning to find the muscle is tight and hurts when you move it, and you decide that you're not going to use it until it's really well, then what should be a minor injury can become as devastating as a really severe tear. With muscle injuries in athletes at least, *the way you treat the injury determines disability much more than the magnitude of the injury.* A small tear that you coddle, babying it while it heals on its own, can be a lot more disabling than a substantial tear that's dealt with effectively.

As a general rule, *muscle injuries won't heal as quickly if you just leave them alone. You have to work to get well.*

That work can be easier than you think. One notable by-product of being injured is that you soon come to realize the many ways in which that injury connects with everything else that's going on in your body. You never dreamed that moving *that* would make it hurt *here*. Well, if you do something that makes the injured area hurt, you must be doing something right. More likely than not, that something involves stretching the injured part. Simply keep it up. You don't have to know any anatomy, don't even have to know just what it was you injured. If getting out of a chair or out of bed, or into a shower or the car, hurts, you'll know what you need to do to stretch the muscle. Don't shy away from your activity. Find the motion that gives the most discomfort and gently repeat it, stopping just short of real pain. That way your rehabilitation can become part of your daily activity, rather than something you do specially. You just naturally keep the muscle stretched and active, in contrast to avoiding activities that hurt. If it doesn't hurt, you'll know that you're not exercising the muscle at all. You'll pay for that later.

Restrengthening the muscle involves executing the opposite motion. If you stretch out your injured hamstring by extending your leg when you step into the shower, you can strengthen it by bending the leg. If it's a torn quadriceps and bending your leg to get into your car stretches the muscle (again, you'll know because it will hurt), then extending your leg out straight after you close the door will strengthen it. It involves listening to your body. Don't worry, it'll tell you the truth.

If you prefer a more formal rehab program, here's one: To stretch the hamstrings, do a hurdler's stretch. While standing, straighten your leg out in front of you and rest it on a chair, a coffee table, or the hood of your car. You *don't* want your leg out to the side, so keep your hips square—at right angles to your extended leg—and slowly lower your chest to your thigh far enough so that the back of your thigh starts to hurt. Hold that position for fifteen or twenty seconds, then lean forward a little more, again until it starts to hurt, and hold the stretch for about the same amount of time. (Just make sure the appropriate muscles are hurting. Stretching your quadriceps and feeling your knee hurt indicates you're doing the stretch wrong. Likewise with stretching your hamstrings and feeling the front of your hip hurt.) You may find, soon after the injury especially, that you can't bend over the leg much at all without pain. That's okay—simply do as much as you can. In time the muscles will stretch and your flexibility will increase. Do this stretching in the morning, during the day, and before you go to bed—if you stretch at night, you won't be so stiff in the morning. And as the muscle stretches and heals, bend farther and stretch more often.

To strengthen the muscle, bend the leg against resistance. That resistance can be your other leg, a chair, the floor, an inner tube. Work to the point of fatigue, when the muscle starts to burn, and then back off. As with stretching, three series of ten contractions is a reasonable schedule. Combine the two when it's comfortable to do so. Stretch, strengthen, and then, because the muscle will tend to tighten after being contracted, stretch again.

Do all this through a *comfortable* arc of motion. It's *not* necessary to go from a straight knee to your heel pressing up against your buttock. If you're able to accomplish half that range of motion, or even 10 percent of it, that's fine. Your leg may hurt so much at first that you can't bend it at all, and you may have to do the exercises isometrically, by simply tightening the muscle. It'll still do some good.

For quadriceps tears, simply reverse these procedures. The quadriceps and hamstrings complement each other. When you bend your knee, the hamstrings contract and the quads stretch; when you straighten your knee, the quads contract and the hamstrings stretch. They're always working in opposite directions. So to stretch the quads, do the exercise that tightens the hamstrings—that is, bend your leg. Here's a good way: while standing, bend your injured leg and grab the foot with your hand (make sure it's the hand of the opposite arm—right foot, left hand; left foot, right hand). Then pull back on the leg. As with the hamstrings, you may only be able to bend a little bit at first, but greater ability to bend will come. Remember the stretch or discomfort should be felt in the front of the thigh, *not* the knee. To strengthen the quadriceps, extend the leg against resistance, at first only as much as you can handle without hurting, then, as the muscle heals, increase the resistance and the number of repetitions.

Perhaps the best exercise technique of all is contract-relax stretching. To exercise the hamstrings, lie on your back and have a friend extend your leg up toward your head until it begins to hurt in the injured area. Then push your leg back against your friend's resistance, using the muscle, contracting it a little, but not too much. Hold the contraction for fifteen seconds, then relax. Then ask your friend to extend your leg farther toward your head. Surprise! You've picked up another fifteen degrees of flexibility. Stop when you again feel discomfort and again push back against the pressure. Stretch again, and stop.

With this exercise you momentarily tire the muscle so that it gives up the ghost for a few seconds, then you pick up the slack and stretch it again. It may be the most effective stretching exercise you can do (it feels good, too), but its disadvantage is that it usually requires two people. However, with some ingenuity you can do contract-relax exercises by yourself. You have to get in a position where you stretch yourself against something rigid—a table leg, say, or a door jamb. Push against the table leg, then relax, move forward to take up the slack, and push again. Contract-relax exercises are the way a physical therapist would stretch you.

So, you've worked on your injury, it's started to come around, and you're back to the activity that injured you in the first place. A couple of things might happen. One is that the muscle might hurt at the beginning of the activity, but as you exercise it loosens up and things get easier. That's likely with ankle sprains, where you milk some of the swelling away as you move and gradually your range of motion increases, but it's not so common with muscle injuries. More likely with muscle injuries is the second possibility: you'll be partway through your workout, a couple of miles into your run, say, and your hamstring will tighten up. If you try to run through it, it just gets tighter and tighter, to the point where you have to stop running or risk hurting yourself again. A way to cope with that kind of problem is to stop running (or stop playing tennis, step away from the barre, or drop out of aerobics class), go off to the side, and do three or four good, long, slow stretches right on the spot. Then start running again. In nine out of ten instances, the leg will be comfortable once more. It may only stay comfortable for another few minutes, however, in which case you simply stop and stretch again, then continue your activity.

If you keep up this regimen, the intervals between stretching will become longer and longer. If during the first couple of days you have to stop and stretch every quarter of a mile, the next week you may only have to stretch every half mile, and the third week every mile and a half, to the point where you may only have to stop once during your run, or not at all. It can be a bother to have to put up with all that stopping and stretching, at least at first, but it can be a very effective way of getting back to your activity.

But only if you can do the activity comfortably. If the tightness comes on and you can't stop it by stretching, *don't continue*. The muscles will just become tighter and tighter, may cause you to change your gait, or your stroke, or your technique, and you'll eventually either reinjure the muscle or injure something else. Instead, discontinue the activity, do the home stretching and strengthening regime, and gradually try again. Ease back into the activity, slowly, and with patience. *Don't* try and force muscle injuries. They'll get you in the end.

A couple of words of caution:

1. **Stretch the injured side specially.** This is crucial when you rehabilitate a muscle injury. Always stretch each side separately and appropriately to its level of fitness. Otherwise, the stronger and more flexible side is always limited by the lack of flexibility and strength of the injured side.

2. **See a doctor.** This is your only recourse if you're treating your injury on your own and it continues to get worse. That kind of situation can be

ominous, nothing to trifle with. Happily, however, such is not usually the case. As long as you exercise good judgment and listen to what your body is telling you, you'll be okay. And you'll be on the road back to your activity sooner than you may anticipate.

CHEERLEADER'S HIP

This injury occurs in young people, often for the same reasons as muscle tears. Overstretching or overcontracting, sudden, unexpected demands on the muscles, cold muscles being forced to work too hard—all these things that would most likely do no more than injure a muscle in an adult can do something quite different in a growing person. They can pull the muscle away from its tether, popping off a piece of bone in the process. Bouncing into the splits can do it— thus the name cheerleader's hip. This injury can pop the hamstrings or the adductors (the muscles in the upper, inner thigh) away from the pelvis. If the quadriceps contracts violently, the portion of the muscle that connects to the pelvis, the rectus femoris, can pull a piece of bone away.

Why will the same incident pop off a piece of bone in a young person and only tear a muscle in an adult? Because in young people bone is still forming. It's geared to grow and heal. Accordingly, it's covered with a dense, blood-rich tissue called periosteum. Adults' bones are covered with periosteum as well, but whereas in a grown person the periosteum is usually paper-thin, in a child it can be as thick as one sixteenth of an inch. In kids the muscles and tendons, where tears occur in an adult, are stronger than their interface with the bone. So if anything is going to pull loose in a child, it will be bone. That's just what happens in cheerleader's hip.

So all of a sudden a piece of periosteum and bone as big as your thumb finds itself no longer connected to the pelvis but floating somewhere in the muscle-tendon area. "What am I doing here?" it asks itself. "I should be doing something." What it does is the only thing it knows how to do: it makes more bone.

So into the doctor's office comes a teenager with a lump of bone the size of half a baseball in the buttocks from, say, a hamstring tear. The unhappy kid is very uncomfortable, only sits on the uninjured buttock, and hurts whenever she moves. And besides the discomfort caused by the lump of bone itself, a bursa that formed over this bone to provide a cushion has become irritated and is swollen to the point where the poor teenager feels as though there are two baseballs in there.

✛ What to do about it ✛ See a doctor. But make sure that the doctor is used to treating athletes, and young ones at that. In an x-ray these bone growths can look just like malignant bone tumors, and it's not uncommon to hear of people being operated on and biopsied because the physician feared the worst. As a doctor, if you don't know that these sorts of injuries can happen to kids in athletics, especially teenagers in the middle of growth spurts, and you don't ask a lot of questions to find out exactly what happened, the x-rays can scare you to death. Here's one situation in which experience can make a big difference.

Sometimes surgery is required. The wayward piece of bone can be screwed or stitched back to the pelvis. Sometimes the piece of bone will build up and then taper back down by itself, and by taking it easy you can wait it out. But the important thing is *to know* what the problem is; then you can act accordingly. See a doctor.

CONTUSIONS

Contusions, or bruises, are almost as common in the thigh as in the lower leg. They're the result of direct blows, the kind of charley horse you get from being hit, and are the bane of contact sports such as wrestling, football, and even soccer, basketball, and baseball. They almost always occur in the quadriceps.

A contusion usually affects people in one of two ways: either it's so devastating, hurts so badly, that you can't do anything but lie there and suffer; or, more often, you take the blow, continue what you're doing for a while, and then pause for half a minute or so, during which time the muscle goes into spasm and ceases working very well. Then it's obvious that it's a serious injury. In a few hours the pain will be accompanied by swelling and soon after by black and blue splotches.

✛ What to do about it ✛ The pain, swelling, and discoloration are the result of ruptured blood vessels below the skin bleeding into the muscle, and massive amounts of blood can accumulate very quickly. With contusions in the lower leg, ice and compression together can slow down the bleeding and reduce swelling. In the meatier thigh, it's harder to apply either effectively—there's too much fat and muscle around the injury. So don't neglect to ice contusions in the thigh, but don't expect miracles. The best way to apply compression to a thigh injury is to put your hand over the point of the blow and lean on it for ten to fifteen minutes.

More effective still is stretching the injured muscle. If you're injured in the quads, you can stretch the muscle by bending your knee. Stretching the muscle stretches the fascia surrounding it as well, tightening the fascia and turning it into a kind of internal tourniquet. You apply compression from within, inhibit bleeding, and get a head start on stretching the muscle, all by simply bending the knee and keeping it bent for the first twelve hours or so after the injury.

Then take it easy. In contrast to muscle tears and strains, with contusions you *do not* want to push to the point of pain. Keep the muscle stretched and start moving in ways that are comfortable. And you might see a doctor as well. These can be painful injuries, and you don't want to overdo and make the problem worse.

MYOSITIS OSSIFICANS

This is the contusion equivalent of cheerleader's hip. If you're hit while the quadriceps muscle is contracting (and it usually is during contusions), the blow not only crushes the muscle and ruptures blood vessels, but because the muscle is under tension from being contracted, it can pull away from the bone. Except for one portion (the rectus femoris, which connects to the pelvis), the quadriceps wholly begins in the thigh. It connects to a good two-thirds of the front part of the femur. And that's muscle to bone connection. There are no tendons here to act as intermediaries. More to the point, it's muscle to periosteum, that dense bone covering that's supposed to heal fractures and otherwise keep things ship-shape.

So when the muscle pulls away from the bone, it takes some periosteum with it. Meanwhile, the ruptured blood vessels are pouring blood into the area, bathing the periosteum, which has set up shop in the muscle an inch away from its former home in the femur. In the face of such adversity the periosteum knows how to do just one thing: make bone. And with so much nutritious blood around it does so at an unbelievable pace. You can see new bone on an x-ray within a couple of weeks of the injury—that's almost unheard of. It can grow as large as a flashlight and often has very sharp edges. And the bone is forming precisely where it shouldn't, inside the muscle. Needless to say, all that does not promote good muscle function. What it does promote is pain.

✚ What to do about it ✚ The best thing to do about myositis ossificans is prevent it from happening in the first place by flexing (bending) the knee as far as possible and keeping it bent for the first twelve to twenty-four hours after the injury. You can wrap an Ace bandage around your thigh and leg to help you sustain this bent-leg position.

Next, see a doctor. The problem is that there's no way of knowing at the beginning whether your contusion will develop into myositis ossificans—which literally means "bone forming in muscle"—or not. Again, here's an instance where it's particularly important to see a doctor who's had experience with such things, because the way you treat the contusion from the beginning will most likely have a bearing on if, or how badly, bone forms in the muscle. If the bone is already there, a doctor who's not used to treating athletes might easily draw the wrong conclusion from x-rays which show a rapidly forming mass that looks suspiciously like a malignant tumor.

Usually these injuries are *not* treated well; in fact, they're abused. Someone— a high school football coach, say—decides that it's nothing more than a bruise, and tells the athlete to work through it, get in the whirlpool, get into a massage program. Yet often this injury can lead to another, simply as a result of mistreating the myositis—by vigorous massage, say, or too much activity. Like simple contusions, this injury should be rested. Pain is *not* gain when it comes to myositis ossificans. Once the bone forms, you have to wait until it's run its course and formed all the bone it's going to form. Usually, it will reverse itself and reabsorb nearly all the bone, a process that can take from three to twelve months. And the muscle will eventually reattach to the femur. You simply have to wait it out.

If it doesn't reabsorb, then surgery might be the only answer. In any case, don't muddle through this one on your own. Have a doctor look at it.

HIP POINTER

Blows to well-protected bones like the femur are painful enough; a blow to the virtually naked bony ridge of the pelvis can be devastating, one of the most painful athletic injuries possible. If you run your fingers along your hip just below the belt or skirt line, you'll run into this ridge. There's little between it and your fingers but skin. When this exposed bone is given a whack by a football helmet, or baseball bat, or a sharp fall, the pain can be unbelievable, frequently requiring injectable drugs to help people tolerate it. In fact, if we could get detailed enough x-rays, we'd probably see that the bone is actually fractured, even crushed.

And it's not just impact pain that causes the problem. The abdominal muscles attach to this ridge, and the blow causes bleeding into these muscles, just as in myositis ossificans (without, in this case, the added complication of displaced bone). In reaction to the bleeding, the abdominal muscles go into spasm, and when the abdominal muscles go into spasm, they *really* go into spasm. The entire front of your body becomes absolutely rigid. You don't want to breathe, to laugh, to cough, or, God forbid, to sneeze. To the inexperienced eye this injury may look like a ruptured appendix or colon because these problems are accompanied by a rigid abdomen as well. It's one of the most dramatic illustrations of the interconnectedness of things in the body, a reminder that most people would be happy to do without.

✛ What to do about it ✛ See a doctor. You'll hurt so badly that it won't cross your mind to do anything but. And be patient. It's important not to go back to your activity too soon. Too many people have gone back too quickly and, to compensate for continued pain, have altered their gait, or their stroke, or their throwing style. The upshot can be another injury to another part of the body, one that may be more serious in the long run than the hip pointer.

OTHER ACUTE PROBLEMS IN THE HIP

There aren't many other acute hip problems. And those are so obvious that, as with hip pointers, it would be surprising if you had to be persuaded to see a doctor. Fractures fall into that category, as do other, less well-defined problems with the hip joint itself. As a general rule, if you have a serious hip joint injury you'll experience substantial loss of motion, and you won't be able to bear weight on the joint. It will hurt, a lot, deep in the hip. These injuries should be seen by a physician.

OVERUSE INJURIES

Overuse injuries are the problems that creep up on you, that begin with the slightest of irritations and build to the point where they can be more painful, and more difficult to deal with, than the kind of dramatic injuries we've been discussing. They're usually the result of overusing a particular muscle or tendon (or bone, even), and they often come about because of some change in your activity. A change

✛ Hip Replacement ✛

These days we see active older people placing heavy demands on their hips. That can take a toll. Older hips are often compromised by degenerative arthritis. One way of dealing with the problem is to replace the joint.

In general, there seem to be two kinds of people who want hip joint replacements. The first experience pain during strenuous activities such as singles tennis, hard skiing, or running, but not many problems during daily living (they're rarely if ever awakened at night, etc.). They *want* a hip replacement, so they can better carry out their abusive behavior.

The other people have severe pain problems all the time, are awakened frequently, can't sleep, can't walk the dog, etc., but are frightened of having the operation. Well, the operation, while a big one, is remarkably effective, affording substantial pain relief to more than 90 percent of patients. Many, however, will enjoy similar improvement—regardless of how bad their x-rays look—if they simply strengthen the muscles surrounding the hip.

This is a no-lose proposition. If you get stronger *and* more comfortable, great—you might stave off the need for an operation for a while. If you get stronger but continue to hurt, then surgery may be the answer (and you can never be too old for a joint replacement). The added strength you've achieved will help you recover sooner from the operation.

in distance run, number of classes taken, sets played, rehearsals attended, terrain traversed—even a new instructor, or a new racquet or pair of shoes—any of these changes can bring on an overuse injury. Most people ignore them until they're so painful or debilitating that they simply can't ignore them any longer. By then something minor may have turned into a serious problem. Especially so as these injuries tend to migrate, and what began in the quads, say, might lodge in the hip. You may be able to treat the latest symptoms, but it's harder to track it all back to the source. And if you don't get back to where it began, it'll just keep recurring.

The single most common source of overuse problems from the waist on down are weak quadriceps. We've discussed how weak quads can affect the knee (see chapter 5, "The Knee"); they can cause problems in the hip as well, and most overuse problems in athletes are in the hip rather than the thigh. Probably the only people who have lots of overuse injuries in the thigh are track and field athletes, and these are often residual problems from old thigh tears and strains. Overuse injuries usually lodge at one end or the other of the muscle where it attaches to tendons—in this case, the hip area, where so many muscles begin. (Muscles that begin at the femur lack tendons. The muscle connects directly to the bone.)

To treat overuse injuries effectively, you have to be aware of these changes, aware of the subtle beginnings. That's where a doctor who will take the time to talk with you, to ask questions and listen to answers, can be of real service in helping you monitor your activities. But it may not be necessary to go to a doctor for many of these things. If you don't, you must become your own monitor. For the only lasting way to deal with overuse injuries is to find out why they occurred, to track them back to their source, and eliminate them there.

GLUTEAL PROBLEMS—PIRIFORMIS SYNDROME

We now focus on that solid wad of muscle in the buttocks, so important in athletics, and so prominent in dancers, skaters, and gymnasts. It's primarily made up of three specific muscles, the gluteus maximus, gluteus medius, and gluteus minimus. That is, the "greatest," "middle," and "smallest" rump muscles—glutes, for short. The glutes are responsible for rotating your hip and leg outwards and for extending the hip and leg backwards. When a dancer does an arabesque, it's the glutes that pull the leg back, up, and out. When a skater glides over the ice, it's the glutes that both rotate and extend the legs. When you run or walk uphill, the glutes provide the power to push your body ahead of your trailing leg. When you do a dolphin kick in the pool, it is the glutes that pull your legs up against the water.

But the glutes don't do all this by themselves. Smaller muscles in the buttocks, muscles that lie beneath the glutes, assist them in rotating and extending the hip. One of these is the tiny piriformis muscle, only a couple of inches long. These small muscles can be irritated along with the glutes for a variety of reasons. For example, if your quads aren't strong enough to tighten your knee on their own, the glutes can be called upon to help—not their preferred task. Similarly, weak hamstrings can lead to overused gluteal muscles. And overuse of the muscles' natural functions can also lead to irritation.

You'll know it when it happens—painful and aching buttocks are no fun—but the problem is often misdiagnosed. This interesting tale involves the piriformis muscle. In about 20 percent of the population, the sciatic (sigh-*at*-ic) nerve—that large nerve that supplies sensation to much of the body from the hips downward—descends from the lower spine and runs right through the piriformis muscle on its way down the legs to the feet. In the remaining 80 percent of us, the nerve runs over the muscle. Either way, if the piriformis goes into spasm, which is what muscles like to do when they're irritated, it can squash or pinch the sciatic nerve.

That can mean pain that runs down the back of the thigh and calf all the way to the foot. The condition is called sciatica, and it can be accompanied by numbness and tingling as well. Meanwhile, the piriformis and the other muscles in the buttocks are in spasm, which means that you have pain in the hip that is particularly sharp when you try to rotate or extend your leg. Not only do you hurt in ballet class, but it's getting pretty tough even to get out of the car or out of a chair. And then the muscle tightens further, which throws your leg into a semipermanent external rotation. You start favoring the hip, altering your gait, moving and bending in strange, awkward ways, all of which starts to affect your back.

Finally you sort it all out and go to the doctor, who says, "Where does it hurt?"

"Well," you answer, "my back is killing me, and I have this pain in my buttocks that goes all the way down my leg to my foot."

"Aha!" the doctor replies. "Disk disease."

For such are the classic symptoms: back pain caused by a degenerating or abnormal disk that pinches the sciatic nerve to produce pain all the way down the foot. And heaven help you if x-rays expose a bulging disk that you may have had for fifteen years and that never bothered you all that time. It's off to the operating room. It happens all too often, and it can be scary.

But you may not have disk disease. You may not have a back problem. Your problem may be the little ol' piriformis muscle. And what may be necessary is not surgery at all, but the kind of treatment that works so well for muscle and tendon injuries: stretching and strengthening.

How can you know? There are a couple of ways to test yourself. Lie on your stomach with your knees together and bent, so that the soles of your feet point heavenward. Then just let your legs fall apart, out to the sides. The motion causes your hips to rotate *inward*, stretching the *external* rotators, the gluteal and piriformis muscles. If the muscles hurt, it's a pretty good chance you've located the problem—the piriformis.

Another test is to sit in a chair or on the floor, place the heel of one leg against the outside of the knee of the other leg, and pull the knee of the first leg (which should be on the side where it hurts) toward the middle of your chest. You should feel a good stretch in the buttocks in any case, but if it really hurts, you may be looking at irritated glutes and/or piriformis muscle. (An interesting thing about this test is that if you really and truly do have a disk problem, this stretch probably *won't* bother you. And doubly interesting is the following: the common test for disk disease—caused sciatica is something called the positive straight-leg raising test. That involves lying on your back and lifting your leg straight up and back, which, if you do have a disk problem, should cause sciatic pain. But if you pull up your leg with the knee bent, there should be no pain—if the problem is caused by a disk. However, if the piriformis or glutes are at fault, then the sciatic pain will occur in *either* case, leg straight or bent. So, if you get the same pain, knees extended or bent, you might look to the muscles and think about canceling your appointment with the back surgeon.)

✛ What to do about it ✛ Stretch and strengthen the muscles. It's easy to do. One strengthening technique is to lie on your stomach and raise your leg behind you. You may find that you're only able to raise the leg a few inches off the ground, or not at all. It doesn't matter. Do the best you can if that means only tightening the buttocks at first. If you stay with it, you'll start to notice results.

Another way to strengthen is by reversing the stretching motion discussed earlier. If you're sitting in a chair, the heel of your injured leg resting outside the knee of the other, and you pull the knee of the injured leg toward the middle of your chest to stretch the gluteal muscles, strengthen them by pushing your leg back against your hand. The more resistance you offer with your hand, the harder it will be to push against it, and the greater the strengthening.

You can do contract-relax exercises this way. Pull your knee toward the middle of your chest as far as is comfortable, then push back against your hand. Hold the push—which contracts the muscle—for about fifteen seconds, then relax. Pull the knee toward you a bit more, then push back with your leg. Hold it for fifteen seconds. Relax. You may have to start with a relatively straight knee and hip, then gradually work the knee back toward the chest. The more the knee and hip are bent, the greater the glutes are extended, and the greater the stretch. It's pretty slick—you can stretch and strengthen the muscles all by yourself with the same test you used to determine the cause of the problem in the first place.

But remember, once you're relatively pain-free and back to your favorite activity, the only way to stay that way is to deal with whatever it was that caused the problem. And with gluteal injuries, that something may have begun in the thigh—weak quads or hamstrings—or might involve the way you go about your activity. Getting rid of the symptoms, no matter how much relief it may bring you, won't guarantee that you might not face the same problem again. The only way to escape that merry-go-round is to find out why you hurt yourself and change the way you go about things accordingly.

A caution: it's certainly worth your while to see if sciatic pain is the result of a piriformis or gluteal injury. But if you try the things we've suggested and the pain persists, or you have a great deal of numbness or tingling, and you feel weakness along your leg—strange sensations you've never experienced before— then don't assume that you've done the exercises wrong and should give them another try. See a doctor.

Sciatica is nothing to play around with. Nor is numbness, tingling, or weakness, no matter where it might show up. If you have any of these sensations, *see a doctor.*

CHRONIC GROIN INJURIES

The adductors, those fanlike muscles in the groin and upper thigh, are responsible for pulling your legs together. There are few sports that demand such movement (equestrian sports come to mind—it's the adductors that allow riders to tighten their legs against the horse—and soccer, where much of the kicking force comes from these muscles), but people experience adductor problems because the muscles have another job as well: they work to stabilize the hip. Ballet dancers use their adductors a lot as pulling-up muscles, very subtle rotators. And the adductors change their function depending on how much you flex or extend your hip. They're good-sized muscles, and they're used, and abused, more than you might imagine.

Some adductor injuries can be awful. Although stretching and strengthening probably will help most adductor problems, the rest seem never to get better. Some people hurt for *years* without relief. They may improve, but whenever they get to a certain level in their activity, back comes the pain again. These cases are a mystery to everyone involved.

✚ What to do about it ✚ Stretching and strengthening the muscles is the best bet. You can stretch the adductors in a number of ways. If you're standing, simply pull your leg out from your body—the farther the pull, the longer the stretch. To strengthen, pull the leg back to the midline and then beyond, crossing your legs in front of you. An inner tube looped around a table leg can provide resistance, as can someone holding on to your leg.

While the adductors are best stretched and strengthened with the knees and hips straight, as when standing or lying down (this places the muscles in the position in which they're actually used), you can also gain some benefit by sitting on the floor with your knees bent and the soles of your feet together. Hold your feet with one hand and with the other gently push against the injured leg—the inside of the leg, not the knee. The longer the push, the greater the stretch. To strengthen, pull the leg back against the resistance of your hand. You can do contract-relax exercises in this way as well.

If the muscles don't respond, see a doctor. You may be in that 50 percent or so whose injury is a bear to treat. If so, you and your doctor can struggle through the dark together.

TENSOR FASCIA LATA INJURY

There's a little fist-shaped muscle in the hip, right under the bony ridge of the pelvis, where your pants pockets begin. It's called the tensor fascia lata. It hooks on to the iliotibial band, the long tendon that runs all the way down the outside of the thigh, across the knee, to the lower leg. Small though it may be, this muscle helps extend your knee, going to work during the last 15 percent of movement and then holding on to help keep your knee extended. (If you tighten your knee and hold it front of you, you can feel how tight the muscle and tendon become. Simply run your fingers from the muscle just below the point of your hip down the outside of your leg to the knee.)

When you bend your knee, the tensor fascia lata helps flex it as well. But if your quads or hamstrings are weak, the tensor fascia lata is forced to bear too much of the load. Weak thigh muscles can lead to irritation of the tensor fascia lata, as well as to iliotibial band tendinitis (see "Iliotibial Band Tendinitis," p. 106).

✛ What to do about it ✛ Strengthen the thigh muscles, the quads especially, and stretch and strengthen the tensor fascia lata. Side-leg raises will strengthen the muscle; crossing your leg *behind* the other—the cross-leg stretch—will stretch it. (See pp. 129–131 in chapter 5, "The Knee," for illustrations of exercises that stretch and strengthen this muscle.)

STRESS FRACTURE OF THE FEMUR

The femur is the largest bone in the body, and it's monstrously strong. It's almost two kinds of bone, really: the shaft, which gets its strength from being an almost rigid cylinder, and the neck. The neck is very sophisticated in structure. Because of its curve and the stress it has to endure, it's built like a bridge, with bone laid down in complicated arches. It's a spongier kind of bone than in the shaft, but still very strong for what it's designed to do.

> **✛ Hip Dislocation, or Not? ✛**
>
> It is common to feel as if your hip were dislocating, when it's probably just the iliotibial band tendon snapping over the greater trochanter. The tendon can be so tight, and is so big and prominent, that when it snaps it can feel as though your hip is shifting in position. It isn't. But the muscle and tendon are, and the abrupt change can be striking and disconcerting.
>
> Treatment involves stretching and strengthening the muscle. Best to see a doctor about it.

But as mighty as this bone is, stress fractures can be its undoing. Stress fractures are almost invisible cracks that invade the bone (for an extended discussion of stress fractures, see chapter 4, "The Lower Leg") and in the worst scenario can spread all the way through it, actually severing one part from another. The stress fracture can become a real fracture, and it's not unusual for it to knock off the head of the femur. That can be devastating. In young people especially, the severed portion can lose its blood supply and die. You can be looking at a hip replacement at age twenty-two.

The problem is made more difficult by the fact that stress fractures are tough to spot because they don't have any particular symptoms. The strongest diagnostic criteria are that there *aren't* any diagnostic criteria. You have pain somewhere in the thigh, usually the upper part. It's worse when you exercise, better when you don't—well, that sounds like a lot of things. You try all the treatments you know, and nothing works. Finally you go to a doctor who, after hearing your frustrating story, gives you an x-ray—still nothing. Finally, if you're lucky, the light dawns, and your doctor gives you a bone scan. And there it is, a tiny crack that you can't believe could cause so much trouble.

It can. We see femoral stress fractures in runners and aerobic dance teachers primarily (not students—the number of classes makes a difference), at a rate of two or three a year. They show up with some frequency in the military, which is so cautious about them that you'll find yourself in bed before you know it and after that on crutches. They seem to be caused by overuse—running, jumping, perhaps changing surfaces and terrains—and training errors, trying to do too much too soon. They can show up anywhere in the femur, from the neck all the way down the shaft, and we really don't know why it's one place and not another. (You can also get stress fractures of the pelvis where the muscles begin. These, too, are often missed.) They all take a long time to heal, sometimes as long as six to nine months, and, if the fracture is in a particularly hazardous spot, it may require surgery to pin the bone together.

✛ What to do about it ✛ See a doctor, and once you have, it's vitally important to do what you're asked to do—in most cases, not much of anything. That's what makes things hard. Active people don't like to do nothing. It's hard enough to get active people to slow down, much less stop doing their favorite activity, but that's just what you have to do with a femoral stress fracture. You have to make the area free of pain so the bone can start to heal, and that may involve crutches and a wheelchair around the house. No fun. The rule of thumb here is that if it's not hurting, you're not doing anything wrong.

Then, when the pain is gone, try to get back to as much activity as you can without hurting the area again. The tricky thing about stress fractures is that the bone originally broke because it wasn't strong enough for the demands you put upon it. So it's not enough simply to let it heal, you've got to exercise it to the point where it's strong enough not to break when you impose those demands again but not to the point that you reinjure it while trying to rehabilitate it. Risky business.

So, the tip-off is activity-related pain in the thigh that you can't put a finger on and that doesn't respond to treatment. If that describes what's happening to you, see a doctor.

SNAPPING HIP

And now, welcome to the haunted house of sports medicine, a world in which things happen for no apparent reason and quit happening just as mysteriously.

How many dancers (and others, too, but mostly dancers) have to get up in the morning and pop their hip before they can go ahead and dance the rest of the day? It's a common thing. It's lucky that most snapping hips don't hurt because we don't know why they pop, and we don't know why they feel better afterwards.

One theory says that tendons snap across the front of the pelvis, or each other, as they change positions during activity. If they snap enough, they can become irritated. And that can mean swelling and pain—the symptoms of tendinitis.

✚ What to do about it ✚ If it doesn't hurt, ignore it. And count your blessings. If it does hurt, see a doctor. The task then will be to find out what tendon or muscle is involved, and then do the familiar things: stretching, strengthening, even using ice and anti-inflammatories. But we may be in the realm of cracking knees, ankles, and toes here. You learn to live with it.

SNAPPING HIP—OUTSIDE VARIETY

There's another kind of snapping hip that's on the outside of the joint, by the greater trochanter, which is a protruding knob at the upper end of the femur, just below where it goes into the hip joint. We know about this one—it involves the tensor fascia lata muscle and the iliotibial band. The muscle helps to flex and extend your hip, and, as it works, the iliotibial band can snap over the greater trochanter, which sticks out from the bone just asking for it. Especially in lean people who don't have much fat to lubricate that sort of movement (there's a bursa in there to help out, too, but sometimes it doesn't), the tendon can become irritated.

It can also occur in people who lie on their hip and move their leg, as in aerobics and calisthenics. The pressure can push the bone against the tendon and irritate it that way. These people feel the irritation right next to the skin.

What to do about it. This one is something you can deal with on your own because it usually involves tendinitis, or a muscle that's too tight or too weak. Stretching, strengthening, icing, and anti-inflammatories are what's required.

MERALGIA PARESTHETICA

Another little thing that can cause big problems. One of the nerves that supplies sensation to the front of the upper thigh comes out of the spine and crosses over the bony ridge of the pelvis. It's called the lateral cutaneous nerve, and it doesn't take very much to bother it. Just enough pressure barely to pinch it against the bone will cause pain down the upper front of the thigh. This shows up once in a while in dancers and other performers who wear costumes that are very binding across the hips. Occasionally we'll see it in a man wearing a dance belt or in people with skintight jeans, even in people whose running shorts have too much elastic. It doesn't take much.

The pain is always hard to pin down. It isn't muscle pain, it doesn't respond to treatment, and it comes and goes depending on what you have on. Once the nerve is irritated and inflamed, though, it'll stick around for a while.

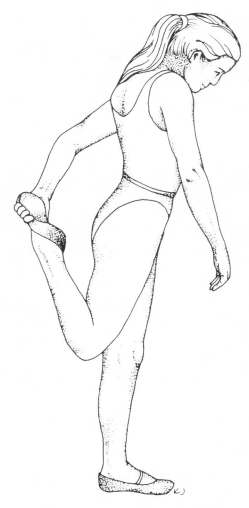

QUADRICEPS STRETCHING EXERCISE

✚ What to do about it ✚ The treatment is pretty simple: get rid of the pressure. A change of clothing and anti-inflammatory drugs will usually calm it down. But it can take some doing to arrive at that point. It might be best to see a doctor, just to be sure what the problem is. It can masquerade as other things, but it doesn't respond like other things. One test involves tapping across the bony ridge of your pelvis. When you come upon the irritated nerve, you'll feel the pain down your thigh like an electric shock.

Fortunately, this problem is rare.

REHAB EXERCISES

For patellar tendinitis (jumper's knee)

For muscle strains and tears of the front of the thigh: Grasp the foot and pull the leg and thigh back. The goal is not to put the foot on the buttock but rather to extend (pull back) the thigh. If done correctly, you will feel the stretch only down the front of the thigh.

For piriformis syndrome

The knee should be pulled toward the opposite hip. The stretch should be felt deep in the buttock.

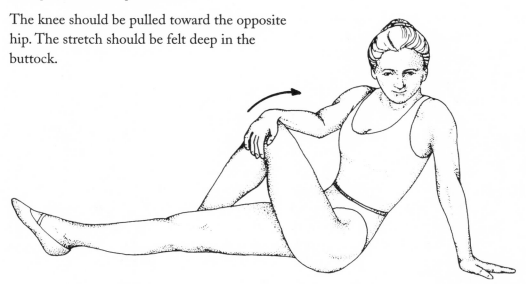

GLUTEAL AND PIRIFORMIS STRETCHING EXERCISE

THIGH LIFT

Strengthening exercises for thigh strains

The exercises that follow (except the last) are all all-purpose hip strengthening exercises. A frequent use is for people who are developing arthritis and becoming weaker due to the pain.

Once weak, the muscles become tight and motion is lost.

Take care not to overarch your back. This strengthens the hip flexors (rectus femoris and iliopsoas).

The thigh should be brought straight forward taking care not to arch the back.

For gluteal strains

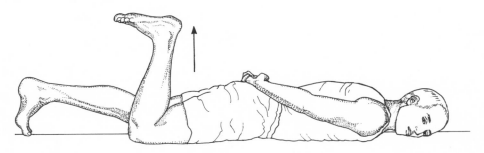

GLUTEAL STRENGTHENING EXERCISE

Lie on your stomach, bend your knee ninety degrees, and lift your leg up. Hold at least six seconds. This is an antigravity exercise; the next exercise utilizes a weight machine to accomplish the same thing.

Be sure to place the pad behind the knee. Do not place the pad below the level of the knee—the knee bears too much strain that way.

THIGH LIFT

For iliotibial band tendinitis

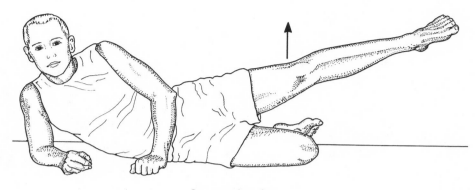

OUTSIDE LEG LIFT

Lie on your side with both hips straight. Lean your body upward on your elbow, and lift your leg up from the side. This and the following exercise strengthen the muscle involved in this tendinitis.

Be sure to place pads at knee level or above. When pads are lower than the knee, they direct too much force to the knee, especially if it's bent at all, which decreases its stability.

STANDING OUTSIDE LEG LIFT

For groin strains

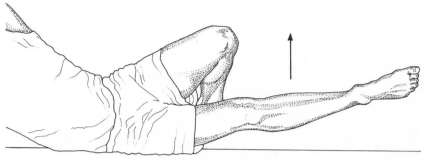

INSIDE LEG LIFT

Lie on your side with your upper hip and leg bent (to get them out of the way). Lift your lower leg into the air.

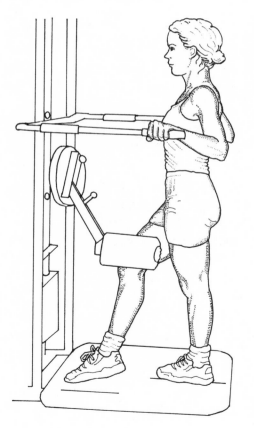

Be sure to place pads at or above the level of your knee. Lower than that, the pads direct too much force to the knee, risking injury.

STANDING INSIDE LEG LIFT

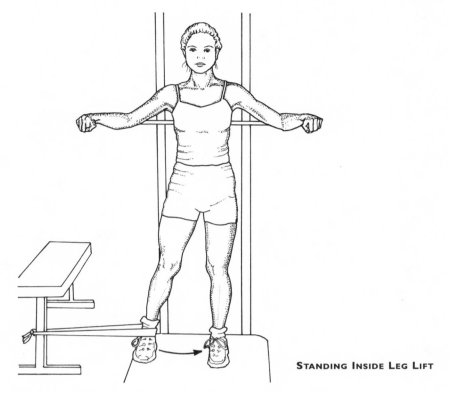

STANDING INSIDE LEG LIFT

Pull your leg toward the middle of your body against resistance.

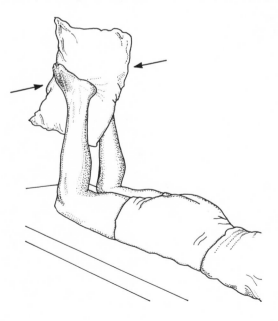

For piriformis syndrome (turnout muscles)

Lie on your stomach with your knees bent at a ninety-degree angle. Place a pillow between your ankles and attempt to crush it by pressing your ankles together. Be sure to keep your knees and thighs together. You should sense your buttocks tightening during the exercise.

HIP, INTERNAL ROTATOR ISOMETRICS

CHAPTER SEVEN

The Back and Neck

ALMOST EVERYONE, in or out of sports, has had back or neck problems. Most are things like stiff necks or sore backs rather than anything really serious—which is lucky because serious problems involving the neck and back can be ominous. The reason, of course, is the backbone, which is, among other things, a conduit that houses the spinal cord, that stalk of nerves that connects all parts of the body with the brain. When you get involved with nerves—with sensation, electrical impulse, the brain's ability to control the body—you're entering a fragile world, the disruption of which can have frightening consequences. From paralysis to partial loss of bodily functions, the hazards of spinal injury are real. But they represent a small minority of all back problems. This chapter will not deal with these relatively few serious back problems because they're obvious, often the result of contact sport injuries or other equally violent accidents, and they *absolutely* require professional care. No home treatments here.

The back is more than a spinal cord conduit, however. It's the body's lodgepole, its center of support. You might compare the backbone to the center pole of a circus tent. Much as the pole holds up the tent, radiating guy wires in all directions, the backbone must support the entire upper body. It provides attachment for guy wires—the muscles in the back and elsewhere—and internal stays—like the pelvis, the rib cage, and the shoulder bones.

+ WARNING +

If You Experience Any of These Conditions, Seek Medical Help

+ Back or neck pain that radiates down your arm or leg;
+ Any numbness or tingling in your arms or legs;
+ Weakness in your arms or legs (for example, you can't stand on your toes);
+ Back, neck, or extremity pain that gets sharply worse with coughing, sneezing, or straining to move your bowels.

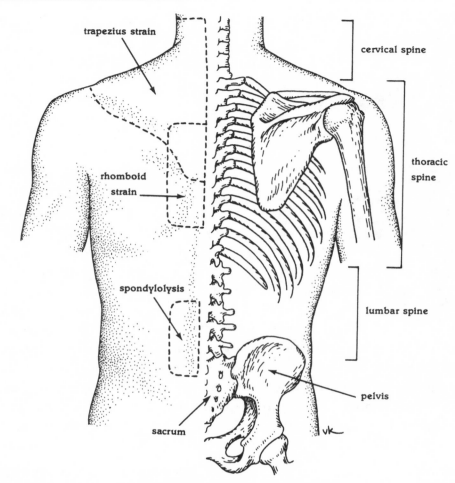

trapezius strain

cervical spine

thoracic
spine

rhomboid
strain

spondylolysis

lumbar spine

pelvis

sacrum

BACK VIEW OF THE BACK AND NECK

Still, it must do more than that. In contrast to a circus tent pole, the backbone must bend. Forward, backward, side to side, twisting double on itself, and
all variations in between, the backbone must be flexible as well as strong. Thus a
reason why it's not simply one rigid bone but a series of twenty-five blocks called
vertebrae, connected by hinges called facet joints, cushioned by spacers called
disks, and held upright against any strong wind by its structure of muscles and
bones. At this point all comparisons fall away. The backbone is unique.

And that's not all. As we've discussed, the backbone must perform yet
another vital task: channel and protect the spinal cord in its journey from the
brain to the pelvis and provide outlets for the nerves that branch off along the
way. So the backbone is a conduit as well.

A lot to ask. It's a wonder there aren't even more back and neck injuries. Yet, for all its success in providing a myriad of services simultaneously, almost anything you read about the backbone suggests that it's not well designed. That is, it's not designed for an upright posture. In this view, the backbone works best when supported at both ends, as with most animals, and as with us humans back a few years when we too scurried around on all fours. Although we readily made the jump to getting around on two legs, our backbone did not.

It's a debatable contention, made all the more difficult to prove one way or the other by the fact that it's hard to ask other animals if their backs are bothering them (although we do know that there are certain breeds of dogs that have frequent disk problems). But whether or not we should be wearing two pairs of running shoes instead of one, it is true that many back problems have to do with the way the backbone is designed.

To explain: in contrast to the center pole of a circus tent, the backbone is not perfectly straight. It curves front to back—it's designed that way. To begin at the top, your neck, which is supported by what's called the cervical spine, curves forward. The part of the backbone to which the ribs are attached, the thoracic spine, meanders backward, and then the lower backbone, the lumbar spine, moves forward again a bit. The effect is a gentle, S curve.

The vertebrae are cut at just enough of an angle to sustain this curve, likewise the cushioning disks between. The guy wires—the muscles—are just taut enough on every side. And although the backbone is very flexible, at rest it returns to this gentle curve.

That is, it should. Problems arise when for one reason or another the backbone is forced into positions that stretch and strain the muscles and bones that hold it in place, so that it remains out of line and, therefore, out of sorts. The reasons include disease and injury and are often unavoidable. Some suggested treatments follow a bit later on. But often you *can* avoid mistreating the backbone. The keys are twofold and very simple: keep your back straight (that is, don't accentuate its normal gentle curve) and strengthen your stomach muscles.

THE IMPORTANCE OF A STRAIGHT BACK

Many people dread back injuries, but they're common and usually not terribly serious. Of the twenty-five vertebrae in the backbone, the ones in the lower back, the lumbar spine, cause the most trouble, three or four times as much trouble as those in the rest of the back. In fact, in athletes these five vertebrae, particularly the lowest three, cause more problems than all the other vertebrae put together.

It's hard to know just why that's so, but it's probably because these largest verte-brae in the backbone are not connected to stabilizers, like the ribs, that help secure them in place. There's a lot of movement in the lumbar spine, just as there is the cervical spine, the part of the backbone in the neck. But in contrast to that upper part of the spine, which only has to support your head, the lower back has to worry about almost half the weight of your body. And it's subject to terrific stresses. The twistings and turnings of the torso above and the legs below can deposit hundreds of pounds per square inch of force on the lumbar spine. So it's potentially a troublesome area, and that potential is made greater when people inadvertently accentuate the lumbar spine's already existing curve.

Everyone has seen a swaybacked horse. People, too, have swaybacks, which are nothing more than overarched backs. Some of us come about our swaybacks naturally—we're born with them—but more often we give ourselves temporary swaybacks without realizing it. It's usually a function of fatigue or lack of strength. Next time you go to a fitness center, watch people work out on the weight machines. Invariably, whether it's back exercises, leg presses, or arm con-ditioners, as people become tired or stack too many plates on the machine, they begin to arch their backs (many people simply arch their backs from the begin-ning—they've never been taught otherwise). Take a peek into the free-weight room. The experienced lifters know better, but novices, especially those who are trying to take on more weight than they can handle, arch their backs with each lift. And it doesn't have to happen at the gym. Whenever your back is involved in lifting (and when you think of it, there are few times when it is not), be it rearranging the furniture, carrying out the garbage, picking up the dog, or just supporting the weight of your body, if you're tired or not strong enough you arch your back. It's a way of trying to get more of the big muscles in your torso to help out.

Not good. As long as the vertebrae in your backbone are stacked as they should be, they absorb force effectively all along the chain; compressing one onto the next as they are designed to do. But when you overarch your back, distorting the backbone's normal curve, you stack the blocks off center. They sheer off course when they compress and tend to want to slide *off* rather than *against* one another. (It's awfully hard for them to do that, of course, as they're locked together at the back by the facet joints. But it's not good for the joints to undergo such stress. These connectors are pretty small compared to the forces against them.) In this position, you lose the advantage of bony stability, and suddenly you have to stabilize your back purely with muscles. The muscles will only tolerate that kind of overwork so long. Then you start having problems. At the least you can develop temporary back pain, at the worst a real injury.

And it's not just in lifting activities where the tendency to arch the back shows up. In gymnastics, especially in women, the arched-back, bottom-out pose is *de rigueur* when finishing a routine. In ballet, dancers without enough turnout tend to tilt their pelvis (and sometimes bend their knees, too) trying for more; when they straighten up, their back arches and bottom sticks out. And the need for good turnout isn't limited to ballet. Gymnasts, figure skaters, even discus throwers depend on turnout. Overarched backs are common here also.

An arched back doesn't just show up in turnout problems. Dancers whose hip flexor muscles—like the sartorius and rectus femoris, those muscles in the front of the pelvis—are overly tight tend to overarch their backs. Many dancers are in this category. Their hamstrings are plenty flexible—they can pull their feet up to their ears—but they don't have as much flexibility in the other direction. The demands of arabesque and attitude simply don't stretch out the hip flexors as much as they might. The result can be a tendency to tilt the pelvis forward, which in turn accentuates the arch in the back.

Aerobic dancers, too, overarch their backs. Often it's because the students tend to do what the teacher does, not what she says. So the teacher introduces an exercise, a donkey kick, say, which should be done with a perfectly flat back, perhaps even with elbows on the floor. While demonstrating, she looks up to see how the students are doing, thereby arching her back. The result? A studio full of students donkey kicking with arched backs.

Ballet teachers try to circumvent the problem by teaching students to pull up through the pelvis and stomach and tighten their buttocks. Physical therapists tell you to tuck your tail beneath you. Either technique works, and both strive toward the same end: keeping the lower back as straight as possible. The straighter the lower back, the more abuse it will take, which is a real boon because most of the activities athletic people do abuse the lower back.

Pelvic tilt

It's important to know what it *feels* like to have a straight back. Many of us don't know; we're too used to the other. One way is by learning to do a pelvic tilt. Lie down on your back and bend your knees toward you. That's all, just bend your knees. The mere act of bending them tilts your pelvis forward and correspondingly flattens your back into the floor. If you want to tilt your pelvis even more, all you have to do is curl up into a ball (a very good way to stretch your lower back, by the way). Now you've reversed the curve of your backbone, which is just the ticket to stretch out your overly contracted muscles.

But it's hard to go through life on your back with your knees bent. It's that *feeling* of flattening the lower back that you want to remember, so that you can reproduce it anytime. Have a friend slide a hand underneath the small of your back, and then push your back into the hand, knees bent or no. That's the feeling. You can do this exercise standing against a wall as well. You don't even need your friend's hand—simply flatten your lower back into the wall. Just the act of doing it is good exercise, and eventually you'll be able to tilt your pelvis and straighten out your back anytime.

You can make it a conscious thing: when standing, think about tilting your pelvis backward; when sitting, neither slump or overarch—simply keep your back straight. If you're sitting in a straight-backed chair, press the small of your back against the support. When lifting, bend from the legs, not the lower back (another way of saying, keep your back straight). And when you're working out on weight machines, be sure to flatten your lower back into the backrests of the equipment. Always aim to *feel* the pressure of the back support against your lower back. If you can't, you're arching too much.

And there's another thing you can do to prevent overarching. It's not obvious, like straightening your back, and it may even be surprising. Yet perhaps it's the most important thing of all: strengthen your stomach muscles.

THE IMPORTANCE OF STRONG ABDOMINAL MUSCLES

Back to the circus tent. The center pole not only supports the guy wires radiating from it, it's supported by them as well. If the guy wires on one side pull too tightly, the pole leans in that direction, even bows out in the center. A similar fate can befall your backbone. If any one of the groups of muscles that attach to the backbone is significantly stronger than the others, it can exert undue influence on the backbone, pulling it out of shape.

The two main muscle groups that influence the backbone this way are the strong ropes of muscles that run along the spine, the paraspinous muscles ("near to the spine" muscles—which you can easily feel on either side of your backbone; when well developed, they surmount the spine like banks of a canal), and your stomach muscles. Although these abdominal muscles attach at the pelvis and ribs and so don't pull directly on the backbone, they still act as guy wires. For life to be pleasant for your backbone, the paraspinous and abdominal muscles must complement one another. Unfortunately, while the paraspinous muscles tend to be strong in everyone, kept toned and conditioned by the everyday demands of living, the same can't be said for the stomach muscles. As beer drinkers and sweets eaters know all too well, the stomach muscles can easily become soft and weak. And when that happens, it's no contest—the back muscles take over. When unopposed back muscles contract, they tend to shorten the distance between the skull and pelvis, just as a drawn bowstring shortens the distance between the two ends of a bow. The result: an accentuation of the spine's curve. You need strong stomach muscles to keep things in balance.

So, when you're talking about prevention or treatment of back injuries, you have to be flexible and strong, but not only in the back. You have to strengthen the muscles in front, too. A good abdominal strengthening program will probably prevent, and treat, more back problems than any other course of action. A good way to go about it is by doing curl-ups.

BACK STRAINS

You're a little tired. You're playing one more set than you usually play, and you lunge to get your racquet on a ball at your shoe tops. It's your best shot of the day, worth the extra half hour on the court and your mounting fatigue. But as you stretch to make contact, you feel something odd happen in your back.

Nothing much. It feels weird, but it certainly isn't going to stop you from playing. You finish the game, then walk off the court for a drink of water before changing sides. And there, while you're standing by the side of the court cooling down a little, resting for a moment, it happens: your back tightens up and suddenly doesn't work very well.

You finish out the set anyway, gutting it out; then go home with a throbbing back and go to bed. In the morning the sun rises, but you don't. You discover that what used to be a human being is now a pretzel. You not only can't get out of that position, you can't even get out of bed. All this for one extra set and an incredible passing shot.

It doesn't have to be tennis, of course. Running, swimming, team sports, dance, weight training—anytime your back becomes weary, or when you do something to it that it isn't accustomed to, the result can be a back muscle strain. It can happen to a football player doing pass-blocking drills or to a gymnast practicing one routine over and over (gymnastics puts backs into horrible positions, but its saving grace is that it involves several different activities, and the variety of demands they make probably saves the day as far as even more frequent, and awful, back problems are concerned). Dancers attempting new or especially strenuous roles are subject to back strains, particularly men whose shoulders and arms aren't strong enough for the demands of dancing with a partner. Often they have a tendency to muscle their partners up with their backs, much like trying to lift too much weight in a gym.

Wrestlers strain their backs by doing arches in an attempt to gain more back strength. A tough aerobics class can cause a back strain, as can something as mundane as working too long on your tennis serve. At the top of your preparation to serve, when your racquet's all the way cocked, your back is hyperextended, a position it doesn't exactly savor. And when you think of all the ways your back is mistreated around the house—digging in the garden, moving furniture, mopping the floors—it's easy to see how it doesn't take much of any athletic activity to push it over the edge.

What doctors think happens with a muscle strain is that you tear at least a few muscle fibers, which then bleed into the muscle. As muscles aren't used to encountering blood except in vessels, where it should be, the blood acts as an irritant, and the muscle goes into spasm. And these are big muscles, dense, long cords with diameters of a good inch and a half or more. When they go into spasm, they *really* go into spasm. There is no muscle injury more debilitating.

They're going to stay in spasm, too, because they're trying to protect themselves. They don't want you to get in positions that might cause further injury, so they do their best to keep you from moving. Very successfully. These muscles clamp down so hard your back feels like a rock.

The strain doesn't have to be in your back, per se. It can show up in your neck as well. You might wake in the morning and find that, because you overstretched a muscle by sleeping in an awkward position, your ear is pressed to your shoulder and you can't do a thing about it. Or a strain in the neck can result from doing something the day before to one of your trapezius muscles (the big shoulder-neck muscles), or to another muscle in the shoulder-neck area. With stiff necks the cause can be mysterious but not so the result.

✛ What to do about it ✛ The only way to deal with strains in the back and neck is to stretch out the afflicted muscles. You want to break up the muscle spasm as soon as possible, for two reasons. One, of course, is pain and disability. As long as the muscles are in spasm, you're going to hurt, and you won't be able to do the things you like to do because your back will be tight as a knot. The other is that the longer the muscle remains in spasm, the harder it is to get out of spasm, and the weaker it becomes. Which means that you'll be a long time working to restrengthen the muscles, and they'll be especially prone to reinjury in the meantime.

If there is anything good about a back strain, however, it may be that because it's so disabling, you're likely to get around to doing something about it more quickly than with strains elsewhere in the body. It's one thing limping around with a hamstring strain. It's another not being able to get around at all. So it's more likely that you won't allow the back muscles enough time for much weakness to develop, and restrengthening the injured muscle might not be as daunting a task as it can be in other places. It's simply hard to ignore things that happen to your back.

So, what to do: as elsewhere in the body where there's pain and perhaps swelling involved, anti-inflammatory drugs can help. Icing? Almost always the answer would be an unqualified yes. But the back is one area where there may be some legitimate disagreement about ice as opposed to heat. Usually you'd never want to apply heat to an injury that involves swelling, as heat tends to increase the blood supply, which increases swelling. Conversely, ice shuts down the blood vessels, helping to keep swelling to a minimum. If your injury occurred dramatically, suddenly, the pain appearing immediately, then icing is probably better because you most likely tore quite of bit of the muscle. In that case, you want to keep the bleeding down as much as possible, and since you can't really compress the back muscles, icing is the next best thing to do.

But if your back strain is similar to the one we described earlier, one that doesn't seem like much at the time but later clamps down and bends you out of shape, then it may be that getting into a nice, warm whirlpool bath or hot tub is just what you need. As long as you *do something* in that nice, warm water. Muscle strains demand an active effort if you're going to get over them. *Stretch* the muscle in the warm water. Take advantage of the wet warmth for something other than just comfort.

So, ice if that feels best; use heat if that's the ticket. Go with what works, always remembering that you have to break up the spasm before the injury will get any better.

It's easy to stretch the back muscles. If your injured back bends you in one direction, then stretch in the other. For example, if your ear is glued to your right shoulder, then putting it on your left shoulder is the way to stretch that muscle. If you're stooped to the left side from back spasms, then bend over to the right. The way to do it is with long and slow stretches. It may take you three or four minutes to get a decent stretch at first—be patient and stay with it. Once you break the spasm, it will be easier the next time.

If the pain is in your lower back, there are a number of ways to stretch, all depending on how flexible you are and how much you hurt. One way is to curl up in a ball. Simply lie down, grab the back of your thighs, and very slowly curl up. Another is to slowly pull one leg at a time toward your chest. In both these exercises, bending your head and shoulders to meet your legs increases the stretch. If you hurt too much to be able to do these stretches, just lying on your back and bending your knees automatically tilts your pelvis, providing a gentle stretch. An even more gentle method than that is simply to lie on your back with a firm pillow underneath your knees. Just raising your knees the thickness of a pillow helps to tilt your pelvis, providing some relief. Any of these simple movements will allow the spastic muscles a bit of relaxation.

For people who are in such lower back pain that it hurts even to make contact with the floor or a bed, another way to stretch is to slowly lower yourself from a standing position into a toe touch (or as close to a toe touch as you can manage). This kind of stretching can feel very good because it takes no effort on your part. Gravity and the weight of your head and arms and upper torso gently pull you down. The problem is, however, that it can be hard to get out of that position. Gravity has stretched you out, but now you have to use your inflamed muscles to pull yourself back up. Don't. Simply bend at the knees, then straighten up. It won't hurt at all.

Sometimes just pressing on the injured muscle for thirty or forty seconds will give it some reflex relaxation. Then you can stretch it. It's like a bit of mini-massage or self-acupressure. And you'll know where to press. A strained muscle will have a hot spot, a place that's hard as a rock, the bull's-eye of the whole area.

Sometimes just doing pelvic tilts or abdominal strengthening exercises can help back injuries, even the worst ones. Curl-ups might bring relief. Anything, as long as you're able to break up the muscle spasm, and the sooner the better. And then as soon as you're able, go about your business. If your back or neck starts to tighten up, just flop down and do the stretches no matter where you are (it can take some courage to roll into a ball on the office floor, but, after all, what's more important, your image or your back?). At first you may have to stretch every ten minutes for the first two hours, then every twenty minutes, then thirty, and so on. In time, stretching before you go to bed, stretching when you get up in the morning, and stretching before and after any athletic activities will probably do the trick. And once you've learned what kind of exercises work for you, you have become in effect your own physician and exercise therapist. You can use the same approach the next time and most likely prevent the frequency of next times. Again, if you get to back muscle strains early, you'll save yourself untold grief and wasted time.

Strains account for probably three quarters of the back problems we see, maybe more. Unaccustomed activity, unaccustomed positions, staying in one position too long, reaching for something too quickly, not being prepared for any particular movement—the causes of back strain are many, and the results are all too similar. Get on them quickly. But, again, although the muscles may be very uncomfortable, they *should not radiate pain or numbness or tingling, produce any weakness in the extremities, or become worse when you cough or sneeze or otherwise strain.* Those symptoms can indicate a serious problem. In that case, see a doctor right away.

STIFF NECK

You need do nothing more than sleep in an awkward position to have a stiff neck (although you may "legitimize" it by having an athletic dream), or it can come from something very active, like practicing your serve for an hour after playing a couple of sets. All that looking up and over your shoulder can cause the muscles in your neck all sorts of fatigue, with the result that you wake up the next morning with your ear plastered to your serving shoulder.

✚ What to do about it ✚ The best remedy for a stiff neck is to stretch out the muscles so that they can't stay in spasm. Your neck goes in six directions: forward, chin on chest; backward, looking at the ceiling; to either side, ear to shoulder; and it twists, looking over shoulder. Those are the directions to stretch, opposite from the way your neck is tilted. If you wake up looking over your right shoulder, stretch by turning to the left. If your ear is tilted toward your left shoulder, tilt to the right. All these motions should be long and slow.

You can contract-relax stretch your neck as well. Stretch, then push the other way against your own arm, then stretch some more. And isometric neck exercises are easy. Push your head and neck against the resistance of your arm.

CONTUSIONS

Contusions, or bruises, are the result of direct blows. The impact can cause blood vessels below the surface to rupture and bleed into the muscle—that's why the area becomes discolored and swollen. If the blow is strong enough, the muscles themselves can tear. And, as we've seen so often in this book, when muscles tear and are confronted with blood that isn't contained in vessels, they know how to do only one thing: contract violently and go into spasm. And when the muscles in the back go into spasm, you know it.

Back contusions usually involve football players struck with a helmet or knee. Sometimes they're the result of larger collisions—from inadvertently running into your tennis partner to serious contact sport things, like a tackle in football. And once again, football players are conspicuous among those who suffer this kind of injury. Contusions can also result from bizarre accidents, such as a gymnast landing on the balance beam on her back.

At the worst these collisions can break body parts that are much better left unbroken. These can include the little bumps of the backbone that you can feel just under the skin, the spinous processes. They're little nubbins of bone, maybe an inch to an inch and a half long, that are used as muscle attachments. They're a long way from the spinal cord, so breaking one is not a big deal. Breaking your back, per se, is awfully hard to do.

Not so breaking your neck, however. You can break your neck pretty easily if it's in the wrong position when you receive a blow. Diving into shallow water is probably the most common cause. Broken necks also show up in equestrian sports—being flipped off a horse and landing on your head—and just occasionally in wrestling. Trampolines produce more than their share of broken necks, from very skilled people using them for training—pole vaulters, high jumpers, gymnasts—to kids playing on them. (That's why you don't see many trampolines.)

In football, if you take enough force, your neck can break even though it isn't in an awkward position. All you have to do is hit somebody hard enough with your head and the vertebrae in the neck can literally explode or slide apart. The results can be devastating because this relatively small section of the backbone doesn't protect the spinal cord as effectively as elsewhere. When these vertebrae break, the danger is that the spinal cord can tear or be severed as well. At the worst such a tear can cause paralysis of the arms and legs—quadriplegia. Probably three quarters of the football injuries that have led to quadriplegia did not result from the player having his head in an awkward position, but from the simple fact that he hit somebody with his head.

It's illegal to tackle with your head at the high school and college levels— illegal under any circumstances in high school; illegal if done intentionally in college. You're supposed to be penalized for a head tackle, but as a rule these penalties are rarely called. Still, it's better than it used to be. The rate of football injuries leading to quadriplegia has been decreasing, and it probably could be even lower if the rules were more stringently enforced. If nothing else, football coaches are pragmatists. The first time they had a couple of players thrown out of a game for hitting with their heads would be the last time. The technique would never be used again, intentionally or accidentally. But, as it is, things have started to improve.

✛ What to do about it ✛ Treat contusions the same way you treat muscle strains. As with muscle strains, it's important to break up the muscle spasms as soon as possible and try to keep the bleeding, and therefore swelling, to a minimum. If you can apply ice to the injured area, fine. More effective still is stretching the muscle. Whichever way it hurts, that's the direction in which to stretch. Make the stretches long and slow. That will not only break up the spasms, it will help control swelling by compressing the muscles from within. (See the previous section for more detailed suggestions.) But if your contusion is severe, with a lot of pain and swelling, it might be best to see a doctor.

If there's ever any possibility that someone may have suffered a neck injury—a person falls, say, and lands on his head or neck, and is unconscious or unable to move his arms or legs—assume the worst, a broken neck. It's very important that you not do anything except try to make the person comfortable, *keep him from moving, and get help.* Don't try to diagnose the problem, don't try to treat it, don't try to straighten his back or neck, don't remove his helmet or uniform—*just get help.* If it's raining, cover him up. If it's sunny and hot, supply some shade. Above all, *get help.*

DISK PROBLEMS

Everyone has heard of such terms as ruptured disks and slipped disks, but few people know what they mean or what disks really are. The popular image of a spinal disk may be one of a hard, round, flat piece of bone or cartilage somehow wedged into the backbone, performing some obscure function, and ready at any moment to "rupture" or "slip" or otherwise bring about disaster.

Well, the shape is right—disks are disklike—but the consistency is wrong. Rather than being little round blocks, disks are more nearly like undersized jelly-filled Danish pastries (ones that have been left standing too long and have gotten a bit stale on the outside). The outside is tough, fibrous tissue; the inside a watery, gelatinous material. As you bend your back, the disks act as cushions, spacing the vertebrae in the backbone and allowing them to twist and bend without bumping and scraping against each other. The jelly in the disk acts something like a kitchen sponge between plates—at rest the sponge holds the plates apart, but if you press them together it displaces to one side or another according to the pressure you exert.

As we grow older, this jelly loses some of its fluid, becoming stiffer and less effective as a shock absorber. And under the constant pressure exerted by the movement of the backbone, it can begin to push against its fibrous outer surface. If there's a defect in the tissue, the surface will bulge out like a worn inner tube. Sometimes it can even fragment, a piece of disk breaking free. Thus, a ruptured, or "slipped," disk.

By itself the bulging or fragmenting isn't much of a problem, as long as it doesn't impinge against anything important. However, the backbone shelters something *very* important: the spinal cord. If the disk bulges toward the front of the body, you're safe. There's nothing there for it to interfere with. But if it presses back, or back and to the sides, it will soon encounter the spinal cord (that is, if the disk is at the level of the first lumbar vertebra or higher—the spinal cord only descends that far into the backbone) or press against nerve roots branching off from the cord. The spinal cord sends off two nerve roots at the level of each vertebra. Where it ends at the first lumbar vertebra, the cord then trails nerve roots, like the tail of a kite, into the four remaining lumbar vertebrae and then into the sacrum and coccyx, which form the "butterfly body" in the pelvis. Those roots continue to escape the backbone two by two and descend into the rest of the body, supplying all our sensations downward.

The nerve roots exit the bony cage of the spinal column through little holes in the bone called foramina (for-*aye*-mina), which are hardly bigger than the nerves themselves. If a disk protrudes in that direction, two things can happen: it can crimp the spinal cord itself, or it can bulge into the foramina, squashing the nerve root against the bone. Either obstruction brings about a similar result, radiating pain and loss of nerve function. And when you move, stretching the nerve over the bulge in the disk, it hurts all the more. That's why one test for disk problems is straight-leg raising. If you raise your leg up and down, and that causes pain from your foot to your back, it's likely you're pulling the nerve back and forth over a protruding disk. Other tests look at strength and reflexes—heel and knee jerk, for example. If the nerve's ability to conduct impulses is in any way impaired, you'll lose your ability to function as usual. And if the problem is at a certain level in your lower back, the loss can even include bladder and bowel function. All this from an undersized jelly-filled Danish losing its shape and mucking up your electrical system.

✚ What to do about it ✚ See a doctor. Disk problems are *not* something you should ignore or try to manage yourself. The stakes are too high.

Treatments vary. Sometimes long periods of rest do the job, with the help of a corset or back brace to stabilize you in the meantime. Sometimes anti-inflammatory drugs (cortisone is often used here) can reduce the swelling of the disk enough to get rid of the pressure. Sometimes a disk problem leads to surgery, and even then the treatment can vary. The procedure is called a laminectomy, and it involves removing the part of the disk that's ruptured. Sometimes people remove the entire disk, sometimes fuse vertebrae together. And sometimes less-invasive techniques—laser disk ablation, microsurgery, "small incision" diskectomies—can deal with the problem. There's a lot of controversy among doctors over the best way to manage disk problems.

But that controversy doesn't extend to your best course of action. If you're experiencing numbness, tingling, pain radiating into your extremities; if you have any weakness in your limbs, and bowel or bladder dysfunction; if your back hurts more when you sneeze, cough, or strain, then there's only one thing to do: *see a doctor right away.*

STRESS FRACTURES—SPONDYLOLYSIS

Stress fractures, those hairline breaks that result from chronic overusing or misusing the bone rather than from any one dramatic incident, show up in the backbone, too. In the spine they're called spondylolysis (spon-de-lo-*lie*-sis)—literally "vertebra loosening."

Spondylolysis occurs near the little knuckle-sized facet joints at the back of the spine, and most often in the lower lumbar vertebrae, just before the backbone descends into the pelvis. The tip-off is usually pain when you arch your back (indeed, spondylolysis may be caused by overarching—more on that in a minute). Dancers may feel pain in their raised leg when they do an arabesque or in their lower back on the raised-leg side. With this problem, any activity that demands arching the back may produce pain.

No one knows just what causes spondylolysis, but there's an interesting piece of information to back up the suspicion that it's a result of overarching. High-level teenage girl gymnasts, who overarch as a matter of course (nowhere more obviously than when posing after dismounting an apparatus), suffer from spondylolysis *four times* more frequently than females their age who are not gymnasts. It may be that football lineman, who tend to overarch when they come out of the down position to block, suffer it more frequently than other people, and ballet dancers most certainly do. And it may also be more common in figure skaters.

But perhaps it's not only overarching that causes spondylolysis. In ballet and figure skating you don't arch that much, as having your back swayed and rear end sticking out is not considered aesthetically desirable in these activities. It may be jumping that does it, or simply the constant pounding the lower back undergoes in these kinds of demanding activities. There's obviously something more to it than we yet understand.

Some people think that tight hamstrings or tight hip flexor muscles are the culprit. And it's true that among not-so-serious athletes tight hamstrings will show up in association with spondylolysis. But it's hard to know which is the chicken and which is the egg. It may be that tight muscles are the result, rather than the cause, of the problem.

And it may be that the older you are the less likely it is that you'll have to do anything more about spondylolysis than read this section. Most of the bone scan evidence of the problem is in young people, teens and upward. When it shows up in adults it most likely has been there for some time and is surfacing because of some recent change in activity. But, again, we're just not sure.

✚ What to do about it ✚ It depends on how much it hurts. If your back doesn't bother you a lot, then there's no reason to do much of anything except be careful. But you certainly should spend some time working on straightening your backbone—doing pelvic tilts and curl-ups—because the more you arch your back, the worse the problem will be.

If it does hurt, see a doctor. The important thing here is to have the problem diagnosed correctly. For even though it may not be absolutely killing you now, like any stress fracture it will get you later if you don't treat it effectively. And that treatment involves staying away from activities that hurt. Again, the barometer is pain.

The good news is that in a good third of cases the bone will heal as a result of nothing more than keeping the area pain-free for a length of time. The bad news is that the time required can be as long as six months. For most of us, that might be an inconvenience; for a young person seriously involved in an activity a six-month layoff can mean a twelve-month departure from meaningful competition or performing. And that can mean a devastating gap in a budding career, if not the end of it.

So, spondylolysis is one of those problems that may be no problem for some, an inconvenience for most, and a serious blow for the rest of us. As a general rule, once you stop the activity the provoked the problem, spondylolysis disappears (even though a bone scan may say differently). The difficulty is getting along without your favorite activity. And this condition may not carry any horrible long-term implications. Although people with spondylolysis likely will have more frequent back complaints through the years than people without, the likelihood of them having to endure surgery or other major disruptions is very small.

And, again, this is one of those problems that responds well to using the backbone as it was designed to be used. Straighten your backbone and strengthen your abdominal muscles.

SPONDYLOLISTHESIS

One thing that can happen to people with stress fractures (but rarely to athletes) is that the crack in the vertebra can become so pronounced that one part of the spine separates from another and, if you have cracks on both sides of the spine, causes one vertebra to actually slip forward onto the other. The word spondylolisthesis (spon-de-lo-*liss*-the-sis) means "vertebra shift," and that's exactly what happens. In the worst cases, the vertebra can slide forward as much as an inch and a half. That's a long, long way when you're talking about a space as confined as that of the backbone.

Fortunately, this shifting tends to occur in the lower vertebrae, below the level of the spinal cord, so there's little danger of pinching or chopping the cord in two. At these lower levels there are only nerve roots, and they float inside the spinal column with more than enough room. So rarely do you see any disastrous problems with spondylolisthesis, and rarely does the vertebral shift ever come all at once. It tends rather to slip up on you over a long period of time.

✚ **What to do about it** ✚ The tip-off is lower back pain, and, again, it's *how much* pain that counts. With spondylolisthesis, it probably will hurt enough to motivate you to see a doctor. In milder cases, the treatment can be rest and perhaps some kind of body brace. If the vertebral shift is really bad, it may require surgical fusion so it can't slip any further.

SCOLIOSIS

Despite the fear the word generates, scoliosis is a common and, in most cases, insignificant condition. It literally means "a curve," and it denotes just that in the backbone, but a curve in a distinct direction—lateral, or side to side. Whereas the backbone is designed to curve front to back, it isn't supposed to curve side to side—that is, not to remain that way. And with scoliosis you never get just one lateral curve, as your body will not tolerate your spine bending in just one direction. It will figure out a way to keep your skull centered over your pelvis, and that usually means that your spine will make another lateral curve in the opposite direction from the first one, either above or below it, or both. So although your head stays perfectly aligned over your hips, all sorts of interesting things may be going on in between.

Scoliosis curves are not just side to side, however. Usually they also have some rotation, and it's the rotation that testers look for in school kids. They have the kids bend over and sight along their backs. If one side of the back is higher than the other, then it's likely the kid has scoliosis. And they'll find it in quite a few of them. It's a disease most common to teenage girls. More than one teenage girl in ten has some degree of it. Why, no one knows. In fact the most common kind is called idiopathic scoliosis, which means that we don't know what causes it.

In the worst cases the curve can be severe to the point of deformity. It can get so bad that it can actually collapse a lung and part of your chest. Those cases may have to be treated with braces and even surgery. But most of the time the curvature is so mild that it's almost unnoticeable and certainly not disabling. There are people dancing professionally who have significant scoliosis. Professional skaters have it, as do top-level gymnasts. Frequently women will notice it when they try on pants, and one hip is more prominent than the other. Or when one breast is higher than the other. Women forty years old may notice it for the first time, but it's never bothered them before and probably never will.

You can get temporary scoliosis from muscle spasms in your back. When one of the big ropes of muscles on either side of your spine goes into spasm, it will pull the spine to one side just like a bow. So one of the offshoots of the kinds of back injuries we've been discussing can be scoliosis.

✛ What to do about it ✛ In the case of a temporary, muscle injury-caused scoliosis, do the things we've suggested to treat the muscle injury. Or if pain is severe, see a doctor.

In the case of idiopathic scoliosis, you probably won't even know you have it unless someone calls your attention to it, perhaps during a physical exam. In that case you're already with a doctor, and it's a good bet that there's nothing much to do about it, anyway. For more pronounced cases, see a doctor for sure. There are treatments that may preclude the necessity for bracing or surgery. One of these is applying an electrical charge at night to the muscles opposite the curve. The charge stimulates the muscles, causing them to contract and pull the spine back to normal. The technique can be helpful if applied early enough. And, contrary to what may be the popular perception of scoliosis, it's good for people with this problem to stay active.

OSTEOPOROSIS

Osteoporosis, a loss of bone strength affecting primarily postmenopausal women, is in the news these days. It's the result of hormonal changes and can, in extreme cases, lead to a collapsed spine because of increasingly soft bone. What isn't as well known is that some of the same problems show up in young, high-level female athletes, whether menstruating or not. It's almost like a kind of youthful menopause. Unfortunately, it can happen even with normal periods, good diets, calcium supplementation, and the like.

✛ What to do about it ✛ See a doctor. Often women who suffer from osteoporosis are also calcium-deficient. So, if you're a serious female athlete, it may be a good idea to supplement your diet with a multivitamin and additional calcium and iron. Antacid tablets are a cheap and readily available source of extra calcium. Two a day provide the right dosage of calcium in easily absorbable form.

SCHEUERMAN'S DISEASE

How many parents are constantly nagging at how many teenagers to stand up straight? Well, some of those gooselike necks and rounded shoulders actually may be beyond the beleaguered kids' control. They could be a result of Scheuerman's disease. It's an odd malady affecting the growth centers in the vertebrae. It is in these areas that new bone is formed, which then pushes out to lengthen and thicken the existing bone. In the case of this disease, however, the growth centers fragment and produce wedge-shaped vertebrae rather than squarish building blocks. As the wedge shape increases over time, the backbone curves forward, the shoulders round, the neck sticks out—and parents start harping.

✢ What to do about it ✢ See someone. It can be diagnosed by x-ray, and there are some things that can be done. Sometimes a brace can help. But it's a rare problem. Most of the teenagers who slump don't have back problems, don't need a brace, and probably don't need to see a doctor

BACK INJURIES IN GENERAL

You can deal with the vast majority of back problems yourself, *if you catch them early*. Again, it comes back to *being aware* of what's going on in your body and, rather than ignoring it, *doing something about it*. Your approach should be two-pronged:

1. **Figure out what's caused the problem.** It may be easy to do. Your neck might be stiff, say, because you've been practicing serves more than usual, and the constant looking up and over your shoulder has over-worked the muscles. Or it might be a tough task, worthy of a medical detective (in which case seeing a doctor can produce real benefits), all because of the body's persistent predilection, much discussed in these pages, for being everywhere connected to everything else.

2. **Stretch and strengthen the muscles involved.** The way to stretch is to move in the direction that hurts—that is, the direction opposite to that in which you're frozen. If you're twisted to the left, turn to the right. If your chin is down on your chest, look up to the sky. If you're bent over at the waist, lean back. Curling into a ball can help alleviate lower back pain, or possibly hanging down to touch your toes will help. All these stretches should be long and slow. If you can manage only a few inches at first, keep at it, and your flexibility will increase as your pain decreases.

And try curl-ups right away. Few people have stomach muscles that are as strong as they should be, so the curl-ups can do nothing but help you. Remember to do them properly. The key is to keep your back flat against the floor. Have a friend periodically slide a hand under the small of your back as you're learning. If there's room for a hand, your back is arched and you're not doing the exercise correctly.

Then, when you're no longer hurting too much, ease back into your activity. Go slowly at first; then gradually build up steam. Continuing to stretch and strengthen the back and stomach muscles will go a long way toward preventing your back problem, whatever it is, from happening again. But if it should, or something similar, then attack it as you have this one. The sooner you get to back problems the better.

And, once more for good measure: *if your back pain radiates into your arms or legs; if you feel numbness or tingling in your arms or legs; if you notice sudden weakness in your arms or legs; if coughing, sneezing, or other straining makes your back pain worse—see a doctor.*

✚ A Note About Home Exercise Equipment ✚

It's safe if it is used correctly. But that's a big "if." After spending a lot of money on equipment, the tendency is to go home and immediately see what you can do. After all, an investment like this should produce tangible results, and quickly, right? So you hit it hard, too hard, piling too much weight on top of too much weight, checking the scales and taking measurements as you go. And if they're not what you're looking for, you hit it even harder. All with no supervision, no one to remind you that, in all likelihood, as you pile the weights high, you're committing the cardinal sin of lifting: arching your back.

Insufficient supervision may be a problem at fitness facilities as well. In the best of circumstances it's not easy for a few staff people to keep track of the crush of bodies in the weight room, and often those staff people, dependent as they are on commissions for attracting new members, are busy giving tours, answering questions, and making juice drinks rather than advising members on their lifting techniques. But at least at fitness facilities there *are* people around—at home there's no one. And often at home there's no mirror to help you keep track of yourself. As a result, the risk of back problems is greater at home.

A rule of thumb: *if you can't lift without arching your back, drop back to a weight you can handle with your back flat.* Press the small of your back into the backrest of the apparatus, and make sure it stays there for the duration of the exercise. Remind yourself to *feel* your back against the support. And go on to a heavier weight only when you can handle it with a flat back.

It's not how fast you proceed from level to level that counts, but if you're doing the exercises correctly. So perhaps one advantage of home equipment is that there's no outside pressure motivating you to progress too quickly. If you're secure at home, with no brute next to you lifting fifty pounds more than you did, or are spared from the embarrassment of someone half your size doubling the weight on the machine you just vacated, then maybe you can relax and go at your own pace. Whew! What a relief. Just remember to keep your back straight.

COMMONLY ASKED QUESTIONS
ABOUT BACK INJURIES

When I stretch my back by flexing forward or rolling into a ball, it hurts. Is there another approach that might work better for me?

Yes, there is. We've found that perhaps as many as 15 percent of the people we see get more relief from extension exercises than flexion exercises. Another name for extension exercises might be press-up exercises, or controlled arching. If you lie on the floor, flat on your stomach, and slowly arch your back by pressing up with your arms, you're doing extension exercises. Although these exercises actually contract the back muscles rather than stretch them (they do stretch the

---

+ Curl-ups +

When it comes to strengthening stomach muscles, there's a difference between curl-ups and sit-ups. It's not that there's anything wrong with sit-ups—along with push-ups and chin-ups they're among the most universally done strengthening exercises. It's just that if strengthening the stomach muscles is your aim, there's nothing more effective than curl-ups. And nothing safer. They have a built-in warning system. When you reach the point where you're too tired to continue exercising safely, you'll find that you can't do the curl-ups correctly. In that case, simply stop.

Here's how to do curl-ups the right way: Lie on the floor with your hands resting together over the lower part of your chest. (Don't put your hands behind your head, because the tendency then is to pull your head up with your arms, rather than with your stomach muscles.) Tilt your pelvis, pressing the small of your back into the floor, and *slowly* curl your head and shoulders up to the point where your shoulder blades have cleared the floor and then just a little beyond. Hold this position for a count of six, then *slowly* curl back down to the floor. Try it again. If you're

doing it right, you should feel it in your stomach and no place else.

If you hook your feet, under a sofa or some other restraint, you won't feel the curl-ups in your stomach as much because you'll then have created a fulcrum that allows you to use your hip flexor muscles as well. That dilutes the exercise as far as your stomach muscles are concerned. So if you don't hook your feet, then you can't cheat by letting other muscles help pull you up. Curl-ups keep you honest.

As for V-ups, when you V-up you use your stomach muscles, but you also use your hip flexors. Any time you involve your hips in an exercise, you shortchange your abdominal muscles. There's nothing wrong with V-ups, certainly. It simply depends on what you're exercising for. If it's to strengthen stomach muscles to provide more stability for your back, then curl-ups are the ticket. It may be that you'll want to do curl-ups together with your usual sit-ups or V-ups.

Count to six as you curl up, hold for a count of six, then curl down to a count of six—all very slowly, always making sure that your back is flat.

abdominal muscles, although not very well), they open up the front of the disk space between vertebrae in your backbone, allowing the gelatinous center of each disk to shift into a different configuration than that which it's used to. At least, such is the logic behind extension exercises.

Whatever the reasons, the approach does work for some people. If you're one of those people, you should learn the techniques from a physical therapist rather than experimenting at home. The key here is *controlled* arching. With all the problems that could be caused by overarching your back, you don't want to run the risk of overarching on purpose.

If I have a weak back, how do I make my back stronger?

By making your stomach muscles stronger. For the most part back muscles are pretty strong. They may be too tight, and stretching them might be in order, but

---

CURL-UPS (CONTINUED)

That's the important thing: your back must be flat, pressed into the floor. As soon as your back begins to arch, and it will when fatigue sets in, then stop. In contrast to sit-ups, during which people do all sorts of things just to keep going—arching their backs, throwing themselves into the exercises, speeding up to be able to finish—curl-ups shouldn't be done if you can't do them correctly. And that means slowly as well as with a flat back. If you do them slowly, you can't cheat. The whole point is to strengthen the stomach muscles to provide better support for your back. Anything other than a pure curl-up brings in other muscles to help out, in which case the exercise won't do as much for your back.

So slow, flat-back curl-ups will do your back a lot of good. Five reps three times a day is a good number to shoot for, but don't be discouraged if you can't do that many at first, or even later. Curl-ups are tough. One is worth at least fifteen sit-ups. If you can do even five at a time you're doing very well. Years ago we tried out curl-ups on a junior national gymnastics team (a number of whom went on to the Olympics). These were some of the best-conditioned athletes in all sports, people who can do

200 conventional sit-ups just like that. *Not one of them could do five curl-ups.* It wasn't that they didn't have muscles. One look at these athletes dispelled that notion because their muscle definition strained belief. It was just that these well-defined muscles weren't functioning as back stabilizers. They were conditioned to do other things. When they were called into play in curl-ups, which condition the stomach muscles to work for your back, they weren't equal to the task. So as virtually all gymnasts have some back pain to contend with, curl-ups work for them as well. A number of gymnastic clubs now incorporate them in their conditioning routines.

You can even use curl-ups on an occasional basis. If your back aches from bending too long over your desk or drafting table, or over the stove or a sawhorse, a few curl-ups on the spot can clear things up. Again, the cardinal rules are: (1) be sure your back is flattened into the floor; (2) do the curl-ups slowly; (3) don't worry about how many you can do—it doesn't matter as long as you do them correctly (if you're doing 200 of these, you're doing them wrong); and (4) when your back starts to arch from fatigue, stop.

because we constantly use them for everything from lifting to bending and twisting to just holding us upright, our back muscles rarely need much extra strengthening. It's the stomach muscles that often aren't doing their job to stabilize your back. Try curl-ups.

What activities are dangerous for my back?

Whenever you can't quite handle an activity, you wind up using your back wrong. It's very interesting—if something's too heavy to lift, you misuse your back lifting it. If your shoulders aren't flexible enough to twist around and hit a serve, your back bends to compensate. If your hip muscles cramp and tilt your pelvis, your back suffers the displacement. If you wrench your knee and limp around too long, eventually your back will go into spasm. If you're not strong enough, you use your back, and if you're not flexible enough, you use your back—never correctly. The poor back takes it in the seat of the pants whenever something's wrong elsewhere.

So, the most dangerous activity for the back is *doing any activity incorrectly.* Get the rest of your body in shape, and your back will stay in shape.

When are my back problems bad enough to go to the doctor?

Three tip-offs you can't ignore:

1. When it hurts so bad you can't sleep. If you don't get a good night's sleep, you'll never get better. You need a window of comfort in the midst of your misery to make any improvement. Often a doctor can provide that.

2. When you've tried the home remedies described in this chapter for a few days and things aren't getting better. Or they're getting worse. That's a tip-off that either your approach is not the right one, or the problem is too difficult to handle on your own.

3. When you experience any of these warning signs: (a) the pain is not just in your back or neck but radiates into other parts of your body; (b) you have numbness or tingling in your arms or legs; (c) you notice sudden weakness in your arms or legs; or (d) coughing, sneezing, or other straining makes the pain worse. See a doctor.

REHAB EXERCISES

Abdominal strengthening exercises for low back strains and pain

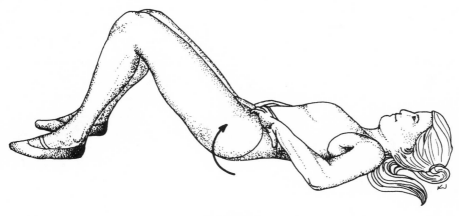

PELVIC TILT

Do this exercise first and hold it while doing curl-ups.

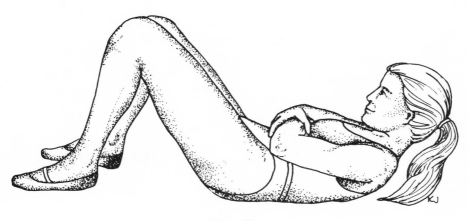

CURL-UPS

Stretching exercises for low back strains and pain

LOW BACK STRETCHES

First do with both legs, then with each individual leg. As with all stretches, hold for thirty seconds.

For strengthening back muscles

These are progressively more strenuous exercises. They *must not* produce any pain or discomfort.

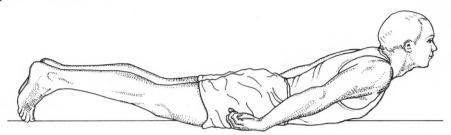

Lie on your stomach and begin a reverse curl-up exercise. Stop part way and hold the position.

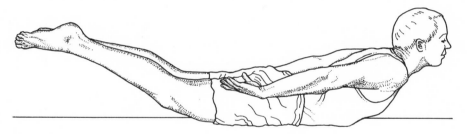

Lying on your stomach, pull your torso and legs into the air. Be careful to make a gentle arch along the entire back instead of jerking upright and bending primarily at the lower back. At first you can do the exercise most easily by keeping your arms at your sides and raising your torso only.

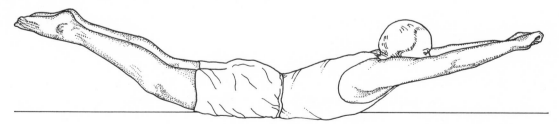

The next step, when you're strong enough, is to raise both torso and legs, still keeping your arms at your sides. The exercise is most difficult when you extend your arms above your head and raise both torso and legs.

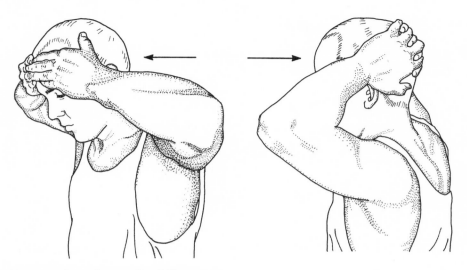

For neck pain and stiffness

Push your head against the resistance of your hand. There are six possible directions: bending your head to the front, the back, and each side, and turning your head to each side. Hold each isometric contraction for five to six seconds.

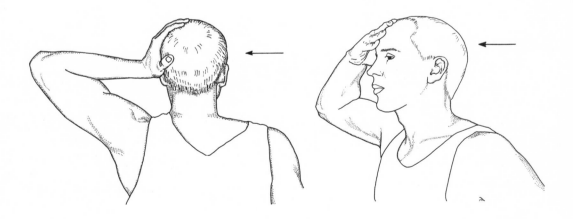

NECK MUSCLE ISOMETRIC STRENGTHENING

CHAPTER EIGHT

The Shoulder

THE SHOULDER is the most flexible joint in the body. We can rotate our arm in a full circle. We can throw a baseball or football, serve a tennis ball, swim the freestyle. We can do a 360-degree rotation on the side horse, lift a ballet partner, scoop a basketball from the floor and dunk it far overhead (a few of us can, anyway). What's more (and absolutely vital to athletics), we can navigate this huge range of motion with power. The shoulder is able to back up its extraordinary mobility with a lot of muscle.

People who hurt their shoulder quickly discover how limited, and frustrating, life can be without a properly functioning shoulder. And not just in athletics. Think of combing your hair, tying your shoelaces, driving your car, brushing your teeth, turning the pages of this book—all the inconsequential daily movements we take for granted—without the freedom and strength provided by the shoulder. Unfortunately, there are many people in this boat. For the trade-off the shoulder makes for all its flexibility is in the realm of stability. The shoulder is at once the most mobile and the least stable of all the joints in the body. And, not only that, what stability it does have is maintained only by constant vigilance on the body's part.

In contrast, the knee is not the most stable joint in the world. As we've seen, it too must make a compromise between flexibility and stability. But what stability it does have is reasonably constant, provided

---

+ WARNING +

If You Experience Any of These Conditions, Seek Medical Help

+ Your shoulder is locked—you can't move it at all or in any specific direction;
+ Shoulder pain is accompanied by numbness or tingling in your arm or hand;
+ Your shoulder looks or feels deformed;
+ You can't raise your arm from your side;
+ Shoulder pain keeps you awake (or awakens you) at night.

by its elaborate network of ligaments, all four of them. The knee joint capsule, too, provides some firmness, as do the muscles and tendons—sometimes they even step in and take over for the ligaments. But the knee is held together primarily by the ligaments, guy wires, which are there first and always to provide support.

The hip, on the other hand, is very stable. If you had no ligaments, muscles, tendons, joint capsule, or anything else surrounding the hip joint, it would still hold together very nicely, thank you. With its ball in its deep cup of a socket, the hip is *mechanically* set up to stay in one piece. It's a simple, direct, efficient design (which is why hip replacements are more effective than those of other joints).

Now, to the shoulder. In its defense we must repeat that neither the hip, nor the knee, nor any other joint comes close to the flexibility the shoulder offers. But not only doesn't the shoulder offer the mechanical stability of a deep ball and socket, not only doesn't it offer the guy wire stability of an elaborate network of ligaments, but it offers no stability at all—except for that provided by the constant interrelated tension of the muscles and tendons crisscrossing this area of the body. If something drastic should happen to these muscles and tendons, some evil sorcerer come and cut them in two, say, your shoulder would simply fall apart. And were your shoulder muscles to completely relax, as they do under anesthesia or in deep sleep, and somebody gave your arm a sharp pull, the joint would come apart.

These are unlikely incidents, of course, evoked here to make a point. But as it is, in real life, the shoulder *does* fall apart—that is, dislocate—more frequently than any other major joint. That injury is common in contact sports. Even more frequent are less dramatic injuries to the muscles and tendons, which must constantly work just to keep things together, even when you're not moving your shoulder. Strains, tendinitis, inflammations of one kind or another, these sneaky kinds of problems often attack the shoulder. And when they do, they can be particularly debilitating because a healthy shoulder is so important in everyday activities, not to mention athletic ones. If your knee is in a splint, you may not be able to run, but you can get around, well enough to function from day to day. But if your shoulder is out of commission, there goes not only the tennis game, the swim, and the run, too (all that jarring is readily transmitted up to the shoulder), but day-to-day tasks as simple and necessary as opening a door, lifting a cup to your mouth, or buttoning your shirt.

Yet the shoulder joint, like the hip, *is* a ball and socket assembly. Why then doesn't it hold together as well as the hip? The answer is that there are balls and

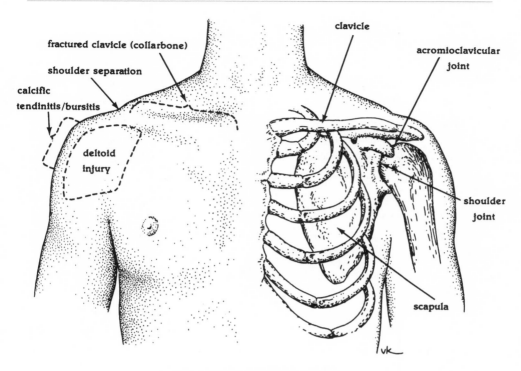

FRONT VIEW OF THE SHOULDER

sockets and balls and sockets. The hip joint is like a tennis ball stuffed into a teacup so firmly that it can turn but not pull free. The shoulder's ball and socket, on the other hand, is more nearly like a racquetball on a silver dollar-sized saucer. The ball is the end of the upper arm bone, the humerus. The saucer is part of your shoulder blade, or scapula. And the ball rests *against*, rather than on, the saucer because the saucer is no more than a vertical depression in the shoulder blade. Besides that, the saucer is much too small and shallow to provide the ball any support, although, at the same time, its very size and shallowness allows the ball to swivel and turn almost without limits. The crux of the design problem is how to secure the ball to the saucer—it's vertical, after all, so gravity hinders rather than helps—and still allow such broad range of motion.

The body's solution is to run muscles and tendons across the joint, as though securing a group of wires to the ball and the edge of the saucer. When the wires are suitably tight, the ball remains in the center of the saucer where it should be. But if any one of the wires should come loose or break or, conversely, tighten too much, the ball tends to move away from the center of the saucer. And the saucer is so small that the ball may even tip off the edge of it.

So, a constant interrelated tension among the muscles and tendons acting as guy wires for the shoulder joint is absolutely essential. Otherwise, the ball will not remain in the center of the socket. It doesn't need to, really, when your arm is hanging to the side. But once you raise your arm and move it through all the loops the shoulder is capable of, the joint will not function effectively if the ball and saucer are not properly aligned. The off-center ball explores new ground, runs into things it should stay clear of. The result: pain.

One of those things the wandering ball may run into is another part of the shoulder, the acromion. A combination of two Greek words meaning "tip of the shoulder," the acromion is just that, a bony shelf that juts up from the shoulder blade to provide a kind of protective roof over the shoulder joint, and which connects to the collarbone, or clavicle, at a small joint called the acromioclavicular—or A-C—joint. (See "Shoulder Separation" later in this chapter.)

And now comes an even more curious tale. First, to backtrack: all other joints are secured to the body by bony attachments. The hip joint is part of the pelvis, which is itself part of the backbone, really. The knee connects to the femur above and the tibia below. The ankle connects the lower leg bones to the bones in the foot. And so it goes, all solid, substantial connections. But in the shoulder, bless it, the only bony attachment to the rest of the body is through a bone, the collarbone, that's not much bigger around than your index finger and connects to the shoulder through a little joint—the A-C joint—about the size of your fingernail. The entire remaining shoulder assembly—the shoulder blade with its bony ridge that includes the acromion, and the ball and saucer shoulder joint itself, and thus your whole arm—is attached to the rest of your body by muscles only. As you move your arm and shoulder, the whole shebang—shoulder joint, shoulder blade, collarbone and all—moves up and down, back and forth along your chest wall.

That makes for super flexibility, but it must be apparent by now that it can also make for problems. If you're not in very good shape, or if some of the individual muscles involved aren't in very good shape, or if the *relationship* among those muscles is out of kilter, then the shoulder can't twist and turn and move and slide as it must if you're going to do all the things you like to do. These can be subtle discrepancies, minor things that by themselves might not even be noticeable but when functioning in concert with the rest of the shoulder's complex interrelationships can throw things decidedly out of tune. And that's not to mention acute incidents, sudden dramatic injuries that can produce the kinds of well-known problems associated with the shoulder like broken collarbones and shoulder dislocations.

So, there's no other place in the body where rehabilitation is as important as in the shoulder. You can brace your knee and tape your ankle or fingers and still function—people do it all the time. Professional athletes often brace and tape themselves for extra support even if they're not injured. But you can't brace your shoulder, not if you want to be able to move it easily. With the shoulder you're stuck with the consequences of injury. As debilitating as injuries in the rest of the body can be, in the shoulder they can *really* change your life. It pays to try to head off these things before they happen by being good to this joint.

OVERUSE SHOULDER PROBLEMS— TIP-OFFS TO TROUBLE

A very nice thing about the shoulder is that usually it gives you ample time to head off problems before they head you off. It'll give you little hints that something is up, and if you act on those hints—slow down, start rehabilitating *before* the problem gets out of control—you can often arrest the process before it gets started. As in other areas of the body, most gradual-onset (that is, overuse) problems are the result of *change*—lifting too much weight, adding too many repetitions, driving too many balls on the range, practicing your serve too long. The muscles holding things together grow tired and stop functioning normally.

And overuse problems can actually arise from underuse. This can happen when, for whatever reason, you fail to use your shoulder in a normal fashion. Having your arm in a sling for an elbow or wrist injury is one example. Another is after surgery on the arm or even the chest (women may develop shoulder problems following breast surgery, either for cancer or cosmetics). A period of even a few weeks of reluctance to move the shoulder—for fear of chest wall pain or of disrupting a surgical incision—is enough to make the shoulder weak enough to be prone to overuse injuries.

The prime indicator of shoulder problems is how you use your shoulder. If, while raising your arms to the side, you hunch your shoulder toward your ear, or tuck it forward toward your chest, or do a bit of both at the same time, then there's almost certainly some problem in the shoulder that you're trying to compensate for. The mechanism works like this:

Usually the first thing that goes when you start having shoulder problems is the ability to bring your arm up from the side comfortably. The shoulder joint itself is only involved in this motion for the first 85 degrees or so—that's all the flexibility you have there. For the remaining 100 degrees or more that your arm can normally navigate, you're dependent on movement from the rest of your shoulder assembly—your shoulder blade slides up a good three or four inches as you continue to raise your arm. You can watch this process unfold in the mirror. Put your hand on top of your shoulder as you raise your arm and feel those relationships. They don't change. Every time you raise your arm, your shoulder girdle, as it's called, will start to move as your arm comes straight out from your body. You can see your shoulder blade, and the rest of the assembly, slide up as you continue to raise your arm.

That is, your shoulder blade *should* start to slide at about the point that your arm is at a right angle to your body. But if something is amiss around the joint itself, something that restricts movement in the ball and saucer, your shoulder girdle will be obliged to start its motion earlier. The result of that premature motion is less shoulder mobility. Because the shoulder girdle has had to move too early, by the time you raise your arm to the point at which your shoulder blade should start sliding, it may already be halfway to your ear. And by the time your arm lifts to the point that would normally cause the shoulder girdle to be halfway to your ear, it may be wedged up against the top of your neck. And that means no more movement. Your arm may only be three quarters of the way to its destination, but that's it. It will go no further.

You can get away with partial shoulder mobility in some activities, but not those in which line is important, such as dance, gymnastics, and figure skating. There it's important to keep the shoulders relaxed and down. Any hunching at all is immediately apparent. Not only does it look bad, destroying your form, but it reduces arm movement and can throw your head out of line.

So early movement of the shoulder girdle is a tip-off that there may be an injury around the joint area. And soon the injury may become so ingrained that you start carrying your shoulder hunched up all the time. You won't need to raise your arm to discover the problem. A quick peek in the mirror will suffice.

Another warning sign can be the habit of rolling your bad shoulder to the front, kind of tucking it into your chest. The muscles in the front of your shoulder are stronger than those in the back—look at the difference in size between the chest muscles and those that surround the shoulder blade in the back. Weight lifters walk around with their shoulders rolled forward and in because their chest muscles, strong to begin with, have become even stronger through training and pull the shoulder forward. You may not be a weight lifter, but if there's an imbalance between your chest and back muscles—and there often is—the chest muscles can become overly tight and pull your shoulder forward.

Again, a quick look in the mirror can tell you a lot. The key is to compare one side with the other. An injured shoulder not only has a tendency to hunch up, it rolls in and forward as well. And, of course, it goes without saying that sooner or later these tip-offs will be accompanied by pain. If you're like most people and don't make it a practice to conduct regular exploratory examinations of yourself, then it's likely that you won't look for tip-offs until pain and stiffness finally motivate you. By then the tip-offs are largely superfluous. You've got a shoulder problem.

✚ What to do about it ✚ The first thing is to get rid of the pain. Don't make the mistake that many of us make all the time, that of deciding that whatever it is that's bothering you will surely go away by itself. And then the next day, when it's still there, you decide that just one more day will clear it up, and so on and so on. Until a couple of weeks or a month later it's no longer just a minor ache, it's a major injury. Attend to shoulder problems promptly. If you're hurting for a couple of days in a row, come to grips with it. Knock off whatever it is that's bothering you until your shoulder is again comfortable. Just doing that, and the exercises we're about to suggest, may be all you need.

If you let things go on too long, the plot thickens. Then knocking off for a while may bring you some comfort, but when you go back to your activity it'll take less to bring back the symptoms than it did to develop them in the first place. Because by now your shoulder won't be in as good shape as it was in the first place. The muscles will have weakened and lost the ability to work together efficiently during the weeks you compensated for the pain (and misused your shoulder) to be able to continue playing.

Now it may not be so easy to get rid of the pain, either. You may find that what was once restricted to a particular activity now shows up almost all the time. Everything you do hurts. To try and escape the pain, you use your shoulder abnormally all day. That's no good, not only for comfort's sake, but for your ability to get rid of the problem. It's hard enough to rehabilitate other places in your body when you're hurting—it's almost impossible with the shoulder. If everything you do is going to hurt, including rehabilitation exercises, you'll continue to use your shoulder abnormally even when you do the exercises. And that'll nullify any gains you get from rehabilitation. So, it's important to pay attention to shoulder problems right away.

Again, the first step is to stop doing the things that hurt. Sometimes, especially if the problem is well along, that means doing absolutely nothing that involves your shoulder. That can be pretty hard to manage unless you put your arm in a sling. As cumbersome as that might be, it can be worth it. It's not that a sling will absolutely immobilize your shoulder—nothing will do that but a body cast almost—but it'll force you to think about what you're doing. Instead of automatically shooting out your arm to open a door, or shake hands, or reach for the check, you'll have to think twice and use the other arm. Anti-inflammatory drugs can help during this period as well. Just don't cheat on yourself. Let the shoulder rest.

The next order of business is to rebalance and restrengthen the shoulder muscles. It can be hard to pinpoint, but the likelihood is that the crucial interrelated tension among the muscles in your shoulder has been thrown out of whack. When these muscles don't work well, your shoulder doesn't work well. Without the consistent tension of these guy wires, the ball in your shoulder joint may no longer be centered in the saucer. When you move your arm, the ball rolls around and bumps into things it shouldn't. (Interestingly, if you use a weight or rehabilitation machine, something that forces your shoulder to stay in a perfect arc of motion, you may have no pain at all. It's just when you leave it to the muscles themselves to balance things, and they're not working right, that you have troubles.)

It used to be that people did surgery to correct this problem, going into the shoulder and taking off part of the acromion, the bony shelf above the joint, to provide more room. But in most instances you really don't need to that. It's possible to reseat the joint through exercise therapy rather than surgery—a great boon to everyone.

So, you've rested the shoulder and finally gotten to the point where you're free from pain. Now it's time to retune everything so you'll be able to stay that way.

Here is a series of four exercises. They're to be done without weights or resistance, simply by utilizing the weight of your arm. By the time you do all of them, you will have run through the entire range of motion of the shoulder, and, if you do them as often as we recommend, you'll not only begin to restrengthen and balance the muscles but to develop endurance. They're awfully good exercises, and most likely will do the trick. All they demand from you is perseverance.

1. Bend over at the waist and let the arm on your injured side hang in front of you. Then start swinging it in a clockwise motion. Not too hard or too

fast. Use just enough muscle to kick your arm in motion and keep it swinging lazily.

At first you may only be able to bend over a little bit. That's okay. Continue to circle clockwise, then counterclockwise, bending over farther and farther as you go, until your torso is at right angles, parallel to the ground. The key here is: *don't do anything that hurts*. If it hurts to bend too far, don't bend too far. If it hurts to swing in a circle, don't. You may have to make an ellipse, or an egg shape, or some other figure that feels all right. Then gradually work toward a complete circle, both clockwise and counterclockwise.

2. Stand up straight. Pretend that you're on one end of a double-handled saw and start sawing. Back and forth, in and out, way out and way back. As with all these exercises, the more repetitions you do, the more your range of motion will increase. You're stretching at the same time as you're strengthening. (And the exercise also puts your elbow through a complete range of motion.)

3. Let your arm fall straight down to your side. Then raise your arm up and to the side at right angles to your body and let it back down, up and down, as though you're slowly flapping an injured wing. These are called abduction swings.

    Raise your arm only to a comfortable level. Even if you can only bring it up a foot or two from your side to start with, keep at it. As you continue, you'll become more flexible. And if it hurts too much to swing your arm up at all, start out by bending your elbow to form a chicken wing. Then flap it up as far as is comfortable. After you develop flexibility that way, gradually straighten out.

4. Last but not least, shrug your shoulders. That's all, just shrug your shoulders and while at the top of the shrug pull your shoulders back and your shoulder blades together as though you're trying to squeeze a tennis ball between them.

Nothing to it, right? If you're having a fair amount of shoulder trouble, start out by doing the exercises ten times each, twice a day—in the morning and evening, say. And increase as you grow stronger and more flexible. What you're shooting toward is 50 of each exercise, three times a day. That's 750 reps. When you start doing that many, these deceptively easy exercises turn into quite a workout. Don't worry if you work up to about 35 and figure you must have lost count because nothing so easy could be so difficult. Only pretty good athletes can do that many reps readily. Use that number as a goal, a motivator—although getting rid of your shoulder problem should be motivation enough.

A week to ten days of these exercises is probably enough. You may find that you can go back to your activity, always taking it easy, of course, working into it a little at a time. But if you go back and find that your shoulder still bothers you, it's time for special exercise therapy to deal with the specific muscles involved. And for this you should see a doctor or physical therapist. You have to do these more specialized exercises against resistance, in very specific positions, in order to isolate one muscle or another. They're best taught in person. You'll find, though, that at the very least these general exercises will tone and strengthen your shoulder. They'll make you use everything and use it right.

To give credit where credit is due, these exercises were developed by Robert Kerlan, a Los Angeles orthopedic surgeon who for years probably took care of more baseball players than anybody else has. He used the exercises as part of a rehabilitation program for pitchers. But they're so good, they'll work for anybody. And you can use them as a general toning procedure, a preventive regimen that you can perform anytime. Of course, these exercises can be boring, and people don't like to do boring things, especially such simple boring things. They'd rather do boring things on a complicated machine. But at the onset no machine is going to do you any more good than these simple exercises. Save your money and start circling, sawing, and flapping. Later, to really build more muscle, weights or machines will often be necessary—something you can undertake at almost any fitness club or weight room.

RHOMBOID STRAINS

Now to more specific injuries. There are a couple of strains that recur with some frequency in the shoulder and are easy to diagnose. One of those is a rhomboid strain. The rhomboids are muscles in the center of your back that attach the edge of your shoulder blade to your spine. They help to pull the shoulder blade upward and toward the spine. (See the illustration on p. 164, chapter 7, to pinpoint the location of a rhomboid strain.) People sometimes complain of back pain when the culprit is really the rhomboid. The muscle will go into spasm, producing little knots. You can feel them—hard, painful spots in the center of your back. And because your shoulder blade no longer can move much, you'll have a tough time doing things like raising your arm.

Modern technology has helped make problems such as this even more common. Working on a keyboard, for example, pulls your shoulders forward (especially if your workstation isn't properly set up) and stretches your rhomboids. This is part of the reason for the nagging upper back pain that often accompanies a day in front of the computer.

✚ **What to do about it** ✚ As always with muscle strains, the strategy is to rest the muscle, stretch it out, and restrengthen it. Since the rhomboid muscles pull your shoulder blades together, the best way to stretch them is by forcing the shoulder blades apart. Simply hug yourself. Reach around to your back with both arms, grasp hold of the shoulder blades, and stretch. It's a good way to relieve the pain. Another way is to grab the arm on the side of the body that hurts and pull it across your body with your other arm. Pull it high, middle, or low, depending on where you feel the stretch the most.

A good way to strengthen the rhomboids is by reversing the stretching motion (as everywhere in the body, the motions of stretching and strengthening are the reverse of one another). While leaning forward at the waist, pull your shoulder blades together. You can start by folding your arms like chicken wings and flap backwards. Then, as your strength and range of motion improve, straighten out your arms, thereby increasing their weight, and pull your shoulder blades together. Doing the exercises bent over at the waist enlists gravity as an aid, making your arms heavier, and thus further strengthening the muscle. Make sure you're not pulling your *arms* back, just your shoulder blades. Think again of squeezing that tennis ball between your shoulder blades.

TRAPEZIUS STRAINS

The other recurrent shoulder strain is that of the trapezius muscle. The trapezius is a huge flat, triangular muscle that reaches almost from the base of your skull out to your shoulder, and then down to the middle of your back at the belt line. The top part of it forms the web that descends from the side of your neck to your shoulder. It moves your neck from side to side and helps move the shoulder blade as well. (Again, see the illustration on p. 164, chapter 7.)

It's this double duty that accounts for many trapezius strains. For example, let's say your shoulder bothers you. Your body's natural inclination is to try to protect it. How? By tucking it forward, out of harm's way. What muscle do you use to do that? The trapezius. But because the top part of that muscle is attached to your neck, the motion affects the neck, too. And as the trapezius struggles to keep your shoulder tucked in, little by little you may find that your neck doesn't work very well. In time it may hurt more than the shoulder did in the first place. All this because another muscle (or tendon, or joint) acted up and the trapezius tried to make things better.

✛ What to do about it ✛ Again, rest, stretch, and strengthen. When you've stopped doing whatever it is that hurts long enough so that you're comfortable again, start gentle stretching. A good way to stretch the upper trapezius is to bend your neck away and a little bit forward from the side that hurts. Long, slow stretches will unknot the muscle.

Then strengthen. Shoulder shrugs will strengthen the upper part of the trapezius, because it's that part of the muscle that shrugs you. The lower trapezius is more difficult to strengthen, but it's not as frequently injured. If the shrugs don't seem to help, then it might be a good idea to see a doctor. In fact, it's a good idea to have a pretty solid idea of what's happening with injuries such as these, and as often as not the person to see for that is a physical therapist. A therapist knows how to do very discrete muscle testing and will be able to show you sharp, discrete muscle-strengthening techniques.

BURSITIS

Yes, this shows up in the shoulder too, as there's a large bursa between the acromion and the joint. But rarely does it appear in athletes. For years almost everything that hurt on the outside of the shoulder was called bursitis, but most likely these were other things—tendinitis or muscle strains.

✛ What to do about it ✛ If your shoulder hurts on the outside, rest it until the pain is gone then try the circling-shrugging exercises we've discussed. More likely than not the pain will stay away. If not, see a doctor. If bursitis is truly the problem, a shot of cortisone may help a lot.

CALCIFIC TENDINITIS

Sometimes a bizarre thing happens with shoulder tendinitis. Besides the tendons becoming inflamed and irritated, the body deposits calcium in the injured area, so much calcium that you can see it in x-rays. It looks just like bone, and that's disturbing to see in a spot where there shouldn't be any. (When you operate you find it's much like toothpaste in consistency and color.) The body's reaction to these calcium deposits is predictable: it wants to get that foreign stuff out of there. So the area becomes even more inflamed, which causes it to lay down more calcium, which causes more inflammation, and so it goes. It can turn into a bad situation, with reduced movement in your shoulder and much pain. In fact, it can be one of the most painful injuries possible, in the same league with passing a kidney stone. Often even drugs won't help.

✛ **What to do about it** ✛ Like true bursitis, calcific tendinitis is frequently treated with cortisone injections. Successfully, too, as the cortisone stops the inflammation, which in turn stops the calcium deposits. Sometimes the body will then absorb the calcium, sometimes not. If not, or if the inflammation just won't quit, surgery can be the answer.

But sometimes people with large amounts of calcium deposits don't even know they're there. You may x-ray their shoulder for other reasons, and, lo and behold, the calcium shows up. The real problem is not the calcium itself but the tendinitis that causes it to deposit. Calcific tendinitis is more than anything a visible evidence of chronic tendinitis. Nobody quite knows why the calcium forms, but we do know why people get tendinitis: overuse and abuse of the joint. So although a shot of cortisone may get rid of the immediate problem, it won't prevent the calcium from forming again. The only thing that'll do that is getting rid of the tendinitis, and the only thing that'll do *that* is the kind of rehab program we've been talking about. Try the exercises. If the problem persists, see a doctor. Just be careful not to confuse temporary relief with a long-term solution.

THORACIC OUTLET SYNDROME

As with anyplace else in the body, *if you have numbness, tingling, or weakness in your shoulder or down your arm, you should always see a doctor.* Those are the symptoms of problems involving nerves, which in one way or another lead back to the spinal column, and you never want to risk serious injury in the spine.

In this case, despite the name of the injury, the problem begins in the cervical spine, the seven vertebrae in the neck. All the nerves to your arm come from the top part of this portion of the backbone, exiting the base of your neck (thus thoracic "outlet" syndrome) to form big trunks of nerves deep in the armpit. From there the nerves run down your arm and do all the things that nerves are supposed to do. Along the way from the spine to the arm, the nerves go over and around a lot of muscles. As with piriformis syndrome in the hip and thigh, if any of these muscles are injured, in spasm, or if you just hold your shoulder in an abnormal position, you can stretch and pinch the nerves. The result: pain, but not necessarily pain in the shoulder.

Nerves are interesting. If you hit a nerve in your elbow—that is, your crazy bone—you don't just feel it there, you feel it in your fingers although you haven't done a thing to them. The same is true with your shoulder. If you irritate a nerve in your shoulder, you may feel the pain in your elbow. Sometimes what people think is tennis elbow is really a result of thoracic outlet syndrome. If you stretch your neck in a certain way and your thumb starts tingling, it may not be your thumb that's causing the problem. If every time you reach over the back seat your fingers hurt, it may not be the fault of your fingers.

✚ What to do about it ✚ See a doctor. Although the culprit may be a stretched nerve in your shoulder, it could be anything, even a disk problem. You want to be sure just what the injury is. If it is thoracic outlet syndrome, then stretching and strengthening the muscles involved may be the ticket. Again, it's important to find out just what the problem is.

CONTUSIONS

Contusions—direct blows—usually occur in contact sports. Football, wrestling, lacrosse, and soccer can all produce a contused shoulder, as can such accidents as skiing into a barrier or colliding against a stage set or another dancer. A contusion can be a painful injury, but in and of itself it's rarely serious. The reason is that contusions almost always affect the deltoid, the big muscle that caps your shoulder, and the only one that you can see reasonably well. It's the muscle that bulges impressively in bodybuilders, that fills out the shoulders of tight T-shirts. But its very visibility is also the cross the deltoid must bear. The other muscles and tendons in the shoulder either lie sheltered beneath the deltoid or cluster in front and in back of the shoulder blade. So when a blow is on the way, it's the deltoid's lot in life to receive it.

The deltoid is the unsophisticated hulk of the shoulder. The muscles beneath it, the rotator cuff muscles, are the fine-tuners. The deltoid is responsible for doing most of the gross work, but the rotator cuff muscles hold the joint in the right position, balancing things so that work can be done. It's more critical if these smaller muscles are injured by the blow, but almost always they're not—thanks to the sheltering deltoid.

Since the deltoid only spans one joint, it rarely tears from the force of the blow. (Remember that muscles that span one joint, like the deltoid, are less likely to tear than muscles that span two joints, such as the biceps. More on that soon.) But like muscles anywhere it will go into spasm, which means that soon you won't be able to use your shoulder properly. Thus starts another of the body's seemingly endless number of vicious cycles, and the reason why although contusions usually aren't serious in themselves they can lay the groundwork for lots of other problems.

Your shoulder hurts, and you can't raise your arm. So you start enlisting other muscles to do what the battered deltoid is no longer able to do. You start moving your shoulder blade too early, say, and learn all sorts of other ways of cheating to keep your shoulder functioning. That may be okay temporarily, but once the shoulder learns how to cheat, it won't stop even when the original injury heals. One of the real problems with tennis and baseball players, and football quarterbacks, too, is that once the injury heals they continue to throw or serve as though their shoulder were still hurt. It may have been the only way they could function during the injury, but now it's an inefficient way. And, more than that, it can be a harmful way, because misusing the muscles can lead to other problems.

In effect your body has said to these muscles, "Stop doing what you usually do, I have a new job for you. The muscle that usually does this job isn't working very well. I want you to take over." But your shoulder is designed in such a way that muscles do their original tasks best. Once new muscles step into situations they're not designed for, they more easily get injured. Or, because your shoulder now hurts, the muscles surrounding it, like the trapezius, find themselves asked to hold your shoulder in ways they're not used to—all hunched up, say, to reduce the pain—and they themselves might start hurting. Often people go to the doctor complaining of neck or back pain, and the real culprit is the shoulder. These can be tough problems to handle, because you have to work backwards to the source. And it can be hard to set up rehab programs to cover such a multitude of sins.

So the real danger of a contusion is the far-flung problems it can set into play. That's why it's not a good idea to ignore the injury.

✚ **What to do about it** ✚ It's important to get on contusions right away by stretching out the injured muscle. The circle-shrug exercise regime (described earlier) is a good way of stretching and strengthening any of the muscles in the shoulder. For more specific rehab exercises, you'll have to see a physician or physical therapist. But it may be difficult to find someone who will offer you the time and expertise you need. Many doctors can provide cortisone shots, anti-inflammatory medications, and even surgery for shoulder injuries, but few as readily give good rehab advice. Unless you see a doctor who is used to taking care of athletes, information on what to do about your shoulder over the long term can be hard to come by. And that's too bad, for, as we've seen, the shoulder is one area in which the healthy interrelationship of muscles is crucial. But as far as the importance of muscle functioning and rehabilitation is concerned, knowledge about the shoulder is probably about a decade behind that of the knee. The upshot can be shoulder problems that don't go away for a long, long time.

So, it's very important to keep the shoulder healthy and to rehabilitate it as quickly and efficiently as possible after an injury like a contusion. We've offered some suggestions as to how. It's a good idea to see a doctor who regularly takes care of athletes to find out more.

BROKEN COLLARBONE

Probably the most common accident involving the shoulder is falling on your outstretched arm. And the most common result of that is a broken collarbone. The collarbone is the single most frequently fractured bone in young people. And that's not just from athletics, but as a result of play—falling out of a tree or the upper bunk bed, or racing down the sidewalk, tripping, and reaching to break the fall.

The collarbone, or clavicle, is the only bony link between your shoulder and the rest of you. If you cut all the muscles away from your shoulder, the only thing left connecting it to your body would be the collarbone. As a result, any stress on the arm and shoulder is transmitted to the rest of your body through the collarbone. So if you're skating, say, and you stumble and reach out to break your fall, the force of the impact, fueled by the weight of your entire body, goes right up your arm, through your shoulder to the collarbone, and, finally, to the spot where the collarbone attaches to the rest of the body—your breastbone, or sternum. Except that often the force doesn't reach all the way to the sternum. The collarbone, the weak link in the chain, so slender it's hardly thicker than your finger, breaks first.

You'll know it when it happens. It hurts like crazy when you touch the end of the fracture, which is almost always in the middle third of the bone, and the whole area becomes tender. Soon it'll swell, and you'll have trouble moving your shoulder at all.

✚ **What to do about it** ✚ Applying ice may help reduce swelling, but there's little else to do except see a doctor. The bone must be set right for it to heal right. People usually set the break the same way it was done years ago, in a figure-eight dressing that pulls your shoulders back and puts some traction on the fracture. We've recently discovered, however, that most patients don't use their figure-eight braces after a few weeks, once they've become more comfortable. Consistent use of the brace may well reduce the ultimate deformity of the clavicle, but the vast majority of breaks heal even if the brace is discarded in a few weeks. Almost all broken collarbones heal, and they all heal with a bump.

Collarbone fractures are something like rib fractures that way—they rarely need any kind of surgical intervention. If your collarbone line is important to you, you might as well get used to the fact that a fracture will produce a lump, although it probably will get smaller over time. But there's little to do about it. Surgery may not decrease the size of the lump, and it will give you a scar over the spot. And it's a bad place to operate, especially in women, as the weight of the breast stretches the skin, causing the scar to spread.

SHOULDER SEPARATION

The joint that connects the collarbone to the shoulder is called the acromioclavicular joint—"acromio" for acromion, the bony ridge of the shoulder blade, "clavicular" for clavicle. You can feel it. With your fingers just follow your collarbone toward the shoulder—the little bump just before the end is the joint. It's tiny, only about the size of your fingernail, but well tethered by ligaments. Still, it's so small that falling onto the tip of your shoulder can sometimes push the joint apart, separating the collarbone from the shoulder. By a ratio of ten to one, it's a male sports injury. Wrestling, football, lacrosse, hockey—anytime a person's shoulder is driven into the ground or he falls on the outstretched hand, the shoulder can separate. As with a broken collarbone, the force travels up the arm to the joint.

Usually a shoulder separation is either bad or not so bad, with little in between. You may tear out the whole A-C joint, completely separate the collarbone from the shoulder, or just partially tear the ligaments. In the case of a complete separation, the collarbone, no longer tethered to the shoulder, can stick up as much as an inch. If the tear is minor, the lump will be less severe. In either case, it hurts, especially when you try to lift your arm above your head or bring it across the front of your body. And if you press on the A-C joint itself, look out.

✛ **What to do about it** ✛ In the case of complete separations, the strategy is obvious: see a doctor right away. But the minor varieties can be deceiving. Although the injury is painful at first, it soon gets better and can be easy to forget. But a quarter of the people with minor separations still suffer discomfort as late as five years later, especially when doing things that carry the arm across the body, like throwing a ball or setting up for a backhand shot. The motion pushes together the sides of the joint, which has degenerated over the years, causing the bones to rub against one another and hurt. And what's really a minor disability can lead to other problems because, as elsewhere, your body tries to compensate for the pain by enlisting muscles and tendons to do jobs they're not supposed to do. They can then become irritated and inflamed, which leads to more discomfort, which leads to . . . . And so it goes.

So it may be worthwhile to see a doctor if you even suspect the possibility of a separation no matter how slight. It used to be that many separations were treated with surgery designed to tether the clavicle back where it belonged. Recently we're finding that many of these injuries heal adequately on their own—usually with the bump remaining on the top of the shoulder. So a doctor may simply put your arm in a sling until it's comfortable, then lead you through a rehab program and wait and see what happens.

If the A-C joint should remain painful, surgery might be in order. The outer end of the clavicle, just the last half-inch or so, can be removed with little or no loss of strength or function. You can go back to almost any activity without the end of your collarbone, and your shoulder looks better without the lump that would be there if the bone remained.

(Recently we've been seeing more and more patients with arthritis of the A-C joint. Sometimes it's the result of an old minor sprain or partial separation. It even may be the consequence of intensive weight-training programs. Many times patients with degenerative arthritis of the A-C joint can't recall any injury. The nagging pain, often not severe enough to merit a doctor's visit, can result in improper shoulder use. And the result of improper use, as we've seen so many times in this book, can be tendinitis or other problems that exacerbate the original injury.)

DISLOCATIONS

Back to the old ball and saucer, the shoulder joint itself. And back to the theme of this chapter: there's no such thing as a free lunch. The shoulder enjoys nearly unlimited flexibility, but what it must sacrifice for that is stability. And there's no better evidence for this lack of stability than the fact that of all the major joints in the body, not one of them dislocates as frequently as the shoulder.

The causes are many and varied. Wrestling can wrench your arm out of the shoulder socket. So can arm tackling in football, catching a ski pole in the ground, or leading a horse that suddenly rears back. We recently saw a fellow who dislocated his shoulder when all of him except his arm fell through the hatch of a sailboat. But the most common cause is falling on your outstretched arm. If you fall just right (or just wrong), you can squirt the ball of the shoulder joint away from the saucer. It doesn't take much.

Again, the reason is that the shoulder joint is held together not by a securely fitting ball and socket, nor by stiff, reliable ligaments, but by the constant inter-related tension of the muscles and tendons around the joint. We just don't real-ize how protective of our shoulder we are, all the time. Just relax completely for an instant, and the shoulder will dislocate a bit (that is, sublex) all by itself, sim-ply from the weight of your hanging arm. After shoulder injuries, when the mus-cles are really weak, people often walk around with their shoulder hunched up to their ear, because they can sense that if they relaxed, their shoulder would slide out. And it would, maybe as far as a half an inch. Combine that natural insta-bility with an outside force, and it's easy to see why shoulder dislocations are so common.

You'll know, immediately, that something has happened to your shoulder that you never want to happen again. The shoulder muscles go into spasm, and any motion of your arm hurts. You have a tendency to hold your shoulder close to your body for protection. And the most telling sign is that you lose the ability to rotate your arm. Other injuries may cause you to hold your arm close, but noth-ing but a dislocation or fracture will take away your ability to rotate it. The area may appear swollen and become tender. Nothing feels right, neither straighten-ing up, nor crouching down. There's a strong sense that something is badly out of alignment.

✛ What to do about it ✛ See a doctor. The first thing that he or she will do is relocate, or reduce, the dislocated joint. Any other treatment comes later.

Most likely you'll never need to know how to reduce a dislocation by your-self, as most people are within reasonable reach of a doctor's office or emergency room. But what if you're on a camping trip, say, miles from any doctor? In that case reducing the injury can be vitally important. There are a number of ways to do it. Here's one that's both effective and safe: clasp the fingers of both hands in

+ Swimming +

Swimming is the country's most popular athletic activity by far. From jumpers and splashers, to competitors of all ages, to rough-water swimmers, or people rehabilitating injuries, the water offers an environment that is at once refreshing, supportive (no gravity to fight against), and safe—once you learn to swim, that is.

But don't ask competitive swimmers about the joys of their sport. They're too busy to answer you—busy staggering around trying to catch up with homework, meals, and sleep. Too busy trying to keep up with a regimen more tyrannical than that of almost any other activity. We're talking up to five hours a day of virtually nonstop stroking and kicking and gliding and turning. For what? For the privilege of racing a few minutes once or twice a month. For the ability to swim 50 to 400 yards flat out (there are longer races, of course, up to 1,500 yards, but the bulk of competitive swimmers don't swim those). Nowhere else in sports is the contrast between performance demands and training methods more drastic.

Yet swimmers carry on this way, day in and day out, year in and year out. No wonder so many of them burn out, and no wonder so many have shoulder problems. It may be that well over half of all serious swimmers have had shoulder problems at some time or another. They're mostly overuse injuries—tendinitis, inflammation, rotator cuff tears, a condition called "swimmer's shoulder"—and they probably result from the length and frequency of workouts. Whereas in most sports, overuse injuries usually come from some kind of change—new shoes, new

front of you (*if* you can get the hand on the dislocated side in front of you—it can take some doing), then pull your knee up to your chest and grasp it, and just relax. Let the weight of your leg stretch your arm away from your body. It may seem that that's the wrong direction, but you have to remember that when your shoulder dislocated, the muscles went into spasm. Now they're actually holding the joint apart. You've got to stretch out those muscles. When you do, in most instances the joint will pop back together.

Old hands at dislocations learn such tricks. And there are old hands because for years one dislocation meant that there was between a 75 percent and 90 percent chance that you would have others. Doctors were so convinced that one dislocation was the prelude to many that they went ahead and operated on athletes as young as teenagers, hoping that surgical reconstruction would keep the joint in place. However, a doctor named John Aronen has cast doubt on that approach. He took a group of U.S. Naval Academy midshipmen with shoulder dislocations, immobilized their shoulders for about three weeks in a sling and bandages, then started them on a couple months' program of combined strengthening and stretching. Then he sent the men back to their normal activities, which included demanding physical conditioning and sports. After three years, when according to previous records most of the recurrences should have occurred, only 25 percent of these men suffered new dislocations.

So, there is hope. But once a dislocation does recur, all bets are off. Then the likelihood of recurrences gets high again.

The moral to the story is that it's important to find a doctor who knows about these things and will set up and supervise a really good rehab program.

This is one situation in which you don't want to do it yourself. Dislocations don't have to recur, and they don't have to be treated surgically. If someone tells you they do, get a second opinion.

SHOULDER SUBLUXATION

A subluxation no more than a minor dislocation. Pop, it's out; pop, it's back in—all by itself. Your shoulder hurts for a moment, then feels pretty much as before. Then within hours the pain returns, and soon it's hard to move the shoulder. The causes are similar to those of dislocations.

✚ What to do about it ✚ See a doctor who knows how to rehabilitate such injuries. Like dislocations, subluxations can be difficult to handle, with high recurrence rates (but probably a much lower recurrence rate if you rehabilitate well). The treatment is exactly the same as that for dislocations, even though the joint doesn't slide out as far: immobilize it, then rehabilitate.

Because the injury doesn't seem as bad, it's a temptation to ease off the rehab program. Don't. It can mean the difference between suffering or escaping an endless round of recurrent subluxations.

ROTATOR CUFF TEARS

The *rotator cuff* is much in the sports news these days. Baseball pitchers who a few years ago would have been described as having sore shoulders now suffer from injuries of the rotator cuff—whatever that is. Well, it's a cuff of four tendons that, like a hood, cover the shoulder joint. They're connected to muscles, none of which you can see, that attach at one end to the shoulder blade and at the other to a little ridge around the upper arm bone, the humerus, just below the ball portion.

SWIMMING (CONTINUED)

track, new racquet, new training regimen, new floor, new teacher—in swimming they come from simply wearing out the shoulder joint.

The only way to treat such injuries is to drop down to a level of activity that no longer hurts, give the joint some rest (continue working out by changing to a stroke that doesn't cause symptoms, while avoiding high-impact turns), and carefully begin to stretch and strengthen the muscles involved.

In an effort to manage swimming injuries, just about everything else has been investigated except the length of the workout itself. Perhaps coaches should lean more toward the quality of the workout rather than the quantity. Toward more stroke work and less yardage. More tapering and less building up. Swimming fresh rather than tired. Taking time off rather than increasing time on. In any case, as far as preventing injuries is concerned, it's just about the only thing left to try.

That, and taking a look at stretching. Swimmers are great ones for stretching, maybe as a result of the notion that swimmers need long, flexible muscles. And not only do they stretch themselves before workouts and meets, they stretch each other. A common sight is one swimmer twisting and extending the arms of another. But swimmers never use these extremes of flexibility in the water. There's no stroke that demands that kind of range of motion. The stretching serves no functional purpose. Still, swimmers do it anyway, with the result that they often injure themselves by stretching before they even jump in the water.

These are the muscles that rotate your arm—thus, rotator cuff—and that keep your joint stable. They keep the ball centered in the saucer when you move your arm, stabilizing the fulcrum that allows the other muscles to do what they're supposed to do.

With any kind of violent movement you can tear the rotator cuff, but most of these injuries are attritional things. Anytime your arm is in an upright position, the tendons may rub against the shoulder blade, causing minute tearing and inflammation. The more your arm is overhead—pitchers, quarterbacks, and tennis players come to mind, but perhaps none so much as swimmers—the more wear. But you don't need to be an athlete to have rotator cuff problems. Everyday activities will do just fine. A startling statistic is that more than half of everyone over fifty years of age has rotator cuff tears. In people over seventy, the rate is up to over 70 percent. It seems to be one of those realities of life that most of us can look forward to if, indeed, we haven't experienced it already. Happily, however, most of us will never know we have this type of damage.

The tip-off is pain in or on the side of the shoulder, especially when you raise your arm above shoulder level. In the worst cases you lose the ability even to bring your arm up from your side. But most people handle rotator cuff tears without too much difficulty. Just another thing to adjust to as we age.

+ What to do about it + The circle-shrug exercises we discussed earlier can do you a lot of good here. But if the pain is really severe, you should see a doctor. Sometimes rotator cuff tears are treated surgically. A professional athlete may find it the only recourse, but recreational athletes should be wary of surgery. The likelihood of a big-league pitcher coming back after a rotator cuff repair is not high at all. And that's somebody who has a lot of time to devote to rehab and is dealing with people who really know their stuff. It may be that for most of us, unless it's a large tear with a lot of disability, a strong and specific strengthening and stretching program will do the most good.

RUPTURED BICEPS

It's about the only muscle in the shoulder that frequently ruptures, and this usually occurs in older people. Often the injury is not connected with an athletic activity at all. You'll be lifting or moving something—the refrigerator, the piano—and all of a sudden you feel a pop. It's not particularly painful or disabling, but when you look down at your arm your biceps bulges like Popeye's after he's eaten a can of spinach.

What happens is that part of the biceps snaps off the shoulder and rolls down into your arm like one of those party favors that coils back when you stop blowing into it. Two parts of the biceps connect to the shoulder: the short head, in which the muscle itself ascends high into the shoulder and attaches to the front of the shoulder blade with the help of a short tendon, and the long head, in which the muscle ends below the shoulder and relies on a long, snaky tendon to go up the rest of the way through the joint. It's that long tendon that ruptures and causes the sudden bulge. The rest of the muscle stays in place, but your arm looks like Popeye's.

✛ What to do about it ✛ There isn't much you can do about it. No one can put the tendon back where it was. If someone does operate, the idea is to tether the tendon into the humerus and let it go at that. But often the same thing happens naturally—the ruptured tendon simply connects to the bone by itself.

Then it's just a matter of letting the dust settle and gradually getting back to your activity. The body uses the half of the biceps that's still attached and recruits the other muscles that bend your elbow to do more than their share of the work. The result may be less efficiency than before, but we don't use our biceps for that much anyway. If you can tolerate a lumpy muscle, in time you may forget that you injured it. You can go back to tennis, swimming, a reasonable level of weight lifting—almost any activity—with a ruptured biceps. But you'll always look like Popeye.

(Interestingly, the biceps tendon is often inflamed along with rotator cuff tendinitis, but when this tendon ruptures, much of the shoulder pain disappears. So some good may come even from a ruptured tendon.)

PECTORAL TEAR

The big muscle on the front of the chest that forms the fold over the front of the armpit is called the pectoralis major (to differentiate it from the pectoralis minor, which lies above it). This is the muscle that allows you to draw your arm across your chest. It can tear, usually in weight lifters, sometimes in gymnasts, causing real pain and disability. Just as a torn biceps snaps back to form a sharp bulge, so does a torn pec. If your pain is accompanied by a big knot on one side of your chest, there's a good chance you've torn a pec.

✛ What to do about it ✛ See a doctor. It's not a common injury, but it can be serious enough to require surgery.

COMMONLY ASKED QUESTIONS ABOUT SHOULDER INJURIES

If I dislocate my shoulder, do I need an operation?

Maybe not. It all depends on what you do following your dislocation. A really good rehabilitation program is the key. Make sure that whoever treats the dislocation sets you up with a physical therapist who can give you thorough, specific rehab instructions. And make sure that you follow them faithfully—especially with a first dislocation. Once this injury recurs, the more likely it is to continue to recur. And the more often it recurs, the more likely that you will, indeed, find yourself on the operating table.

Do I have a torn rotator cuff?

The answer is, yes, if you're male and age fifty or above, you probably do. If you're younger than that and do a lot of activities that involve raising your arm above your head—like tennis, swimming, and throwing sports—yes, you probably do, too. The rotator cuff seems to be one of those structures that wears out.

The important question is, however, does it matter? And the answer to that one is, most likely not. Most people go through life with a torn rotator cuff very well, thank you. The fact that evidence of tearing may show up during a shoulder examination or with an MRI is not necessarily reason to do anything about your rotator cuff—not if it doesn't bother you. Odds are that through the years you've noticed some changes in how your shoulder operates, and you've adapted to them in such a way that you're still doing what you like to do pretty well. Discovering that you have a torn rotator cuff doesn't change that one bit.

That is, it shouldn't. Some doctors like to treat x-rays or MRIs rather than symptoms. If it shows up in an exam, better do something about it—no matter that you may never have known there was a problem. Be careful of encountering such an attitude. The bottom line is, or should be, this: if your shoulder isn't hurting, and you don't have to compromise your strength or range of motion, then you shouldn't have anything done to your rotator cuff.

Will I ever be able to use my frozen shoulder?

A frozen shoulder—that is, a shoulder that simply won't move—rarely shows up in athletes. We see the problem in people who injured their shoulder in one way or another and then stopped using it. If you keep your shoulder in one position too long, it'll resist moving into any other position. It may be because the soft tissue capsule enclosing the joint develops adhesions, kind of hunkers down and adheres to itself, preventing movement.

The antidote is to start moving your shoulder. The answer to the question is, yes, you will be able to use your frozen shoulder, but it can take a long time—months or even years—to regain the flexibility you once had. Some doctors put you under general anesthetic and manipulate the shoulder, breaking the adhesions that way. You can do the same thing yourself just by exercising the joint, although it can be a slower process and it'll hurt, especially at first. But motion isn't enough. You must restrengthen those tight muscles, or the shoulder will just freeze up again.

The best thing, of course, is *never stop using your shoulder in the first place*. If you injure your shoulder, see someone or rehabilitate it yourself, but don't stop using it. That's asking for real problems.

Will my shoulder *ever* get better?

Yes, most likely it will. It'll just take a while. The shoulder involves the most intimately interrelated group of muscles and muscular functions in the entire body. It can take time to get over problems in this area. In the shoulder little glitches can make big problems, and, because one thing leads to another here more than anywhere, you often have to deal with secondary problems at the same time you're trying to come to grips with what started the whole thing.

And it's so hard to rest the shoulder, to give it a chance to regain its equilibrium. If your knee is in a splint, then you limp around for a while, but you still limp *around*. If your shoulder and arm are in a sling, there go more of your daily functions than you ever dreamed possible.

Perseverance helps, that and patience. But having a shoulder problem does have one advantage: you can do the majority of rehab exercises on your own. No need to run over to the therapy center or the fitness club for weight and rehab equipment. With the shoulder, weight and resistance aren't as important as the mere act of motion.

So, look on the bright side. Circles and sawing, anyone?

Why *isn't* my shoulder getting better?

That's the flip side of the previous question, and therein lies an interesting tale: one of the biggest problems we see with shoulder injuries is that *people tend to manipulate their activities so that they stay at the same level of discomfort.*

Sounds crazy, no? But it's true. People that we've put on a rehab program will come back month after month and say, "My shoulder feels the same. It hurts just as much." It can be depressing, all this lack of improvement, until you learn to ask an important question: "Is my activity level the same month after month as well?" And there the answer will probably be, "No, I'm doing more than I did before."

Without thinking, people will start playing more or harder tennis, or they'll work back up to 3,000 yards in the pool, or they'll start opening doors again, or pick up the typewriter in the office and move it around—things they never would have done a couple of weeks ago. If it's a knee injury, they might increase their laps on the track, or start parking five blocks away from the office instead of in the parking garage in the basement. A dancer may start using the injured leg as her weight-bearing leg at the barre, whereas before she only used it as her free leg—again, all this without thinking about it.

So, it may be that, no, you're really not getting any better. If so, it's time to have things reevaluated. But it may be that, yes, you're getting lots better. So much better that you've been able to increase your level of activity without even noticing that you've done so. It's just that people find a pain level that they can live with and then in one way or another conspire to stay right there.

Do I really need a physical therapist?

With shoulder problems you're more likely to need such assistance. Effective range-of-motion exercises and strengthening programs designed to combat your specific weaknesses often require the expertise only found with physical therapists. You don't necessarily need to go every day—just often enough for therapist to follow your progress and modify your exercise program accordingly.

REHAB EXERCISES

For shoulder problems in general

This general exercise program moves the shoulder joint through its entire range of motion and utilizes virtually all of the shoulder muscles (including those of the rotator cuff). Do a minimum of twenty-five repetitions twice a day for *each* exercise—only through a comfortable range of motion. These exercises will help many shoulder problems disappear if started as soon as pain and discomfort begin.

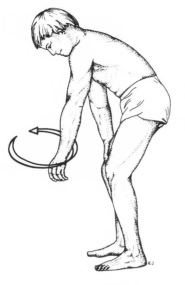

CIRCLES

Bend over at the waist and let the arm on your injured side hang in front of you. Then start swinging it in a clockwise motion: not too hard or too fast—it's not like stirring a vat of molasses. Use just enough muscle to kick your arm into motion and keep it swinging lazily.

At first you may only be able to bend over a little ways. That's okay. Continue to circle clockwise, then counterclockwise, bending over further and further until your torso is at right angles, parallel to the ground. The key here is *don't do anything that hurts.* If it hurts to bend too far, don't. You may have to make an ellipse, or an egg shape, or some other figure that feels all right. Then gradually work toward a complete circle, both clockwise and counterclockwise.

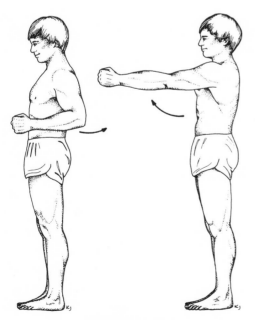

SAWING EXERCISES

Stand up straight. Pretend that you're on one end of a double-handled saw, and start sawing. Back and forth, in and out, way out and way back. As with all these exercises, the more repetitions you do, the more your range of motion will increase. You're stretching at the same time as you're srengthening. The exercise also puts your elbow through a complete range of motion.

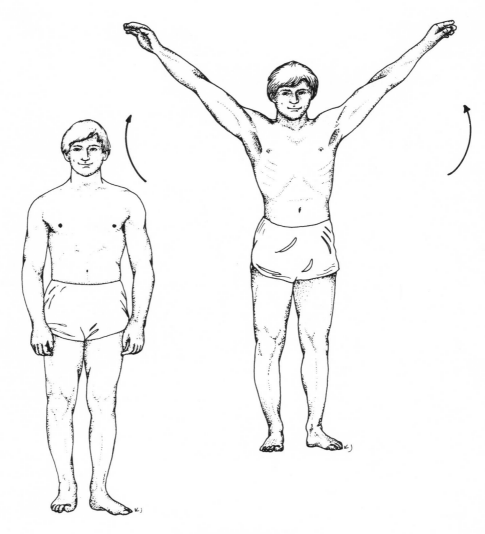

ABDUCTION SWINGS

Let your arm fall straight down to your side. Then raise your arm up at right angles to your body and let it back down, up and down, as though you're slowly flapping an injured wing. Raise your arm to a comfortable level only. Even if you can only bring your arm up a foot or two from your side to start with, keep at it. As you continue, you'll become more flexible. If it hurts too much to swing your arm up at all, start out by bending your elbow to form a chicken wing. Then flap it up as far as it is comfortable. After you develop flexibility that way, gradually straighten out.

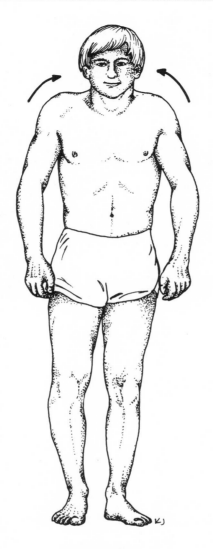

SHOULDER SHRUGS

Last, but not least, shrug your shoulders. That's all, just shrug your shoulders and, while at the "top" of the shrug, pull your shoulders back and your shoulder blades together as though you're trying to squeeze a tennis ball between them. If you want to get fancy about it, you may want to roll your shoulders up and forward then down, or up and back then down, again making clockwise and counterclockwise circles. After doing so much sawing and circling and flapping, you may feel like shrugging your shoulders anyway.

General shoulder rehab exercises

These exercises strengthen the deltoid muscles—those that do much of the "work" of the shoulder.

VARIOUS RAISES AND PRESSES

With arms straight, raise dumbbells a little above shoulder height.

Lying on your stomach with elbows locked and arms straight, raise dumbbells to shoulder height.

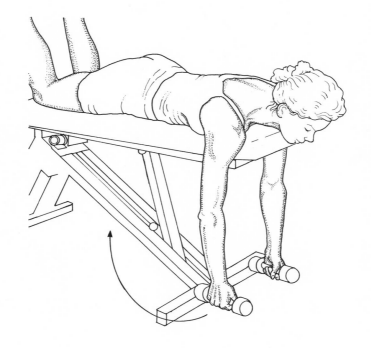

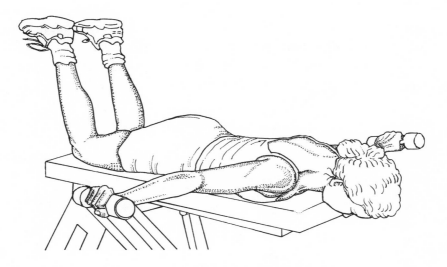

POSTERIOR DELTOID MUSCLE EXERCISES

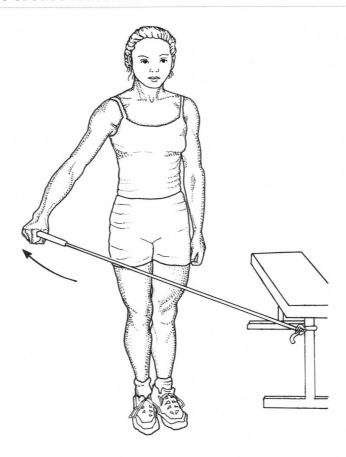

Here is the same exercise as shown on pp. 218, only done with a Thera-Band®
or surgical tubing. Stand with your arms at your sides and pull your injured arm
up and out against resistance. Pull only as far as is comfortable. As you grow
stronger, you'll be able to pull higher. Then increase the resistance. Do two sets
of ten repetitions every day.

CHAPTER NINE

The Elbow

THERE MAY NOT BE many different kinds of elbow problems, but they're persistent. Part of the reason is the way the joint is constructed. It's lucky that whoever designed the elbow doesn't moonlight hanging doors, because although the elbow is a great hinge, it's a crooked one. You can see for yourself. Bend your elbow as far as you can, so that you're touching your shoulder with your fingertips. Now slowly straighten your arm, keeping palms up. Surprise! Your arm doesn't extend absolutely straight. It veers out to the side from the elbow, especially in women. That crook away from the straight and narrow is called the "carrying angle," and herein lies the seed of one of the elbow's two dominant ailments. In large part because of this carrying angle, when you serve a tennis ball or throw a baseball, the inside of your elbow tends to open up and the outside collapses in on itself. Were the elbow a more balanced hinge, it would more efficiently distribute the forces stirred up by these activities. But it's not, and it doesn't. Thus, Little League elbow, which, combined with tennis elbow, is one of the most common injuries of the entire upper body.

But that's just one of the elbow's peculiarities. It's really two joints: a joint that lets you flex and straighten your arm and a joint that allows you to rotate your wrist and hand—at the same time if need be. To

+ WARNING +

If You Experience Any of These Conditions, Seek Medical Help

+ **Elbow locking (abrupt pain, inability to straighten the elbow);**
+ **Sharp, catching elbow pain, for no apparent reason;**
+ **Swelling and redness at the point of the elbow;**
+ **A fall resulting in any deformity of the elbow (it looks different than the other side);**
+ **Numbness or tingling in the forearm or hand.**

watch the elbow rotate, place your hand and arm, palm up, on a table in front of you. Your thumbnail should be touching the table. Then, without lifting your arm, turn your hand over so that the other side of your thumb now lies flat on the table. That's called pronation. Now rotate back again—supination. That's a full 180 degrees of rotation at the wrist. Crooked hinge or no, the elbow is a versatile, efficient instrument.

This joint that's really two joints connects the humerus, the upper arm bone, to two bones in the lower arm—the ulna and radius. That there are two bones in the lower arm is important. It's what makes possible the elbow's ability to bend *and* rotate. The ulna, the longer of the two, allows the elbow to bend. You can feel it run all the way from your elbow to your wrist along the inside back of your forearm. It cradles the end of the humerus in a comfy hollow with a shoehorn-like extension that allows the two bones to work with one another as a hinge, albeit a crooked one. If you place your cupped hand (which represents the ulna) over your fist (the humerus) and then increase and decrease the angle between your arms, you'll get the idea.

Little League elbow

MEDIAL VIEW OF THE ELBOW

The shorter bone, the radius, sometimes runs parallel to the ulna, sometimes across it like an X, depending on what your wrist and forearm are doing. Again, rest your arm on a table in front of you, palm up. In this position your forearm is flat, with the two bones lying docilely side by side. If you rotate your wrist, however, interesting things begin to happen. Your forearm develops a transverse swelling, a small ridge running from the outside of the elbow to the inside of the wrist. This muscular ridge indicates what the radius is doing underneath it—that is, pivoting against the humerus and rotating around the ulna, which itself doesn't move much at all relative to its partner.

The radius's ability to rotate is a function of its shape. Whereas the ulna cradles the humerus, the radius abuts it. The end of the radius is shaped something like an ice-cream cone, the top of which has been hollowed out by pressing the scooper into it. It's an ideal shape for traveling along the convex end of the humerus, which the radius does to a lesser or greater extent, up to 140 degrees of rotation, every time you twist your wrist. So, there's a lot going on inside your elbow all the time: bones not only swing against each other as in a hinge, but

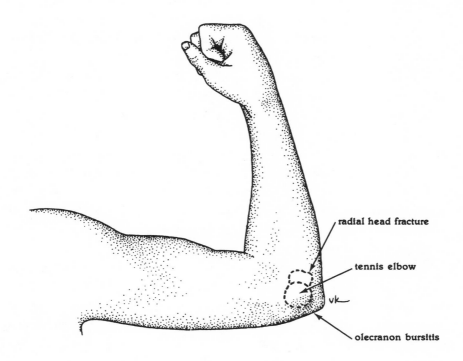

LATERAL VIEW OF THE ELBOW

rotate along an arc, constantly changing relative position, all within the confines of a pretty tight space. Two joints, indeed.

TENNIS ELBOW (LATERAL HUMERAL EPICONDYLITIS)

All of which brings us to tennis elbow, perhaps the dominant elbow injury. Its name to the contrary, tennis elbow is more common off the court than on—it shows up more frequently in the trades or industry than in athletic settings. People who work with impact wrenches, hammers, and staple guns are susceptible to tennis elbow. Framers, automobile mechanics, and assembly-line workers suffer from it. Ditto those who do nothing more strenuous than put up jam for the winter. Clinics are swamped by epidemics of tennis elbow during the fall canning season. So here's the $64,000 question: auto mechanics, homemakers putting up preserves, tennis players—what do all these people have in common that leads to tennis elbow?

The answer is that they all tend to do things that demand sharp, quick twists of the wrist. A mechanic tugging a wrench against a stubborn spark plug, a canner twisting closed the top of a jar, a tennis player hitting (or mishitting) a backhand—all of these movements put demands on the wrist that sometimes it can't handle.

Which leads to the next question: what does all this wrist stuff have to do with the elbow? It comes down to interrelationships again. The muscles that bend back your wrist and straighten your fingers all begin at the elbow. In one spot. A spot no bigger than a dime. It's the bump on the outside of your elbow, the very spot that hurts so much when you have tennis elbow. It's called the lateral humeral epicondyle (literally, "the outside top of the knuckle of the humerus"), and, accordingly, tennis elbow is also called lateral epicondylitis. This spot is where almost 40 percent of the muscles of the forearm begin—all that from an area not much bigger than a fingernail. Not the greatest mechanical arrangement in the whole world. No wonder it hurts.

The scenario goes like this: tennis players are taught to hit a backhand with their bodies, using their arms as a rigid lever. They're taught to step into the ball, with elbow and wrist frozen, and to swing through it using the legs and shoulder to provide power. The impact of the ball against the racquet then travels up the length of the arm and dissipates into the entire body. Makes sense. So what do we do instead? We forget the body and arm the ball to death, leading with the elbow—our first mistake. Then, to compensate, we use the wrist to whip the racquet through the ball—mistake number two. The muscles in the forearm, which are perfectly able to hold the wrist rigid, simply can't produce the power necessary to drive the racquet into the ball and handle the impact as well. And because we're not keeping the elbow rigid, but letting it remain loose and flexible, the bulk of the impact doesn't travel up the rest of the arm and into the body but goes up the muscles and tendons of the forearm and slams into the elbow with considerable force. Where? Right into the lateral epicondyle, which is simply incapable of absorbing so much force. The result: tennis elbow.

It's probably unnecessary to describe how this feels, as so many people have experienced it. The tip-off is pain, of course, centered at the epicondyle and resulting from almost everything you do with the wrist and elbow. From opening doors, to shaking hands (tennis elbow is a politician's nightmare), to picking up your kid, the cat, or the evening paper—not to mention hitting a backhand—the pain is there. For perhaps one or two out of a hundred people, it arrives with a single backhand. In one stroke, these people may tear part of the tendon that connects the muscles to the bone, popping off a few fibers. They're the ones who may receive a cortisone shot and suddenly are good as new. What happens is that the cortisone quickly decreases the inflammation, which in turn gets rid of the pain, which, in an injury like this, is the real problem rather than the tear itself. Although it's likely that they've only torn a few of hundreds of fibers, the danger is that because of the pain they'll be unable to use the joint, and so the muscles can quickly weaken. With the pain gone, they're able to go out and use the elbow and keep the muscles strong.

But most of us have to cope with the sneaky kind of tennis elbow, the overuse variety, that comes on gradually from almost imperceptible beginnings and is much more difficult to get rid of. At first your elbow hurts a little after your match but is better the next day. The weekend player then forgets all about it until the next weekend, when it starts to hurt before the match is over and keeps hurting a day or two later. And so it goes, until finally it hurts so much, all the time, that you can't play tennis at all, and, not only that, you stop doing even the simplest everyday things. There's no single treatment as effective as a cortisone injection for this problem. But it may be even easier—and healthier—to get rid of. The crux of the matter is attending to it quickly.

✚ What to do about it ✚ The earlier you catch tennis elbow the better. When you first notice the pain, that's the time to do something about it. The first thing may be to figure out if it's actually tennis elbow that's bothering you rather than something else. One test is to put the backs of your wrists together and see if one bends more readily than the other. A stiff wrist might indicate tennis elbow. Another is to stretch the muscle involved by straightening your sore arm in front of you with your palm and wrist down and then pulling your hand under the arm and toward you. If your elbow hurts, you may have tennis elbow. And if none of these tests seems to sort things out, there's one other. Again extend your arm out in front of you with your palm down. Place your other hand over the top of your hanging hand and then push up against this restraining hand. If your elbow hurts when you do that, you've got tennis elbow for sure.

Now's the time to ice your elbow and stretch the muscles. Do it again, before and after your next match. A good way to stretch is by repeating the exercise you used to test for the problem—that is, hold your arm out in front of you, elbow straight, palm down, and with your other hand pull the hand on the injured side under as far as possible. That may hurt; if you do this stretch with your elbow bent, it's easier on you. So you may want to go through a progression by starting with the elbow bent and gradually straightening it as you go. The muscle is stretched the most when your elbow is straight.

Icing and stretching ought to head off tennis elbow, but if the pain comes back again, and yet again, better see a doctor right away. Not a medical doctor—a tennis doctor. In other words, *get to the tennis pro and take some lessons.* Professional tennis players almost never suffer from tennis elbow. The reason? Their fundamentals are sound. The best treatment for tennis elbow, better by a long shot than any kind of medical treatment—ice, stretching, cortisone shots, anti-inflammatory drugs, surgery, anything—is a series of lessons to improve your backhand. That, combined with ice and stretching (done early enough so that the muscles don't have time to weaken and tighten), will cure virtually any bout of tennis elbow. It's almost foolproof.

But let's say, like most of us, you haven't done anything about your tennis elbow, and now the pain has increased to the point where you can't ignore it any longer. Perhaps you've tried various treatments prescribed by your friends in the locker room. (And lots of people do get well with these treatments; they're certainly not to be scoffed at. It's just that they often work for some people but not necessarily for everyone else. Tennis elbow is like shinsplints in that way—there are almost as many suggested treatments as there are cases.) But if none of these treatments worked for you, now what?

You must make the elbow comfortable enough so you can rehabilitate it. That usually means that you need to stop doing those things that hurt, tennis first and foremost. If you hurt, you're not going to use the muscles properly, even in rehab exercises, and if you don't use the muscles properly, they won't get any better but will simply continue to hurt. It's an old refrain with overuse injuries like this. Sometimes we put people in a sling, not because there's anything magical about a sling, but because it makes you think about how you're mistreating your elbow before you go ahead and do it. If you don't even try to open doors or pick up heavy objects because the sling reminds you of your mortality, you're ahead of the game.

Once the elbow stops hurting, you can start stretching and strengthening the muscles that attach to it. We've already talked about how to stretch the muscles. The best way to strengthen them is by doing reverse wrist curls. Rest your arm on a table with your wrist and hand hanging free over the edge. Then curl your wrist back as far as possible. If you run your fingers along the top of your forearm, you can feel the muscles contracting from the wrist all the way to the elbow. Repeat the curl ten times, say, and do three sets of these. If your elbow remains pain-free, then gradually add resistance in the form of a dumbbell or a piece of surgical tubing. Increase the weight of the dumbbell or the resistance of the tubing as you grow stronger. These treatments will help.

Of course, there's no need to wait until your elbow hurts before getting around to strengthening the muscles in your lower arm. (Contrary to popular belief, squeezing a tennis ball will not do much for tennis elbow. That exercise works on the muscles that flex your wrist, rather than the extensors. Not only are these muscles not involved in tennis elbow, but they're usually relatively strong already.)

Now to the nether world of tennis elbow remedies, those things that may or may not do anything for anyone, depending on your mood and the phase of the moon. Many locker room cures fall into this category.

Some people swear by a certain brand or composition of racquet or, with equal fervor, avoid others. Aluminum racquets, graphite racquets, wood racquets, composite racquets; mid-sized, large, regular; tightly or loosely strung—nobody has ever been able to sort out which does what to whom. In fact, so many kinds of racquets have been accused of causing tennis elbow that probably no one kind is the culprit. It's more likely that it's a change from one racquet to another that helps cause the problem, much as a change in running shoes, floor surface, or bicycle pedal alignment can help bring about tendinitis.

So if you're going to change racquets, it's a good idea to do so as an experienced runner changes shoes—gradually. Use your new racquet for just fifteen minutes the first day, then go back to your old one. The next time use it for twenty-five minutes, the next time forty minutes, and so on, until you can finally put the old one aside for good. The same strategy applies for a new grip size. There's some data to suggest that using a slightly oversized grip decreases the amount of torque transferred to your arm, thereby decreasing the amount of force your elbow must tolerate. But make a change in grip size gradually as well. Let your elbow and the rest of your arm ease into these things.

Of all the tennis elbow appliances, the bands and braces and magic amulets, the most effective is the band. Nothing more than a strap, sometimes called a counterforce brace, that wraps tightly around the muscle just below the elbow, it seems to help most people. It may simply squeeze the muscle enough that you use it a bit differently, or change the direction of the pull on the muscle—no one knows. But as long as it works, who cares?

Just don't make the mistake of using these aids as cures. If they control your pain so that you can play, great. But *treat* your tennis elbow in the meantime. If you don't, you may find that what controlled the pain for a while no longer works, and your elbow hurts more than ever. Stretching and strengthening, perhaps taking anti-inflammatories, icing after you play—all these treatments will help. And, again, don't neglect the most important remedy of all: take a tennis lesson; improve that backhand. (Interestingly, you almost never see tennis elbow in people with a two-handed backhand, because a two-handed backhand is really more of an opposite-handed forehand than anything else. It may be that when all the younger players who now use two-handed backhands reach their forties, prime tennis elbow age, we'll see much less of it.)

If you deal effectively with tennis elbow early on, you should never have to see a doctor—except the tennis "doctor," that is.

LITTLE LEAGUE ELBOW OR GOLFER'S ELBOW (MEDIAL TENNIS ELBOW)

If lateral humeral epicondylitis is the tennis elbow of recreational tennis players, medial humeral epicondylitis, pain on the *inside* of the elbow, is the tennis elbow of really good players. Pros and top amateurs rarely get the lateral variety of tennis elbow because their fundamentals are sound. Rather they tend to get wear-and-tear tendinitis on the inside of the elbow—but not from their backhand. They get it from their forehand or serve, that big, sweeping, overhead stroke that happens to be very similar to the motion of a baseball pitcher. So it's no surprise that medial tennis elbow is better known by its other names, Little League elbow or golfer's elbow.

Here we return to the carrying angle, the elbow's tendency to resemble a crooked door hinge, with the forearm veering out to the side when you straighten your arm. When you follow through after making a pitch or hitting a tennis serve or forehand, that tendency to veer to the side is amplified. In the elbow this outward force causes the inside portion of the joint to open up. It literally tries to pull itself apart from the inside out, especially when you throw or hit from the side rather than over the top. But the ligaments and muscles holding the joint together won't allow such a catastrophe; they hold on tight. Elbow opening up, muscles and ligaments holding on—something's got to give. As usual, that something is the weak link in the chain, the tendons (and, occasionally, the ligaments, too). Over time, with pitch after pitch and serve after serve, these tendons weaken, stretch, and give a little. The result is tendinitis of the tendons attached to the medial epicondyle. You experience it as pain on the inside of your elbow.

So it's the inside (or medial) equivalent of the more common lateral tennis elbow, with one important difference: whereas tennis elbow is muscular in origin, that is, it comes from too much being asked of the muscles that attach to the elbow, Little League elbow begins in the joint. The joint itself tries to pull apart, with the muscles doing their darndest to hold things together.

With young people, the problem becomes compounded, as their tendons connect to a growth center in the bone. Classic Little League elbow is really a kind of Osgood-Schlatter disease of the elbow (see chapter 5, "The Knee," for a discussion of Osgood-Schlatter). As the elbow opens up and the tendon strains at the bone, the area not only becomes irritated but enlarged as well. A third of all Little League pitchers probably have an enlargement of the inside of the elbow, but it's no more of a problem than the tendinitis itself. There are no long-term consequences from this enlargement. It's usually something that shows up in x-rays but might go unnoticed otherwise.

The notion that throwing curveballs at too young an age is the cause of Little League elbow may be true, but it's more likely that elbow problems are the result of the sheer quantity of throwing rather than what is thrown. Little League elbow is not so much the result of specific muscle overuse but of general overuse of the entire arm. And it simply takes longer to learn how to throw a curveball than it does to throw a fastball. If it takes you 100 pitches a day to learn a fastball, it may take 400 to learn a curve. It's that extra hour and a half after dinner spent snapping off curveballs with your dad or older brother that causes Little League elbow, not the kind of pitch you throw.

The tennis equivalent is the grocery cart full of balls or the ball machine. Hitting too many tennis balls causes elbow problems. With one can of balls, it's hard to get in trouble because you spend half your time chasing and picking up balls. But if the pro stands across the net with a cart full of balls, or the machine spits them at you rapid-fire, you'll hit more forehands and backhands in a half hour than you do in a couple of weekends of three sets a day, especially if you play doubles. And most people encounter the grocery cart or ball machine at a particularly unfortunate time, the beginning of the season when they're trying to get back in shape. Wham! From months off watching it rain or snow to hundreds of balls coming at you. Your poor elbow can't win.

The tendon involved in Little League elbow attaches right next to your crazy bone—really the ulnar nerve—which runs in a groove behind the elbow and down into the forearm and the outside of your hand. If the tendinitis is really bad, the inflammation can move over into the nerve groove and irritate the nerve itself. Then it's as though you're hitting your crazy bone all the time, and your little finger and ring finger may become numb and tingly. If the tendinitis becomes chronic, the tendon gives way to scar and degenerative tissue, a condition that can require surgery to clean out the area and reattach the tendon.

Sometimes Little League elbow (and lateral tennis elbow, as well) can lead to numbness and tingling all up and down the arm and sometimes to pain that doesn't come from the elbow at all but from the shoulder. Interrelationships. If your elbow hurts, you use your arm differently; and if you use your arm differently, you may start using your shoulder differently. As we discussed in chapter 8, "The Shoulder," using your shoulder in unaccustomed ways can lead to thoracic outlet syndrome, a stretching and pinching of the nerves passing over the muscles in your shoulder on their way down to your arm. Those irritated nerves then send messages of grief to the ends of the circuit (nerves aren't shy—if there's irritation in one place, you may feel it in another). So sometimes what's needed at first is not elbow treatment but shoulder rehab. Such cases can become complicated fast.

✚ What to do about it ✚ Elbow surgery is reasonably effective, but it *is* surgery. With almost any kind of major joint surgery, people never quite come back to their previous level of ability. In the elbow, the primary by-product is often a reduced range of motion.

But most bouts of Little League elbow don't require surgery. As with lateral tennis elbow, resting your elbow is the first thing to do. Icing it after use can help, as can taking anti-inflammatory drugs. Stretching and strengthening the muscles involved is good. You can do the same exercises as with lateral tennis elbow, but in the opposite direction. The exercise that stretches the muscles involved in lateral tennis elbow—dropping your wrist and pulling your hand underneath your arm—will *strengthen* the muscles involved in Little League elbow (see illustration, p. 238). Cocking your wrist up and pulling your hand back will *stretch* the muscles involved in Little League elbow.

Little League pitchers who complain of elbow pain should stay away from throwing for a while and then only gradually get back to playing when the pain subsides, all the while icing, stretching, and strengthening as suggested. But if the elbow continues to hurt, they should definitely see a doctor and probably have x-rays. The rule of thumb, especially when it comes to kids, is *never ignore joint pain*. If you do, by the time the kids are sixteen they may have a chronically injured elbow, one that could bother them for the rest of their lives.

When all is said and done, because Little League elbow is a function of overuse rather than poor technique or lack of strength, it may be one of those things that simply comes with the territory. If you hurt but want to continue playing baseball, say, you certainly should try the treatments we've suggested, and see a doctor if things don't clear up. But you should also realize that it may be a problem you simply have to live with. It comes down to weighing what's important to you—playing with some pain, or playing less or even not at all. It's the kind of dilemma that soon becomes very familiar to people involved in sports. And the only person who can decide which road to take is you.

+ Kids and Joint Pain +

We've said it before, but it bears repeating, especially with kids: if joint pain lasts more than a couple of days, especially pain in the "naked" joints—the elbow, knee, ankle, and wrist, those not covered by muscle—better see a doctor. Muscle pain is usually no problem. As long as it doesn't show up all of a sudden—as with a muscle tear—it's probably sore from being overused and can for the most part be ignored. Not so joints. Pain there can mean real problems.

Especially with kids. Because they're growing, kids' joints are looser than those of adults. Just as bones grow faster than muscles, so do joints. In fact, it sometimes seems that muscles are the last to know when *anything* important is happening. They are the simpletons in the family. Joints are much smarter than muscles; so are ligaments. They anticipate rapid growth spurts and loosen up in preparation. Meanwhile, the muscles go merrily on their way, tight as ever, oblivious to the whole thing. You have to loosen up your own muscles; joints loosen up by themselves.

No one has been able to document that there's an increase in injuries due to that looseness, and certainly if there is it's not substantial, but prolonged pain in these loosened joints still should make you suspicious. Don't let it persist in your child without trying to find out why it's there.

JOINT MICE—SEVERE LITTLE LEAGUE ELBOW

"Joint mice" are the little loose things that scurry around in your elbow (in the knee, "knee mice," in the shoulder, "shoulder mice," etc.)—in other words, bone chips. They're caused by repeatedly snapping your elbow into full extension, as when pitching a baseball or serving in tennis. They can result from a bad case of Little League elbow. Again, because of the elbow's carrying angle, which causes the inside of the joint to fly apart, the outside of the elbow tends to collapse in on itself, grinding the bones together. It's this smashing, the action of the head of the radius colliding with the humerus, that can cause little pieces of bone to chip off into the elbow. And the more tired you get, the less able your muscles are to absorb the shock and fend off this smashing and crashing.

The role the muscles play in decelerating movements and thus absorbing shock is not as well appreciated as their ability to get things started in the first place, but it's no less important. It's a very sophisticated function, an *eccentric,* or lengthening, contraction—almost a contradiction of terms. The muscle must be able to work against the direction of the movement, to contract at the same time as it lengthens, and all very rapidly. For example, when a pitcher follows through, the muscle that cocked the arm, the biceps, must now cushion the arm as it straightens. It must mitigate the effect of the muscle that extends the arm, the triceps, and the momentum of the movement itself. Otherwise, like a car without shock absorbers, nothing dampens the movement, and your arm can snap straight with an impact that can chip bones.

Joint mice can lead to pain and swelling, and the loose pieces of bone can lodge in the joint, making it impossible to use your elbow. Out of the blue you get this terrible pain, like being hit with an ice pick, and you can't do anything with the joint. Then, as quickly as it came, the pain disappears as the loose bone chip gets out of the way. The problem can be especially serious when combined with osteochondritis dissecans, that strange tendency of bones to die in spots and simply flake away (see chapter 2, "The Ankle," for more on this condition). Pieces of loose bone as large as a marble have shown up in the elbow—almost half the volume of a joint that small. Children are more prone to this problem than adults, but, fortunately, it's very uncommon.

✛ What to do about it ✛ See a doctor. Sometimes the mice have to be removed surgically. The arthroscope is especially handy for this kind of operation. We can also intentionally overstrengthen the biceps. We put them on what otherwise might be an ill-conceived rehab program that makes them a little bit muscle-bound, so that the muscle will decelerate and cushion more strongly than usual, thus preventing bone from bashing into bone.

Once more, with feeling: both tennis elbow and Little League elbow become more frequent as we age. Women more than men are afflicted with tennis elbow; men more than women with Little League elbow. One third to one half of all tennis players over forty years of age have some symptoms of one or the other. The likelihood of encountering either is related to how often you play now, how often you've played in the past and for how long (you've probably developed some degenerative changes in the tendons if you've played a lot), and the level of your technique. With tennis elbow, technique and strength is very important. The more of both, the less likelihood of getting tennis elbow. Little League or golfers' elbow strikes without much regard to either. It's wonderfully democratic that way. It's pure overuse.

BURSITIS

Ever wonder why the skin at your elbow moves around so easily? One reason is that there's lots of it. It has to cover your elbow when it's bent as well as straight, and to do that it has to have lots of slack. The other reason the skin slides over the elbow so readily is that there's a bursa in there, a slippery fluid-producing sac that, as we've seen in earlier chapters, tends to show up whenever something in the body needs to slide over something else. It's called the olecranon bursa because it covers the olecranon process, that shoehorn-like extension of the ulna into which the humerus fits. The bursa functions like a little pallet of ball bearings, reducing the friction between the bone and skin. We'd be much like a tin man without lubricating oil if we didn't have bursas.

The trade-off is that bursas can be irritated easily, and in the elbow, with its bony, exposed prominence, the olecranon bursa is often bumped. From bumping, the bursa produces more and more fluid, which causes it to swell, sometimes to the size of a chicken egg. A swollen bursa is annoying more than anything else, and it has a tendency to stay irritated because we so often rest our elbows against things.

In the elbow bursitis is sometimes compounded by the fact that because the skin in the area is not only plentiful but thin (take a couple fingers' full and pinch it together—even in double thickness it's not very thick), the hair follicles are very close to the bursa. If a follicle gets irritated from all the swelling, it can become infected and in turn infect the swollen bursa. Elbow bursas are the most frequently irritated bursas in the body. And an infected bursa, already swollen and distended, adds pain to annoyance. They're no fun.

Sometimes, after a swollen bursa finally goes down, people will complain of what feels like tiny bone chips in their elbow. What happens is that the bursa isn't elastic, so when the fluid disappears you're stuck with a sac that's too big. The loose bodies you feel in the elbow are really the wrinkles of the now over-sized sac. In time the wrinkles dry and harden, and then they feel even more like bone.

+ What to do about it + Ice can help reduce a swollen bursa. So can anti-inflammatory drugs. That and being careful not to bump your elbow—a tough task.

If the irritation doesn't go away, you may have to see a doctor. Sometimes the only recourse is draining the bursa; sometimes doctors inject them with corti-sone. The last resort is surgery to remove the thing.

RADIAL-HEAD FRACTURE

A fall on your outstretched arm and hand can break the head of the radius, that bone shaped like an ice-cream scoop that rotates against the humerus. The injury is the result of the force of the impact traveling up the arm to the joint, where it attacks the point of least resistance—in this case the end of the radius. You'll know it from the pain on the outside of the elbow, and soon the joint will stiffen and swell. This may be the most common acute elbow injury that recre-ational athletes suffer.

+ What to do about it + See a doctor. Usually it's not a serious injury. You may not even have to immobilize your elbow but simply protect it until it heals, which it tends to do very quickly.

EPIPHYSIAL FRACTURE

Since there are a number of growth centers (or epiphyses) near the elbow, young people sometimes fracture these areas. Usually the culprit is a fall and a landing on the outstretched hand.

+ What to do about it + This is a painful, obvious injury, nothing that you'd ever dream of waiting out. See a doctor, right away. With this kind of frac-ture there can be some potential problems with injury to the vessels or nerves that cross the elbow and supply your hand. So it's a medical urgency, if not an emergency. Leave the elbow in whatever position it's in and call a doctor, or 911, or have someone get you to an emergency room. Again, *don't ignore sudden painful injuries to the elbow, or any other joint.*

DISLOCATIONS

Elbow dislocations show up in contact sports like football and wrestling, and, in particular, gymnastics. Because of the elbow's carrying angle, a fall on your out-stretched arm can push the joint apart rather than transmit the force all the way up the arm to the shoulder. Female gymnasts, especially, are prone to disloca-tions, as their carrying angle is greater than that of males and so many of them have hyperextended elbows as well. A dislocation is terribly painful, as it involves stretching or tearing of the ligaments around the joint that causes the muscles to go into spasm in an attempt to hold things together.

✛ What to do about it ✛ See a doctor. Often the treatment involves put-ting your elbow in a cast at a ninety-degree angle for three weeks or so. For female gymnasts, however, that treatment might not work. The reason why offers yet more evidence of how sensitive the elbow is to injury.

With any injury, and especially after surgery, the elbow loses some of its abil-ity to bend and straighten. For most of us, the loss of the extremes of elbow motion does not present a major problem. We can continue running, tennis, swimming, biking, pretty much as before. Not so the gymnast, however. Arm flexibility is crucial in this sport, especially so because gymnasts need the stabil-ity provided by a locked elbow. Carrying angle and all, if you can lock your elbow out straight, you can use it as a support (in tumbling, say, or on the bars), much as a locked knee provides support—all without the necessity of muscle power. A locked knee or elbow is much like the spinal column in that it provides the sta-bility of one bone perched on top of the other.

If you can't extend your arm straight, however, you're forced to support your-self with the muscles that extend the elbow, primarily the triceps. Well, the tri-ceps is not the world's strongest muscle, and female gymnasts in particular lack the upper body strength to rely on muscles alone. Males are better able to do it, but all gymnasts need skeletal stability.

So with female gymnasts, even though it's a bit more risky and requires a lot of attention, we cast dislocated elbows at less of an angle than we might other-wise. The hope is that when the injury heals the elbow will be able to extend farther than if it were bent at a greater angle in the cast. In any case, flexion comes back more readily than extension. Your biceps is stronger than your triceps. It'll crank your elbow into a bent position even though the joint may be stiff. So, for athletes who absolutely need to fully extend (straighten) the elbow, we try to provide people with extra extension.

REHAB EXERCISES

For tennis elbow

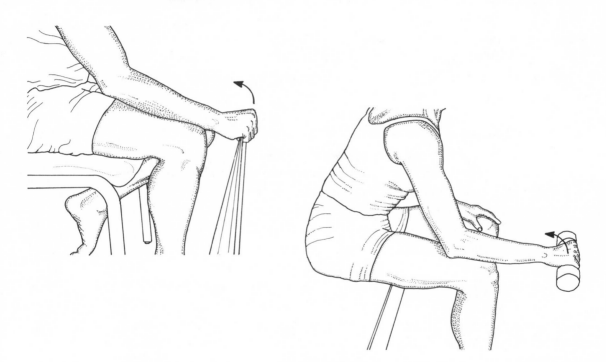

REVERSE WRIST CURLS

Reverse wrist curls strengthen the muscles in the forearm that extend the wrist. Rest your arm on your knee with your wrist and hand, palm down, hanging free. Curl your wrist toward you, using as much weight as is comfortable.

You can begin doing reverse wrist curls with your elbow bent. Then, as you become stronger, straighten your elbow. A straight elbow enhances the workout as you stretch your muscles, making them more flexible—and making the exercise more difficult.

CHAPTER TEN

The Wrist and Hand

IT'S HARD TO ESCAPE wrist injuries. Even sports in which the wrist is not involved have a surprisingly high number of them. For example, in-line skating and skateboarding are notorious for causing wrist injuries. Why? Because skaters and skateboarders fall, and the most common reaction on the way down is to thrust out a hand to break the fall. Well, you may break your fall that way, but you may break something else as well—your wrist. We've finally gotten to the bottom of this transmitted-force business (which affects your arm from the shoulder on down) that we've been talking about in chapters 8 and 9. Here the force is not transmitted—it's direct, and the wrist, or the hand, is the recipient.

A fall is just one of the ways in which you can injure your hand. There are lots of others. Jamming your fingers is the most common; blows to and by the hand are not far behind. Dislocations, fractures, tendinitis, sprains—it's an impressive assortment. In fact, there are more acute injuries in the hand than anyplace else in the body. And that's just counting the injuries that show up at emergency rooms or doctors' offices. The bulk of hand injuries never see the inside of a doctor's office. People treat them by themselves—usually pretty successfully, but not always. The number of permanently twisted, crooked, bent, and gnarled fingers around testify to that.

The hand and wrist may be small in comparison to other parts of the body, and their injuries not as dramatic as some we've discussed, but injuries to wrist and hand can be as disabling as any of the others,

> ### ✚ WARNING ✚
> **If You Experience Any of These Conditions, Seek Medical Help**
>
> ✚ **An injury results in any deformity;**
> ✚ **You experience numbness or tingling in the hand or fingers;**
> ✚ **You experience weakness—for example, dropping things.**

especially for an athlete. A jammed finger can put a quarterback, pitcher, or basketball player out of commission as surely as a dislocated shoulder or torn-up knee. A sprained thumb can as effectively prevent a dancer from partnering, a boxer from entering the ring, or a tennis player from stepping onto the court, as can a sprained ankle. And if any of you athletes out there are musicians, or secretaries, surgeons, or artists, forget it. Hand and wrist injuries can be the kiss of death.

THE WRIST AND THE HAND

They're the body's last outpost, in a way the culmination of everything else that has allowed you to run, jump, bend, and stretch. The twist of a wrist and touch of a finger can make or break the entire body's athletic effort. From pool players to tennis players, handball players to bowlers, gymnasts to baseball players, how well your hand and wrist works is the key. A lot to ask of twenty-seven little bones, eight in the wrist and nineteen in the hand, even ones so artfully arranged.

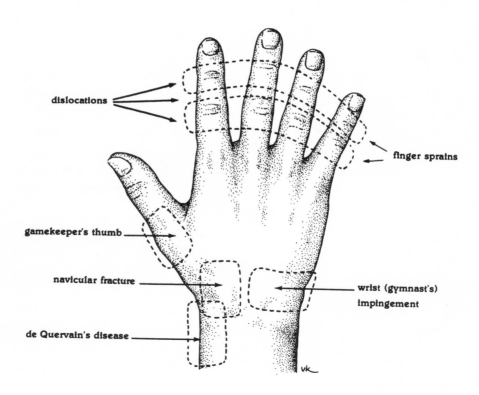

TOP VIEW OF THE WRIST AND HAND

The two forearm bones, the ulna and radius, are lashed together by ligaments at the wrist in a kind of shallow cradle. Sitting atop that cradle is a slightly oblong wedge of eight small bones arranged in two rows of four, called the carpus. It's this junction of the forearm and wrist bones that is the joint proper; it allows the wrist its super flexibility. The wrist can bend up and back almost 180 degrees and along with the forearm can rotate fully as much as that. As in the elbow, the radius rotates around the ulna to turn the wrist, but whereas in the elbow the radius slides along the humerus, which remains relatively stationary, here it takes the wrist along with it. When the radius rotates, the wrist rotates, while the ulna stays pretty much where it is.

The wedge of small bones in the wrist is itself capable of some rotation, but its primary job is to provide a stable base for the hand and its fingers. Five columns of bones make up the hand, four bones in each finger's column and three in the thumb's. The top three bones in each column (two in the thumb) are called the phalanges (from the Greek for "battle lines"). The lower echelon of

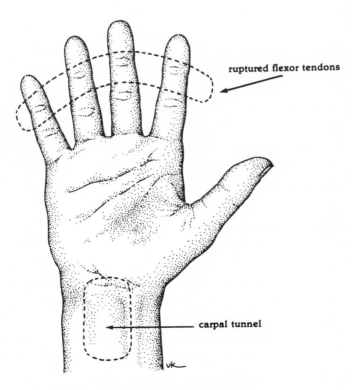

ruptured flexor tendons

carpal tunnel

BOTTOM VIEW OF THE WRIST AND HAND

bones, the metacarpal (or "beyond the wrist") bones, is masked by the fleshy part of the hand from wrist to knuckles, but you can easily feel the bones by running your fingers over the back of your hand, and, if you wiggle your fingers, you can see the dancing tendons that connect the bones to muscles in the forearm. There are muscles in the hand itself, but most of your hand's power comes from these muscles in the forearm, which operate as if by remote control, their controlling agents long tendrils of tendons. One group of tendons runs up the back of your hand to extend your fingers and thumb; another group moves through your palm to enable you to bend your fingers. And a web of ligaments holds the bones in alignment. The great majority of hand and wrist injuries in one way or another subvert this usually happy working family of bones, tendons, and ligaments.

NAVICULAR FRACTURE

It's the most common of the bad things that can happen to the wrist from a fall on an outstretched hand. And it's probably the worst. The carpal navicular, or scaphoid (both words mean "boat shaped") is a bone that lies at the base of the thumb, just beneath the hollow in your wrist that's accentuated when you extend your thumb. The bone is tiny, about the size of the last joint of your little finger, and it's the lowest bone in the wedge of eight (the carpus) that comprises the wrist. The navicular directly abuts the radius. This positioning is important because when you fall on your wrist, the force may travel through the other bones in the carpus because they have some give to them, but when it reaches the navicular, all bets are off. The navicular has no place to go, except right into the end of the radius. And in a test of strength between the navicular and the radius, the radius will win every time. The upshot is that often the little navicular will break on impact.

That's not good. The navicular has a bad reputation for not healing. And because it's such a small bone, almost all of it is surface and in contact with other bones. That means that any kind of irregularity in this bone can cause even more trouble than it might otherwise. One of the first things that happens when you fracture your navicular—besides pain, that is—is you lose the ability to fully bend the wrist—*permanently*. There's no getting around it, navicular fractures are nasty. They're particularly common in wrestling and football.

✚ What to do about it ✚ See a doctor. Any fall on your outstretched hand that bends the wrist back and hurts for more than a day or so, not necessarily with a lot of swelling, should be seen by people who know what they're doing.

And it probably should be x-rayed. This is one instance in which you should overreact and see a doctor more quickly than you might otherwise and take more x-rays than you might otherwise. If the x-rays don't show anything and your wrist still hurts three weeks later, go back and get it x-rayed again. The adage in orthopedics and sports medicine is that anything that looks like a wrist sprain, particularly if it hurts on the thumb side of the wrist, is not a sprain until you've absolutely proved that it isn't a navicular fracture. Some doctors feel so strongly about this injury that even if your x-rays are negative, if your wrist is sore on the thumb side, they'll put you in a cast and bring you back in three weeks to x-ray again, just to be sure. (A bone scan three or four days after the injury can be a quicker way of finding these elusive fractures.)

Still, even after doing all that, it's a tough injury to pinpoint. It's hard to x-ray the navicular. Frequently people miss the injury, sometimes because they x-ray the wrong bone, sometimes because they x-ray the right bone but the fracture line simply doesn't show up (which underscores the advisability of getting another x-ray later on if the pain continues, as the fracture may be more visible once it's

> ### + Other Wrist Bone Injuries +
>
> There are many different kinds, but they don't occur very often and are the result of very specific situations—nothing as general as falling on your outstretched hand. They, too, can be tough to live with, as the smallest displacement in the eight tiny wrist bones can cause fits. Any wrist injuries that don't soon calm down should be seen by a doctor, maybe even a hand surgeon.

started to heal). Once you are sure of the diagnosis, there are two primary ways of treating the injury. One is to put your wrist in a cast and simply wait for it to heal. Some athletes, football linemen, for example, can get away with playing and wearing a cast at the same time. The drawback with this approach is that it can take nine to twelve *months* to heal. The navicular is a slow-healing bone, lacking a good blood supply to provide nutrients. The other treatment is surgery. Probably more than any other bone in the body, a navicular fracture that won't heal requires surgery.

So the moral of the story is, if you fall on your outstretched hand and it hurts beyond a day or so afterwards, especially on the thumb side, see a doctor. Overreact on the side of caution. As difficult as the injury is for a professional to treat, it's that much more difficult, and dangerous, to ignore it and try to live with it.

TENDINITIS

A variety of forms of tendinitis can afflict the wrist, sometimes from nothing more offensive than taping your wrist too tightly. The most common wrist tendinitis is called de Quervain's disease, after the nineteenth-century Swiss surgeon who first identified it (and, incidentally, introduced iodized table salt as well). It affects the tendons that connect your thumb to the muscles in your forearm. These tendons allow you to extend your thumb, so that you can hitchhike. You can easily see and feel them. There are three of them, two of which run closely together, and they straddle the hollow below your thumb that covers the navicular bone.

These tendons can become swollen and painful to the point that it seems as though they're infected. The cause can be any repetitive activity—tennis, weight lifting, gardening, rowing (feathering can bring it about, as you use your thumbs to help rotate the oars)—and the problem can become so bad that surgery is necessary. Using computer keyboards is another source of these problems. (In fact, keyboarding may well be the most common cause of both tendinitis and, as we'll see in a moment, carpal tunnel syndrome.) The sheaths that the tendons run in can become so scarred and restricted from the irritation that every time you move your thumb they squeak. That's one tip-off. The classic experiment, called Finkelstein's test, is to wrap the fingers of your hand around your thumb and squeeze toward your little finger. If you have de Quervain's disease, it'll hurt even to touch the thumb, much less squeeze it.

Another form of tendinitis affects the tendons on the bottom side of the wrist, those that allow you to flex your fingers. As with tendinitis anywhere in the body, it's the result of overuse or abuse. Again, tennis, lifting weights, rowing, any repetitive activity can bring it about. Tendinitis on this side of the hand, however, carries with it a special wrinkle. The tendons to the fingers, all eight of them (two for each finger), and one of the tendons to the thumb go through the carpal tunnel, which is literally a tunnel in the wrist and palm that protects the tendons on their long journey from your forearm to your fingers. But the tendons don't have the tunnel all to themselves. The median nerve that supplies sensation to part of your palm runs through there as well. Now the plot thickens. If the tendons become irritated, swell, and fill up the tunnel, they can squash the nerve, which is the only soft thing in there. It starts out about the same size as the tendons; if they get irritated, it gets scrunched.

So carpal tunnel tendinitis can not only cause soreness and swelling, it can bring about numbness and tingling from the thumb side of your palm all the way back to your forearm. And your hand might feel more swollen than it really is, just because you no longer have normal sensation in the area. It's most common in people with rheumatoid arthritis in their hands and in women, usually older women, just before menstruation (because of the tendency to swell easily from water retention), but you see it in athletes as well. You can test yourself for it by tapping the area to see if you can reproduce the pain, by holding your hands with wrists cocked in prayer position, or just by letting them hang limp. If your wrist hurts in any of these positions, you most likely have carpal tunnel tendinitis.

✚ What to do about it ✚ The most important thing is to catch it early. Almost any tendinitis will do well if treated early enough.

Icing after activity will help. Contrast baths—four or five repetitions of warm water for four minutes, ice water for one—two or three times a day can be very effective. Just make sure you move your hand in the warm water. Anti-inflammatory drugs can help. Wearing a splint will rest the tendons and promote healing, and many splints such as the "gymnast's" wrist splint can actually be worn while performing activities. Then, after the pain disappears and you're comfortable, gentle stretching is a good idea. To know which way to stretch, simply move your wrist and hand in the direction that hurts.

If you don't attend to the injury early, you'll have to wait until the swelling goes down before doing any stretching. Ice and contrast baths can hurry the process along. If the muscles go into spasm, you'll want to immobilize the joint in a splint or removable cast to protect it. A good idea in any case is to splint your wrist at night—taping a little pillow around your wrist will do the trick—because your wrist can get in strange positions when you're sleeping and stay that way for a long time.

Again, you want to get rid of the soreness and swelling right away. Ice after activity, contrast baths, anti-inflammatories, and maybe a splint. Then, once you're comfortable, on to gentle stretching. But if all fails, see a doctor.

IMPINGEMENT

For a gymnast, impingement in the wrist can be a real problem, but most of us, athletes or otherwise, wouldn't even know it if we had it. It's one of those specialized sports medicine injuries that affects athletes who use their arms and wrists to bear weight, and none so much as gymnasts. Like a dancer who must be able to bend at least ninety degrees at the ankle in order to plié, a gymnast must be able to bend at least ninety degrees at the wrist to do a myriad of things. If you can't bend your hand back over your arm at a right angle, then all those tricks like handstands, cartwheels, and back walkovers, and many more of the gymnastic repertory of flips and twists, become awfully difficult, if not impossible. If you can't dorsiflex—that is, bend back—at ninety degrees, then you've got to do all sorts of spooky things with your elbow and shoulder to try and compensate for your stiffness. Otherwise, you can't get your body over your wrist.

It's not that bone builds up, as in the ankle, impinging upon your dorsiflexed wrist; rather the soft tissue in the area becomes scarred and chronically swollen from the constant pressure exerted upon the wrist. And a gymnast with problems elsewhere, in the elbow or shoulder, may call upon her wrist to bend even more than ninety degrees to compensate for those other troubles. That added pressure upon the wrist can lead to just what the gymnast can least afford: impingement. (Impingement also shows up in dancers and skaters who are partnering. It's definitely a weight-bearing injury, but it may not be your own weight that you're bearing.)

+ What to do about it + Like tendinitis, impingement responds to a regimen of rest, ice, contrast baths, anti-inflammatories, and, later, gentle stretching. Another thing we try to do is make the muscles on the bottom side of the wrist, the ones that pull the wrist down, so strong that they act as a brake and protect the wrist from unnecessary pressure. The logic goes like this: If you're not very strong, and you do a cartwheel or any of the other tricks that load your body weight onto your wrist, then the wrist tends to sag until the soft tissue becomes so tight that it won't let you go any further or until the bones run into each other. That's not good. It's a kind of passive restraint that can lead to just the kind of irritation that causes impingement. If, on the other hand, you're really strong, then your muscles will prevent you from sagging over quite that far. That's active restraint, and it can help reduce the pressure on the soft tissue of the wrist by holding back the body's weight a little.

You can further provide an external bolster by wrapping tape around your wrist, and there are mechanical aids, such as splints, that can help protect the joint. But don't expect that, as in ankle impingement, an operation might solve the problem. Impingement in the wrist just doesn't respond well to surgery. Sometimes the only way to deal with the problem is by wearing a splint for everything except actual competition and to simply grin and bear it during that time. Some people manage very well that way. It's simply one of those things that you may have to live with as best you can.

GANGLION

This problem is fairly common in racquet sports or handball, but it's no big deal. A ganglion is a little fluid-filled cyst that grows on the back of the wrist. It's about the size of a marble and is especially prominent when you bend your hand down. People now feel that it's the result of a ligament injury that has somehow gone awry while healing. It's not malignant, really no cause for great concern, but it can become tender and bothersome, probably because it's pushing things out of its way as it grows. And it can cause tendinitis in the back of the wrist because now the tendons have to navigate around this obstruction, and, as we've seen over and over in this book, any unaccustomed demands can irritate and inflame tendons.

✚ **What to do about it** ✚ The traditional treatment involves the family Bible. Not prayer, but smashing the Bible onto your wrist and breaking the ganglion. The fluid absorbs away after a few days, and, if you're lucky, that's that.

These days, nontraditionalists tend to have ganglions aspirated or surgically removed. And sometimes they'll just go away by themselves. The thing to ask yourself is if the ganglion is bothering you. If not, it'll cause no harm; you might just as easily ignore it.

JAMMED FINGER

It's the most common finger injury. You jab your finger into a wall, catch a ball wrong, fall on the finger, inadvertently run into someone—the causes are many. The results are the same: a painful, swollen, stiff finger. It's probably a sprain, a stretching or partial tearing of the ligaments and capsule surrounding one of the finger's joints. The difficulty is that these are tiny joints, so a little swelling can go a long way to completely disable the finger. And it seems to stay that way forever. Jammed fingers stay swollen for months, even if they're not very serious. And there really isn't much you can do about it.

✚ **What to do about it** ✚ What people *do* do about it, unfortunately, is try to get it back to normal as soon as possible. A swollen joint won't bend as far as a normal one, but people develop the habit of *making* it bend by prodding it with the other hand. That irritates it more and makes it swell even more. People will come into the doctor's office complaining of a finger whose swelling hasn't gone down in four months, all the while pushing and pulling at it with their other hand as they talk. No wonder it hasn't gone down.

The thing to do with jammed fingers is to leave them alone. That and contrast baths and anti-inflammatories is about all you can do. The next thing is to realize that even if you didn't jam it badly, it may stay swollen for a long time and you may lose a little bit of the bend in it. But if you just can't bear to sit around doing nothing, then use the finger muscles themselves to exercise the joint rather than your other hand. Hold the rest of the finger still and just move the tip, or whatever joint is injured. In that way you won't bend the joint more than is safe to do (because the muscles won't flex more than is comfortable), and you'll be strengthening the finger at the same time.

But, above all, patience is virtue. Nine times out of ten the finger will come all the way back and the swelling will go all the way down. But you have to be nice to it in the meanwhile. And the meanwhile can last an awfully long time.

DISLOCATIONS OF THE FINGERS

These are very common injuries. The causes are the same as those of jammed fingers: hitting a wall (dislocations are the bane of handball players) or someone else, falling on your finger, catching a ball wrong. And the results are similar as well: pain, swelling, stiffness in the joint. In fact, many jammed fingers are just shy of being dislocations, in which the joint capsule and ligaments tear enough that the joint actually comes apart. You'll know it when you have a dislocation rather than simply a jammed finger. It hurts more, and it just doesn't feel right. Something feels, and looks, out of place, askew. And that something is, of course, the joint, usually the middle joint in the finger.

+ What to do about it + Since only about one in ten dislocations ever sees the inside of a doctor's office, people must be doing a good job of treating them by themselves. Most of them are popped back into place by the injured person or a friend, and most don't lead to any long-term problems. Some do lead to permanent instability in the affected joint, but the fact remains that there are so many dislocations out there that heal and are forgotten that it's hard to recommend any more than reasonable caution concerning them.

Icing is important because these are little joints, and a little swelling can cause a lot of disability. Contrast baths, too, are an effective way of getting rid of swelling. And probably the best thing you can do is splint the affected joint, either by using a splint made for that purpose (never splint your finger on a tongue depressor, for example—the finger should not be straight), or by simply taping the finger to an adjacent finger. Like toes, fingers offer built-in splints because the joints of one finger are seldom at the same level as those of the finger next door. The fingers lie comfortably against one another, joint against bone.

Tape above and below the dislocated joint, and remember to allow the finger to bend a little. You should splint in the position into which it falls naturally. Keep the finger splinted for two to three weeks. A word to the wise: don't remove the splint at night. It may be a great temptation to do so, as it can be tiresome to have your finger splinted all the time, but people often flex and extend their fingers while sleeping. If you leave your finger unsplinted, you may be awakened out of a dead sleep by a painful and throbbing dislocated finger tightly clenched into a fist. Keep the splint on until you can comfortably bend the finger. Then stretch the finger gently and gradually get back to your activity.

If there's any question about the injured joint, if it doesn't seem to improve and the pain just won't go away, then see a doctor for sure. It may be more than a dislocation—a fracture, say—and your fingers are too valuable to take any chances with them. See a doctor.

BASEBALL FINGER

This is another common injury, also called mallet finger. It can happen when, instead of catching a ball in your hand, you catch it against your finger. The impact drives the end of your finger toward the palm of your hand and pulls away the tendon that attaches near the fingernail. Your injury may feel much like a jammed finger or even a dislocation, the other common finger injuries, but you can recognize baseball finger by the fact that you can't straighten your finger. You may be able to bend it—the tendon on the uninjured side is still attached—but you can't straighten it. It's important to check for this right after the injury happens because soon the finger will straighten a bit just from the pressure of swelling.

✚ What to do about it ✚ If you can't straighten your finger, see a doctor. At the least your finger may have to be splinted for six weeks before the tendon completely reattaches, which it will usually do. At the worst the impact may have pulled off a piece of bone with the tendon, in which case surgery may be necessary.

For most of us this is not a horribly disabling injury; it's just annoying not to be able to straighten your finger. But for athletes who depend on their hands, it can be much worse than that. It can be a career-threatening problem. See someone.

FLEXOR TENDON RUPTURE

This is the football equivalent of baseball finger. This injury involves the opposite tendon, the one that flexes the finger rather than straightens it. In football

+ Miscellaneous Injuries +

Cuts in your hand can be a problem, especially if they're any place in the palm. The tendons in the palm are right under the skin's surface. A cut need only be three or four millimeters deep to reach a tendon. And, as with feet, the blood supply to the hand isn't so great. Infections can be another problem. Even blisters bear watching. Don't just ignore lacerations in the hand. Keep them clean, covered, and watch for infection.

There are a lot of little muscles in the hand, but not much goes wrong with them. You can, though, get a lot of bleeding inside the hand from something striking it, or from the hand itself doing the striking. The base of the thumb is an especially good place for internal bleeding. The bleeding, and the swelling that comes from it, can be very disabling temporarily but is not of great consequence otherwise. Ice and compression will do the most good.

Bleeding under a fingernail can result from a blow. Sometimes the resulting pressure can hurt a lot. Just as in the toenails, an easy way to get rid of the pressure is to puncture the nail with a hot paper clip or a tiny, sterilized drill bit.

No matter what the injury, if it comes on dramatically, with a lot of pain and disability, it's a good idea to see a doctor. If you've lost any function in your hands—you can't curl your fingers down, can't make a fist, can't straighten your fingers—or if you get lots of swelling or any squeaking or cracking in the hand, then ice it for a day, and if the problem disappears, fine. But if it doesn't, *see a doctor.* Your hands are simply too important to risk.

it's usually the result of a player grabbing the jersey of another, then getting his finger stuck in it while the other player moves away. The force can pop loose the tendon beneath the finger. With this injury you'll be able to straighten the finger but not bend it.

+ What to do about it + See a doctor. It may be that baseball finger will heal by itself—not so this injury. The tendon usually must be reattached, and the only procedure that can accomplish that is surgery. Again, the test is to see if you can curl your fingers into your palm. If one finger sticks out, you've torn loose the tendon.

FRACTURES

Usually fractures in the hand or fingers are pretty obvious. They grate, they hurt, they swell. They're often caused by hitting something—or someone. An easy way to tell if you've fractured a finger, or even a bone lower down in the metacarpal area of the hand, is to straighten your fingers and just tap the tip of the one that hurts. If you feel a pain lower down in the finger, or into the hand, you've probably fractured it.

+ What to do about it + See a doctor. The danger of fractures in the hand is that the severed bones can rotate against one another, changing the alignment of the injured finger. If, for example, you bend your fingers toward your palm and one veers out in a different direction, it's the result of rotation, and you're in for a problem. A rotated finger can keep you from having a powerful grip, which can be a handicap in more than simply athletics.

Sometimes a splint will treat the fracture; sometimes surgery is necessary. Again, see a doctor.

GAMEKEEPER'S THUMB

This is the most common injury of the thumb, and it may be the most frequent injury in skiing (it's hard to be sure, since, as with most hand injuries, people usually don't tell a doctor about it). It's a sprain of the ligaments at the base of the thumb, right where the web between the thumb and index finger begins. It's often called gamekeeper's thumb, which is what we'll call it rather than a sprain of the ulnar collateral ligament of the metacarpal phalangeal joint. The term comes from the custom of gamekeepers in jolly olde England of wringing the necks of birds and other small game animals between their thumb and index finger. If you wring enough pheasant necks, you'll stretch out the ligament, and you'll end up with a joint that opens *way* up.

The problem is that when you lose the ligaments at the base of the thumb, you lose the ability to pinch the tip of the finger to the side of the thumb. The joint is only supported by ligaments in this direction—no muscles back it up. So although these are small ligaments, an injury to them can be thoroughly disabling. Imagine trying to grip a bat, or a tennis racquet, or a ski pole without being able to exert any pressure with your thumb. Which brings us back to why this is the most common ski injury, and why ski poles aren't made with straps any longer. People commonly acquire gamekeeper's thumb by falling with the pole in their hand. The impact slams the pole into the thumb, forcing it away from the rest of the hand and stretching or tearing the ligaments at the base. With no straps to tether the poles to their hands, skiers are free to jettison their poles before falling.

✚ What to do about it ✚ If your thumb is really tender, better see a doctor. The more torn rather than stretched the ligaments are, the more likely the necessity of surgery to reconstruct them. (If your thumb *really* hurts, you could have a fracture rather than simply a sprain. In that case, you should see a doctor for sure.)

Otherwise, treat gamekeeper's thumb as you would any sprain: rest, ice, compression, contrast baths, and anti-inflammatories. Then, when the pain subsides, stretch gently and gradually begin to use the joint again.

CHAPTER ELEVEN

Exercising to Stay Fit

FOR MOST PEOPLE, increased exercise and better conditioning help prevent cardiovascular disease, some forms of cancer (colon cancer, for example), diabetes, osteoporosis, and depression. Most people who exercise claim that it just makes them feel better. And it's fun to do.

Besides these general benefits, exercise can help you in the sport of your choice. Combining conditioning with actually playing the sport allows you to build strength and endurance in the muscles you most need, whereas solely using the sport itself for conditioning increases the likelihood that you'll suffer overuse injuries. And the older we get the more important this additional conditioning becomes.

For most people in the United States, especially women, the most popular form of exercise is aerobics. Estimates are that aerobic dance alone involves as many as twenty-three million people. There are more women doing aerobic dance than any other organized exercise activity, more even than in all the high school competitive athletic programs in the country put together.

And for good reason. Aerobic exercise can do all sorts of good things for your body. It helps lower blood pressure and cholesterol levels. It tunes up the cardiovascular system. Over time it actually changes your metabolism so that you tend to use accumulated fat for energy. Aerobic exercise will help you do other athletic activities better (even if those activities consist of nothing more than walking up the three flights of stairs to your office without feeling as though you're going to collapse). And for many people it promotes a more healthy sense of self—you simply feel better.

Hefty benefits from such a simple activity, for aerobic exercise really is simple. All that's required to achieve a training effect is to keep your heart rate between 65 and 80 percent of maximum for as little as twenty minutes three days a week.

It doesn't matter what you do. Running, rapid walking, cycling, swimming, dancing, rowing—these are the most common aerobic activities, but anything will do. Some people climb stairs (although you need a lot of stairs to keep it up for twenty minutes), some people skip rope, some people shoot baskets. As long as you *sustain* your heart rate at 65 to 80 percent of maximum for twenty minutes, you're in business.

Anything less than that certainly won't hurt. There's no magic in twenty minutes. It's just a guide. Twenty minutes three days a week will give you consistent benefits from your training. That's not to say that nineteen minutes won't give you some benefits as well, or that ten minutes isn't better than nothing. In fact, any activity—be it mowing the lawn, walking the dog, or washing the car—is better than nothing. They all add up to fitness enhancement.

You should approach aerobic activity with the expectation that you should break a sweat but always be able to carry on minimal conversations (except while swimming, of course, at once the most antisocial and non-sweat-inducing of sports). If you're biking with friends and they can't understand what you're saying because you're simply too short of breath, you've probably gone beyond aerobics. If you can't ask your aerobic dance neighbor a question or can't respond to what she says because you're out of breath, you've probably gone beyond aerobics. If you finish your run in a pool of sweat, unable to move or talk, you've gone beyond aerobics. It's such a *civilized* activity, so reasonable and doable—thus its appeal.

All of that is not to say that finishing your run sweaty and out of breath is bad for you (not necessarily, that is, but it can lead to injuries, depending on how you go about it), but it probably isn't aerobic exercise. The term aerobic comes from the Greek words for "air" and "life"—aerobic exercise involves breathing, the utilization of oxygen. Sounds obvious. We're always breathing, right? But when we're out of breath, our intake of oxygen can't match our output of energy. The demands of our activity outstrip our ability to fuel it by

+ How to Find Your + Aerobic Heart Rate

How can you figure out what heart rate to sustain? A rough method to determine your maximal heart rate is to subtract your age from 220. So a 40-year-old person's maximal heart rate is about 180 beats per minute. Now figure 65 to 80 percent of that: let's say 125 beats per minute (about 70 percent of maximum). If you're 40 years old and you can keep your heart pounding along at 125 beats per minute for twenty minutes, you're giving yourself a healthy dose of aerobic exercise. If you're 60 years old, a good rate would be about 110 beats per minute. If you're 20, 140 beats per minute will do—and so it goes. An easy way to measure your heart rate is by feeling the pulse in your neck, just below the jawline. Count the beats for ten seconds, then multiply by six. Twenty beats during that ten-second interval indicate about 120 beats per minute—right on the money for a 40-year-old.

breathing. Then the body must rely on its stored energy sources. Thus, the term anaerobic—"without air life."

Activities such as sprinting, whether on a track, a bike, or in a pool, are anaerobic. A runner may not even breathe once during a sixty-yard dash. A swimmer may take one breath going out and a couple more coming back during a fifty-yard sprint. All that time the body uses its stored up carbohydrates to keep going. This kind of exercise hurts more than aerobic exercise. Your muscles burn because you're depleting the available fuel and all that's left are waste products like lactic acid. "Go for the burn" means to exercise to the point at which you hurt. Any serious athlete deals with that kind of hurt daily.

Done to excess, any aerobic exercise can become anaerobic, and there's nothing wrong with that. It all depends on your reason for exercising. Anaerobic exercise is the name of the game for building strength in specific muscles. When you abuse a muscle to the point where it burns, you begin to build strength in that muscle. Bodybuilders bring their muscles to this point all the time. It's what pumping iron is all about. But if your intent is general fitness—lowering blood pressure and cholesterol levels, tuning up the cardiovascular system, inducing your metabolism to use accumulated fat for energy—aerobic exercise is an efficient and reasonable way to go about it. The results are not as quick and dramatic as building muscles with anaerobic exercise, but they're attained at less cost of time and effort. And if you stick with it long enough, the benefits become measurable and lasting.

They show up in subtle ways. Some people exercise in the hope of living longer, but there's no real evidence to suggest that you're likely to live one month longer if you do aerobics than if you don't. It's the quality of your life while you're still around that increases. The odds are that you'll simply feel better. You'll find that you're able to ski longer, say, or survive an extra set of tennis. You'll be able to take a hike in the mountains without getting winded as easily as before or walk up the hill to the office without huffing and puffing. Your weight may not change too much—aerobic exercise is not an efficient way to lose weight though combining exercise with diet control can produce results—but slowly that weight becomes distributed differently. Muscle begins to replace fat. Muscle is heavier than fat, so you may not lose much weight, but the weight you have will look better than fat. Muscle is more dense and takes up less space, so the exchange of a few pounds of fat for a few pounds of muscle can improve your appearance. And although none of these benefits show up immediately, you don't have to wait too long either. Pulse rate and blood pressure changes often occur in a couple of months. Weight loss takes longer. The change in metabolism that allows your body to burn off accumulated fat more readily becomes measurable in three to six months.

But exercise, any kind of exercise, is not for everybody. Some people simply hate to exercise. Being browbeaten into it by a physician, a spouse, or a book like this can actually decrease the quality of one's life rather than improve it. If you'd rather curl up with a good book in front of the pool than swim laps, that's okay. It depends on what you want from life. And the same reasoning applies to exercise. It's important to remember that any kind of exercise may be good for you. It all depends on your reason for doing it.

HOW TO PICK YOUR OWN STYLE OF AEROBIC TRAINING

You need to know what you want from your exercise and how much you enjoy doing it. The activities usually associated with aerobic conditioning are those that are constant through a period of time—running, rapid walking, swimming, cycling, rowing, dancing—in contrast to tennis, say, which involves spurts of rapid activity combined with spurts of preparing for and recovering from action. But it's crazy to decide that swimming laps is going to be the exercise for you if you hate the water or are trying to get in shape for skiing. By the same token, there's no sense running a few miles a day if you don't like to run, or if you're preparing for tennis season. And there's certainly no reason to do either activity if you don't like to be alone. Besides, lower body workouts don't do that much for upper body sports and vice versa, specially if you don't enjoy what you're doing.

So if you have goals in mind for your conditioning, best match the exercise with the goal. If it's skiing you're after, then running will help—cycling maybe even more so. (Exercising on a Nordic Trak machine can help your cross-country skiing.) If it's tennis, then an upper body conditioner like swimming or rowing might be the way to go (some running won't hurt, certainly). If it's general conditioning, then pick an activity you like to do and one that's convenient for you. If you live in San Francisco, say, and you can't manage running hills, it may not be worth it for you to have to drive twenty minutes to flat terrain, run for twenty minutes, and then drive another twenty minutes home. On the other hand, there's not one person in San Francisco who lives more than fifteen minutes from a fitness facility. In that case, aerobic dance might be the ticket for you, especially if you like the companionship, the idea of having an instructor, and don't mind paying for the privilege. Running and brisk walking, of course, are free.

Previous medical problems can determine what activity you chose. If you have knee problems, then running up and down hills may not be a lot of fun, nor will pumping a bike for a few miles. Lower back problems may not be the ticket for the jarring involved with running or the stretching demanded by the rowing machine. Hundreds of shoulder revolutions in the swimming pool might not be the best thing for chronic shoulder problems. You may have to give these activities a test drive; experiment a bit until you find what's right for you.

On the other hand, just because you've had a bad experience with one or another of these activities doesn't mean that they're out of the question forever. You simply may have to modify your approach. For example . . .

Running

Often people complain about running on a track—it's boring, it hurts, it gives them shinsplints. Well, it can be boring, that's for sure. In fact, if aerobic conditioning is your aim, it may not be such a good idea to run on a track at all. Besides the fact that running through town or through a park can be much more interesting, some tracks simply are not designed for training. They're built for competition (synthetic tracks fall into this category), and although they may feel soft, they're actually too hard and unyielding for the constant pounding produced by frequent runs. The result of training on these tracks can be nagging injuries. If you must run on a track, be sure it's cinder or dirt, not synthetic.

Sometimes people complain of not being able to find a grassy area to run on. Well, today's shoes are designed to run on asphalt. The idea of the cushioned sole is to make asphalt as easy on the body as grass. You can even run on concrete in these shoes, but asphalt is much better. It's softer, and the subtle irregularities of the surface allow your shoe to sink, providing even more cushioning. So, if possible, run in the road rather than on the sidewalk. Alternate directions, however. Always running against traffic is all well and good, but some roads are heavily crowned, with the result that you're always running on a hillside with the right side of your body at a higher level than the left. The discrepancy can take a toll.

Many coastal dwellers prefer to run on the beach. As glorious as it can be to jump into the waves at the end of your workout, beach running has a couple of problems. One is that the soft sand converts your shoes (or bare feet) into negative-heeled footwear because your heels sink into the sand as you run. There's nothing intrinsically wrong with a negative heel—some shoe companies have made their mark by claiming that it's a desirable commodity—but when you're used to having your heel raised above the rest of your foot, as is the case with almost all of the shoes people wear, suddenly dropping your heel below that level can put a lot of strain on your Achilles tendon and calf and hamstring muscles. If they're not pretty flexible, look out. Tendinitis and muscle strains can be the result.

The other problem at the beach is similar to that of running on the road: you're always navigating a sidehill. The best thing to do is pick a beach that slopes as gradually as possible and stick to the moist, hard sand. Low tide is often a particularly good time to run. And if you start out going in one direction, be sure to take the time to come all the way back in the other. Equalize the effect of the slope.

Cycling

Lots of people have had bad experiences with cycling, especially people with knee problems. True, the nature of pumping a bike—up and down, back and forth, against resistance—can be hard on the knees, but more people suffer from cycling than need to, most likely because they haven't set up their bikes well.

Before you take off for the first time, you should adjust your own bike. The shop where you bought your bike may not have set it up well for you. Often they adjust things for greatest efficiency, as though all their customers, like themselves, did 100-mile excursions on their days off. That approach may not translate into the greatest safety and comfort for someone with a knee problem. And it can be a good idea to set up on an exercise bike to start with. It's easy to control, easy to adjust, and you don't have to carry a wrench and socket set around in your back pocket for the duration of your ride.

Begin by finding the ideal seat height for you. The higher the seat, the straighter your knee when the pedal is most distant from you. The lower the seat, the more bent your knee. You know when your knee hurts—find the position that bothers you least. (In general, your knee should be about fifteen degrees shy of full extension when the pedal is farthest away.) Then check your foot placement. That's a consideration that can be crucial to being able to cycle comfortably.

Although bike pedals and toe clips point straight ahead, most feet don't. Most people's feet turn out, at least a little. Some people are pigeon-toed—their feet turn in. Yet bike designers don't seem to acknowledge the discrepancy. The pedals lie square to the sprocket, toe clips secured to the front, inviting the foot to slip in and stay there, parallel to each other and the bike. Yet forcing feet to be aligned that way would be like making runners fit into parallel, shoe-wide troughs. That would be ludicrous, but cyclists do the equivalent all the time.

Don't let yourself fall into that trap. You can tell which way your feet fall by sitting on a table with your knees bent and legs hanging. Notice which way your feet point. That's the way they should point on the pedals. Although they may not look it, toe clips allow you to vary the angle of your feet by about five to eight degrees in either direction and still stay secured. That's enough for most people. Hard-core cyclists spend lots of time and money making sure that their cleats are attached at precisely the right angle for comfort on the pedals. Less serious bikers can do much the same thing by gouging out a ridge in their cycling shoes so that their feet fit onto the pedals the same way all the time. Don't do it, though, until you're sure you've found the right angle.

Once you're situated properly, with feet comfortably placed and height adjusted, you may find that most of your cycling problems fade away. If some still persist, it may be wise to try another sport. There are lots of ways to get your aerobic conditioning.

Rowing

Watch out for similar things in rowing. Are your feet situated properly? They don't have to point straight ahead in a rowing machine, either. The boot supports that oarsmen use often are angled for specific foot demands. You should similarly be able to adjust the slide distance on a rowing machine to accommodate your particular frame. It may be that bending forward is rough, or perhaps it's pulling all the way back that hurts. Do whatever's comfortable for you. Again, for general aerobic conditioning it's not so much what you do as whether your heart rate is high enough for long enough. Even a relatively short rowing stroke can offer you a good aerobic workout if you go at it hard enough.

Skiing

Between 85 and 90 percent of all ski injuries result from falls, and the kinds of injuries those falls produce can be serious and long term. For example, skiing produces a higher percentage of fractures than any other sport. So, given that most skiers, especially beginners, are going to fall once in a while at least, you want to do everything you can to keep those spills to a minimum. Here are a few suggestions.

Become a better skier. The better you are, the less chance you have of getting hurt. Studies have shown a strong correlation between increasing levels of skiing ability and decreasing levels of injury. Like the tennis player who takes a lesson to get rid of tennis elbow, take a ski lesson to avoid ski injuries. It's one of the best safety investments you can make.

Shorter skis are safer than longer skis. It used to be that anyone who was anyone used long skis. If your skis weren't taller than you were, there was obviously something wrong with you. Short skis, if available, were the sign of lack of ability, extreme youth, or some other unattractive characteristic. Now that equation has turned around. Short skis are in, and available, and much easier to ski on. There may be some benefit from the short ski acting as a smaller lever arm during falls, subsequently transferring less force to your legs, knees, and ankles, but, most importantly, short skis lead to fewer falls in the first place. They require less energy and strength to manage, can be manipulated more readily, and don't tire you as quickly. So if you're going to use your old skis for the first time in years, or are contemplating borrowing a pair from your parents or aunt or uncle, you might be better off buying or renting a new, short pair. Your legs will thank you.

Proper binding tension is vitally important. The bindings are the link between you and your skis. Assuming that despite your lessons and good skis you're going to fall anyway, you'll want to be able to jettison your skis right away. Falling is the source of most ski injuries, and falling with your skis attached is the best way to make sure that the injury has a pretty good chance of being serious.

The most deadly fall for beginning and intermediate skiers is a slow, twisting fall. When the people at the ski lodge set your bindings for you they usually test the release by whacking the side of your boot. If the binding releases after such a blow, they send you off to the slopes. If you happen to fall with such an abrupt force, the binding will set you free. But that's not the fall that's going to injure you. It's the slow kind that's most dangerous, and it's likely that your binding will hold on tight during one of those, trapping your foot on the ski.

You should be able to snap your foot out of the bindings all by yourself. To test them, have somebody firmly hold the tip and tail of the ski as you stand on it. You should be able to twist the toe of the boot out of the binding simply by turning your foot to the inside. It should take some effort, but not so much that it hurts. If you can't get out, the bindings are too tight.

Once you've set your bindings, test them every day before you ski. Don't assume that setting them once will set them forever. Bindings are engineered precisely and can change their adjustment just by being jammed into a locker or strapped onto a car. A good thing to do is make sure you can twist out of them just before you step into the lift line each morning. And remember, you want to twist to the *inside*. Most falls will push your skis outwards; you want your foot to be able to come free to the inside.

Some people object to having their bindings set too loose because they might let go inadvertently. It's no fun to be skiing along and have a binding come loose for no reason. Falls from inadvertent binding release can be traumatic—the binding comes loose, you know you're going to fall, and, as though it's all happening in slow motion, you have time to think about all the horrible possibilities. But few people are badly hurt by such falls—far fewer than those injured during falls in which the binding releases late or not at all. If you're a beginner you might just accept the fact that it may be your lot in life to spend a lot of time putting your skis back on. Better that than the six weeks or so you'd have to spend in a cast and the months of rehabilitation afterwards. So, if you've been falling a fair amount and your bindings are not coming loose, you'd better look out.

(Unfortunately there's not much evidence that even ideally functioning bindings do much to prevent that most famous of ski injuries, the anterior cruciate ligament (ACL) tear. We can, however, offer a couple of suggestions. One is to avoid skiing with your knees sharply bent and your weight back on the tails of the skis. ACL tears seem to accompany this position. Another no-no is to try to recover from, or ride out, a fall. Perhaps the simplest and best advice is, don't fight it—learn how to fall.)

After you check your bindings, warm up. Slide over to the bottom of the slope and sidestep up about fifty feet. Then ski down, making a couple of turns on the way. Then turn around, sidestep up on your other side another fifty feet, and ski down again, turning along the way. Finally, herringbone up, make a turn, and come down. It'll take you about five minutes and is well worth the effort.

Most skiers don't do any such thing. They climb out from their cramped position in the car directly into the cold, put on their skis, get into the chairlift and assume another cramped position for the ten minutes or so of the ride, then suddenly unfold to ski down the ramp, which, for beginners, may be the steepest slope they see all day. Then, if they're still in one piece, they expect to be able to ski a mile down to the bottom without hurting themselves. It's absurd. No one would attempt a few sets of tennis without stretching and hitting a few balls first; no one would set out to run a few miles without getting the blood flowing and muscles relaxed and stretched ahead of time. In fact, there's not another athlete in any other activity who would dream of doing anything as demanding, and with as high an injury potential, as skiing without any stretching or warming up exercises. But skiers do that all the time. Not smart. A disproportionate number of injuries occur in the first portion of the first run of the day.

When you do fall, try to keep your legs together. Most injuries occur when one leg splays away from the other. Two legs held together splint one another, reducing the chance of harm. Sometimes you simply have to sit down in the snow while you're still in control rather than trying to ski through an oncoming fall. Sometimes you have to hold back a bit and better gauge your ability to stay upright. But sometimes you just don't have any choice. Even if you follow every suggestion we've made, you might be injured. Injuries will attack the best-prepared, smartest, and best-conditioned people. That's the nature of the sport.

Some serious ski injuries are not terribly painful. About half the people with medial collateral knee ligament tears ski down the slope by themselves, and many with anterior cruciate ligament tears have no idea how severely they've injured themselves. If you're hurting badly, you should see someone who can help you, obviously; and even a joint that feels loose is reason enough to get

---

+ Cross-country Skiing +

Skiing began as ski touring—what we now call cross-country skiing. For years, during the growth and peak popularity of Alpine skiing, cross-country skiing was a sport reserved for the true enthusiast, the person who hiked and camped and donned skis for something other than whizzing down a slope at top speed. These days, with the costs of ski equipment and lift tickets and lodging going through the roof, Alpine skiers are looking elsewhere for things to do in the snow. Many of them have discovered cross-country skiing, a much more economical sport. So now there are a number of people who are not woods-wise setting off on mountain trails. For these people, a few words of caution:

Don't ski too long or too far. Especially early in the year, as you're getting into condition, it's much better to go out and come back twice than it is to go out and not be able to come back at all. The Alpine skier is used to skiing until tired and then just sliding downhill and home. Ski touring doesn't work that way. You can't simply go on until you're tired—you still have to make it back, a task that can include navigating uphill slopes and difficult terrain. Rather, pick a specific distance, or a time, and then turn around. Go out for forty minutes and then come back. As you grow stronger and begin to learn your body's limitations, you can increase the length of your excursions. Until then, frostbite, exposure, and just plain fatigue can be very real problems.

Be careful when using cross-country skis on Alpine slopes. It used to be that most ski areas wouldn't let people with cross-country skis onto lifts, as they fig-

medical help. It might be fully as serious an injury, if not more, than one that is more painful.

If you hurt your leg or ankle, don't take your boot off. The boot provides compression to minimize swelling, and, if your leg is broken, the boot can be a handy tether for a splint or traction device.

Don't ski alone. That admonition may seem unnecessary on jam-packed Alpine slopes, but be cautious about wandering off onto little-used trails, especially late in the day. In any activity in which the environment is not hospitable, and which requires special means to get around, it's always wise to have a friend around for help if the conditions get the better of you.

ADVICE—APPROACH IT GINGERLY

For people who exercise, especially beginners, the woods are full of advice. Most of it is well meaning, some of it is actually well taken, but much is not terribly well founded. The advisory columns in the national fitness magazines can fall into this category. They are often written by people who are in the upper echelons of their sport and are trying to wring that last one tenth of a percent of efficiency from their activity. For such a person, subtle or not-so-subtle alterations in foot position

---

CROSS-COUNTRY SKIING (CONTINUED)

ured—rightly—that cross-country skiers were a hazard on the slopes. Now, perhaps for economic reasons, that policy has changed in a number of areas, and the resulting injuries are beginning to roll in—serious injuries, fractures and the like.

The reason is that cross-country skis are designed to go in straight lines primarily and not to make the quick, sharp turns demanded by Alpine courses. Turning in a cross-country ski demands technical expertise and a lot of room. If you're zipping down an Alpine slope and are suddenly confronted with a little ravine, a grove of trees, or another skier, you better be a ski touring expert, or lucky. So if you want to practice with your cross-country skis on Alpine slopes, pick a slope that's gentle, relatively unpopulated, and open, so that if

you don't execute a turn you won't end up in the trees or off a cliff or tangled up with another skier.

A less dramatic problem in ski touring occurs with *muscle strains,* and not just in the legs. People forget that in contrast to Alpine skiing, cross-country skiing is a lower *and* upper body sport. You use your arms to pull and push as much as you do your legs. It's important to condition the entire body for this sport. A rowing machine in combination with bicycling might be an effective off-season conditioner. Better yet is a ski touring trainer, a commercially available treadmill device that requires you to use your arms and legs in working out. These are tremendous exercise devices and not just for ski touring. We've used them to help rehabilitate knee surgery patients.

and arm swing may pay real dividends. But for the rest of us mortals, those of us who are happy to run our few miles, get our heart rate up, and enjoy the scenery along the way, any conscious attempt to alter our form may lead to disaster.

If you look like a duck when you run, it's probably because your hips and knees are built in such a way that your most efficient form is ducklike. If your legs bow and feet point in when you run, so be it—that's the way you're built. For someone to suggest that your feet should point straight ahead, or your hips remain straight, or your neck and head stay motionless can be ludicrous and dangerous. Sports medicine physicians make a good part of their living seeing people who tried to change their running gait.

There is a time for refining technique, of course, but for the recreational athlete it shouldn't come at the expense of what feels comfortable. A word to the wise: when beginning any activity, or sustaining one for recreational purposes, *do what comes naturally*. And for heaven's sake don't change just because somebody advises you to. The idea for most people is to enjoy what you do, remain comfortable and free of injury, and realize the benefits of exercise at the same time. Remember, it doesn't matter how you get your pulse rate up or how you look doing it—the benefits will come.

AN APPROACH TO WORKING OUT

All right. The moment has come. After numerous fits and starts and solemn promises that you're going to start anytime now, the day arrives. You've locked the office, run the errands, paid the bills, washed the car, picked up the kids, and fed the cat—no more excuses, time to get going. You're wearing your new running shoes, matching shorts, latest tank top. It's a beautiful day, not a cloud in the sky. Everything's set. There's only one problem: now what do you do?

Some people simply decide, "I'll run a mile to start with." Well, assuming you're fit enough to run a mile—and many people are, at least the first time they try—how long will it take you? Eight minutes? Eighteen minutes? A half hour? Remember, in aerobic exercise it's not how far you run but how long and at what heart rate that counts. So, you set off on your mile and, pride being what it is, you push hard the whole way. You arrive back home in fifteen minutes—not long enough for a good aerobic workout but a significant length of time, nevertheless—with your tongue hanging out. No matter. At least you survived. The first day has been a success. And a few minutes later, shoes off, supine on the sofa, a cold glass in your hand, you're comfortable enough to wonder what the big deal about this exercise business is, anyhow. It wasn't so hard. One mile today, you'll push up to two tomorrow. Who said you weren't in good shape?

The next morning you can hardly get out of bed. And as the day wanes, so do you. You're too tired even to think about running. Best take a day off and get back to it tomorrow.

The next morning comes—you're worse. You hurt in places you didn't know existed. If you were simply too *exhausted* to move yesterday, today you're too *sore* to move. It hurts to climb out of bed, hurts to straighten up, hurts to open the refrigerator door, hurts to bend getting into the car. And by the end of the day these general hurts have coalesced into specific hurts: your calves and Achilles tendons feel as though they're on fire, and your lower back feels as if it was used for a punching bag when you weren't looking.

Finally, a week later, you've recovered enough to entertain the thought of moving again, maybe even running again, and a few days after that you once more pull on your running shoes and matching shorts. What have you gained? Nothing. Not only have you trashed your body, perhaps planted the seed of a problem that could persist and turn into something bigger, but you haven't even started on the road to conditioning because you've had to wait so long before you were able to go out again. Now, as you face setting off on your run, you're back where you started, perhaps even behind, and, to make matters worse, after a couple of weeks of beautiful Indian summer, the weather has turned. Today it's gray and drizzling, hardly running weather. You wonder, what's the big deal about this exercise business, anyway?

If a goodly portion of the income of sports medicine doctors comes from people who try and change their natural way of doing things, another sizable chunk comes from people who refuse to work into condition gradually. You simply have to start gently. So much so that it can seem almost ridiculous at first.

If twenty minutes of running is your goal, begin by working up to rapid *walking* for twenty minutes. Start with five minutes of walking the first day, two and a half minutes out, two and a half minutes back. (This is a good strategy for any aerobics activity. Distances really don't mean anything in aerobics, time does. If you split your time in half—half out, half in—at least you know you'll always make it home.) Then do seven total minutes, and a couple of days later do nine. Go up a couple of minutes every other day, and in a couple of weeks you'll be walking for twenty minutes at a good, rapid pace without hurting anything or suffering the next morning. At that point you've already begun to enjoy your aerobic workout.

Then start exchanging running for some of your walking. Run the first five minutes of your workout and walk the last fifteen. A couple of days later run the first seven minutes and walk the last thirteen, then nine and eleven, and so on.

Build up just as you did with your walking, and in a couple of weeks you'll be running the entire workout with no ill effects afterwards.

Always remember to do the running at the *beginning* of your workout. Warm up and stretch, and then get right to the running. Don't do what most people do—leave the tough stuff until last. There's no worse time to change your activity to one that's more stressful than when you're tired. It's hard enough for your body to have to worry about running instead of walking. Don't make it deal with fatigue at the same time.

This principle holds true for any stressful change. If you're training for the San Francisco Marathon, say, and you know you have to get used to running up and down hills, add the hills to your workout at the beginning, then run the flats. If you're going to add some sprints, do the fast stuff early in the workout rather than at the end. And so it goes. The less fatigued you are, the better you'll be able to handle change.

It's good to remember that you lose the benefits of training at least twice as fast as you gain them. If you've been unable to work out for a few days, you shouldn't start right back in where you left off. Those few days of idleness have deconditioned your body twice as much as a comparable amount of exercise would have built you up. You don't have to start all over again, necessarily, but you should drop back to a level that's slightly less than that which you feel able to handle and then gradually increase to your normal speed. The good thing about such a step backwards is that after a short layoff you'll be able to come back to top speed more quickly than it took to get you there in the first place.

If the reason you can't work out happens to be illness, then it's especially important to start back gradually. You've not only missed time and have suffered the deconditioning that mere lack of exercise brings about, but your body has been torn down by illness as well. You can hurt yourself by starting back too hard. Being in bed for a week with the flu is much like being in space—you actually experience a decrease in muscle size and capability.

Remember also that the more fit you are, the more it takes to drive your pulse rate up high enough to be able to realize aerobic benefits. It's the bittersweetness of aerobic training: as you become stronger, your heart is able to function effectively with less effort, and the things you did yesterday to drive up your pulse don't necessarily do the trick anymore. You simply have to work harder to sustain the same benefits. Similarly, a fit body will readily relax. Your pulse rate will drop back to normal at the slightest break, rather than race to catch up as it used to when you took a breather. So if you're involved in an activity that changes pace often during those twenty minutes, you may not be realizing twenty minutes of aerobic conditioning. During a significant amount of that time, your heart may have dropped back to a nearly normal rate.

For most people, training every other day is enough. There's nothing wrong with working out every day, but you really don't need to—not for aerobic conditioning reasons, that is. Three to four days a week are enough to provide solid benefits. And, interestingly enough, after four times a week the increase in benefits doesn't keep pace with the increase in time and energy. Whereas working out four times a week may be 33 percent better for you than just three times, training five times will not be 25 percent better than four. And training eight times won't be twice as good as just four. After a certain point, the rate of increase in the benefits of training flattens out. If you're a competitive athlete, then yes, it may be worth it to grind out five, ten, or even more workouts a week for the relatively small increase in conditioning that the extra effort gleans. But for those people who exercise for general fitness rather than with specific athletic goals in mind, the only real reason to do aerobic conditioning more than four times a week is if you enjoy it—which, all things considered, may be the best reason of all.

WEIGHT TRAINING

Aerobic conditioning is not the only valid kind of exercise, of course. In fact, it's a good idea to combine aerobic exercise with other kinds, even alternate them day to day. A solid course of exercise for just about anyone might include an aerobic workout every other day and weight training every other day. Aerobic fitness is primarily cardiovascular conditioning; weight training concentrates on the muscles themselves.

People usually go into weight training for two reasons. One is to build strength. If you're a serious athlete, weight work can help you better perform in your sport. If you're a skier, for example, you've got to have rock-hard quadriceps. Weight training can help strengthen those muscles. If you're a tennis player, you need strong legs and shoulders. If you're a male dancer, you've got to have strong shoulders and arms for lifting your partner. Running, gymnastics, swimming— weight training can help in just about any sport. And it may be that you simply want to be stronger for general, everyday reasons. You're tired of being exhausted for days after moving the furniture around, say. You want to be stronger for yard work. Weight training can zero in on any particular muscle group and help build strength.

The other reason is to look better. Muscle is better looking than fat. You can work with muscle, tone and develop it. You can't tone fat. In fact one kind of fat, the infamous and dreaded cellulite, is much like having an injection of lard under

+ Weight Training +
for Ice Skaters

Weight training is probably a good idea for skaters. Certainly for men some work on the arms and torso can be a help, as male skaters are required to lift their partners more and more. For one thing, lifts often look bad if the man isn't strong enough to let the woman down slowly; secondly, injuries can result from such a lack of strength. As with male dancers, back problems are common among male skaters, and the women can suffer stress fractures in the lower leg if they're consistently let down too quickly or too hard.

your skin. Weight training offers a way to attack these areas and, if not eliminate them (you can't really spot reduce through weight or aerobic training), at least firm them up. Any area of the body will look better if the muscles underlying it are firm. You'll feel better as well.

(And for some women there's another very good reason to train with weights. There's good evidence that for postmenopausal women weight training can halt the progression of osteoporosis.)

How should you approach weight training?

Gradually. One of the real problems with fitness facilities is that frequently they're run by people for whom lifting weights is a way of life rather than a means to an end. For these people the idea is to be as muscular as possible and to *look* as muscular as possible—all of which is fine, of course, but those may not be your goals. Yet often these instructors create programs for you that are similar to the ones they themselves follow in order to look that way. These programs are geared to the development of muscle bulk, and bulk may be the last thing you want. Runners don't want bulk. Tennis players don't want bulk. Certainly dancers don't want bulk. And often these programs emphasize rapid increases in weight-lifting capabilities. It's very impressive to pull your chart and see that in three months you've increased the weight you can lift 300 percent. Gives you a feeling of accomplishment.

But such huge percentage increases can be misleading. If you begin a free-weight program able to bench press 50 pounds, say, and in a few months are hoisting 150 pounds, that's a 300 percent increase. But, as in anything, the easiest gains are the early ones. Another person, someone who's stronger to begin with, may begin at 150 pounds and during the same amount of time increase to 175 pounds. That's less than a 20 percent increase. Does that mean that the first program is better than the second or the first person is in better shape than the second? Nonsense. It all depends on where you start and what your goals are.

Similarly, weight-training instructors often push you hard. The usual approach is that as soon as you can handle twelve repetitions at any given weight, add a plate. Well, if you're not very strong to begin with and you're only lifting thirty pounds on the knee extension device, a full ten-pound plate represents a 33 percent increase. That's a big jump. A number of such increases, all of which are certainly possible in the beginning stages of a lifting program, look great on the progress chart. You'll probably notice some new muscle. You may also notice some new knee problems.

Our usual recommendation is that you shouldn't increase anything, ever, by more than 20 percent, And even that's a large increment. Ten percent might even be better. That rule of thumb pertains not only to lifting weights, but to distance and time as well. And it's wise to at least do twenty-four to thirty repetitions before adding weight. That's asking a lot—people get bored doing too many reps—but it's even more boring being hurt. (A way to hedge the bet would be to do fewer reps and add only a half a plate at a time.)

The better fitness facilities increasingly offer the services of exercise physiologists, and more and more the instructors themselves have had some training in the area. Still, the most important aspect of any fitness program is that you yourself know why you're doing it. Is your goal to bulk up or trim down? To prepare for a particular activity or to gain overall strength? To develop a particular muscle group or to keep in shape during the off-season? The more you've thought about why you're exercising, the more accurately an instructor can tailor a program for you, and the more readily you'll attain your goals. The reason *why* you're there in large part determines *how* you should use the equipment.

How to lift weights

It's a discussion we probably wouldn't be having were it not for Nautilus equipment. Nautilus is as much responsible for the success of the fitness movement as anything because it was the first to offer uniform equipment with uniform training programs. It took the weight room out of the smelly, boxing-style gym where women couldn't go and transformed it into the shiny, chromed, and mirrored little palaces that are rapidly replacing singles bars as preferred places for the sexes to get together. The equipment is attractively and invitingly designed, and, not only that, it offers a solid workout. Because of its eccentric cam, Nautilus was the first to offer equipment that loaded the muscle appropriately through the whole range of motion. This equipment provided less resistance at the extremes of motion, where you're weaker, and more during the midrange, where you're stronger. Whereas people used to do the bulk of their lifting through the midrange only because no one was strong enough to handle extremes, with Nautilus it was possible to lift uniformly through the entire range of motion.

Moreover, if you used the equipment correctly it *forced* you to go through the entire range and to stretch to get into the machine in the first place. So, properly used, the equipment provided strengthening and stretching. Now, of course, there are a variety of Nautilus-like weight machines. Any of them can afford you a good workout. Nautilus was simply the first.

So much so that with modern weight equipment you may not need to stretch quite as much before beginning to lift. Still, stretching before any exercise is a good idea. It's one of the eight cardinal rules of lifting. They are:

1. **Stretch before and after lifting.** You'll feel much better afterwards.

2. **Always lift weights that you can control.** If you start quivering when you lift, you're probably working with more weight than you can handle. A muscle that quivers is approaching its breaking point. And that's when the body begins to compensate by arching the back as well performing other ill-advised tricks. Not good. Keep your lifting under control.

3. **Have somebody watch you.** Lifting weights with a friend is a good idea because then someone can check on your technique and alert you to any bad habits. One of the problems with many fitness facilities is that they just don't have enough people (or the people don't have enough time—they're too busy trying to bring in new memberships) to properly supervise the weight room. If you lift weights incorrectly—arching the back is the primary offender (see chapter 7, "The Back and Neck")—you might as well not lift at all. Partner up.

4. **Lift deliberately.** If you lift ballistically, that is by bouncing into the weights, you're not going to gain the full benefit of the lifting because you're using momentum to help you. More than that, you can actually tear a muscle by bouncing into a weight that's too heavy.

    But "deliberately" doesn't necessarily mean "slowly." There's an advantage to tailoring your training as closely as possible to the pace of the activity. If you do high-speed things like sprinting, swimming, dancing, or gymnastics, then it can be a good idea to do high-speed repetitions. Slower, endurance activities like long-distance running may demand slower reps but more of them. But, in any case, lift deliberately, come down deliberately, always keeping your back pressed into the backrest. It's the coming down, the eccentric contraction, that is the most effective strengthening technique.

And go through the entire range of motion. Don't cheat yourself by using the cheater bar when you should be using your muscles.

5. **Work up to heavier weights in small increments.** A 20 percent increase is plenty. Ten percent may be even better. Sometimes it's impossible to increase so gradually, as facilities don't always have equipment with half increments. But do the best you can within the limits of your particular facility. No matter the temptation, don't think that you can add two or three or even more plates each time you increase. Step up gradually.

6. **Find equipment that's the right size for you.** Smaller men, many women, and kids often have been the odd people out in many cases—the equipment simply has been too large for them. Now equipment designed for women is available, and the better nonspecialized brands are adjustable. Lifting with the wrong size equipment can lead to injury.

7. **Don't hurry through your workout.** When you race through a lifting program you start to do things wrong—you get tired, begin to arch your back, use less than the full range of motion—and the result can be diminished benefits at the least, injury at the worst. Not to mention the fact that hurrying through is no fun. Give your workout the time and concentration it needs.

8. **Give yourself proper rest.** The ideal program might involve alternating lifting every other day with aerobic workouts every other day. Although it's often advertised as such, weight circuit training usually isn't aerobic. When you're actually using the equipment, you're probably doing anaerobic training (pant, pant), and the breaks between stations can bring your heart rate down. So combining weight training with aerobic training is a solid way to go.

How to decide which muscles to strengthen

First you have to know why you're exercising. Is it for a general tune-up or to get in shape for a specific activity? If the former, you may want to hit the entire circuit of stations. If the latter, then take your cue from the way you feel after doing the activity. For example, if you're working out to get—or stay—in shape for tennis, then simply remember how you felt last year when you went out and played for the first time *without* getting in shape first. What hurt? Where were you sore the next day? Those are the areas to work on.

With tennis, it's likely your calves will hurt because you're using your soleus and gastrocnemius muscles to keep you up on your toes. Your back may hurt from all that bending and stretching. And your shoulder will most likely hurt, for obvious reasons. (And if you can't remember all this from last season, drag yourself out on the court for a refresher—it will come back quickly.) Armed with that information, simply find the equipment that works out the muscles in question and emphasize those stations in your workout. If in doubt, consult with a staff member. It's that easy. And other activities will just as clearly communicate their needs. Come the new season, you'll likely find yourself toned and ready to go.

FINDING YOUR LEVEL

There *are* limits. Hard as it may be to accept, each of us has a point beyond which we can't do more. If that weren't true, people would be running two-minute miles and bench-pressing 1,500 pounds. We just can't go on forever. But people assume that they can. If I can lift 150 pounds on the knee extender today, why can't I lift 175 pounds tomorrow? And 200 pounds soon thereafter? But the fact is that if you work at it, you'll arrive at a point where you're in good shape, and to go beyond that point probably means that you're going to get hurt.

All the more so because after the age of twenty-five, we probably get 1 percent weaker and 1 percent less flexible every year. Part of the reason for that is cultural—until the fitness boom we became much more sedentary as we became older—but for the most part it's just the way things are, one of the "joys" of aging. So if you want to keep doing what you've always been able to do, it'll take that much more effort just to hold your own as you age.

But, you may ask, what about professional athletes? They're always trying to do more. They don't attain a certain level and stay there. True enough, but they pay a high price. To begin with, pushing the limits is a full-time job. And secondly, successful athletes are a millimeter away from disaster all the time. They train to be always on the edge—push a little harder, and they're liable to fall off. Top athletes constantly must deal with injuries. It's an occupational hazard for them but not the happiest situation for recreational athletes who are trying to get some fun out of their activity, hold down a job, and cultivate relationships with other people at the same time. You just can't do everything. Try, and you'll be injured too much of the time.

So, it's important to find a level that agrees with you and not worry because you aren't constantly doing more and better. Remember, the more fit you are, the more grudging your gains. At first your progress can be spectacular. It's easy to get used to 20 percent gains every week. But that kind of euphoria just doesn't last. If in the beginning you can almost measure improvements by the day, soon you're only able to measure them by the week, then by the month, and after a while you may not be able to measure them at all. The road to fitness looks something like this: Spectacular gains at first and then the long,

hard road. So, stay with it, but don't expect improvement forever. Realize that what happens during the first two weeks will never happen again. Find a level that is satisfying and reasonably free of injury, and then best of luck in trying to stay there.

STRETCHING

Nobody thought very much about stretching until about forty years ago. It was then that people in football (which is the origin of many of the things we do in conditioning) decided that weight training should be an integral part of getting in shape. In those days it was mostly free weights, and, in order to maximize the amount of weight they could lift, people only lifted through the minimum range of motion. The result: muscle injuries. And the result of that was the stretching programs that we still see. These programs became popular not because football itself necessarily tore muscles but because the weight programs, ill conceived and sometimes ill performed, developed substantial but tight muscles (thus the term muscle-bound), and these muscles readily tore. Stretching programs were an attempt to alleviate the problem. If muscles were well stretched beforehand, maybe they wouldn't become so tight and tear so easily during lifting.

+ WARNINGS +

+ **Joint pain.** If you hurt where you bend—in the knee, ankle, wrist, or elbow—then you may be in for trouble. These joints are pretty much devoid of muscle. Pain there is not a good sign.

+ **If you hurt where you rotate**— in the shoulder or hip—you're on somewhat safer ground. Both joints are embedded deep in muscle and other soft tissue. Pain here may well be muscular, something you might be able to stretch out and work through.

+ **Pain just doesn't go away.** Better think twice . . . exercise can be terrific for someone who's healthy. But if you work out an injured body, you invite real problems. And no matter how important it may seem to keep up your regimen, nothing is worth serious injury. See a doctor.

In time, the fitness industry boomed and stretching became more than simply an attempt to prevent football players from injuring themselves during ill-advised weight sessions—it became a way to prevent injuries, and, more than that, an end in itself. Now we have stretching books, stretching TV shows, stretching classes. People go into stretching programs for stretching's sake. There's no goal, no end in mind. You just want to become more and more and more flexible. But when are you flexible enough? Certainly you'll never be as flexible as the instructor—she's been at it for years—but there she is, day after day, twisting her body into pretzels that you'll never come close to matching.

Still, you try, and the result can be an injury. We see lots of problems with these programs. You can only be so flexible. Like weight training, endurance training, and any other kind of training, there's a point beyond which you cannot go without hurting yourself. Too much stretching can do more than stretch muscles and tendons—it can stretch ligaments and muck up joints. You have to decide how flexible is flexible enough and stay at that level. And, for better or for worse, some of us are just not destined to be very flexible. Somehow or other we survive.

If you're in an activity that requires a certain degree of flexibility, that is, if your stretching is a means to an end, then it's a different story. Gymnasts have to stretch because they're going to put their bodies into abnormal positions. Baseball pitchers have to stretch their shoulders because they pull way back before releasing the ball. Tennis players rear back before serving. Dancers likewise need flexibility—stretching is a way to attain it. And people who are simply going to jog around the block, swim a few laps, or lift a few weights can profit from stretching. It's a way to loosen up, get the blood flowing, tone the muscles. It's a good thing to do after exercise to keep your tired muscles from contracting and being sore the next day. And it can be important to rehabilitate a previously injured muscle or get it ready for exercise. But to approach stretching as a goal in itself, a way of dealing with other sins—no. There has never been anyone who has been able to document that a stretching program will prevent injuries to muscles not injured before. It may be that the opposite is true: stretching for its own sake can cause more problems than it prevents.

Let your body be your guide. In any activity, listen to what it's telling you. It rarely lies. Rather than setting a goal and conforming to a schedule, it may be wiser—and safer—to proceed at a pace your body feels comfortable with. It never hurts to push a little, but when your body's shouting "Stop!" or "Slow down!" it doesn't pay to ignore it.

Rather, it *does* pay, if your business is sports medicine.

CHAPTER TWELVE

How to Choose a Sports Medicine Doctor

THOSE TWO EXTRA WORDS—"sports medicine"—make a difference. A doctor who may be perfectly able to treat all manner of life-threatening problems might *not* be the one to best deal with your bum knee. Or your swimmer's shoulder. Or your tennis elbow. Although one body resembles another, and an aching elbow may look much the same whether it's the result of tennis or carpentry, the treatment afforded that elbow may vary a lot. One doctor may accurately diagnose the injury as tendinitis of the elbow and suggest, rightly, that the problem will disappear in time if you quit tennis. But you don't want to quit tennis. Athletes go to sports medicine doctors to find ways to recover from their injuries *and* continue to perform their athletic activity.

Sometimes that's simply impossible, neither practical nor good medicine. But most often you *can* get back to your sport, if the treatment is based not only on a thorough understanding of the way the body works but on a no less thorough understanding of the activity that caused the problem in the first place. In sports medicine, the injury and the activity are forever wedded. You can't treat one without understanding the other.

Better, then, that your doctor should say, "You have tendinitis of your elbow because your backhand is lousy. You'll never get rid of the problem until you improve your backhand. Go take some lessons. Meanwhile, you've got to regain strength and flexibility. Here are some specific exercises to start you on that road."

Contained therein are all the ingredients that characterize a good sports medicine doctor: someone who gives you a precise diagnosis, looks for the cause of the injury, suggests, precisely, how to get rid of the injury and keep it from happening again, and gets you safely back to your athletic activity as soon as possible. In other words, someone who not only treats your tennis elbow but helps you get back on the court.

QUALITIES TO LOOK FOR IN A SPORTS MEDICINE DOCTOR

Let's look at them, one at a time.

A sports medicine doctor should offer a precise diagnosis. It's not enough simply to say, "You've hurt your elbow." *You* know you've hurt your elbow; what you want to hear is what, precisely, is wrong with it. It's true that some people aren't really interested in what goes on inside the body; they just want to get well. And it's also true that medical terminology can be forbidding to anyone outside of medicine—a little bit of "tendinitis of the lateral humeral epicondyle" can go a long way. But your doctor should at least make an effort to explain to you what it is you've done to yourself, accompanied by definitions of terms (just what is "tendinitis," anyway?) and, if necessary, a guided tour of the body (as in, "The lateral humeral epicondyle is that bump on the outside of your elbow, the one that hurts").

If your doctor doesn't explain your problem to you, ask questions. He may not have had much practice in having to explain himself, as often people become cowed and meek when they enter doctors' offices. The same person who won't drive his car away from the mechanic without finding out what was wrong, or who demands a precise accounting from her child's teacher of what's been going on in the classroom, suddenly turns mute in the doctor's office in order not to seem a bother. It's your body at risk and your money—ask questions.

A hint: write down the answers. It's too easy to nod your head in understanding in the heat of the moment and then later on forget everything that was said. Another hint: don't go in with a written list of questions. In these days of malpractice suits, a written list might make any doctor very nervous. Memorize your questions ahead of time; then write down the answers. Your doctor should answer all your questions. If not, it might be time to look for another doctor.

The doctor should look for the cause of the injury. In sports medicine, the cause is critical—it plays a large role in determining the treatment. Not so much in the case of acute injuries. If you break your leg or blow out a knee ligament, managing the injury isn't going to be much different whether you did it skiing, playing football, or tripping over the family cat. But most sports injuries are not acute; between 65 percent and 75 percent are overuse problems, the kinds that sneak up on you. With these, the cause is not obvious. But unless you know how it happened, you won't know how to treat it so that it won't happen again.

And that takes time. It takes time for a doctor to talk it over with you, to ask the questions that lead back to what caused the injury in the first place. It can be tricky. A dancer's back problem, for example, can be the end result of a chain of difficulties that started with forcing turnout. Treating the back pain may get rid of the problem for a time, but unless you go on and do something about the turnout issue, it won't be long before you're hurting again—and finding yourself right back in the doctor's office.

The two minute office consultation just doesn't work in sports medicine. Unless your doctor is prepared to spend time with you and get to the heart of your problem, you may well be advised to spend time finding another doctor.

The doctor should tell you, precisely, how to get rid of the injury and keep it from happening again. How many people with sprained ankles have been told, "Wrap the ankle, ice it, and stay off of it"? Period. Not how to wrap it so it doesn't end up looking like a sausage, how to ice it so it everywhere receives the benefit of the cold, and how to keep the muscles strong in the meanwhile so they don't simply waste away. Yes, you can recover from a sprained ankle—more or less—if you wrap it, ice it, and stay off of it, but you can recover sooner, more thoroughly, and with less chance of spraining it again if you receive some instructions as to how to go about it effectively. And if such is the case with an obvious injury like a sprained ankle, how much more important is it to deal precisely with a more obscure injury, a injury, say, that may have its roots elsewhere in the body? A large number of sports injuries are just so. Don't shortchange yourself with anything less than a precise course of treatment.

And it's the physician's responsibility to set you up with a rehabilitation program as well. If you've had a severe injury, if you're involved in any kind of reasonably high intensity athletic activity, or if your injury has nagged you for at least a couple of weeks (making it virtually certain that you've been favoring something for those two weeks, forcing other parts of your body to perform inappropriate functions to compensate), you're going to have to rehabilitate yourself, restrengthen yourself, regain your flexibility. Your doctor may have a physical therapist in his office actually devise the program for you, or he may send you to someone else, but it's his responsibility to set something up. If no such rehab program is forthcoming, it may be another strong hint to look elsewhere.

The doctor should get you safely back to your activity as soon as possible. Otherwise, why bother? Rest, staying away from what hurts, will cure many problems, but you can rest on your own. Besides, if you're willing to stay away, much of what we've been talking about doesn't apply to you. Athletes, from pros to recreational types, are often characterized by an almost fanatical devotion to their activity. If they can't do it, they suffer. You can't tell a swimmer, "Don't swim. Run instead. You'll derive the same cardiovascular benefits." It won't work. Swimmers like to be in the water. By the same token, runners feel cheated unless they feel their feet pounding on the ground, tennis players like to wield racquets, skiers want to race down slopes, dancers immediately look for a barre. For these people, recovering from injury is only half the battle. The rest is being able to quickly get back to their favorite activity.

Facilitating all that can be quite a trick. And it must be done safely as well. If not, you're right back where you started at the least, and probably even worse off. It can take a great deal of ingenuity on the part of the doctor, combined with a thoroughgoing understanding of the body and the activity involved. It's not easy. Still, it's what you look for in a sports medicine doctor. What reason is there to settle for less?

A FEW MORE SUGGESTIONS

Beware of the instant cure. With many injuries—in particular overuse problems that involve inflammation and swelling—a cortisone injection or some other kind of dramatic medication can effect a seemingly miraculous cure. Suddenly you're well—for about forty-eight hours anyway. Then it's right back to where you were.

In some cases there may be a good reason for such treatment. A professional tennis player on the eve of an important match may opt for this kind of temporary solution, ditto the dancer who doesn't want to bow out of a performance— always with the understanding that long-lasting treatment must come later. But if there's no overriding reason to temporarily eliminate symptoms this way, and for most of us there really isn't, people would be well advised not to go this route. It does no good in the long run and can even do some harm. At best it's a highly calculated risk. When it comes to sports injuries, the true instant cure is exceedingly rare. Usually all you're doing is putting off any real treatment of the problem in exchange for a temporary, and risky, elimination of symptoms.

Most injuries don't require surgery. And of those that do, only a few require urgent surgery. So if your doctor announces that you have to undergo an operation, you should always ask whether there are alternatives.

There *are* alternatives, almost always. They may not be what you want to hear, however. An alternative to knee surgery may be to give up skiing, or running. An alternative to shoulder surgery may be to give up tennis. An alternative to ankle surgery may be to give up dancing. Or worse. Or, in many cases, much better. But the point is that if someone tells you there's absolutely no choice in the matter, except in the rarest of instances that's simply not the case. It's during times like this that a second opinion may be just what the doctor ordered.

You want a doctor to schedule a follow-up visit. Medical fees being what they are, a return visit may seem something of an extravagance. Who wants to pay more than is absolutely necessary? But in this case a return visit—and the fee that it entails—may be a good investment. You want your doctor to stay involved with your injury until you're well. That is, you want to know what to do if things *don't* go as planned. Who's going to offer that information? It should be the doctor who treated the injury in the first place, and a return visit indicates his willingness to do just that.

If there is no follow-up visit scheduled, at the very least your doctor should offer to make himself available if things go wrong. Any indication that your doctor is involved with you and your problem is good. With today's increasing demands on sports medicine facilities, it's all too easy to encounter just the opposite.

A sports medicine doctor doesn't have to be an orthopedic surgeon. Most sports medicine doctors probably are orthopedic surgeons, but it's not necessary. What is necessary is that the doctor have as solid an understanding of muscular-skeletal anatomy as an orthopedic surgeon and a solid understanding of athletic activities (which orthopedic surgeons may or may not have) as well. Of course, a non-orthopedist won't be able to do surgery, but maybe only one in twenty people needs surgery, anyhow. What's important in surgery is that the doctor be competent and experienced, rather than strictly a sports medicine surgeon. Doing an operation well is a function of how often you've done it, not whether the reason for it is sports-related. How the injury is managed afterwards, what kind of rehabilitation is involved, and even whether or not to do the operation in the first place—all that involves sports medicine more than the actual operation. And your sports medicine doctor, whether or not he actually performs the surgery, can be involved in those decisions. The important thing is finding a good sports medicine doctor, no matter his specialty.

But, if you're lost, or just starting your search for a sports medicine doctor and you don't have anywhere else to go, it can be a good idea to start with an orthopedic surgeon. Orthopedists deal with the anatomy of the muscular-skeletal system all the time. At least you'll have someone who knows intimately how the body moves.

Physical therapists should not passively make you well. That is, if a therapist wants you to come in every afternoon for an hour of ultrasound, or galvanic stimulation, hot packs, ice massage, or any of the other tricks of the trade (all of which, when applied appropriately, can be very effective), and doesn't give you a rehab program to do at home, ask for one. If the therapist refuses, it may be time to go elsewhere.

You *can't* get over your injury without actively working at it. True, you may recover well enough to go back to work or school, but you aren't going to be able to get back on the court or the track, or into the gym or studio. Without an active involvement on your part, you'll never get all the way back to where you were before injury.

But, it's so comforting to have someone else take care of you. Kind of like crawling back into the womb. So nice just to lie there and have someone massage and knead and bathe you with all sorts of relaxing unguents. Yes, and as a supplement to the hard work you're doing on your own, these ministrations can help you along. But by themselves they're simply not enough.

Why then are some therapists so reluctant to set up home rehab programs? For a number of reasons. It takes time to set up such a program, time to instruct you, time to make up handouts and written instruction, and in a busy therapy center time is at a premium. The irony there is that although it may seem bad business to have people do things at home, it's really the smartest approach therapists can take. People get well that way, and the more people you help back to health, the more people recommend you and come back to you. After all, it's better business to see fifteen people for five visits each than it is to see one person twenty times.

+ Your Fitness Facility + & Getting Over Your Injury

Physical therapy can be vitally important in helping you recover from your injury, but the sad reality is that your insurance company is unlikely to pay for all the rehabilitation you may need to get back to your favorite activity. That's where fitness facilities come in.

As a place to put the finishing touches on your rehab, fitness facilities can be ideal. If you've had some specific physical therapy already, odds are that by the time you approach a fitness facility what you need is the kind of generalized rehabilitation that exercise and weight machines can provide. There's no better place to find those than at fitness facilities.

Even if you have fitness equipment at home, almost certainly you don't have the variety offered by a fitness facility. And that variety can be important. For example, if it's generalized fitness you're after and your injured knee hurts when you use a cross-country ski machine, you can use an exercise bike instead. If the bike hurts your knee, you can change to an elliptical trainer. Or better yet, you can use all three pieces of equipment, rotating them so as to enjoy maximum training while minimizing discomfort and injury.

The moral of the story: rehab therapy should be active, centered in the home, and supplemented at the therapy center.

FINDING A DOCTOR

So, all that said, how do you go about finding the kind of sports medicine doctor you want? Where do you begin?

The best place to start is with other athletes. Legitimate athletes, serious athletes, not just someone who works out once in a while and has been hurt occasionally. Ask another athlete to recommend a good doctor. The athletes' underground is usually a pretty good source of information.

It used to be that college and professional team physicians were the best sources, primarily because they were the only doctors who had had any experience taking care of sports injuries. No longer. The majority of sports medicine physicians don't take care of professional teams—there simply aren't enough teams to go around. And these days professional teams make money from their medical care—physicians, sports medicine facilities, and hospitals often pay the team for the privilege of taking care of them. So the team doctors may be the highest bidders but not necessarily the most expert or experienced.

There's another reason why using professional athletics or sports team affiliations may not be of much value. Many physicians have at one time taken care of a team, often while they were training at a large sports medicine facility—that doesn't mean they're experts at it. In addition many team affiliations result from doctors volunteering their time—not necessarily an indication of either experience or excellence.

And now with the Internet, the task of finding a good sports medicine doctor is even more difficult. You have to remember that there's no quality control as to what is put into Web pages. Perhaps look-

---

FITNESS FACILITY (CONTINUED)

As far as specific exercises are concerned, fitness facilities have machines for every specific muscle group and often have free weights as well. These riches allow you to focus your rehab. (All the rehab exercises we recommend in this book can be done in fitness facilities.)

Finally, fitness facilities have instructors, and most also offer personal trainers. These people can help map out an exercise/rehab regimen for you. If it's tennis you want to get back to, for example, they can suggest specific exercises and even guide (or browbeat, if necessary) you through them. They can work with you to modify your regimen as you recover and regain fitness. And they can remind you what to do if you forget. And, in general, you can trust the advice you'll receive from these people. Fitness facilities are doing a much better job than they used to in providing qualified instructors.

Back to cost. With insurance companies becoming ever more reticent with their payments, from a money standpoint alone fitness facilities can be a good deal. Often you can sign up for a two- or three-month introductory period at a fitness facility for less than it would cost for a week or two of physical therapy.

ing to sports medicine societies is the best route to take. There's a society for almost every discipline—orthopedic surgeons, podiatrists, physical therapists, and so on—and at the least the practitioners who belong to these groups have been interested enough to pay dues, go to some meetings, and subscribe to a journal. Probably the most reliable of the groups for the purpose of finding a sports medicine doctor is the American Orthopedic Society for Sports Medicine, as orthopedists have more experience being team physicians and the like than other doctors (phone: 847-292-4900; fax: 847-292-4905; home page: www.sportsmed.org).

The American College of Sports Medicine, even though it consists of a number of physician members, may not be the best place to go for a recommendation. Many of the members are Ph.D.'s and exercise physiologists who don't deal with injuries. If you want to find out how fit you are, then this group can most likely find you someone to measure your physical condition; but it might be wise to look elsewhere for someone to take care of your injury.

Simply going to a facility that calls itself a sports medicine clinic might be better than going elsewhere—and it might not. There are no regulations where such designations are concerned. There are some physicians who have had a great deal of experience in dealing with sports injuries and so legitimately call themselves sports medicine doctors; there are others who are trying to attract athletes and so label themselves sports medicine doctors no matter their expertise and experience. So, in a way, you just have to pay your money and take your chances. But at the least the title, "sports medicine doctor," is something to look for rather than just going to someone cold.

Going to a doctor who is himself a runner, say, or who regularly attends the ballet, doesn't necessarily mean that the person knows anything about how to treat ballet injuries, or how to treat any running injuries other than his own, if that. Seeking out a physician who happens to be an athlete, or enjoys athletic events, is no guarantee that you're going to find a sports medicine doctor. Again, experience with treating sports injuries is what counts. That, and the ability to make a precise diagnosis, the readiness to look for a cause, the willingness to explain to you what you're supposed to do to participate in your treatment and what to do if the treatment doesn't work, and an interest in helping you safely back to your activity as soon as possible.

There's no foolproof method to finding such a doctor. Perhaps the best way is to talk to other athletes who have been happy with their medical care. Nothing beats word of mouth.

CHAPTER THIRTEEN

So, You're Going to Have an Operation

WE MIGHT HAVE CALLED this chapter "So, You *Want* to Have an Operation?" because when it comes to athletic activities, people do strange things. One of those things is to dive into surgery with the eagerness of a skier diving into a hot tub. An injured athlete often will do any-thing—*anything*—to get back to an athletic activity as soon as possible, and if that anything involves surgery, so be it. In fact, maybe all the better. Some athletic types have a pecking order based on experience in the operating room. A red badge of courage complete with impressive scars. And if it's *arthroscopic* surgery . . . well, you just can't do any bet-ter than that. The scars are even more impressive for being tiny. And what's more, you'll be good as new in a few weeks, right?

Wrong. We're not out to scare anyone, for there are good reasons for sur-gery—we've been talking about them throughout this book—but the reality is that surgery not only entails risks, it rarely makes things in the injured area as good as they were beforehand. It all depends on why you had the surgery in the first place. If it's to enable you to run or walk again, that's one thing. If it's to enable you again to be the star of the noon pickup basketball game, that might be another. The point is that surgery should not be rushed into without consid-erable thought. Short-term impatience is not the best reason for having a long-term operation. Nor is the desire to stand out in your social set. There is much to consider before you decide to bare yourself to the surgeon's knife.

SURGERY FOR SPORTS INJURIES

In general, there are two kinds of operations in sports. One involves *repair*, the other *removal*. For the most part the removal operations work the best because you're taking out something that doesn't belong where it is. It may be a torn piece of meniscus that's jamming up a runner's knee, a bone spur in the back of a dancer's ankle that prevents her from going on pointe, a lump of bone and gristle in the front of the ankle that prevents a gymnast from beginning or landing jumps. Some of these things, like bone spurs, shouldn't be there in the first place; others, like torn cartilage, are simply in the wrong place. Once they're removed, the body is able to resume its usual activity. The knee and ankle bend and flex as though nothing were ever the matter—or pretty nearly so. And as a number of these procedures can be done with the arthroscope, the period of recovery is often shorter than with other kinds of surgery.

Repair operations are never this successful. In these, surgeons attempt to repair things that have been torn, stretched, or otherwise put out of commission—ligaments and tendons mostly. Once you tear a ligament, it's never going to be as tight as before. And it's not the fault of the operation. Whether you treat these injuries surgically or not, they simply don't come back all the way. It's the nature of the beast. The best the surgeon can do is try to improve a situation that without help might be much worse. Gains are relative, and there are no guarantees.

But what about all the well-known athletes who come back from major operations? The answer is that sometimes major repair surgery can be successful because few athletes, even the best ones, operate at 100 percent efficiency anyway. So they may lose 10 percent of their ability after surgery but with more diligence and harder work afterwards might approach their previous level of functioning. Still, you always lose something, and the people who come back strongly from big operations probably fall into one of two categories: they're either so much better than anyone else to start with that they can afford to give away 10 to 15 percent of their ability and remain on top, or they're willing to ignore bad news. Many athletes fall into this latter category—they get back to their activity in record time, but they really shouldn't have. Not only are they no longer performing anywhere near their former level, but they're going to pay the price later on. Ask any number of retired football players how their knees feel now.

Many athletes are aware of this trade-off and consider it an equitable one, especially if they make their living with their bodies. A few more years of prime earning power—even if you can perform at no more than 75 percent on a team that just can't find anyone else to do 76 percent—is worth all the problems that are sure to follow. But most athletes are not professionals. Not only do they not depend on their bodies for their livelihood, but they don't have available the same round-the-clock medical care that professionals enjoy (more on that in a moment). Nevertheless, their thinking—or lack of it—ignores these differences. A skier hobbles into the doctor's office, leans the crutches against the wall, struggles onto the examining table, and announces, "I've got to ski again next season. Do whatever is necessary, Doc." Well, this skier, flushed with the stories of professional athletes returning to action after all sorts of horrendous injuries, and ready, as many people are, to lie back and let the doctor work medical magic, should be appraised of a few interesting bits of information.

1. **There are certain injuries that just don't get better**—or better enough, anyway, to allow a return to the activity that caused them. No matter how successful the treatment, no matter what ingenious things the doctor does, some people are simply not going to get back to skiing—or running, handball, tennis, dance, or whatever their favorite activity might be. In such cases, you must modify your life to accommodate your injury, not the other way around.

2. **You're going to play a larger role in recovering from your injury than that of the operation.** Sometimes the opera*tor* doesn't bother to tell the opera*tee* about this. Often people ask, "How long am I going to be in the hospital?" Well, you may stay in the hospital for only three days, or not at all, but that's the least of your worries. With some of the more involved operations, what you better be ready to face is six months of daily hour-and-a-half supervised rehabilitation sessions. That's what the professional athletes do, and if you want similar results, you have to do the same.

   But pro athletes have nothing better to do than work to get back into action—it's part of their life. In the real world, an hour and a half of daily rehab translates into nothing less than a part-time job. By the time you get yourself to the physical therapy facility, park, change clothes, do the exercises, take a shower, change clothes, climb in your car, and get back to work, half the day is gone. And the exercises themselves are *tough*. There are many more enjoyable things in life than pitting your slowly recovering knee against the Cybex machine. So there are more things to consider about surgery than the size of the resulting scar and the number of days in the hospital.

3. **Sometimes the operations don't work.** The most reliable surgical procedures are successful no more than 90 percent of the time—pretty

good odds but no guarantee—and for other operations the rates are considerably lower. Your injury may prove to be more extensive than first thought, or you may have developed secondary problems as a result of trying to compensate for initial injury. Even in the most successful removal operations this can be the case. A dancer may have a bone spur in the ankle removed, for example, theoretically allowing her to flex and extend to a degree she hasn't experienced in years. But just because she hasn't been able to use that full range of motion in so long, her body may have tightened up to the point where it could take her another full year to stretch out enough to be able to enjoy the benefits of the operation.

4. **People die during surgery.** It doesn't happen often, not in sports-related operations, anyway, but it *does* happen. Surgery, no matter how minor, entails risk.

So, approach surgery with your eyes open. Guard against the "if I have an operation all my problems will be solved" type of thinking. They won't. Surgery should be considered a last resort. If possible, explore every nonsurgical means of treatment before considering it. In most cases you can wait on surgery until the problem simply can't be dealt with otherwise, but you certainly can't undo an operation once it's been performed. And even if it does come to surgery and your operation is a complete success, you'll be faced with the need to rehabilitate your injured part. Don't let anyone tell you otherwise.

SOME QUESTIONS TO ASK YOUR DOCTOR WHEN CONSIDERING AN OPERATION

Are there any nonsurgical alternatives?

The answer is yes. There always are alternatives. What you have to decide is if the alternatives are more or less palatable than the surgery itself.

It may be that an alternative to surgery is for you to give up tennis, for example, or dance. And it may be that for you giving it up is simply out of the question. Or it may be that you can live *without* tennis more readily than you can live *with* a difficult operation and a long rehab period, during which you won't be able to do much of anything anyhow, and after which the odds of getting back to your previous level are not very good. If you have a knee problem that prevents you from playing in the noon basketball league, say, then it may be that an alternative to surgery is to take up racquetball. Or it may be that the alternative to surgery is the pain and disability of continuing to have your knee lock up on you, whereas a relatively simple operation could relieve you of all that. It all depends on why you're considering surgery.

In all these cases, it's important that your doctor is thinking along the same lines as you are. The doctor should know why it is that you may want the operation. He should present you with the alternatives and ask you what your priorities are. And he should offer a recommendation one way or the other. But remember that orthopedic surgeons make their living by performing operations. The more operations, the better the living. If your doctor seems too eager to put you under the knife, doesn't explain the alternatives, or, at the least, doesn't advise caution, it may be time for a second opinion.

So, a good reason for surgery may *not* be that you can't dunk the basketball any longer or serve at ninety miles per hour. Instability in your knee, a good reason. Inability to dunk, not a good one.

Why don't we try the alternatives first?

When it comes to athletics, surgery is often an elective procedure. There are seldom any life or death issues involved. At stake is performance in a certain athletic activity or, possibly, pain and disability. So if the alternative to surgery is an exercise program that only works in 10 percent of the cases, what's the disadvantage in giving it a try? You may be among the 10 percent.

In any case, it's important that your doctor make you understand how urgent the need for any possible operation might be. Again, in most cases you can give surgery a try after all else fails. But you can't undo the consequences of the knife.

What are the odds that the operation will work?

This question has several corollaries: If the operation works, to what degree will it work? Will it allow me to go back to the same high level of activity? Can I work out daily? Do I have to take any special precautions?

You want these answers beforehand. You want to go into surgery knowing as much about the likely results as possible.

A good way of judging the success of any operation is by talking to someone who's had it. We make a point of contacting patients at least a year afterwards. "Now that you've gone through all this," we ask, "now that you've been to the hospital, had to leave work or school, gone through all the rehabilitation, made all these visits to the doctor—knowing what you know now, would you have the operation again?" If the answer is "yes," that's one thing. But—stability during examination, muscle size, x-rays, MRIs, calibrated strength, and all the other clinical determinations to the contrary—if the answer is, "I sure wouldn't go through all that again," then you've got to think long and hard about the worth of it all.

Operations are simply no fun. And they aren't glamorous in the least. Especially if something goes wrong.

Can the operation make me worse?

The answer is yes. There's always a chance. *How much* of a chance is the issue. What are the odds? And, what, *exactly,* could go wrong? These are the kinds of questions people rarely ask. They don't like to hear bad news, even if it's only potential bad news. But these are the kinds of things you need to know.

Again, here's where getting a second opinion can make sense. And if your doctor throws a tantrum when you mention a second opinion, then you should be even more determined to get one. Besides, more and more insurance companies are beginning to require them.

How extensive will rehabilitation be?

If someone tells you that you won't have to do any rehab work, look for a second opinion. Some kinds of operations require less rehab than others, but all require *something* on your part. Anyone who says otherwise is simply not being realistic.

And along with this question should come others. How long before I can go back to work? How long before I can take a shower? How long before I'm back to my athletic activity? Will I be able to rehab at home, or do I have to come to the physical therapy facility all the time? And will my insurance pay for physical therapy? This can be more expensive than the surgery itself.

What about a second operation?

Sometimes it takes a long time to realize benefits from an operation, even a simple one. And sometimes patients and doctors become impatient. If you're looking at an *unplanned* second operation (sometimes two-part operations are planned in advance—that's a different story) for the same problem within three to six months after the first surgery, then you might well get a second opinion. It simply may be that not enough time has elapsed to find out if the first operation worked or not.

If enough time has gone by so that it's clear that the first operation didn't work, be aware that it's even less likely that the second one will do the job. The surgeon would have done the second procedure the first time if it were more likely to be successful. It may be that there's something else going on, a problem that neither you nor your doctor yet understands.

If the person who's going to operate on you is unwilling to answer your questions, for whatever reason, then you better look elsewhere for care. When you pay thousands of dollars for surgery, you're not just paying surgeons for their two hours in the operating room—you're paying for them to answer your questions before and after surgery, to schedule return visits following surgery, and to supervise your rehab program. If they're not prepared to do all of these things, you might think twice about having them do anything at all.

And don't depend on your infallible memory to hold on to the surgeon's responses forever. *Write down the answers to your questions.*

ARTHROSCOPIC SURGERY

It may not be magic, but the first time you see the inside of a knee in full color on a twenty-four-inch TV screen, you might think so. "See" is the crucial word here. The most important thing about arthroscopy is that it has allowed surgeons to *see* what they're doing. If you can see what's going on inside the knee (or elsewhere—arthroscopy is increasingly used in other joints, especially the shoulder), then you can figure out *precisely* what the problems are and do the right operations. No more surmising from external evidence and digging into the interior of the knee through a two-inch incision not quite knowing what you're going to find there. With arthroscopy, proof is right before your eyes, in living color. And you can even make a videotape of the procedure for consultation afterwards.

The technology is sophisticated in the execution but pretty straightforward in conception. Why not make a tiny telescope, attach its own light source, add a miniature TV camera, and connect the whole package to a needle-like probe that you can slip into the knee or shoulder through a quarter-inch incision? Voilà, the arthroscope. It took the technologies of miniaturization, fiber optics, and video to make this idea work, and now it's a staple of orthopedic surgery.

Ironically, one of the effects of arthroscopy has been to make people less wary of having surgery. People come in *demanding* the operation and get angry if you tell them that they're not going to need it. You may say to them, "We're as sure as we can be what's wrong with your knee. Even if you were arthroscoped, it wouldn't change the rehabilitation treatment we've set up for you."

"I don't care," they answer. "I want you to arthroscope my knee." Or "I want an MRI."

Well, TV pictures, fiber optics, and high tech to the contrary, arthroscopic surgery *is* surgery. Someone gives you an anesthetic, makes an incision (no matter how tiny), inserts a foreign body into your knee, and probes around in there, often taking something out.

Complications are not very frequent with arthroscopy, but, as with any surgery, they're always a risk. Infection can be a problem, and instruments can break. Yet some people have the impression that arthroscopy is just like getting an immunization shot—you come in, have your procedure, then go back to volleyball the next day. Not so. Most people take four to six weeks to get back to where they were. Plus it will cost you or your insurance company (which ultimately means you) thousands of dollars for your "shot." Even if you're only paying 20 percent of the cost, that's still a lot of money. So it makes economic sense, at the least, to have an orthopedist who prefers to make as many treatment decisions as possible *without* going into your knee. Arthroscopy is not a cure-all. That you can remove a torn cartilage through the arthroscope is nice, but studies have shown that six months down the road it doesn't make any difference whether your cartilage was removed through two quarter-inch incisions or one two-inch incision. Once you've been through a rehabilitation program, it just doesn't matter.

That said, the arthroscope is sure a handy tool. It's so tiny that you can put it into corners of the body that are too remote for a light and your naked eye. And you can do surgery through it. You can take out loose bodies and torn cartilages; you can sew some cartilages back together; and most orthopedists are doing ligament surgery with it. All this through a couple of quarter-inch incisions. Few stitches are required to close things up, and, compared to the two-inch-long scar produced by other surgical techniques, the mementos of being arthroscoped are negligible. Pretty slick. But still, the most important benefit of the arthroscope is that it allows you to plan,

---

+ MRI +
Magnetic Resonance Imaging

MRIs utilize magnetic energy to view what's inside you. Unlike x-rays, which just show bones, MRIs allow visualization of soft tissues such as the cartilage in the knee, blood vessels, muscles, tendons, and ligaments. In fact MRIs allow such precise examinations that we are finding there are more things "wrong" with us than we've ever imagined. Fraying of the rotator cuff tendons is present on nearly all adult shoulder MRIs as is degeneration of the menisci in most adults. Are these findings important? Not if the patient isn't suffering any problems. MRIs are best utilized as adjuncts to diagnosis, not the final word.

Increasingly patients demand MRIs. They feel they're getting less than ideal care without one. Well, aside from the fact that MRIs are expensive (much more costly than a visit to the doctor), they may not help solve the problem. A good rule of thumb is that an MRI can be helpful if it uncovers information that will alter treatment, whether it be surgery, rehabilitation, or both. If the information gathered from an MRI can't be *used,* the MRI is probably not necessary.

precisely, what you need to do to the knee, because you're able to see everything as clearly as though you've slipped in there yourself.

TOTAL JOINT REPLACEMENTS

Total joint replacements—primarily of hips and knees—are one of the biggest orthopedic advances in the past few decades. There are more than a quarter million of these surgeries each year in the United States. Their success—defined as an appreciable decrease in pain and an increase in activity—approaches 90 percent. But these procedures are not for everyone. The primary tip-off that a total joint replacement may help is pain—pain while walking, pain awakening you at night, and so on. While it's true that x-rays reveal severe problems in those undergoing total joint replacement—collapse of bone, loss of space between the ends of bone in joints that is normally taken up by cartilage, and undesirable formation of new bone such as spurs—the decision to undergo joint replacement is *not* based solely on x-rays. *Pain* is the bottom line.

There are many people with dreadful looking x-rays who have little or no pain and, in many instances, participate in sports with only minimal symptoms. One thing these people seem to have in common is strength. In spite of discomfort they have maintained strength in the muscles acting on the joint in question. Should they become weak (contracting the flu, undergoing some other kind of surgery, sustaining an injury), their joint can often become very painful very quickly even though x-rays have changed little, if at all.

So our recommendation concerning joint replacement is to find out how much better you can get by first regaining normal strength and endurance through nonsurgical means. Undergoing a rehabilitation program has no downside. At best your pain will diminish and the operation can be delayed—sometimes for months or years. At worst the exercises will be too uncomfortable to do, or your muscles may become stronger but this does not relieve the pain. If so, you've lost nothing but a little time. Should you resort to surgery, you'll find that you'll come through the operation better and that postoperative rehabilitation is easier because you're already accomplished some of it beforehand.

Some people want joint replacements so they can increase or return to athletic activities. Frequently we see patients who handle the activities of daily life—walking, climbing stairs, getting in and out of chairs and cars—with little difficulty but have knee or hip pain when they play tennis. They want an operation so they can return to tennis. But it is unlikely that a total joint replacement will allow a return to an activity that they've avoided for some time.

And because replacement joints are made of metal and plastic (which wear out because they, unlike our normal joints, cannot repair themselves), and these materials must adhere to the bones into and onto which they've been placed, they will not tolerate the abuse normal—or even degenerating—joints will. You'll have to curtail your activities even with successful joint replacements.

For example, activities to be avoided include baseball, softball, basketball, boxing, football, gymnastics, handball, hockey, jogging, lacrosse, motocross, racquetball, rock climbing, soccer, tennis (singles), volleyball, and power weight lifting. Activities that are usually possible include archery, cycling, bowling, ballroom dancing (recreational, not necessarily competitive), square dancing, golf, hiking, horseshoes, ice skating, low-resistance weight training, low-resistance rowing, shuffleboard, cross-country skiing, swimming, table tennis, and walking. Other activities such as in-line skating, downhill skiing, and jazz dancing can often be undertaken with a physician's approval and prior skill and experience in the sports.

So in certain instances total joint replacements *can* help. But they're not cure-alls.

Ballet

AT FIRST GLANCE you may find it odd to encounter a section devoted to ballet in a book about athletic injuries. Not so. Although not a sport, ballet is most certainly an athletic activity, one of the most physically demanding professions imaginable. It demands strength comparable to that needed in any sport and flexibility that exceeds them all. And it requires that the most mind-boggling feats—stratospheric jumps, dervishlike spins and turns, fiendishly difficult lifts—be made to look effortless. Beyond the intense physical demands, it is the artistry of ballet that sets it apart from other athletic endeavors.

All that leads to a constant barrage of injuries. But outside the narrow world of dance-related literature, there's almost nothing written about ballet injuries. At the Center for Sports Medicine we've long had experience taking care of the injuries of dancers, from the San Francisco Ballet to other Bay Area dance companies and from individual dancers from around the world to ballet students—at once the most vulnerable to injuries and most needful of help. Here's what we've found:

Because so many dance injuries might not even be noticed in the everyday world, it's hard to find a doctor to take care of them. You need someone who knows dance as well as medicine, and those people are far and few between. So much so that, sadly, medical care for dancers is almost a contradiction in terms. Its state-of-the-art is where medical care for football players was decades ago. The big dance companies attract doctors who take care of their dancers reasonably well, but that's about it. The rest of the dance population is forced to fend for itself, and, as anyone knows who has been forced to seek treatment for an athletic injury, fending for yourself may find you a competent doctor but not necessarily one who is used to dealing with sports injuries, much less dance injuries. All too often a dancer with what may be a routine injury in dance encounters a physician who has never dealt with the problem and whose advice is to stop dancing until the injury heals. Well, for a dancer to stop dancing is the kiss of death. You *can't* stop dancing. You may take a break from performing, take class in such a way that you don't risk making the problem worse, but you must stay active if at all physically possible. But the inexperienced doctor (inexperienced with dancers, that is) delivers the dictum: stop dancing. No wonder so many dancers seek help outside the mainstream of medicine—from herbalists, naturopaths, acupuncturists—often with useful results. At the least these practitioners offer the dancer a sympathetic ear and attempt to set up treatments that allow her to continue dancing.

All that is changing, but slowly. For most doctors, there's little persuasive inducement to direct a practice toward dancers. Most dance problems are very specific overuse injuries that require a lot of time and knowledge of dance to sort out. Whereas if you're dealing with contact sports, say, an anterior cruciate ligament tear is an anterior cruciate tear is an anterior cruciate tear. It doesn't matter much if it happens in football or while tripping over the family dog—the treatment is the same. And often that treatment involves surgery, which means big bucks. In contrast, taking forever to figure out that a dancer's lower back strain is resulting from improper positioning of the hip due to overly tight quadriceps and then devising specific exercise therapy that will enable the dancer to continue dancing may be a great boon to the dancer, but it brings home neither the bacon nor referrals that can lead to other high-paying cases for the doctor. And often dancers have little money, so billing becomes a problem. The only real rewards for the doctor are those gained from helping people in general and from dealing with the dancers themselves, who are among the most pleasant, grateful people to step into the office. But, with rare exceptions, a doctor simply can't make a living by building a practice around dancers.

So it's important that dancers search out doctors who know dancing. You want to find doctors who know their stuff *and* try to figure out ways to keep you dancing while helping you recover from your injury. (From a doctor's point of view, this may be a pretty tough trick but good medicine. Doctors just buy trouble if they try to keep dancers out of the studio. The dancers may pay lip service to such treatment regimens, but they're going to get back into the studio sooner rather than later no matter what. Then they'll simply incur more problems later on.) For certain problems the "doctor" to see may be another dancer. Dancers know how to take care of minimal common injuries like foot problems—corns, blisters, calluses, shoes that need modification—better than anyone. More serious problems, however, may require a physician. And now the dancer, or the dance parent, is faced with the biggest trick of all: finding a good one.

FINDING A DOCTOR

For the person new to dance, this can be a daunting task. Often your family doctor's advice, while sound in other areas, may be off the mark when it comes to dance. Indeed, how may an uninformed doctor react when asked if a dancer should continue to take class? What does it mean to "take class"? Sitting at a desk while a teacher rattles on—that's the common interpretation of the term. Many doctors have never seen a ballet class, and that lack of exposure doesn't always produce the best medical advice. So, how do you find someone who knows what's involved in dance?

Step one: if you're new to your locale, or new to dance, a first step might be to comb the yellow pages for someone who advertises as a sports medicine doctor. At the least, such a person is probably used to treating active people who want to become active again. The first couple of minutes of the first interview should tell you if you've made a mistake. If a doctor doesn't respond to dance terminology or gives little indication of interest to learn, it may be you should look elsewhere.

Step two: you might call a local dance company for advice. Unfortunately, in some companies the official doctor may be a financial patron who likes ballet but has had little real interaction with dancers. Again, the initial interview should tell you a lot.

Step three: the head of the dance department at a local college might be able to recommend someone. You might also ask your own dance teacher. People that deal with, and are responsible for, dancers should know what it takes to keep them going.

Step four: talk to other dancers. The best way by far. Dancers have an even better underground than runners do. At the very least other dancers can point you toward someone who will listen to you rather than simply advise you to stay out of the studio. At best you actually may find a doctor who will suggest good treatment. And it never hurts to ask what it was that caused your dance friend to visit the doctor's office and what the treatment consisted of. If your friend's ailment is similar to yours and the treatment was successful, count yourself lucky, and on the right track.

CHILDREN IN BALLET

It probably goes without saying that ballet is a world unto itself. For all its beauty and the dedication it inspires from those involved, it can be a particularly demanding world, and even a forbidding one, especially to people entering it for the first time. And once that world begins to engulf you, it's difficult to retain a sense of perspective. Parents and their children who become hooked by ballet know the phenomenon all too well: the overriding imperative in life becomes *dance!* And as to how much, the answer is always, *more!*

So, for parents and children just entering ballet, and those in various stages along the way, here are some suggestions from a sports medicine point of view.

Beginners

Most kids begin ballet for recreational reasons. As in recreational gymnastics, a class a week rarely hurts anyone. It's probably good because it teaches kids a bit about their bodies and gives them something to do rather than sit in front of the TV. There are virtually no injury problems in recreational ballet.

+ Kids and PE Classes +

Dedicated child athletes probably don't belong in PE classes. If a kid is training himself for a particular activity, let's say ballet, he certainly is getting enough exercise without taking a PE class. Most likely he's getting everything PE is supposed to give him and more, except perhaps social contact with his classmates. And, by not taking PE, he reduces his risk of injury.

There are two major problem with PE classes. One is that, like the rest of school, they're geared for the widest possible student population—a little something for everyone. That approach may not be right for a child who specializes in one particular activity. The training simply may not be appropriate for him. And the other is that PE classes change activities too abruptly. For one quarter they concentrate on volleyball, say, or basketball, two court-oriented jumping games. Then, wham!—it's up and down the field playing soccer, with all the running and kicking that sport demands. Then it's a sudden change of pace to softball—throwing, sliding, and twisting while swinging the bat. For kids who aren't in particularly good shape, the change won't matter much. They can be safe enough in just about any sport. But for a kid who's fine-tuned for one particular activity or another, such an abrupt change can bring on problems. As we've seen so often in this book, it's the abrupt changes that cause injuries. When a body is used to one kind of activity, a quick change forces it

---

Getting serious

When kids start to become serious about ballet, it's usually for one of two reasons: they decide (or mother and father decide for them) that they really like ballet, or they start taking ballet to enhance their performance in other activities, notably gymnastics and figure skating. If the focus is ballet, the path is pretty straightforward. You start to advance and increase the number of classes at a rate consistent with your ability. You have to be able to trust your teacher in this regard. A tip-off as to whether you're progressing too quickly is how you feel. Your body will let you know if it's doing too much too soon. It speaks a pretty persuasive language—it's called injury.

If your interest in ballet is as a means to enhance other activities, however, you'd better watch out. Therein lies danger. It's hard to be half-serious about ballet. If your child takes class once a week just for the fun of it, fine. But if the motivation is more serious than that, one class just won't do—especially if the goal is to complement another sport. It's simply not enough to make a difference. Moreover, the muscles and techniques involved in ballet are different

---

KIDS AND PE CLASSES (CONTINUED)

to reeducate itself too quickly. The body just doesn't like sudden, unexpected demands; it breaks down.

For example, the ballet dancer's muscles are stretched for extreme flexibility. He's geared for sudden bursts of activity separated by slow movements and a great deal of posing. To subject that body to the constant running and jumping and contact of basketball, say, simply because the school calendar demands it, is to invite problems. (The opposite is true as well, by the way. If a basketball player were suddenly forced to achieve the extreme flexibility and quick movements of ballet, she too would quickly find herself hurting.) Yet that's just what many schools demand. PE is held sacrosanct, as though bypassing it means somehow tampering with an entire institution rather than simply dealing with the needs of any particular child most effectively.

We even see injuries as a result of the tests sponsored by the President's Council for Fitness. Suddenly kids are forced to see how far and fast they can run, how many push-ups they can do, how many sit-ups, and so on. Interestingly, it's usually the best athletes, those kids who score best on the tests, who suffer the most injuries from them. As in other things, it's the most finely tuned instrument that breaks down most readily when asked to perform unfamiliar tasks. When that instrument is your child's body . . . well, it may be wise to think about the need for PE.

enough from those of other activities that a casual exposure can hurt rather than help performance elsewhere. The experience of one nationally ranked skater is a case in point: she took a hard ballet class once a week, found she was invariably stiff and aching the next day, yet still had to skate a five-hour workout. The day after that she would hurt so much that for the next couple of days she was unable to skate effectively at all. So she held back during workouts to nurse her body. By the time the next ballet class rolled around, she once again felt good, but then the class would make her stiff afterwards, and same cycle began again. She was taking just enough ballet to tear down her body but not enough to condition it. Rather than attending class only once a week, she would have been much better off not taking ballet at all.

Similarly, a person who takes aerobic dance just once a week has a higher likelihood of being injured than someone who takes class at least three days a week because the occasional dancer never reaps the conditioning benefits. If an athlete takes ballet as a complementary activity, she should take class three times a week and should start during a time when there's not much going on in her other sport. Later, after her muscles have become accustomed to the classes, she may be able to cut down to twice a week. Even then she may not realize all the benefits of the ballet training, but at least she'll avoid the hazards.

The Nutcracker syndrome

Every time early December rolls around, we brace ourselves for an onslaught of ballet injuries. The reason? *The Nutcracker.* Not that there's anything wrong with this old chestnut of a ballet, it's just that for many kids it offers a first chance to perform. Suddenly a child who has been taking class once or twice a week is thrown into a rehearsal schedule that doubles or triples the amount of time she spends in ballet slippers. Even in the youngest children, that kind of rapid onset of activity can bring about problems, usually overuse injuries. They don't develop into long-term problems, but they can assume an importance far beyond their seriousness because of the emotional involvement, especially that of the parents: "*My child* has been chosen for *The Nutcracker!* What do you *mean* she might not be able to perform?" But the sad truth is that because the rehearsal period is often so contracted, sometimes no more than a couple of weeks, if a child is hurt badly enough to see a doctor there's a good chance she won't make the show.

The way to get around this problem, of course, is to begin rehearsals earlier and gradually work up to the intensity of the last couple of weeks. Teachers also might integrate rehearsal work into their classes, thereby avoiding the abrupt rush of work that can bring about overuse injuries. But, given the unstable nature of most ballet schools, and their obligation to do the best they can with the resources on hand, both financial and human, such long-term solutions may not be realistic. Until then, parents and children simply have to get used to some brand-new aches and pains come Christmas time.

Rapid growth spurts

Young dancers who attend summer workshops notice this a lot. The slim twelve-year-old ballerina, the shortest and lightest girl in class, comes back the next summer toting baggage she never had to accommodate before—things like hips and thighs. Or the short, compact dynamo of a fifteen-year-old boy shows up a head taller and with arms and legs that seem to flop around like a rag doll's. The growth spurts of adolescence can cause them, and their teachers, to think that all of a sudden they've been handed new bodies, ones that just won't respond to their commands any longer.

And it's true, they might as well have a new body; during growth spurts things can change that much. Weight distribution changes as you grow, center of gravity changes, and the proportion among body parts changes. Your head weighs pretty much the same throughout life, and your trunk doesn't change as much as your extremities—but, oh, those extremities. A couple of unfamiliar extra inches of leg, or more flesh around the thigh and hips, can make a big difference when you're trying to cut through space as gracefully and powerfully as possible. Coordination, that tenuous art based on precisely calibrated interrelationships, can fall apart pretty easily when new proportions are added to the mix.

Not only that, but the rapidly growing dancer runs a higher risk of injury than otherwise. The skeleton outgrows the rest of the body at such times, making the muscles tight. And, as we've seen over and over in this book, tight muscles are readily injured muscles. Ballet is better equipped than other activities to cope with this risk, however. It may be that there is no other athletic activity that offers a training regimen as thoughtful as ballet. The slow, deliberate progression from stretching at the barre, to practicing the same movements later in the center, to then performing them on stage develops strength and flexibility simultaneously. No other sports activity starts students with the very same movements that they'll be using later when actually performing. And, because by the time they enter their growth spurts serious ballet students are in the studio a lot, stretching and practicing for hours at a time, the transition to awkwardness and increased injury risk may occur gradually.

One good thing that some gymnastic clubs do is keep growth charts on their kids and update them every month. When the young gymnasts start sprouting up, the instructors move them right into practicing a group of specific exercises that stretch the areas most frequently involved in muscle tightness—and in injuries like Osgood-Schlatter disease, Achilles tendinitis, and back problems caused by tight hamstrings. You can do the same thing at home. Put those family height measurements on the kitchen wall to good use. When your ballet student starts growing three inches a year, start her on some stretching exercises. Have her stretch the quadriceps, hamstrings, and calf muscles. The exercises are easy (simply refer to the appropriate sections of this book to find some suggestions) and very effective. Most of the injuries attributable to tight muscles during growth spurts can be prevented if you keep the muscles stretched, strong, and flexible.

Who can dance and who can't—some ways to predict turnout

It's a harsh fact of ballet life that whatever else you have going for you, if you don't have enough turnout (outside rotation) you're going to find yourself on a long, difficult journey. Most ballet students begin training regardless of the suitability of their bodies for the demands of this kind of dancing. It's only later, if they become serious or try to get into a professional school, that the degree of turnout they possess can become a deciding factor.

Proper turnout comes from the hip. When a dancer turns out, there should be no rotation in the knee or ankle—it's the hip joint that must swivel. Some people are born with a lot of outside rotation, others aren't. But in either case, by about eleven years of age, hip configuration is pretty well set. After the age of eleven or so, there's not much you can do about your turnout one way or another. You can change soft tissues after that, develop what turnout you already have, but the bones are set.

So it can be a good idea to test turnout before you get too serious about ballet. That's exactly what the professional ballet schools do before they even admit a student. (They also look for a particular body type—slim, with long limbs, a high instep, and a certain amount of native flexibility.) It can be horribly difficult for a fledgling dancer to find out at the start that she doesn't have the turnout necessary for ballet, but it may be less difficult than to discover this later on after investing so much time and effort. And it's not the end of the world. Other forms of dance—modern, jazz, show dancing, for example—don't have the same kind of turnout demands as ballet. If a dancer knows early on that she doesn't meet the physical requirements for ballet, she can focus in another direction.

How do you go about measuring turnout? Most people have a similar amount of total hip rotation, in the neighborhood of ninety degrees. The crux in measuring turnout is this: on which side of neutral—that is, when your leg is pointing straight ahead—does most of the rotation occur? If your leg rotates most of that ninety degrees to the inside, toward your other leg, that's perfectly fine as far as your general health is concerned and actually may be better for some activities (the strongest kickers in swimming tend to be somewhat pigeon-toed, for example), but it won't cut the mustard in ballet. If, on the other hand, most of the rotation is to the outside, you're probably a good candidate for ballet. The physician for the Royal Ballet in London maintains a requirement that dancers have at least forty-five degrees of external rotation; some people have more.

The way the Royal Ballet determines rotation is by having a dancer lie on a table on her back, with her knees bent and lower legs hanging off the edge. Then they actually turn out her legs and calibrate the amount of rotation. That's tough to do accurately at home, but there's a quick and easy way that's less precise but will probably tell you all you need to know. The dancer should lie down on her stomach with her knees bent and one lower leg pointing to the ceiling. Keeping thighs together, let the leg flop to the outside. Then move it in the opposite direction, toward your other leg. If your leg bends out farther than it bends in, you may not have enough turnout. But if your leg moves farther toward the inside, so much so that your other leg may get in the way, then you're in luck. (Don't be confused. In this position, turning the lower leg to the *inside* rotates the hip to the *outside*. Try it and all will come clear.)

So if your child doesn't have sufficient turnout, then ballet can be fine in a recreational way. Anything more than that is likely to be frustrating. It might be a good idea to start easing her into another kind of dance early on.

Problems of too much turnout

Too much turnout? How in the world can a dancer have too much turnout? Well, it may be that too much is as bad as too little by the time a dancer reaches her late teens and the upper levels of her professional school. Dancers with ideal turnout tend to have more muscle injuries than other dancers once the going gets tough. It may be that they've never become strong enough because it's all been so easy. They simply haven't had to develop their muscles fully over the years—they've always had more than enough turnout to get by—and once they find themselves swamped with classes and rehearsals and the pressure of vying for apprenticeships and corps de ballet positions, that god-given but underde-veloped body tends to break down.

It's nothing major, usually, nothing that can't be dealt with by stretching and exercise. But it's surprising to see hip injuries, for example, in girls with seventy to eighty degrees of turnout. That's the kind of injury you might expect to see in younger dancers who are overusing their hip muscles attempting to improve their turnout. Girls with an abundance of rotation should be able to sail through most every obstacle that comes their way. But they don't; they get hurt. So, dancers with a surfeit of turnout might be well advised to get some additional work so that they can fully develop their strength.

When should you go on pointe?

That's the $64,000 question. There may be no other area that gives rise to so much controversy. Some teachers absolutely refuse to put a student on pointe until a certain age—twelve or thirteen, say. Others are more flexible, preferring to put a child on pointe according to her individual development and talent. And still others are somewhere in between, but no less vehement about their meth-ods. For the poor, confused ballet parent, the question might be, "Why *not* put a child on pointe anytime that's convenient? Why wait?" The answers are similarly diverse and passionately held: going on pointe too soon can cause deformity. It can cause arthritis. It can cause improper muscle development. It can harm the still-developing bone.

Well, all or any of that may be true, but we've never seen evidence of it. We've never seen any permanent problems resulting from going on pointe too soon (maybe people with such problems are no longer dancers and so limp off to get care from doctors who aren't in sports medicine). Being on pointe may cause a few aches and pains, bunions, and blisters, and we sometimes see related knee problems, but these things are associated with dancing in general. If for no other reason, young dancers who go on pointe aren't in toe shoes long enough to cause permanent damage. It's more likely that any long-term injuries will show up in the dancer's head rather than in her feet and legs. It's simply horribly frustrating for a child who may have been a reasonable dancer in technique shoes to go on pointe and not be able to do much of anything and hurt all the time to boot.

So, when *is* a good time to go on pointe? The first thing to know is that you may or may not be able to rely on your teacher's judgment in this regard. The best instructors can simply look at a child at the barre and tell if she should be on pointe or not, but the best instructors are rare. Others, as we've suggested, simply set arbitrary rules—take it or leave it. And still others are so cowed by pressure from students—and their parents—that they may capitulate unwisely and put a child on pointe at the wrong time. (There are pressing economic reasons for such behavior as well. Ballet schools are in a very competitive business. If a student is unhappy at one school, no matter the reason, she may well go to another one cross-town.) It may be up to the parent to decide when it's best for your child to go on pointe. Here are a few suggestions to ease the burden of that decision.

1. The age that's most frequently given is twelve years old, but it's more sensible to say that if a dancer is somewhere around the age of twelve and has had a minimum of three years of serious training, she's probably ready for pointe. It may be, however, that with three years of serious training a particular dancer at ten, or even eight, years of age is ready. And it may be that eight years of serious training by age fifteen isn't nearly enough for others and nothing ever will be. There are some dancers who should never go on pointe and some who take to it as though they were born in toe shoes. The bottom line is the strength of their training and their body.

2. If a student is able to do a solid passé on half-pointe, with a straight, pulled-up knee, she may be ready for pointe. It's a good test, demanding that she bear all her weight on one leg, with full knee extension and full relevé. If she's not solid at that, it may be that she won't have the strength to handle pointe work.

3. If a dancer can go from a grand plié in the center to standing with knees straight, no wobbling, without altering foot position, it may be time for pointe.

4. If the teacher offers—or demands—to go with the dancer for her first toe shoes, it's a good sign. Toe shoes can be difficult to fit. That the teacher cares enough to offer her own time and expertise should bolster your confidence in her good judgment. If she doesn't and simply says, "Go out and get some toe shoes," it may be time to wonder. (In large schools, in which an entire level of students might go on pointe at the same time, it may be impractical for a teacher to thus offer her services. Still, it's something to look for.)

Again, there's no absolute answer. All else being equal, being able to trust the advice of your ballet instructor is by far the best way to go. Failing that, rest assured that it's highly unlikely that any lasting harm will come to your ballerina if she goes on pointe too soon. The saving grace of the whole business may be that toe shoes are so uncomfortable that only the best, and strongest, dancers are able to tolerate them long enough to risk real damage. And they're the ones who are least likely to suffer it.

ADULT BEGINNERS

The truest and kindest advice that one can give an adult beginning ballet student is, don't take it seriously. It's just too late to have lofty aspirations. The die—in this case your body—is already cast. No matter how talented you may be, no matter how quickly you pick things up, if you haven't trained your body for a good ten years or so already, you will never be able to meet or survive the demands of the art.

The crux, as you may expect, involves turnout. For many dancers it's hard enough to develop adequate turnout after having worked on it since the age of eight. It's virtually impossible if you start at age eighteen. And too zealous an effort will only lead to injury. By that age, hip configuration is set for good; any extra turnout you may be able to squeeze out of your body must come from the knees and ankles, which aren't designed for it.

Teachers usually realize the built-in inadequacies of adult beginners and don't stress the need for excessive turnout and flexibility, but sometimes the students themselves are hard to convince. Especially the college student who takes a dance class for the first time (either because she's a PE major and dance is part of the curriculum, or it's her first opportunity to take elective classes) and is swept away by the joy of moving to music. For that blissful innocent the limits of her own capabilities may be less glaring than they will be later on, and the result can be all sorts of problems.

At some point adult beginners come to realize their limitations and, if they want to continue dancing, find the kind of gentle, occasional arrangement that suits them. Until then teachers must be especially sensitive to their adult students' difficulties (is there anything more embarrassing than stepping into class in a leotard and tights for the first time?). Perhaps college dance classes should be considered more an introduction to movement than serious ballet training.

PROFESSIONALS AND SERIOUS PRE-PROFESSIONALS

If one were to rank ballet injuries by their frequency, the list would go something like this:

1. Overuse knee problems, such as chrondromalacia, tendinitis, and turn-out-related kneecap injuries;

2. Overuse ankle problems;

3. Overuse hip problems;

4. Back problems (maybe ten percent of all injuries, and more common in men); and

5. Stress fractures, usually from significant changes in activity levels.

It's obvious from the list that most injuries in ballet *aren't* cataclysms. Rather they're nagging little things that, if ignored, can turn into nagging big things. More often than not, that's exactly what happens. By the time a dancer gets to the doctor, that little problem that could have been cleared up pretty easily has grown into something that threatens the dancer's ability to keep going. Of course, that's why she finally dragged herself to the doctor. Like anyone, dancers tend to ignore problems that are ignorable, preferring to imagine that they will fade away on their own. What makes the situation worse is that, unlike most people, dancers are encouraged to do just that by the hierarchical structure of the dance world: at the top, directors and choreographers who, even though they themselves once danced, are often intolerant of injuries in their minions, and, at the bottom, hordes of young dancers champing at the bit to step in and get their chance to perform. Caught in that kind of dilemma, it's no wonder dancers are loath to own up to injuries.

This reluctance is strongest in high-level students, apprentices, and ballet corps members. This is the most competitive time of a dancer's life, and it's also the time when any lack of proper training, any lack of strength or technique, will rear its ugly head. But who's going to admit it? Falter for an instant and there's an army of others just waiting to nab your spot.

The tendency may be most pronounced, and most poignant, in the veteran corps dancer, the "old" trouper of twenty-five, say, who's beginning to realize that she's never going to break out of the corps and that there are countless eighteen-year-olds who can do almost everything she can and are willing to abuse their bodies to do so. Of course abusing the body is nothing new to her—she's been at it for the seven or eight years she's been in the company—but now, at only twenty-five years old, she's not healing as fast as she used to. The injuries are coming more frequently and lasting longer, and she can feel the breath of the younger dancers on her neck. So she says nothing, dances hurt, and then hurts more, until finally she simply hurts too much to go on.

It's easy enough to empathize with this dancer, even more so when you consider her options—there are none. There's no dancer's union strong enough to fight for her, and what can she look to outside the dance world? It's a meaningless question, for her life has been so strongly directed and sheltered that there is no life outside dance. So, she hurts.

Soloists and principal dancers may suffer as many injuries—in some cases even more because they dance longer and technically more demanding roles—but they're generally more willing to admit their problems and do something about them. They're much more likely than the corps dancer to say to the director, "I'm not going to do it because I hurt." And they're much more likely to get away with this, or the artistic director is likely to choreograph around their injuries. So, as a group, they're the healthiest dancers around. The smart ones won't risk themselves because they can look forward to five or ten years down the line. The corps dancer doesn't know if she can even look forward to next season.

But if dancers and directors only knew, they could do themselves a great favor by admitting and attending to injuries early on. Not only would dancers stay on stage more consistently, but they might do so in reasonable health.

MALE DANCERS

The general consensus is that men suffer more hip injuries than women. That may or may not be true—it's hard to know precisely—but if it's true it may a result of two factors: men usually start ballet later than women, and some companies aren't as selective when it comes to men. There just aren't as many male dancers. Although things are changing, schools and companies may take anyone who's willing. Forget the amount of turnout he may have; if he's a viable boy, take him.

So it may be that in the male dance population there is a higher proportion of individuals having problems with their hips than among the women. The men also may not be as physically suited to ballet as the women in the first place, and, because they usually start dance training later, they have to force turnout even more than women do. The result: hip problems.

Who knows what can be done about it? It may be that when men begin training as young as the women do, and when enough men go into ballet that companies and schools can be as selective as they are with women (and that process has already begun), then hip injuries will show up in men no more frequently than they do in women.

Male dancers also tend to have back problems. Here the cause is clear: lifting. Carrying all those women around all those years takes its toll. But even here the relative paucity of male dancers and their late development play a role. There aren't enough men to go around, and they're usually less advanced in their training and ability than girls of similar age. But the schools have to go ahead and train the girls to be lifted. So, they use the boys on hand over and over until all the girls get their chance to be lifted. Well, the girls may be ready, but most likely the boys are not. Because up to now their training has solely built up the lower half of their bodies, their shoulders and arms are simply too weak. And after they do double, triple, and quadruple duty lifting all the girls, they're even weaker. Ideally they should do these lifts with their shoulders and arms, but as they tire they begin to use their backs. That usually means overarching the back, and, as any weight lifter will tell you, once you start overarching your back you're heading for trouble. This "back-arching" problem becomes even worse when turnout is inadequate because flexing the hips—and arching the back to compensate for it—is a way to make turnout look better.

The problem is compounded because the girls are themselves beginners when it comes to partnering. Women who know how to be lifted do their share of the lifting. They know when to jump, how to hold their body so it's light and alive rather than just dead weight, how to help in coming down. If a woman doesn't help out, even the strongest men have a hard time lifting. But rather than knowing how to help the boys lift, these girls are just getting off the ground for the first time themselves. So it's the worst possible combination: inexperienced boys who aren't strong enough lifting inexperienced girls who don't know how to be lifted. And the boys bear the brunt of the consequences—in their backs.

This problem, at least, may have a solution—or perhaps a partial one. The boys should embark on an upper body strengthening program long before they start partnering. At least one large ballet school now incorporates a universal weight room for just that purpose. So by the time the partnering classes come around, the boys still may not be completely ready, but they'll be in much better shape than otherwise.

That's the part of the solution that's easily implemented. The other may be impossible, given the way things are in the ballet world. Why not teach the girls how to partner with the most advanced boys in the school, or company corps dancers, or even soloists? And vice versa with the boys. Let a boy learn to lift with a corps girl, someone who can help him rather than make things even harder. And only then, after both groups have learned basic techniques from experienced people and the boys have built up their strength, would it be time to put the beginning girls and boys together.

Sounds good, but even if there were time for such company-school interactions, what self-respecting soloist or corps dancer would risk herself in the grasp of a shaky, beginning boy? And what working male dancer, who constantly battles fatigue and an aching back anyway, would make time to lift a class of neophyte girls? It may be that building strength with weights is the only viable course of action, and that male dancers simply should expect back problems as one of the consequences of practicing their vocation—which, given the need to constantly support so much weight with such slow, seemingly effortless movements and to continue dancing and otherwise keeping their own bodies under control in the meanwhile, is one of the most physically difficult professions of all.

Glossary

Achilles tendon: the large tendon in the back of the leg that connects the muscles of the calf to the heel bone. The largest tendon in the body.

acromion: a bony shelf that juts up from the shoulder blade to provide a kind of protective roof over the shoulder joint. It connects to the collarbone, or clavicle, at a small joint called the acromioclavicular—or A-C—joint.

adductors: any muscles that move one part of the body toward another or toward the midline of the body. In particular, the groin muscles.

aerobic exercise: exercise involving breathing and the utilization of oxygen (as opposed to anaerobic exercise).

anaerobic exercise: exercise involving the utilization of stored energy sources (as opposed to aerobic exercise).

arabesque: in ballet, the pose in which the body is supported by one leg while the other leg is extended behind and at a right angle to the supporting leg.

arthroscopy: a surgical technique that involves inserting into a joint a small telescope that projects the view of the inside of the joint onto a TV screen. Arthroscopy is used most frequently in knee and shoulder surgery.

Baker's cyst: a large, fluid-filled swelling in the back of the knee.

baseball finger: tearing of the tendon that attaches near the fingernail. The result is the finger won't straighten. Also called mallet finger.

biceps: a muscle with two heads of origin. Particularly, the biceps muscle in the front of the upper arm from the shoulder joint to the elbow. This muscle flexes the elbow.

black toenail: the result of bleeding under the nail.

blister: a swelling containing watery fluid and sometimes blood. A blister is simply a callus that hasn't been given enough time to form.

bruise: an area of skin discoloration caused by bleeding from blood vessels rupturing underneath the skin. The cause is usually a blow. Also called a contusion.

bunion: swelling of the joint between the big toe and the first metatarsal bone.

bursa: a small, moist fibrous envelope or sac that occurs where body parts move against each other. A bursa helps reduce friction.

bursitis: an inflammation of a bursa.

calcific tendinitis: calcium deposited in an area of tendinitis. In the shoulder, it is one of the most painful injuries possible.

callus: a hard, thick area of skin occurring in parts of the body subject to pressure or friction.

cardiovascular conditioning: exercise that increases the heart's ability to circulate blood through the body.

carpal tunnel: a tunnel in the wrist and palm that protects the tendons that connect the fingers to the muscles in the forearm. The median nerve that supplies sensation to part of the palm runs in the carpal tunnel as well.

carpus: the oblong wedge of eight small bones in the wrist. They afford the wrist its flexibility.

carrying angle: the elbow's tendency to cause the forearm to veer out to the side when extended. Especially prominent in women.

cartilage: dense tissue that usually provides cushioning at the meeting of bony surfaces.

cheerleader's hip: the result of sudden demands on the muscles of the hip that pulls muscle away from the bone, popping off a piece of bone in the process. Bounding into splits can do it.

chondromalacia: wear and tear of the cartilage in a joint. Used to describe problems of the kneecap not tracking effectively. Chondromalacia patella is a roughening of the inner surface of the kneecap.

clavicle: the collarbone.

coccyx: the tailbone.

collateral ligaments: ligaments that run along the side of a joint. In the knee, for example, there is one on each side (lateral collateral ligament on the outside, medial collateral ligament on the inside). They connect the femur to the tibia and prevent the knee from moving sideways.

compartment syndrome: a condition, usually in the shin area of the lower leg, in which a muscle swells, sometimes up to a third more than its usual size, but the fascia compartment surrounding the muscle does not. The result can be serious, a reduced blood supply to the muscle.

constriction tendinitis: tendinitis caused by the pressure of constricting clothing, especially in the foot.

contrast baths: alternating warm and cold baths to reduce swelling and promote healing.

contusion: an area of skin discoloration caused by bleeding of blood vessels rupturing underneath the skin. The cause is usually a blow. Also called a bruise.

corn: a callus that often occurs between or on top of the toes. Between the toes it is called a soft corn.

cruciate ligaments: ligaments that cross within the knee, from the middle of the tibia to the middle of the femur. The anterior cruciate ligament, the forward of the two, restrains the shin from moving forward. The posterior cruciate ligament, the one toward the back of the knee, prevents the shin from moving backward.

cyst: a sac filled with fluid.

deltoid: the thick triangle of muscle that slopes over the shoulder onto the upper arm. It is responsible for raising the arm away from the body. This muscle separates into three leaves. The most apparent is the anterior deltoid.

de Quervain's disease: a common tendinitis of the wrist, affecting the tendons that connect the thumb to the muscles in the forearm.

disk: a fibrous spacer between vertebrae of the backbone.

dislocation: the displacement of bones meeting at a joint from their normal position. For example, a shoulder dislocation involves the separation of the ball of the shoulder joint from its seat in the socket of the scapula.

dorsiflex: to flex the foot, hand, or fingers backward.

epiphyses: growth centers near the ends of bones of young people.

extensor mechanism: the drive train from the quadriceps to the shinbone that allows extension of the lower leg.

facet joints: bony hinges connecting the vertebrae to each other.

fascia: a tough, gristlelike envelope that encloses muscles.

fascial hernia: tiny balloonlike bulges or defects under the skin, often in the lower outside shin area, just above the ankle.

femur: the large bone in the thigh. The body's largest bone.

fibula: the long, thin outer bone of the lower leg.

foramina: small holes in the vertebrae through which protrude nerves from the spinal cord.

fracture: breakage of a bone, either complete or partial.

funny bone: the ulnar nerve, which runs in a groove behind the elbow and down into the forearm and the outside of the hand. Also called crazy bone.

gamekeeper's thumb: sprain of the ligaments at the base of the thumb, where the web between the thumb and index finger begins. The result is a loss of ability to pinch.

ganglion: a small fluid-filled cyst that grows from a joint, often on the back of the wrist.

gastrocnemius: the large muscle in the calf that attaches in the lower thigh, runs behind the knee about one third of the way down the lower leg, and connects to the Achilles tendon.

gelling: stiff, painful movement of a joint, especially the knee.

gluteal muscles: the large muscles in the buttocks, responsible for extending and rotating the hip and leg—primarily the gluteus maximus, gluteus medius, and gluteus minimus.

grand jeté: in ballet a great jump from one leg to the other in which the leading leg appears to be thrown into the air.

greater trochanter: the protruding knob at the upper outside end of the femur.

hamstrings: large muscles in the back of the thigh.

heel spur: a spike of bone up to three quarters of an inch long extending from the heel bone.

hip pointer: a blow to the bony ridge of the pelvis. One of the most painful athletic injuries.

humeral epicondyle: the lateral humeral epicondyle is the bump on the outside of the elbow, the location of tennis elbow. The medial humeral epicondyle is the bump on the inside of the elbow, the location of Little League elbow.

humerus: the upper arm bone.

iliotibial band: a long, thick, rigid tendon that runs from the upper part of the hip along the outside of the thigh and across the knee and connects to the shinbone.

impingement: buildup of bone and soft tissue, primarily in the ankle and wrist, blocking movement.

ingrown toenail: a toenail that curls at the edges and grows into the fleshy part of the toe.

isotope scan: a diagnostic technique involving injecting into the body a radioactive-isotope solution that searches out the healing process in bone.

joint mice: loose bodies in a joint—for example, bone chips in the elbow.

jumper's knee: tendinitis of the tendon attached to the kneecap. It usually occurs at the bottom of the kneecap, where the tendon from the shinbone connects. Also called patellar tendinitis.

lactic acid: a simple sugar that's the end product of anaerobic exercise. It can accumulate in the muscles and cause burning or cramping.

laminectomy: surgery involving removing at least part of a ruptured disk.

ligaments: tough bands of fibers that connect bone to bone.

Little League elbow: tendinitis of the inside of the elbow, at the medial humeral epicondyle. Also called medial tennis elbow or golfer's elbow.

menisci: thick rings of cartilage that cushion the knee and provide shock absorption. Also called fibrocartilage. Each ring is called a meniscus.

meniscus cyst: a fluid-filled sac attached to a torn meniscus.

meralgia paresthetica: irritation of the lateral cutaneous nerve, which crosses the bony ridge of the pelvis. This problem can cause pain down the upper front of the thigh.

metacarpal bones: the five bones of the hand that connect the carpus, or wrist bones, to the phalanges, or finger bones.

metatarsal bones: the small bones between the toes and the top of the foot.

MRI—Magnetic Resonance Imaging. A technique wherein your body (or body part) is placed in a giant magnet and the body's disruption of the magnetic waves is translated into slices viewed on a screen or film. This process, unlike x-rays which primarily reveal details about bone, shows soft tissues like cartilage, tendons, muscles, and ligaments.

myositis ossificans: the result of a blow against a muscle that not only ruptures blood vessels but pulls the muscle away from the bone, taking periosteum with it and resulting in bone forming within the muscle.

navicular: a boat-shaped bone in the foot and hand. In the hand it lies at the base of the thumb; in the foot it rests against the lower anklebone, the talus. In the hand it's also called the scaphoid.

olecranon process: the large end of the ulna, which extends behind the elbow joint.

orthopedic sleeve: a tight, pullover neoprene bandage, often used for the knee.

orthotic: a custom-made shoe insert.

Osgood-Schlatter disease: a form of tendinitis at the end of the patellar tendon, where this tendon goes into the shinbone. It affects growing people, primarily between ten and sixteen years of age.

osteochondritis dissecans: a condition in which a piece of bone and overlying cartilage loses its blood supply and flakes away into a joint, often the knee or ankle.

osteoporosis: a loss of bone strength and density affecting primarily post-menopausal women. Symptoms include stooped and rounded shoulders.

paraspinous muscles: the strong ropes of muscles that run along either side of the spine.

passé: in ballet, a movement in which the foot of the working leg passes the knee of the supporting leg.

patella: the kneecap.

pectoral muscles: the chest muscles. The pectoralis major is a large fan-shaped muscle that draws the arm forward across the chest. The smaller pectoralis minor draws the shoulder blade downward.

pelvis: the bony ringlike structure to which the bones of the legs are attached. Also called pelvic girdle or hip girdle.

periosteum: a layer of dense tissue that covers the surface of bone. In children the periosteum is especially thick and rich with blood to promote growth.

peroneal muscles: muscles that run along the outside of the lower calf. They enable one to pull the foot to the outside.

peroneal tendons: tendons that connect the peroneal muscles, which run along the outside of the lower leg, to the bones of the foot.

phalanges: the bones of the fingers and toes.

piriformis syndrome: irritation of the piriformis muscle, a small muscle that lies in the buttocks underneath the gluteals and assists them in rotating and extending the hip.

plantar fascia: a ligament-like rope of fibrous tissue that runs along the inside of the sole of the foot from the heel to the base of the toes. Among other functions it maintains the arch.

plantar fasciitis: inflammation of a stretched, torn plantar fascia.

plantar neuroma: a pinched nerve usually between the third and fourth toes. Sometimes called Morton's neuroma.

plié: in ballet, bending the knee over the ankle.

popliteus: a tiny muscle in the back of the knee that helps to flex the knee.

pronation: the act of turning the hand so that the palm faces downward.

quadriceps: the muscle group in the front part of the thigh. The body's largest and most powerful muscles.

quadriplegia: paralysis of the arms and legs.

radial head: the head of the radius, convex in shape, which rotates against the humerus.

radius: the outer and shorter bone of the forearm.

rectus femoris: the portion of the quadriceps muscle that connects to the pelvis.

reduction: restoring a displaced part of the body to its normal position by manipulation or surgery. For example, a dislocated shoulder is reduced by centering the ball of the shoulder joint against its seat in the scapula once again.

relevé: in ballet, raising the body onto the toes or half-pointe.

rhomboid muscles: muscles in the center of the back that attach the edge of the shoulder blade to the spine. They help to pull the shoulder blade upward and toward the spine.

rotator cuff muscles: the group of small muscles in the shoulder joint below the deltoids. These muscles hold the joint in the proper position and are responsible for subtle, precise shoulder movements. They are frequently torn.

rupture: tissue that bursts apart or open. For example, an Achilles tendon can rupture. So can the biceps muscle.

sacrum: the fused portion of the backbone at the level of the pelvis.

scapula: the shoulder blade.

Scheuerman's disease: abnormal growth of the vertebrae, causing a forward curve of the backbone.

sciatica: irritation of the sciatic nerve, the large nerve that supplies sensation to much of the body from the hips downward. The result can be pain that runs down the back of the thigh and calf all the way to the foot.

scoliosis: a side-to-side curve of the backbone.

sesamoid bones: tiny bones in the feet within the tendons that run to the big toe.

sesamoiditis: any irritation of the sesamoid bones.

shinsplints: all-purpose category describing pain in the lower leg.

shoulder separation: dislocation of the acromioclavicular joint, thereby separating the collarbone from the shoulder.

snapping hip: popping in the hip joint, sometimes for unknown reasons.

snowball crepitation: squeaking caused by inflammation of a tendon and its sheath. As the tendon moves within the sheath, it squeaks, sounding like the noise made by squeezing a handful of snow.

soleus: the muscle in the lower part of the calf.

spondylolisthesis: a severe stress fracture of the vertebrae that causes one vertebra to slip forward on another.

spondylolysis: a stress fracture of the vertebrae.

spinal column: the flexible bony column extending from the base of the skull to the small of the back. It encloses and protects the spinal cord, articulates with the skull, ribs, and hip girdle, and provides attachment for the muscles of the back. It consists of three parts: the cervical spine, thoracic spine, and lumbar spine.

spinous processes: small bumps of the backbone, just under the skin, an inch to an inch and a half long, that function as muscle attachments.

sprain: an injury to a ligament caused by sudden overstretching or tearing.

sternum: the breastbone.

stress fracture: a hairline fracture, often too fine to show up on x-rays, caused by stress on the bone just to the point of breaking.

subluxation: partial dislocation of a joint, so that the bone ends are misaligned but still in contact.

supination: the act of turning the hand so that the palm faces upward.

synovial membrane: the fluid-producing lining that surrounds joints.

talus: the lower of the bones in the ankle.

tendinitis: inflammation of a tendon.

tendon: the tough cords that attach muscle to bone.

tennis elbow: tendinitis in the elbow, at the point of the bump on the outside of the elbow, the lateral humeral epicondyle.

tennis leg: the ripping away of part of the calf muscle from the Achilles tendon. Also called calf strain.

tensor fascia lata: a small fist-shaped muscle in the hip, under the bony ridge of the pelvis.

thoracic outlet syndrome: irritation of the nerves that begin in the neck and run into the shoulder and down the arm. The result can be pain in the arms and hands, far from the point of irritation.

tibia: the shinbone.

trapezius: the huge, flat, triangular muscle that covers the back of the neck and shoulder. It moves the head backward to either side and is important in movements of the shoulder blade.

triceps: a muscle with three heads of origin. Particularly, the triceps muscle in the back of the upper arm. It contracts to extend the elbow.

ulna: the inner and longer bone of the forearm.

vastus medialis: a tiny section of the quadriceps muscle located just above and to the inside of the kneecap. This muscle is very important in keeping the kneecap tracking properly.

vertebrae: the small bones that comprise the spinal column.

Injuries Listed by Sport

General Index

Alain McLaughlin

Dr. James Garrick is the founder and director of the Center for Sports Medicine in San Francisco, the first hospital-based, multi-specialty clinic dealing with athletic injuries. He founded the Sports Medicine Division at the University of Washington—the first facility of its kind in a major university in the United States. Dr. Garrick is the co-author of *Sports Injuries: Diagnosis and Management,* a book for primary-care physicians, recently published in a second edition.

Peter Radetsky is a former contributing editor of *Discover* magazine and faculty member of the Science Communicaiton Program at the University of California, Santa Cruz. He writes articles on a variety of topics from biology to medicine, space sciences to ecology, sociology to genetics, history to public affairs. Among his books are *The Invisible Invaders* and *Allergic to the Twentieth Century. Anybody's Sports Medicine Book* is his third collaboration with Dr. Garrick.

Jessica Radetsky